Love is Like a Soufflé

ELIE GRIMES

Translated by Eve Bodeux

Printed in the United States of America

First Printing, 2018

ISBN print book: 978-0-9997-1693-9

ISBN digital book: 978-0-9997-1692-2

Sassy Fiction

Flat 703
900, Monroe Street
Hoboken, NJ 07030

www.sassyfiction.com

Originally published in French under the title *Les gentilles filles vont au paradis, les autres
la` où elles le veulent* © La Librairie Générale Française, 2017

Published by special arrangement with La Librairie Générale Française in
conjunction with their duly appointed agent 2 Seas Literary Agency

CONTENTS

1
MELTED BUTTER

"We need to marry these two off—to each other," Great Aunt Vicki said for the thousandth time.

Zoey was able to stop herself from rolling her eyes and continued to smile at her and Vicki's friend Becky Manson. The two elderly women were talking as if she and Adrian weren't actually standing right in front of them.

She knew what was coming but had resigned herself, happy to play the role of the tortured martyr out of the goodness of her heart.

She did love them, but Aunt Vicki could talk endlessly about what was going on in the lives of the younger generation in her circle. She didn't mean any harm, in fact, quite the opposite.

She'd given up on getting any help from Adrian. His long-established technique was to display total apathy in the face of the charming matron's attacks on their status as singles. However, Zoey took the risk of glancing over at him, as Aunt Vicki continued, "Adrian and Zoey live in New York." Zoey sighed, thinking, "*She says it like we live together!*"

"Zoey has her own catering business in the city. And she's only thirty! Her grandmother, my sister Angelina, taught her everything she knows. Zoey's the one catering this party. She never stops working, and that's why she's still single. However, Becky, you and I know, don't we, that the answer's often right there in front of you, even if you're looking for it somewhere else."

Adrian, his hands in the pockets of his jeans, was happy enough to simply exhale and blow the bangs of his brown hair off the side of his nose. He then went back to staring intensely at the far side of the yard.

From the corner of her eye, Zoey could see her mother trying to get her attention with a desperate expression on her face. She was indicating an empty spot in the middle of the table that was a dangerous threat to how balanced the presentation looked.

Aware that of being disloyal, she went for it anyway,

"But, Aunt Vicki, Adrian wouldn't make a good boyfriend. He acts like he's in high school. Look at him. He still wears AC/DC t-shirts!"

Standing next to her, Adrian tensed up and let out a whistle from between clenched teeth. He bobbed his head, letting his rebellious bangs fall back into place to hide beneath them. She knew she'd have to pay for this later.

"Well, all's fair when you're at war," she thought, realizing that that wasn't exactly the way the proverb went.

The older woman started in again at full speed,

"The airlines lost Adrian's suitcase. Did you know that he just got back from Brazil? He came straight here from Rio so he wouldn't miss Zoey's parents' thirty-fifth wedding anniversary. That's why he's wearing those old t-shirts. It's obviously too small. He's a brilliant composer. Just brilliant. He and Zoey were practically raised together. Adrian is Stella and Darryl Peters' son. They are Zoey's parents' friends who live just across the street. There was also Dalton--Zoey's brother, Tina--their cousin, and Laurie--the Hartings' daughter who lives at the end of the street. We called them "the gang.""

"If you wanted me to marry her," Adrian began gleefully, "you should have raised her to be a bit nicer."

Zoey turned her head, just in time to see the look of resentment on her best friend's face. Then, barely acknowledging him, took off to join her mother.

"Nice try, Mozart," she thought fighting off the urge to verbally attack Adrian, whom she'd known her whole life.

She tried not to run since several people at the tables set up in her parents' yard were watching her. She purposely ignored Nana, her grandmother, who was trying to get her attention. Nana fidgeted with the pearls of her necklace while she chatted with Stella Peters, like she always did when the discussion was tense.

Their interaction was nothing, however, compared to what was about to take place.

The closer Zoey got to her mother, the more her mother puckered her lips anxiously. From her own mother, the formidable Nana, Fran Westwood had inherited an attention to detail as well as an authoritarian manner that was magnified by a much more conventional personality than the elder woman's. In contrast to her mother, Fran's social standing was very important to her. Zoey had spent months preparing for her parents' wedding anniversary celebration and thought she'd go crazy every time the phone rang and "Mom" appeared on the screen. Two weeks out from the fateful date, she had seriously thought about changing her email address. Three days before, she'd wondered if it would really be that hard to have a fake passport made so she could flee to Mexico, or better yet France, where she could find a job as a chef in a cute little bistro.

"You haven't labeled the vegetarian dishes," her mother snapped. Her pupils were quivering at a worrying rate as her perfectly made up eyes grew wide.

Zoey looked at the table, then at her mother, and took a deep breath.

"You told me I shouldn't put the vegetarian selections on the same table as the other items."

"I never said any such thing!," Fran exclaimed.

"You said that your vegetarian friends would be appalled at the idea that their food was mingling with meat," Zoey continued calmly, carefully pronouncing each syllable.

"This is ridiculous!"

"I totally agree with you," Zoey responded.

"You need to resolve this right now," Fran insisted, furious. "Most of the guests will be arriving soon. "If Roberta Conner doesn't have her vegetarian fix, my life will be hell in the days to come and all the effort I put into making this an unforgettable event will have been for nothing. You know how much this means to your father."

From the corner of her eye, Zoey saw Joe Westwood help himself to a glass of whiskey while relaxing with Darryl Peters. They were sitting in the sunroom, where they had spent many hours over the years, shooting the breeze about everything and nothing.

"I'll add some labels," Zoey agreed.

However, her mother was still obviously anxious.

"You should fix your hair, sweetheart. I'm going to be very busy from here on out, so, while I have your attention, please be nice to Laurie Harting. Her mother was worried and talked to me about it. Don't forget that you were friends when you were younger and that there's been a lot of water under the bridge since Spencer and you…" Zoey stared at her mother and laughed bitterly, despite herself.

"Since Spencer and I broke up because she did everything she could to make him fall in love with *her?*

It was Fran Westwood's turn to stare at her daughter, as if Zoey had just announced she'd decided to stuff the vegetarian samosas with pork.

"Don't make a scene tonight, okay?" she scolded, after taking a moment to think about it. "Your father really won't like it if our celebration is ruined by a big commotion."

Zoey almost retorted that her father would have a scene all right, but not because of anything she was going to do. But Fran's reaction to something as stupid as using the wrong type of glass during his toast could.

She gave up arguing with her mother, however, since Fran never listened to her anyway, and decided to focus on the task she'd been given.

She mumbled that she was going to go find the food labels and that she'd also fix her hair, and with a touch of irony in her voice, asked her mother if she needed anything else.

The thin line of her mother's lips told her the answer.

She promised to behave herself with Laurie Harting, specifying, before moving toward the house, that she'd avoid any conversation about Laurie's upcoming marriage to Spencer.

"Zoey?"

Her mother, against all expectations, was smiling.

"I hope that Dalton, Adrian and you don't have a surprise prepared for us this time."

The way she emphasized the word "surprise" said a lot about what she thought of the last surprise they'd given her parents for their thirtieth wedding anniversary.

"I think that Dalton is planning to rap for you," she proclaimed with a sweet smile.

She didn't listen to the resulting fallout and moved away with as much dignity as possible, still ignoring Nana waving at her. She'd obviously followed the entire exchange from afar.

Climbing up the few steps to the house, she pushed her mother's Jack Russel, Velter, away with her foot. He'd been patiently waiting for someone to open the door, hoping against hope that he'd be able to snatch a morsel.

"Sorry, Velt, but no dogs allowed in the house. Health code. Complain to your mistress."

In the kitchen a worrisome calm reigned. She went directly to plastic box marked "Zoey's Kitchen" in cursive, to pull out the labels she had used on the table. Sitting in a corner, Sally, her assistant, was peering at her smartphone. Under her chef's uniform, she'd made the effort to wear a skirt that wasn't too short and had pulled back her fiery red curls.

"Is something wrong?" she asked, without lifting her eyes from the screen.

"My mother wants us to serve the vegetarian dishes mixed in with the others."

Sally looked away from the device to roll her eyes, which Zoey pretended not to see.

"Do you need any help?" she said, reluctantly putting her phone down.

"Have you finished everything else?"

"Yes. The miniature quiches are almost done. I think we're just about ready. I just need to know when to bring out the appetizers. Your mother...

"....is going to drive us both crazy, I know. Thanks for being so patient,

4

Sally."

Her friend smiled.

"She's probably the worst client we've ever had," she said. "Sorry."

"Tell me something I don't know." "Quiche and the appetizers. At least we were able to talk her out of the lobster salad."

"Your mother is, let's say, traditional," Sally responded. "Let's hope she likes it." "Well, I wouldn't hold your breath. She'll never be satisfied unless her friends are suddenly filled with the spirit of kindness and concede that the lunch was good, without adding any backhanded compliments. Obviously, if Nana had been the one in charge, no one would dare make any remarks, even my mother. Everything is a double-edged sword in my family. Officially, my mom is doing this to 'help me get on my feet' but I know she's really doing it so that she can criticize me afterward. I am so terribly disappointing."

She suddenly tasted a bitterness rising in her throat.

Since she'd been a child, her relationship with Fran had been a stormy one. To her credit, her mother had always been proud of being independent and active. Nana had taken up the slack, little by little becoming much more than just a grandmother to Zoey. She'd spent the first ten years of her life going from one house to the other, going home to eat and sleep--and sometimes just to sleep--while Fran and Joe stayed late at the office.

Zoey was also passionately independent and her taste for freedom and total lack of interest in being popular made things even more complicated growing up.

She'd always been told, throughout her teenage years, that she should be a good girl--sometimes it was said with a laugh, and sometimes in all seriousness. It depended on who was doing the talking.

It had become Fran's mantra and when she said it, her tone left no doubt about what she meant.

Once she hit 12, with her a clear vision of who she was and Nana's loving indulgence, Zoey had cultivated a personality that was the direct opposite of what a upper middle class suburbanite mother would expect of her daughter. Her teen years had been a roller coaster ride, full of discovery, arguments and sneaking out with her friends as soon as her mother's attention was diverted (and it often was, toward Dalton, which was fine with Zoey).

As an adult, she'd matured--except for where parties and booze were concerned. When she was with Spencer, she'd thought that Fran would be happy enough, even if at the time she swore that her mother's opinion didn't matter to her at all.

The break up with Spencer was just one more reminder of what a disappointment she was.

At this point in her life, she couldn't have cared less about being a "good girl." She'd really tried, but hadn't succeeded. Maybe she didn't know what being a "good girl" meant. According to popular opinion, she though that it had something to do with having a great haircut and not sleeping with every guy that came along. On that last point, she could swear to the fact that she'd been *the best girl in the whole word* this past year.

That being said, nobody was going to give her a prize for her abstinence.

To Fran, she was still a terrible teenager, sloppy, hanging out with Adrian Peters and Dalton (who was far from a saint but who had become devious enough to escape his mother's retaliation, which Zoey had never quite figured out); she was the girl with no style who could never do right and who didn't take life seriously.

"I'm definitely not the daughter of her dreams," declared Zoey, while Sally gave her an affectionate glance.

Even though Sally had become her best friend, she realized that she shouldn't be revealing her family's dirty laundry when they were at work. *It's not very professional.*

With everything going on, however, it was difficult to keep things separate. Since yesterday, Fran had been treating her like a little child, making hysterical comments about how Zoey did things and her lack of organization.

It seemed like Sally was able to follow Zoey's thoughts by just looking at her and she set her phone down.

"Don't worry," she said quietly. "We been through worse and we'll survive, even if this kitchen isn't helping any. It really isn't practical at all. Everything is so…so new. You'd think none of the appliances had ever been used before."

"Welcome to the kitchen of the perfect American family," Zoey sighed. "It drives Nana totally crazy and she refuses to even set foot in here. My mother only uses the steamer anyway. That's why she's so thin. She wants everyone to think it's her metabolism, but, really, she starves herself."

Zoey bit her lip. She couldn't help herself. She thought about her hair. Her mother had already made fun of it twice. The recalled other comments that had been thrown at her throughout her life and that had been even more harsh. Unlike Fran, Zoey was not what one would call *svelte*. She had hips, a butt, rounded thighs and despaired that she'd never get rid of that extra bit of skin at her elbows that her dad good-naturedly called *baby fat*.

On top of that, her brown hair was impossible and out of control. It wouldn't even hold a barrette. It was in striking contrast to the controlled style of her mother's one-hundred percent Italian tresses. The fortune Fran spent on them was obvious.

Unconsciously, her hand went to an unruly section of hair that was sticking out of her chignon that Giuliano, Fran's stylist, had patiently styled this morning. As she bent down to the oven or leaned over the stove top, it

6

had started to flyaway as the day wore on. Then, suddenly, panicked, she looked at her navy dress, the most conservative piece of clothing she'd been able to find in her closet stuffed full of jeans, revealing tops and brightly colored athletic shoes, and noticed, horrified, that her feet were bare.

"You could have told me that I wasn't wearing any shoes!" she cried.

She was glad that Fran hadn't noticed, because if she had, she would have let Zoey have it.

"You love cooking in bare feet," Sally replied, shrugging her shoulders. "And, anyway, it's sweet."

Her friend's comment made her smile. Sally had a gift for lifting her spirits, she was always positive and always there for her.

"I'm okay staying in the kitchen," Sally said, mischievously. And, that way, I can keep my uniform on. Your mother was happy to tell me that, with my red, curly hair, I'd be better off cutting it short."

"I'm really sorry," mumbled Zoey.

"Don't worry about it. My own mother has told me the same thing," Sally said, smiling. "That, and that I was much too old to be just an assistant. We all have a bossy family to manage. At least we have an excuse for our passionate devotion to sugar.

She emphatically swiped a bit of confectioners' sugar from the table top with her finger and licked it off.

"Let's finish these labels so I can face the lady dragon and her evil fairies," said Zoey, sitting down at the clean side of the table. "I sent my mother Dalton's way, but he won't be able to hold her off forever, at least not without being tempted to send her back to me."

Sally's eyes lit up for a moment.

"How's your brother's music going?"

"Dalton's a god!" Zoey responded, laughing to herself. "It was so hot out that he took his shirt off. I took photos. Want to see?"

Sally gave her a look, suddenly turning a deep red.

"You're terrible!" she exclaimed. "I was just being polite."

"Yup," Zoey laughed hysterically. "In any case, I think Dalton is being tortured by my mother's taste in music, like me with the food. And by the heat, too, because you know she's making him wear a shirt--there's no way she'd let him take it off in public. But, if you insist, I'm sure he'd be glad to give you a private viewing."

This was exactly what Dalton would do. As a teenager, Zoey had given up on the idea of having girlfriends the day she'd realized that some girls hung out with her just to have the chance to get close to her brother, or, even better, to bump into him in the bathroom through a well-planned "coincidence." By the time he started high school, Dalton had evolved from a brat whose classmates wouldn't even attend his birthday parties to a real Romeo. Zoey attributed this miracle to her excellent, big sisterly advice, frequently accompanied by a whack to the back of his head. She'd often thought about how he was the recipient of good genes: with his black hair and olive complexion, he was the perfect caricature of an Italian playboy. His mischievous manner and freckles inspired a certain level of indulgence and, somewhat ironically, this made it even easier for him to get his way faster.

Sally picked up a stack of labels and a marker.

"Zoey Westwood, you are the worst friend in the world. You deserve everything your mom says about you."

This time, Zoey burst out laughing.

"What did I say? I don't have any objections to this little plan. I get it—my brother, the little cockroach, in love with himself and his fancy law school diplomas, embodies the perfect man for a certain red head I know."

Blushing and laughing at the same time, Sally asserted, "I don't have any plans for your brother. And, obviously, he doesn't have any for me either, except for when we went out for coffee last year, after which we were never alone again. I mentioned Dalton because I'm your friend and want to hear about everything that's going on in your life."

"Talking about me?" a cheerful voice said from the kitchen doorway

Dalton nonchalantly strode into the room. He actually was wearing a shirt—a light blue one with white stripes. It didn't go at all with his mass of straight, brown hair that he absolutely refused to cut, or with his face peppered with freckles. It went even less with the beige pants he was wearing that looked oddly like the style usually worn by his father, but a couple of sizes smaller. Altogether, the outfit gave him the appearance of a kid dressed up to receive some school award, but was in harsh contrast to the sly look on his face as he stared at the two women.

"We were talking about what a great DJ you are."

Dalton sprawled out on the nearest chair. "Don't even mention that. Mom is driving me crazy."

Sally and Zoey let slip a conspiratorial laugh.

"I pretended I had to run to the restroom to avoid having to suffer through Sinatra's 'Fly me to the Moon.'"

"I actually like that song," Sally mumbled, before abruptly returning to passionately working on her labels.

"Me too," Dalton responded. "But, you know, not when it's in the middle of a full-on Sinatra retrospective. I wanted to play some Harry Connick Jr, to change it up a bit, and Mom wanted to know why my generation has such bad taste in remakes."

Zoey and Sally stifled their laughter.

"Have the other guests arrived?" asked Zoey.

"Yes, they all came at once." You know the rules her rich suburbanite friends follow—everyone is fashionably 20 minutes late." "Hey you traitor,"

8

he added, addressing his sister, "You pawned Aunt Vicki off on Adrian and I think he's about to jump off a bridge. When I walked by them, he was this close to screaming that, just because he never asked you to marry him, it doesn't mean he's gay. I should have saved him, but..."

"You just couldn't face it. Yeah, I agree, you let him down. I love Aunt Vicki, but both Mom and her in the same evening, plus Laurie Harting!"

Dalton gave her a look, suddenly uncomfortable. Zoey knew he didn't like discussing personal matters with her. Since they'd been kids, they could talk about pretty much anything, except that. Dalton, underneath his happy and talkative exterior, could be extremely uptight. Her head still bent over her task, Sally broke the silence without picking up on their awkwardness.

"Laurie Harting?" She looked at Zoey, who had turned somewhat pale. "Does that mean that Spencer will be here?"

"Do you really think that Laurie would pass up the opportunity to parade her fiancé around here?" Zoey replied, a little more harshly than she'd meant to.

"I don't know her," Sally frowned. "But, according to what you've told me, yes, I have the impression that she's the type of person who doesn't really care about other people's feelings, right? As for Spencer, I don't know him either."

Dalton squirmed in his chair.

"Spencer's a good guy."

Sally lifted her head. Her cheeks were flushed again, but Zoey saw the flash of anger in her eyes when she looked at Dalton.

"A good guy?"

"I always thought of Spencer as a friend," Dalton began, but without daring to look at Zoey.

"Spencer? A friend? "He literally broke your sister's heart!"

Zoey had never seen her friend's temper before. She'd seen her aggravated after talking to an annoying client on the phone, or, after doing her most hated task, accounting. She'd seen her offended, surprised, and even upset once or twice, but she had never heard such raw irritation in her voice before, or seen her face wrinkle up in such displeasure, her green eyes gleaming with vengeance.

"A good guy wouldn't dump someone for her best friend from the neighborhood. A good guy certainly wouldn't do it by email."

"I...," tried Zoey, feeling woozy and whose voice went up a bit too high. "He was in Europe, to be fair, and..."

"Let it go," responded Sally, stopping her with a dismissive gesture.

She turned her attention back to Dalton who, silent, was looking at her with an indecipherable expression.

"A good guy has the decency to not show up at the wedding anniversary of the parents of his ex, almost-fiancée. So, Dalton, I agree that we can all have different opinions about people in general, but, in this case, this is really not my definition of a good guy."

She got up, made a pile of the labels, quickly and efficiently, and without another word, left the room.

"What's her problem?" asked Dalton. His face was stiff and so confused that Zoey wanted to laugh.

"I think that Sally is a stickler when it comes to vocabulary," Zoey responded.

Now, Dalton got up and walked around the table, touching the labels Zoey was finishing. He was circling her and she recognized the same hesitation that he'd had when he was about to ask her to cover for him, when they were teenagers before he sneaked out and didn't want to reveal the name of the girl he was meeting.

"Does it really bother you that he'll be here?" he asked quietly. "It's been two years."

Zoey didn't know what to say. She didn't have any experience discussing this type of thing with her brother and she didn't think this was the time to start. As for Dalton, he seemed to be asking the question on principle, and the rigid smile he was showing her meant he didn't really want to hear her response. Or he was getting ready for a deluge of tears, which would have been both out of character and awkward.

"No," Zoey declared, forcing herself to smile. "A lot of time has passed. It's only a memory now. I'm more worried about how Mom will react if I don't get these labels on the table than I am about crossing paths with Spencer and Laurie. Come on, Dalton, before we make things worse for ourselves."

She walked around the table, opened the oven to make sure that the miniature quiches were doing well, and, after picking up her labels, pushed her brother out of the kitchen. Dalton seemed to relax as they fell back into familiar adolescent behavior, pushing each other in the hallway.

Before going out the door, Dalton stopped and turned toward his sister.

"Zoey?" Don't get too worked over it, okay?"

"I never get worked up." Dalton lifted an eyebrow in doubt.

"Listen, I don't want you to think that I don't care about what you're going through, but you really need to move on.

"I have moved on, Dalton. Oh my, are you actually giving me advice on my love life?

Sally made that much of an impression on you?"

Uncomfortable, her brother moved from one foot to the other. When he turned his face to her, Zoey noticed that his jaw was tense and his hands were balled into a fist.

"I don't like being talked to like that. Sally should learn to control herself."

"I thought you liked her."

For a moment, the look Dalton gave her seemed to hold all the fury in the universe. He'd made that same face as a kid when she'd go into his room and take his toys without asking first.

"Have you ever heard me say that?"

"No, I haven't. That's true."

"So, don't start with your analysis that, that..."

"That women do?"

His tense smile transformed into a teasing one.

"That girlfriends do. I know the stuff you talk about when no one's around."

"Oh, Dalton, please…We aren't fourteen."

He opened the door and slid out, and, since Zoey was following behind, turned around and retorted,

"Really?"

Then he avoided Zoey's hand which was still as quick as ever, but not quick enough.

He's not wrong. Sometimes, I do act like I'm fourteen. But I can do it. I can be mature. So can you, you're also an adult.

However, this did not stop her from discretely catching up to her brother as he made his way through the crowd to his turntable, to give him a satisfying pinch before running off to escape retribution.

2
TOUCH OF LEMON

The guests did end up all arriving at the same time. Zoey had to give her mother credit where credit was due: everyone wanted to be seen at her parties. Sally had quickly and discretely rearranged the food. Fran Westwood was busy welcoming her friends. Zoey was able to slip through the crowd clustered in her parents' perfectly manicured yard and verify that everything was in order, from the appetizers laid out on the table to the cocktail fountain she'd set up despite her mother's lack of enthusiasm. She'd finally been able to convince Fran by using the argument that she'd be the first of her friends to have one.

Zoey knew most of the people who were laughing, talking and eating the hors d'oeuvres that she'd prepared herself and that the servers were bringing out from the kitchen, under Sally's strict direction.

Maybe that was the problem.

She shrunk back, behind the table, into the refreshing shadow of the trees. She was suddenly overcome by a desperate need to be alone.

Except for a few strangers like her father's clients, or new neighbors that her mother wanted to bring into her circle, she'd spent her entire childhood with these people that, now, she only saw once or twice a year, at Christmas or for her parents' annual barbecue. This year, the barbecue had been replaced by this extravagant anniversary party and everything was carefully orchestrated, from the white lanterns hanging from the trees to the china stacked at the end of each table.

Adrian had escaped Aunt Vicki but had ended up in the clutches of his own mother. She was pulling on the collar of his too-small t-shirt while talking to him in an animated fashion. Dalton, behind his turntable on the still-empty wooden dance floor, was using his headset to queue up the next song, while glancing around furtively at his mother's friends. They'd apparently decided to heckle him for the rest of the cocktail hour to make sure he played their favorites. Sally had once again disappeared into the kitchen.

Zoey saw her Uncle Malcolm, squeezed into a light-colored suit, and her Aunt Babeth whose form-fitting dress looked just like her mother's. The two sisters, while very different, had dressed alike since they were young girls. Babeth and Malcolm were talking to Laurie's parents.

Zoey made a nervous gesture when she caught a glimpse of Suzie Harting's perfect profile.

The awful Suzie Harting, the worst of her mother's friends, always ready to strike with a backhanded compliment wearing that sweet, practiced smile that never left her face.

But she's nothing compared to her dreadful husband.

Fred Harting was the epitome of the iron-fisted CEO with a heart of ice. His only weakness, or, more precisely, the only one that he'd admit to, with a satisfied laugh, was his only child, Laurie. He saw her as a precious gem--his beautiful, perfect Laurie and her mother's twin. This weakness for his daughter had led to him being particularly unkind to Zoey. He'd considered her friendship deadweight and undeserving of his princess.

As if thinking her name had made it so, Laurie appeared in Zoey's field of vision. The description of "princess" was appropriate. Laurie wore a summer pink dress that fell just above her knee and showed off her perfectly even tan and ash blond hair, carefully crafted waves falling onto her bare shoulders.

Zoey suppressed an exasperated sigh. Just looking at her gorgeous legs could make Barbie hide in her camper, put sweatpants on, and down an entire carton of cookie dough ice cream.

Overwhelmed by such perfection, and suddenly aware that her navy dress made her seem like an overdressed adolescent, Zoey receded further into the trees.

Breathing hard, she was waiting to see Spencer appear and wrap his arms around his fiancée's tiny waist.

However, he was nowhere to be seen, not by Laurie's parents as they gazed at her with undisguised admiration, or anywhere else.

She felt an arm slip through hers.

"I knew you'd be here, my little Zoey," she heard Adrian's voice say.

"Where could I hide? I'm sure my mom would find me even if I were taking a crap in the bathroom."

"Probably with the help of mine."

"We can thank the gods that they are busy torturing their neighbors."

"Or, maybe we should thank the ground in New Jersey that was never able to grow grass in this part of the yard, making it inaccessible to these middle-aged women teetering in their high heels.

If I knew what was good for me, I'd already be up in our treehouse," grumbled Zoey, lifting her eyes toward the branches.

"If I knew what was good for me, I'd *live* in the treehouse," Adrian declared. "I have such great memories of this place."

"Me too. Like that time I made Laurie's nose bleed."

Adrian put his arms around his friend's shoulders.

"So, Laurie Harting's the reason you're hiding in the trees? Her dress is hideous. She looks like Miss Piggy and..."

"Adrian," Zoey interrupted. "Thank for what you're doing. We both know she's sublime. Even that candy pink looks good on her. I look like a wiener dog compared to her."

"Hey, my little wiener dog," said Adrian looking right into her eyes. "Laurie Harting does not have one ounce of your humor, your intelligence or your class." She's got nothing. She's a plastic doll who, trust me, will have plastic surgery before she's twenty-five, and whose husband will cheat on her with his secretary."

"Do you have any other clichés you'd like to share?" smiled Zoey, somewhat comforted by this idea, but, at the same time, feeling petty and mean.

"Will someone notice that she's not a real blond and announce it on her wedding day?

"I think that Spencer has noticed she isn't a real blond."

"I try not to think about that kind of thing," Adrian replied in an amused tone. "She'll be so bored with her little suburban lifestyle that she'll spend her evenings posting cat videos on Facebook."

"I spend my evenings on Facebook."

"Posting cat videos?"

"No, photos of cakes."

"You're not just messing around, though. You're working!"

"Do you post concert videos on Facebook?"

"No," Adrian admitted.

"Well then."

"Wait, I have indisputable proof that you are worth more than all the Laurie Hartings in the world!"

Zoey looked at him intensely, waiting. Adrian's looked so solemn that she wanted to smack him with the back of her hand, like when they were kids, especially when he dropped his big bomb:

"Laurie Harting wasn't the one who got her first kiss from me."

"It wasn't *my* first kiss, Adrian.

It was *yours*."

"I prefer my version."

"I was there, you know."

She specifically remembered how wide and wistful Adrian's twelve-year old eyes had been, at the moment right before their lips touched. They had decided to keep their eyes open. According to Adrian, that's what lovers did. Seeing his eyes so huge, she'd thought he was afraid, but realized several seconds afterward that he'd discovered Dalton spying on them through the treehouse trap door. Dalton jumped toward the ladder, cackling that he was going tell everyone. They'd run after him, and she'd pinned him to the ground. They'd rubbed his face in the dirt until he swore he wouldn't tell. Adrian had never mentioned it since.

Neither had Zoey. But sometimes, during that year, she would daydream about what they'd be like when they were older: kissing each other passionately like the high school seniors did sometimes, even though it was also a bit disgusting, pushing into each other near the trees surrounding the soccer field. Then, from one day to the next, Adrian went back to his role as "best friend."

As both kids and teenagers, they had stayed the same--wild and free, Dalton always at their heels.

Adrian touched Zoey's cheek with his own.

"Are you still in love with Spencer?" he asked.

"Don't be stupid. After two years? No. It's just that Laurie and him together show me what a catastrophe my life is and what a catastrophe I am. If I were thinner, more assertive or, prettier he would never have left me for her, right? We could say that it was love at first sight, that it was written in the stars, blah, blah, blah, but in reality, he left me for her. Because I'm not a Laurie Harting."

"That's true. You are not a Laurie Harting and you will never be. Thank God. She spent her entire childhood trying to play the role of the perfect daughter. While she was practicing perfection, you grew up, learned things about life, and became the imperfect, endearing woman you are today. I didn't want to tell you at the time, because it seemed like you were very in love and very happy, but Spencer is a Laurie Harting, too. The perfect student, the perfect career. They are perfect together. I am sure there is an imperfect guy out there waiting for you."

"Oh, Adrian," Zoey whispered. "You are so you, so perfect."

"That's why I'm not the one for you, and you understood that about three seconds after our kiss."

"*Your* first kiss."

"Yeah, and I see that you were never able to get help with that pathological lying of yours."

Zoey burst out laughing and pinched his arm.

"So," Adrian said, redirecting the conversation, "you can finally tell me who the lucky guy was that you kissed before me."

"Chris Holfer."

"Chris 'Goody-Goody' Holfer? That guy who has five kids and goes to church every week?"

"That's the one. Do you think it's all somehow related?"

"I'm sure of it. After such a traumatic experience, the poor guy's only choice was to take refuge in religion."

She scanned the crowd. All of these people, so well-dressed, successful and prosperous, brought her back once again to her own insignificance. She could count those who were single on one hand. Even Stannie Jefferson, an account manager at her father's firm, had a date even though she was recently widowed. The only person who was proof that she had been part of a couple once, Spencer, was going to get married next year.

"I'm cursed. I'll end up alone, making cakes for other people's grandkids, like Aunt Vicki. And all my exes are nuts."

In a tender gesture, Adrian hugged her tightly. His t-shirt smelled like the laundry detergent Stella Peters had always used, and its odor plunged her into the comfort of the past.

"All your exes?" he asked. "What about Harry Urcman?"

"Apparently, he's an alcoholic."

"Oh, well then...What about Georgie Wilson?"

"He lives with his mother."

"Pete Frydrier?"

"Dead."

"You're joking!"

"Yes. But he is an accountant."

It was Adrian's turn to burst out laughing.

"And Spencer is Laurie's fiancé. There's a logic to it. Listen, my little Zoey, you don't want to become one of those pathetic thirty-year-olds who run after anything that moves in the hopes of shacking up. You're not going to become, for example, your cousin Tina are you?"

He pointed his finger at a young woman who was approaching Fran to give her a hug. Zoey stifled a cry of exasperation. Tina had obviously gone all out: a blue silk dress--Fran's favorite color, high heels as tall as a ladder, sweeping hair held up with a pin that matched her dress. It was ironic that she looked more like Fran's daughter—but without the brown hair did--than Zoey herself.

"I guess the entire neighborhood 'gang' is here now," Adrian said, deadpan. "Laurie, Tina, Dalton, you and me."

"Until we die, Adrian, Laurie will always be the stuck up one, and Tina will always be the annoying one," said Zoey dramatically. "The neighborhood gang! It made our parents feel good to believe that we were a happy group of inseparable friends. But I don't have one good memory of that time, except for things I did with you and Dalton. Not a single one. I

17

have this terrible feeling that I am condemned to relive this nightmare every year.

"Don't be such a pessimist. I still can't stop laughing every time I think about when we tied your cousin to that boat and let her drift around the lake."

"That because you weren't grounded for a week afterward. Your parents weren't as strict as mine.

"Really? Did you regret it?"

Zoey looked at him with as much determination as she could. They exchanged a conspiratorial smile, exactly the same one that they'd shared twenty years earlier, right before they took Zoey's jump rope and tied Tina's wrists after she'd refused to get out of the boat to give them a turn. There had been no need to discuss it. That had been quite practical at the time, since Adrian had been mostly mute.

"Absolutely not!" she exclaimed, with exactly the same fierce cry as that day long ago.

Then she smiled at him.

"Look at her, the phony. How much do you want to bet that she says something catty about the food?"

"Four dollars."

"That's it?"

"I only bet high when I'm sure to win."

Zoey put her head on Adrian's shoulder.

"We look like gossips, hiding here behind the trees. We're going to end up old and bitter, if you want to know what I think. Like those two grumpy old guys on The Muppet Show."

"I always loved those guys. Didn't you?"

"No. My favorite was that dog who played the piano. Because he reminded me of you."

She gave him a quick kiss on the cheek.

"I am a good little doggie," smiled Adrian. "Thanks, Zoey."

"Any time. Just think how easy life would be without Lauries or Tinas. Everything would have been perfect if they hadn't been around, if we hadn't had to hang out with them and if we hadn't been punished because they always found a way to get us and tattle.

"Well, we wouldn't have had the treehouse to hide in if we hadn't had someone to hide from. I hate it when you have regrets. I prefer the Zoey who is mad at the world one minute and laughs the next. Lift your head high and show them who you've become. Give them a lesson on what class means. With your bare feet and your tousled hair, you look like the heroine from the opera Carmen. Go show all the Spencers of the world that love really is a rebellious bird."

"Does my hair really look that bad?" Zoey wondered, suddenly remembering that she had not stopped by the bathroom and that she wasn't wearing shoes.

"A real gypsy. My mother is going to kill me."

Adrian removed his arm from Zoey's shoulder.

"Quick, go put some shoes on. I'll create a diversion."

"You're not going to sing, are you?"

"No. I'm going to go tell Aunt Vicki that I was the first one you kissed. While she's fainting and your mother runs to help her, you can sneak into the house."

"My poor Adrian, retorted Zoey, raising her eyebrows. "Even Aunt Vicki won't believe your story!"

Adrian smiled.

"Go or I'll tell on you!"

He didn't need to say it twice. Making sure that no one was on the way to the bar area, she walked around the trees to her right and moved directly toward the house, as fast as she could. When she reached the table where the cocktail fountains were on display, her heart skipped a beat. Spencer was just a few feet from her, illuminated by the lanterns, talking to Laurie's dad. He was a good head taller than Fred Harting. Zoey had forgotten how tall he was, how blond he was, and how much laughter suited him. However, he had often been serious around her and she'd found that attractive: tall and blond, constantly lost in thoughts that only he understood. She stopped cold, suddenly on the verge of tears and also furious with herself. She'd prepared for this. She'd imagined herself showing up, serene and majestic, holding out her hand (her cheek?) to Spencer, in perfect control of her emotions. She'd gone over what she'd say more than twenty times: modestly listing her successes over the past two years and asking him about his career and his mother. Spencer, blown away by how mature she seemed, would immediately regret all the pain he'd caused her.

But now, she just wanted to curl up in a ball and die right there, shoeless with crazy hair, while shocked guests looked on and her cousin Tina observed her coldly. Tina never missed a chance to remind her how pathetic she'd always been.

"Would you like something to drink?" someone next to her said.

She turned around. The man standing close to her was holding an empty glass and looked at her, expressionless.

"They should have lit the area around the food up a bit more," the guest said. "I can't read the labels."

Those stupid labels. She looked at this unknown man, suddenly certain that her mother was paying him to point out her mistakes. If he kept talking to her, she'd be forced to stay where she was, and her chances of looking presentable when she faced Spencer – even if it was to die at his feet – were dwindling.

"I'm the caterer," she said, taking his glass out of his hand and opening up the fountain faucet. "This one dispenses margaritas. Sound good?"

"These fountains are a great idea.

"Thank you."

"Now it's my turn to serve you," he said elegantly.

His voice was both warm and curt at the same time, like he was hiding an outgoing personality under multiple layers of finishing school manners.

She looked at him directly now and noticed that he was in very good shape and, even though he wasn't smiling, that he was quite attractive. He was wearing a white shirt and well-fitting jeans. His straight, thick hair was a dark brown that made her want to touch it.

Although his face was not quite symmetrical, he gave off an aura of nobility. His strong nose lacked refinement and his mouth was a bit too long, emphasizing his square jaw. The way he carried himself as he came toward her was what made his entire being seem graceful. In a different place at a different time, she would surely have succumbed to his charms. She wondered who he was and why he continued to stare at her in that odd way, with something between interest and suspicion, while he brought his glass to his lips.

"I'm Zoey," she said.

It seemed like he thought about it for a second, then transferred his drink to his left hand and held out his right.

"Matthew Ziegler."

She'd never heard this name mentioned by her parents. He had mumbled it, almost with regret, as if he wasn't certain that he wanted to introduce himself.

"Are you sure?"

"Yes. Very," he replied with a self-deprecating smile.

"Even if this margarita is especially strong."

"I made those too," she specified.

"I like my alcohol strong."

"It seems like you need it."

He smiled at her. Zoey looked at him quizzically.

"What do you mean by that?"

"Well, seeing you like that, standing on the grass, your hand on your heart, in bare feet ..."

Zoey felt her face getting hot. All of the anger she'd been feeling from the beginning of the evening was close exploding. She was drowning in it.

"What is that supposed to mean? Do I look like an alcoholic? Or desperate?"

He was paying attention but didn't have time to respond.

"Does every woman who walks across a yard in bare feet seem like they need a drink?" she continued, agitated. "Is that what you think? That if a woman doesn't wear a thousand-dollar pink dress, she's got to be a poor old thing and you've got to serve her margaritas to make her more agreeable?"

He was standing there, immobile, eyes wide, with his glass suspended in air.

"I only meant to say that it seemed like you'd been hit hard and..."

"Oh, that's it!" Zoey exclaimed. "You think I am one of those abused women who need help from perfect strangers to get back on their feet? This is bizarre! I'm simply walking across my own yard, and all of a sudden, a guy who can't even remember his own name thinks he can psychoanalyze me, all because we're drinking margaritas! You don't even know me. First of all, how do you know I don't have a legitimate reason for not wearing shoes? Maybe I, I don't know, have flat feet! Or, maybe I just like walking around bare foot. Which obviously makes me bipolar!

"I..."

"I'm going to give you some advice: you need to get outside of your bubble!"

She stopped, breathing hard, suddenly aware that she had been speaking loudly in a voice filled with hysteria. Surprisingly, he didn't turn and run. In fact, he let out a discreet laugh, full of mirth. Behind him, several guests, including Spencer who was squinting to see who was responsible for this erratic diatribe, had stopped talking and were looking at them.

"I'm sorry," stammered Zoey, without looking away from Spencer.

"Not as sorry as I am," pronounced Matthew. "Especially if your feet really are flat."

She wanted to be swallowed up by the earth and disappear. Without replying, she did an about-face and ran toward the house for refuge.

By the expression on Sally's face when she saw her come in through the back door and lean against the table, Zoey understood that she must look like a crazy person who'd just escaped from the asylum.

"Your mother figured out that the food wasn't kosher, right?" she asked.

"Please don't joke right now," sputtered Zoey, who chugged her margarita in one gulp, making her cough. "That *was* way too strong!"

"What? What did your mother do now?"

"No, the margarita. Sally, we have to water down the drinks right now or my parents and their guests are going to be under the table before the dancing begins."

"I'm tempted to leave it like it is."

Zoey gave her a dirty look.

"Okay, okay," Sally conceded. "Let me guess. You had a fight with Laurie Harting?"

21

"I look that bad?" Zoey asked, turning over a stainless steel bowl to try and see the damage.

"Let's just say that you are a bit disheveled and totally beet red. What happened?"

"It was awful," Zoey said. "Spencer was there."

"You knew Spencer would be here," Sally objected.

She opened the fridge to take out some lemons and tried to figure out Fran Westwood's complicated, extremely loud food processor.

"I didn't realize I would take it so badly."

Sally rolled her eyes.

"I could have told you that. And? You got all red and ran away?"

"Don't be sarcastic."

"I'm not being sarcastic," Sally replied, seriously. "That's what I would have done."

"Yes, I ran away. But before that, I attacked one of my parents' guests, a guy I didn't even know."

"One of their friends?"

"No, someone our age. Probably the son of one of my dad's clients. Oh my god, they are going to kill me and, this time, they'll be right!"

"Well. It can't be as dramatic as you think. Just find him and apologize and explain that you were under a lot of pressure for everything to be perfect and it was just too much. Use the stress card, that always works. Do you remember his name or did he even have time to introduce himself before you started in on the fireworks?"

"Yes. Matthew. Wait...Matthew Ziegler."

Sally froze and turned toward her. Zoey understood then that this was something even worse than her having made a fool of herself in front of everyone.

"Matthew Ziegler? Tall, dark, sexy?"

"Well, talk and dark, yes. I'm sure he's sexy, when he isn't being yelled at by someone who's hysterical."

Sally set half of a lemon down on her workspace and approached her friend.

"Matthew W. Ziegler?"

"He didn't mentioned the 'W'."

"Wait. Well dressed, very good looking? Acting like everything around him was totally beneath him?"

"Yes. No. I don't know anymore. But who is this Matthew Ziegler anyway?"

"Do you not read the press releases that I write up?"

Sally voice was creeping dangerously high.

"Um, sometimes."

"No, you never do!"

Zoey realized she was guilty and that it was true. She thought press releases were boring, like accounting and really everything that was not directly related to the act of cooking. She'd let Sally manage all the business aspects of the company, and Sally was very good at it, too.

"Matthew Ziegler," Sally repeated. "One of the most influential food critics in New York. Matthew W. Ziegler. He's closed down restaurants in less than 90 words!

Sally's mouth closed tightly into a furious grimace. She took her smartphone out of her uniform pocket and frantically started typing.

"Do you want to hear an example? *Le Crescendo is worthy of its name for several reasons. However, while they may pile food high on your plate, the result is a mountain that sits in your stomach and reaches up toward your throat. Everything it serves is exaggerated, over-spiced, ridiculously "original" and haphazard. Instead of the* pleasant *climax we were expecting as we worked our way through the amuse-bouche to dessert, we ended up with the feeling that we'd been made to climb Mt. Everest and even an ice ax can't keep you from falling when they add insult to injury with the sky-high bill.*

Sally gave Zoey her most mischievous smiled.

"And, sometimes, he does it in three words: *Three stars, really?*

"Oh my god," Zoey choked out. "He criticized my margarita!"

An out of control, nervous laughter was rising in her chest. The tequila's warmth had taken effect and she felt dizzy.

"That makes you want to laugh?" Sally barked, close to having a nervous breakdown. "You just attacked a guy who can make or break your career and close down your business, and that makes you want to laugh?"

Zoey wanted to answer her, but the laughter rising in her throat was preventing her from speaking. Peals of hysterical hooting filled the kitchen and Sally looked at her in total amazement.

"Zoey, are you completely sloshed? What are you thinking?"

"I, no, nothing, it's just that...," a new wave of laughter overtook her.

"I was just thinking that...that he..."

Zoey slide along the side of the stainless steel work table.

"that after that, he..."

Tears were now falling down her cheeks. Sally let out a small hiccup and tried not to smile. Sitting on the tile floor, Zoey took a deep breath so that she could finish her sentence.

"...that he might close down my parents' yard!"

Visibly fighting the urge to strangle her, Sally couldn't help but erupt in giggles too.

3
CASTER SUGAR

Zoey agreed to return to the yard once the lemons had been squeezed, her hair fixed, her feet covered in a pair of horribly uncomfortable flats, and after she'd received ten minutes of animated coaching from Sally. Everyone seemed to have forgotten the incident (or, more likely, denied it had have even happened), because she was welcomed by friendly faces and compliments on the food.

Only Nana, her grandmother, looked at her critically with her green eyes as she approached, the same way she had when Zoey was a child and she would ask the older woman a question that she felt was beneath Zoey's abilities.

Zoey pasted on a warm smile and sat next to her grandmother. The elderly woman had maintained her presence, despite having diminished in size with age. It gave her the strength of authority with one look. It was that look that had kept the entire family in line, except for Zoey with whom she shared a special, light-hearted closeness and to whom she gave plenty of leeway.

"*Errare humanum est, perseverare diabolicum,*" she growled, tapping her finger on the white table top next to a plate of half-eaten appetizers.

Zoey opened her mouth to object that she still didn't speak Italian.

"That's Latin," Nana interrupted, knowing her granddaughter all too well. "It means that it is human to err, but diabolical to persist in error. Can you explain to me what happened?"

"I don't even know myself. I was so angry, and Mom…"

"No, I don't mean the dramatic scene you treated us to earlier. I would think that that young man regrets the lack of respect he displayed toward you, in any case."

"He wasn't the one that showed a lack of respect. I was the one that...oh well!"

"Yes, oh well. *That* is what I'm talking about."

She used her finger to point at a filo appetizer positioned on her plate.

"Is it overcooked?" Zoey guessed.

"It's perfect. But, Zoey! Cheese sauce on top, really?"

"Too dry," admitted Zoey, defeated. "Then they were soggy from the cheese, I guess."

"Didn't I teach you anything?" Zoey wrinkled her nose.

"Of course. But my mother—your daughter—wanted these specifically. I can assure you that they weren't my idea."

"I believe you. You remember my Aunt Tilla, don't you?"

Nana had told her this story millions of times before, but Zoey loved it—even Nana's embellished version.

Nana had spent the first part of her childhood in Naples, in the family restaurant. Her sister Victoria had been in tow then as she was now, decades later. She had often spoken of the smells that had emanated from that kitchen—from *parmigiana* on Mondays, to *frittate di maccheroni* on Sundays, and not forgetting the fish *piatti* on Fridays. Giuseppe, Nana's father, was at the center of the family business. Nana described him as a small, dynamic man with a brash manner. He liked to spend money, had a snazzy black mustache and a cold eye. He ruled the front of the house, but in the kitchen, it was his sister Tilla who held the power. She was two years younger than he was, and in her mind's eye, Zoey confused her with the image of her grandmother as a young woman. Nana's own mother, a kind woman, sometimes helped serve, but was preoccupied with the little Victoria who was already a chatterbox and with Nana who was always trying to escape her mother's watchful eye. She tried to avoid getting caught up in any conflict between her husband and his sister. They were both impulsive and hot headed and, often, their culinary differences resulted in shouting and splattered tomato sauce.

Giuseppe, exasperated, traditional, and, deep down, proud of his younger sister, often complained that she had not married. He decided to take it upon himself to find her a pliable husband. His vigorous pursuit of this goal caused an uproar in their small, quiet neighborhood in Naples that they nourished with their excellent antipasti. Suitors came forward, lured by both Tilla's beauty and the false impression that the family had great wealth.

The young woman dismissed them one by one, resorting to hiding in the water closet at the end of the hallway to avoid meeting them. Enraged, Giuseppe would call to her from the kitchen, her admirer having already fled, frightened off by the idea of marrying such an impetuous woman.

Giuseppe finally resigned himself, but not without first announcing that his sister would end up an old maid, wrinkly like a prune, dependent on him.

One of the points of contention between Nana's father and his strong-willed sister was a certain dish—*genovese* sauce. Tilla had added it to their menu but Giuseppe, a Napolitano to the core, refused to even consider serving it. Despite being only six years old at the time, Nana clearly remembered her father's angry protests and cries that shook the house to its foundations. Most of the time, Tilla was content to offer him a smug smile, arguing that this sauce would be the key to their wealth and glory. She did so with exaggerated confidence and an unyielding will. Her brother would counterattack by suggesting to their customers that they order other selections from the menu. Due to his charisma as well as the credit that he had extended to the regulars, customers stopped ordering this source of their dispute altogether. Tilla was not, however, discouraged.

Every day, in addition to what was expected, she would also cook up the forbidden sauce.

Nana would recount this story from the point of view of a little girl devoted to the aunt who encouraged her to help in the kitchen when everyone else said she was too little to be of any help at all. As seen from a child's perspective, the story had been romanticized into a fairy tale, and then into a legend that no one dared question. In Nana's version, one lovely day, a stranger from Genoa visited the restaurant and sat alone at a table, ordering a plate of pasta. When Giuseppe inquired as to what sauce he would like, the guest replied that he'd let the cook decide. Rebelliously and with a touch of irony, Tilla served her *genovese* sauce. After taking a bite, the man asked to meet her. He congratulated her and left a generous tip. He came back the next day, again asking for the "chef's choice." Giuseppe stayed angry through the entire week and then became used to seeing the well-mannered traveler. A month passed and he asked for Tilla's hand in marriage.

To everyone's surprise, she accepted, captivated by this quiet man who loved her cooking. With a heavy heart, she predicted that her brother would not succeed without her and she followed her intended to Genoa. A year later, the neighborhood suffered hard times and the restaurant went bankrupt. Giuseppe, true to his impulsive nature, sold everything and moved his family to the United States. Once there, he transferred the deep, unconditional love he'd had for his sister to his eldest daughter who was also talented in the kitchen.

After working in someone else's restaurant for several years, Giuseppe opened a new restaurant and prospered.

Nana never saw her aunt Tilla again. As a young woman, Nana had talked about reuniting with her and her husband. Her only memories of him were that he'd worn a gold signet ring on his wedding day. Then, one day, a letter arrived announcing that her aunt had died, most likely from pneumonia. Nana never saw her father grieve, and, to stay strong, never let herself cry either. But, her entire life, in her dressing table, she kept a cameo that her aunt had given her the day she left for Genoa. She had also given her the gift of wit and a stubborn refusal to follow the culinary conventions of others.

"And so?" said Nana, coming back to the present. "What is any chef's greatest asset?"

"A good stain remover?"

Nana repressed a smile.

"Confidence," intoned Zoey. "I should have defended my menu choices. It's not that easy. There's no mysterious stranger to provide support. And, my mom is your daughter, I'd like to remind you."

"Yes, I know, and it never ceases to amaze me. The cocktail fountains were your own idea, right?"

"Yes. And the margaritas are too strong.

Tequila is always too strong. Contrary to what people think, rum makes the best cocktails and tequila makes the best desserts."

Zoey filed this information away. She'd never thought of using tequila like that, and had only thought of using the types of alcohol "approved" for this purpose, like rum or cognac. Her mind started working.

"You should write a new cookbook, Nana."

"Oh, goodness, no! So, tell me, if you could have prepared anything you wanted, what would your menu have been?"

Zoey didn't have to think about it long. When her mother had asked her to cater the anniversary celebration – negotiating a nice discount on the sly – the perfect menu for such an occasion had immediately come to mind.

"I would have chosen a dish from each country in Europe where they'd spent their honeymoon. France, Italy, Spain, Austria and Greece. I would have set up stations where the guests could watch each item being prepared and a cocktail bar like the one they have at the Ritz. I would have served something that was both sweet and salty because Dad loves that, and desserts that guests could assemble themselves."

Nana put her hand on Zoey's arm.

"Lovely. I would have enjoyed seeing all that instead of eating smoked salmon on toast for the hundredth time. Your tartar was excellent, by the way, Zoey. You need to tell me where you found that honey."

Her compliment reassured Zoey a bit.

"Do you think Mom noticed?"

"Your mother didn't eat a thing for three days to get ready for the party. Most of her friends couldn't tell the difference between orange blossom honey and pigeon poop. Well, fortunately, we won't be subjected to chicken cordon bleu."

Zoey gave her a tight smile.

"It's on its way. With the first course."

Nana sighed deeply but her eyes sparkled.

"You have good ideas, my dear. Do not let these imbeciles ruin them. And no matter what, never let anyone tell you what to do using the excuse that you deserve better than the life you have chosen for yourself."

She squeezed Zoey's arm.

"Believe me. A lot of people will think you have a unique approach, because you see the art of cooking as something to be shared, and not as a catalog of conventions and clichés. They will try to make you believe that your talent must be used to serve as many people as possible. That's just not true. When I published my first cookbook, the publisher wanted to divided it into four separate sections. A good cookbook must have enough recipes to prepare dozens of meals that fit a cook's budget and style."

"And you sold thousands of copies."

"Millions, if you count the translations. Even in Europe. An American cookbook. I had to fight for that. Just think, a woman, in that era…"

"You were so avant-garde, Nana."

"No. I cooked for my family every day of my life and I never worked outside the home. Your grandfather thought that kids and toilets cleaned themselves. But, I always held my ground on one thing."

"Your freedom?"

"My choices. Stand by what you think is right, at all cost."

Nana's mouth bent into an amused grin.

"Except for where you mother is concerned. That's a waste of time. Do what you want and just don't tell her."

She touched Zoey's arm one last time.

"That's what you've always done, isn't it? So. Will Adrian be playing something for us this evening?"

"Not unless we make him."

Nana laughed. Most people's laughs rose in pitch. Hers dropped, pure and completely free.

"I've always been fascinated by the way that this boy seemed to detest being forced to play Gershwin at family parties but he would then play an entire concerto masterfully when he thought no one was listening. Sort of like you with cheese gougères. I have often wondered how such conventional people like the Peters and your parents could have given birth to two rebels like you."

"DNA is a roll of the dice," replied Zoey, slightly sarcastically. "Genetic defects often skip a generation."

"Be prepared to have boring kids then if that's true," retorted the old woman in the same tone of voice.

Go on. Your Aunt Vicki and Becky are getting dangerously close to our

29

table. Nobody should have to suffer through that.

Zoey kissed her grandmother on the cheek and slipped away before Vicki could trap her with one of her interminable monologues. She took a moment to make sure the tables still looked good, but more out of habit than because she was actually worried. Sally was keeping a careful eye on everything so that Zoey could enjoy the evening. She parked herself next to the cocktail fountains. It was the only place where she was free from the presence of her parents' oh-so-conventional friends who preferred to be served by the wait staff.

She was joined by a desperate Adrian who clearly had not succeeded in his attempts at finding his inner Zen. Without a word, he offered her one of the glasses he was holding.

"Thanks for thinking of me," she said.

"Actually, that was totally by chance. I'd been planning to drink them both. Did you know that Fred Harting has two new boats?"

"Well, well, I'm sure you couldn't get him to stop talking about them."

"He described them from the hull to the sails."

Zoey gulped her margarita to stifle her laughter.

"That's better! I'll have to let Sally know."

"Send Dalton her way," Adrian advised. Dalton isn't interested in Sally. I feel bad about that. Obviously, I'm not going to tell her that, but you can imagine how uncomfortable I feel when she talks about him."

He glanced at her sideways and went back to sipping his drink.

"Is everything turning out like you'd planned?"

"I haven't had to do much. Now I just need to supervise and not get too bored."

"What? How could you possibly find this boring? If we're lucky, we might even get to dance!"

He mimed a few tango steps.

"I hope Laurie and Spencer will regale us with the waltz they've learned in dance class preparing for their fabulous wedding," sighed Zoey before finishing off her glass in one swig. "Should I get another one?"

"Zoey, Zoey, Zoey! You know what happens when you drink."

"I can hold my alcohol."

To prove it to him, she stopped a server and grabbed a glass from his tray. She emptied that one as quickly as the first, before taking a third.

"Okay. I accept your challenge, Adrian stated, smiling. He then took a second glass too."

"No," she replied, with the strange sensation that her tongue was half numb. "What's coming up next is going to be the real test. Come with me."

Before he could protest, she took him by the arm and dragged him toward a table where several guests were sitting. Spencer had just brought a plate to Laurie and she thanked him silently, her face toward him, with an arm nonchalantly resting on the back of his chair, crossing her endless legs.

"Did you see how she wrinkles her nose?" she murmured in Adrian's ear. "I think that would be so cute...if you were a rabbit."

"Oh, Zoey, please, don't breathe in my face. And for god's sake, do not get anywhere near a candle."

He had to catch her as she slipped on the grass.

"Stupid shoes! She never fell when she was wearing running shoes. All shoes should be banned, except running shoes."

"Zoey, I think that is the worst idea you've ever had. You're half drunk."

"I am not half drunk."

"Right—you're totally drunk, and..."

Adrian was not able to finish his sentence. They had already reached Laurie and Spencer, who didn't have time to get away, seeing that Zoey and Adrian had appeared out of nowhere. They were clones—both with polite smiles on their faces. Right when Zoey was going to open with what she thought was a particularly hilarious 'How's it going?' she noticed in horror that her cousin Tina was leaning in toward Matthew Ziegler, both of them sitting at the same table, in deep conversation. When he saw her, the food critic stopped speaking and a gleam passed over his chestnut-colored eyes. Laurie was the first to break the heavy silence that had settled in.

"Everything is so delicious, Zoey," she said, indicating her plate. "The curry is exceptional. I'd love to know what you put in it."

Zoey was going to respond when Adrian bent toward her and whispered in her ear,

"Do not tell her what you really think, have mercy."

She touched him softly to move him out of her way. At least that's what she thought she did. She'd literally shoved Adrian off into the corner.

"Curry."

"Just curry?" Laurie insisted.

"Well, obviously, no. I can give you the recipe if you want."

"It's really different."

Zoey looked at her for a moment, to make sure she wasn't being sarcastic.

"Not in India, I would think," she replied.

"It's lucky we're in New Jersey then, isn't it!" Tina interjected with a sickeningly sweet smile on her lips.

Laurie turned toward her, hiding the expression on her face from Zoey who didn't doubt for a second that she approved of what she'd said. She had known their little game since childhood.

"So, what's new?" Zoey continued.

She tried to make her tone sound as neutral as possible, but her voice sounded bitter and shrill. At Laurie's side, Spencer raised his eyebrows.

"Spencer just got a promotion!" Laurie announced.

Zoey stared at her ex-boyfriend, waiting for him to say something.

"And what a promotion!" added Tina. "Laurie and he are going to buy a house in the neighborhood. Have you made up your mind yet?"

"Not yet," Laurie mumbled.

"You really liked that three-bedroom one. The other day you were telling me that the terrace filled the living room with light."

"A terrace, great," Adrian interjected. "A house. Kids." (He hesitated and then added:) "A dog."

He winked at Zoey and then put his arm around her waist.

"It was great talking to you. Now, I think Zoey has to go to the kitchen to make sure that everything is going okay. Don't you, Zoey?"

"Everything is under control," she said, her tongue pasty.

Now, her entire mouth felt numb. Spencer gave her a long look, before the nervous tic appeared that she knew so well. The one that came out when he was particularly embarrassed, like that time she'd asked one of his friends, when they were talking about politics, if there was really an issue in Iraq. In that case, her attempts to convince him had ended up sounding suspiciously like the lyrics to "We Are the World."

"How's it going, Spencer?" Adrian asked. Zoey opened her mouth to tell him to be quiet.

She knew him too. He wasn't able to resist making fun of someone he didn't like for long, and every time he did it, he had this weird "calm before the storm" thing going, a seriousness that predicted the worse.

"It's going well," Spencer confirmed. "How about you, Adrian? Do you still play the piano?"

Zoey turned toward Adrian. This was going to be bad.

"Yes, I do, my dear Spencer, and my fingers are like lightning. They rarely strike the same place twice, but sometimes they do. But, I try to stay out of treble."

Spencer didn't understand the joke, but Zoey noticed that Matthew Ziegler, who had been following the exchange with a straight face until then was now suppressing a smile.

"How's your love life?" Tina demanded.

"Still the same. Not enough room for two at my piano," Adrian stated neutrally. "Musicians are solitary."

"I dated a cellist when I was in college," Spencer said. "I was obsessed with how she held her bow."

Adrian opened his eyes wide. The expression "served up on a silver platter" came to Zoey's mind, despite the fog that was beginning to invade her brain.

"Thank you, Spence', for this perceptive musical metaphor. Do you still play the flute, Laurie? Do you finger, tongue and blow at the same time?"

Zoey burst out laughing, but quickly stifled it, because the look her ex gave her at that exact instant made her want to disappear from the face of the earth. Another laugh responded to hers. She lifted her eyes toward Matthew Ziegler and noticed that, this time, he was very amused.

Laurie, however, was furious.

"You are so funny," Adrian, Tina said. "Maybe you could use this particular talent to tell jokes between two

Gershwin pieces in, I don't know, a piano bar, for example?"

"Excellent idea," retorted Adrian. "I hope you'll come watch me play. I'll ask the bartender to show you where the single guys are hanging out. Once your blood alcohol level is high enough, anything is possible, you know."

Tina's lips tightened.

"Anything is possible, yes," she hissed. "It's even possible that people think you actually have talent."

"And you, a brain."

"I think everyone gets it," murmured Laurie. "If you could stop..."

Zoey noticed that Laurie's lovely tan tone had changed to a bright red. She was torn between the desire to torture her some more or prevent her cousin and best friend from making a scene in front of Spencer. The alcohol prevented her from resolving this dilemma and added to her frustration that she hadn't been the one to make the scene.

To her great relief, Laurie's comment seemed to have defused Adrian.

"Spencer, it's always a pleasure to talk to you," he said. "Laurie, Tina and..."

He suddenly realized Matthew Ziegler was there. The delighted expression that crossed his face announced that the final blow was coming.

Zoey gripped his arm to silence him. Surprised, he pulled it away. In horror, she saw herself falling toward Spencer, try to regain her balance and then trip over herself. He elbow collided with her former beau's nose, knocking him over. She tried to catch herself on the edge of the table, missed, hitting the side of the plate Laurie had placed there during their conversation.

It flew into the air. Zoey saw it land, upside down, on Laurie's pink dress, smearing it with salmon and curry. The young woman let out a deafening wail.

The twenty faces around them did an turned as one. Zoey saw her mother's, frozen in a gracious smile that, as she took in the scene, immediately transformed into an angry and disapproving frown.

From that moment, everything happened very quickly.

Spencer ineffectually tried rubbing Laurie's ruined dress and Tina let out a stream of obscenities in her cousin's direction. Matthew Ziegler went in search of paper towels and Suzie Harting rushed over to her daughter with a glass of water while Laurie surveyed the damage with tears in her eyes.

The guests closest to the debacle stared, while Fran was ready to descend on Zoey like the plague.

It was Dalton who saved her. The music suddenly increased in volume and an enthusiastic voice was heard as the first measures of "Strangers in the Night" began. Joe Westwood, who was not aware of what had happened, was looking for his wife to ask her to dance.

This song was supposed to kick off the dancing portion of the party and Fran had drilled this into her husband and her children ad nauseum. Fran had no choice but to take Joe's arm and follow him.

Adrian took the opportunity to grab Zoey by the shoulder and remove her from the scene of the crime, but not before letting her indulge in good laughing fit.

"You can never control yourself," she cried, when they had successfully disappeared into the reassuring mass of guests watching Fran and Joe whirl their way under the lanterns.

"You should thank me," Adrian retorted. "You were going to make a complete fool of yourself."

Zoey dug her fingernails into his hand as they weaved a path through the party goers surrounding the stage.

The only positive thing to come of all this was that, now, she was sober.

"I ruined Laurie's dress and everyone is going to think I did it out of petty vengeance."

"Why would anyone think that?"

"I should punch you," snapped Zoey.

"You already scratched me, you witch!"

Several people turned toward them, including Adrian's mother. She motioned for them to lower their voices.

"We never change," whined Zoey. "Fifteen years into the future, Laurie will be remembered as the poor victim and we will always be the two troublemakers who have to be told to be quiet, because we can't behave like normal people for more than two minutes."

A discreet "shhhh" came out of nowhere, interrupting her. She looked around to see who it was but everyone seemed mesmerized by the spectacle of her parents perfectly executing the choreographed dance they'd been practicing for weeks.

Joe Westwood twirled Fran as Zoey continued,

"You know what I want to do? I'm going to straight up to the margarita fountain and empty it."

"On Laurie Harting's head? To go with the curry?" asked Adrian.

"And after that, I'm going to go home and try to forget this awful evening."

Her parents were graciously spinning in front of her. Fran's eyes were shining and Joe pulled her toward him, hugging her to his heart. Zoey didn't doubt for one second that her mother had spent hours perfecting this moving scene, with calculating precision.

"I suppose that nothing I could say would divert you from your noble goal," Adrian murmured into her ear.

"You've already done enough, I think."

Nodding his head, he conceded that she was right.

"Okay, Carmen," he sighed. "Go empty that fountain full of tequila. I'll stand by you, in sickness and in health."

"Rest assured that I can still find my bed even when I'm falling-down drunk."

She knew she could count him in situations like this. Adrian didn't have any limits

when they verbally went at it, but he had never left her in a truly embarrassing situation or anywhere where she would have been in physical or—like now—mental danger.

When she woke up the next morning, she saw that he had kept his word: she was in her old room, in her twin bed, under her quilted bedspread.

She was surprised, however, to see that Adrian was there too, between her and the wall, one arm on his stomach and the other lost somewhere under the cream and blue ruffled cotton pillows.

The thing that surprised her even more was that she was as naked as he was.

4

ICING SUGAR

She was able to keep from screaming, saved by the jackhammer drilling in her head.

She didn't remember a thing. Well, almost nothing.

She felt to make sure she was wearing her bra and panties. She checked twice and then had to accept that the only piece of clothing partially covering her was Adrian's AC/DC t-shirt thrown over her chest.

Snippets came back to her abruptly as she reached around for her dress which had been thrown at the bottom of the bed. When she had it in her hand, she noticed that something was twisted up in one of the sleeves. She pulled it out and saw that it was Adrian's black boxer shorts.

As if in a nightmare, she could see herself raging on the dance floor with him to the oldie but goodie "Johnny B. Goode." As he focused on the turntable, Dalton's half-amused, half-fearful face appeared and disappeared behind her hair as it jerked to the rhythm along with the rest of her body. No use in asking if her semblance of a chignon had survived.

She slipped her dress back on with difficulty, pushing away various flash-backs, one of which was particularly embarrassing—of her hiking up that same dress to try and climb the treehouse ladder, egged on by an Adrian, barking drunken advice.

She put one foot on the floor and immediately felt nauseous. The room was pitching back and forth more than the deck of one of Fred Harting's boats. She was searching the ground for her panties, fighting the urge to vomit.

She peeked down at her feet. Considering how bad her toes looked, she must not have kept her flats on for very long either.

She vaguely remembered tossing them onto the grass, late at night, when most of the guests had already left the yard.

However, through the waves of throbbing, it was impossible to retrace what had happened between when she and Adrian were trying to climb the tree and when they landed in her bed. This was despite a great effort on her part.

Adrian groaned in his sleep.

She staggered to the door and opened it carefully, to both avoid waking Adrian and the start of another migraine.

Her mother's voice floated up from the bottom of the stairs.

"I'm not sure I can eat anything for breakfast, Joseph. All that food yesterday!"

Stuck between her room and her brother's, Zoey, breathing hard, froze on the landing. In the off chance that her mother hadn't noticed that she'd ruined Laurie's outfit and gotten smashed, she couldn't go downstairs like this, wearing the same dress she'd had on last night, her eyelashes smeared with mascara and guilt on her face.

A low grunt came from her room at the exact moment that her mother's footsteps began to fade. She needed help, and she needed it now.

Surprised at how fast she could move, Zoey darted into Dalton's room, just across from hers. His room hadn't changed since he'd left for college. He was splayed across his teenage bed, under a poster of a sailboat and a bookshelf. Their mother had removed any of her son's reading materials from the shelf that she'd found offensive, and replaced them with collections of English poetry.

Rewriting history was one of Fran Westwood's favorite pastimes.

The chapter entitled "Thirty-five Years of Marriage" would be the subject of many drafts and redrafts, Zoey was convinced. Her mother would torture her in private with a thousand different versions before coming up with the version of the facts to be used for public consumption, significantly whitewashed.

She stopped cold.

Another flashback made her throat tighten. Had she cried during her father's speech? In front of everyone? Before throwing herself into his arms, sobbing on his shoulder?

Okay, she thought as she was overcome with shame.

I'm dead.

Doubly dead if her mother caught Adrian in her room. None of Fran Westwood's children had ever been allowed to sleep with anyone under her roof.

And certainly not to screw a childhood friend in her twin bed.

Even if Fran had never formally expressed this particular rule, even though she expected her oldest child to constantly think up ways to embarrass her, it was surely because she would never have imagined that

Zoey was capable of doing such a thing. This was only because it would never have crossed her mind to consider Adrian as a possible son-in-law.

Zoey hopped over the clothes strewn across the floor to her brother's bed, put her hand on his shoulder and gently shook him.

"Tell Mom I'm not hungry," Dalton groaned, his head buried in the pillow.

"Dalton, I need your help."

"Get lost, Zoey. I played DJ for the entire Country Club until one o'clock in the morning and my ears are still bleeding."

"Dalton, it's an emergency. If you don't get up right now, I'm going to tell Mom that you spent your entire summer internship in college smoking weed with Andrew Mayer on the roof at his dad's office."

Her words were like a cold shower and Dalton sat up before he had even opened his eyes.

"There's nothing I can do for you, he argued in a thick voice. You got drunk on tequila and Uncle Malcolm filmed all of it. If this video of me in a sky blue shirt gets out, I can say goodbye to my reputation."

"You're a lawyer, Dalton, not a professional DJ. You're going to spend your entire life in sky blue shirts. Now, get up! I really need your help."

Dalton opened his sleep-filled eyes to look at his sister and burst out laughing.

"Hellooooo, Alice Cooper!"

"It's no time for jokes," Zoey snapped. "You have to go downstairs right now and make sure Mom stays away from the dining room."

"I could also go get you some makeup remover. That'd be quicker and much easier on my eyes."

"I don't need any makeup remover. I need you to make sure that Mom doesn't go into either the dining room or the yard."

"Why?"

Zoey felt her stomach tighten at the idea of telling her brother that Adrian was sleeping in her bed, naked as all get out and probably still drunk too.

"Why?" Dalton insisted. "I'm not moving until I know why I have to face Mom the first thing in the morning before having coffee."

"Adrian is in my room."

"What?"

The surprised look on Dalton's face immediately transformed into one of extreme amusement.

"In your room? You mean, in your twin bed?"

He pushed the covers off and jumped up.

"Are you joking? You did the nasty with Adrian Peters in your mother's house?"

"I didn't do the nasty with Adrian in my mother's house—you are so

39

disgusting! I can't even..."

Dalton was already on his way out the door.

"Don't be so loud," Zoey begged, on his heels trying to hold him back.

"After 25 years of friendship, you did the nasty with Adrian," Dalton repeated. "No joke?"

He stopped and turned toward his sister.

"Did you take photos for Aunt Vicki?"

"Dalton, I swear, if I make it through this, I'm going to kill you."

"Do you really think I can help you, considering the situation? Do you actually have a plan?"

"You keep Mom in the kitchen and I'll get Adrian down the stairs, into the dining room, and out the French doors."

Dalton looked at her with a mixture of kindness and dismay usually reserved for very young children.

He's looking *at me like I'm an idiot*, thought Zoey.

"Life with you is never boring," he sighed.

Then he left his room and went straight into his sister's, despite her silent protests.

When he saw that Adrian was still sleeping, she had to put her hand over his mouth to muffle the laughter. The struggle that followed ended up with them on the bed. Adrian lifted a scruffy head and gazed at them with a haggard look in his eyes.

"Go play somewhere else," he complained.

"No, hissed Zoey. Adrian, you have to get up."

"What are you doing in my room?"

"You are in *my* room."

Adrian lifted his head again, took in the ruffled pillows, looked at Zoey and at Dalton, who had a huge grin on his face.

"Shit, Zoey, what did you do this time?" he moaned.

"What did *I* do? There are two of us involved in all this, I'd like to point out!"

"I can confirm that," Dalton added. "Even with Zoey's dismal understanding of biology, even she knows that it takes two."

"Of all the pranks you two have ever pulled, this is without a doubt the most pathetic," responded Adrian, yawning.

He lifted the covers and let out a sigh.

"Okay, Dalton. You even took my boxers off. Very funny. Anyway, set me free before my parents put my photo on a milk carton."

"It's not a joke, Zoey exploded."

"Zoey?" yelled her mother's voice from downstairs. "Are you really going to yell at this hour? Your brother is sleeping!"

Zoey darted toward the door.

"Sorry, Mom. I'll be down in a bit. I...I fell out of bed."

"Obviously! Do you have respect for anything?" her mother replied, raising her voice to indicate her sharp disapproval.

Zoey shut the door and turned toward her brother and Adrian. The commotion under the covers indicated that Adrian had found his shorts, and was trying to put them back on, with at least some dignity.

"So, you're saying that it's not a joke...?" Adrian began.

"You don't remember anything?"

The aggressive tone of her voice seemed to freeze him on the spot and this was unusual for Adrian who was usually very calm. He frowned and Zoey continued on in the same tone,

"You don't remember anything?"

"I remember that we tried to climb up to the treehouse but you were too drunk to make it up the ladder."

"Oh, because *you* were totally sober!"

"Apparently, no, but I was able to get up the ladder!"

He wore the ironic smile that he used to throw off people if he thought they were annoying. It was directed at Dalton. This was totally Adrian. He'd just made fun of her and then he excluded her. Just like when they'd had scuffles as kids and Dalton would end up between them.

"Are you planning to discuss this all morning?" Dalton interrupted.

"Dalton's right," mumbled Zoey. "Let's agree to keep remembering nothing, okay? Dalton is going to create a diversion and you're going to leave by the glass doors in the dining room and go home. Discretely."

"My parents are probably right in the middle of eating their breakfast," Adrian objected.

Zoey threw her brother a look dripping with desperation.

"Dalton, go make sure that Darryl and Stella aren't out on their patio."

Dalton crossed his arms.

"And how would I do that? I just walk right into their yard?"

"Figure it out for god's sake!"

"No," replied Dalton. "*You* figure it out. I'm not the one who slept with the neighbor."

"Always the nice guy," sighed Adrian. "I was drunk, but not that drunk."

"I didn't sleep with the neighbor," spit Zoey, her cheeks flushed. "And, first of all, Adrian is not 'the neighbor.'"

"Technically," he is, retorted Dalton, enjoying himself more and more.

"Technically, I am almost sure that we didn't sleep together," said Adrian, tossing the covers to the end of the bed as he got up.

He had a bruise on his right leg and a thin gash on his shoulder that was still bleeding.

Dalton started cackling loudly.

"Because now you remember?" said Zoey accusingly.

41

She avoided looking at his chest, overcome by shame and by a desire to slap her brother.

"First, if we'd slept together, you'd be in a better mood," stated Adrian, with a determined pout. Because...

He bent down to pick his pants up and put them on with a natural, fluid motion, not at all bothered by their presence.

"Because what?"

He went back to take his t-shirt off of the bed and pull it over his head, hiding the bruise and the scratch. Now, Zoey was able to lift her head and treat him to a look of defiance.

"Because, if we'd really slept together, you'd be thanking me. Considering your attitude, I think it's safe to say that that is very unlikely. I would even allow myself to say that it seems you had a very bad night."

He smiled at her playfully and then focused his attention on Dalton.

"Is there still a trellis under your window?"

Dalton nodded.

"It was still holding strong as of last year."

Zoey automatically took note of this information. It could clearly serve as a new means of pressure on her younger brother if he threatened to spill the beans in the coming months.

"Don't go out of your way for me," Adrian announced. "I'm sure I'll figure it out."

He walked in front of them, with a royal gait, although it was a bit unsteady. After he'd left the room, Dalton let out a whistle.

"Adrian has always had a lot of class."

"Yes," admitted Zoey gruffly. "Pure style:

'If we'd slept together, you'd be in a better mood.'"

She heard the noise the window made as it opened, despite Adrian's efforts to be quiet.

"He's going to break a leg," she worried.

Spitefully, part of her wished he would. The other part started making an anxious humming noise.

"The trellis goes all the way down to the ground," Dalton reassured her.

"I don't want to see that," whimpered Zoey, putting her face in her hands. "If Mom..."

"Zoey?" yelled her mother again. "Zoey? Are you bothering your brother?"

"I'm up," Dalton cried.

Zoey whimpered again. A startled noise indicated that Adrian had also heard Fran Westwood.

"I'm coming, Mom!" Dalton added.

Zoey was filled with an intense feeling of gratitude. Thank you, she mouthed to her brother.

"You owe me one," whispered her brother, before leaving the room and quickly descending the staircase. "Mom? Could you make me a cappuccino with the new machine that you bought last month? I really want to try something new! We could make one for Zoey! She loves to try new things too, you know!"

Using as many possible allusions to what he thought had happened in his sister's bedroom, Dalton led Fran into the kitchen. The ostensibly cheerful tone of his voice assured Zoey that he was enjoying every second. She'd have to pay double. Dalton was not the type to forgive debts. She'd known that since they were little, too.

She couldn't even hold it against him. She had also fiercely held onto any advantage won from using good old honest blackmail. Adrian had learned this lesson too, after getting to know them.

Suddenly remembering who had caused all this commotion, she sprinted to her brother's room and found it empty. She leapt toward the open window.

Adrian had disappeared, like she had both hoped and feared. She knew that she wouldn't see him again before he left for New York. At the same time, the voice inside her head, as well as her past post-party experience, whispered that it would be extremely awkward the next time their paths crossed.

She shut the window and caught a glimpse of herself in the glass, yelping in fear and then in horror as she realized that it was definitely her own reflection staring back with wide raccoon eyes under a tangled, shaggy mess of hair. She bolted back to her own room to work on returning to the land of the living.

The thirty minutes she spent brushing her hair did not succeed in calming her down. Every time she was able to find any semblance of peace, she'd remember that she might have slept with Adrian. From time to time, her brain timidly accepted Adrian's explanation. Then, in turn, she was overcome by humiliation. But mostly, she turned around in circles considering the only theory that made sense to her: it had been so dreadful that he'd preferred to deny it had even happened.

Or, it had been so traumatizing that he'd never mention it to her again.

Or ever be in the same room with her again.

She wasn't even sure that *she'd* ever be able to be in the same room with him again.

With this last thought that would stay with her the entire day, she went downstairs, stiff and nauseous, ready to face her destiny, like a martyr waiting for the lions to appear in a Roman Colosseum.

5
EGG WHITES

Despite Zoey's fears, there was no offensive. She ate breakfast alone at the table. Standing in front of her, Dalton and Fran were having a discussion, well, at least what Fran would consider a discussion: she peppered Dalton with questions about his work, his love life, and punctuated his replies with "good" and "great" before continuing to interrogate him.

With Zoey, Fran was content to be simply cordial. Her stand-offish manner was much worse than if she had followed her normal course of behavior and bombarded her daughter with sanctimonious remarks about how she'd acted. From time to time, Zoey felt her mother's eyes on her. She thought that Pontius Pilate must have had the same cold look of determination before sentencing Christ to be crucified.

Relieved, as soon as breakfast was over, she gathered up her belongings and began loading the pickup truck parked at the back of the house.

Sally was already there, her hair carefully arranged over a face that was even more pale than usual.

"Bad night?" Zoey asked.

"I was cleaning up your mother's kitchen until four in the morning," Sally grumbled.

"I'm so sorry, I was..."

"I know what state you were in, her assistant interrupted. Adrian and you came looking for flour at around 2:00 a.m."

The image of Adrian and her running after each other on the patio throwing flour back and forth returned to her in full force. They were too drunk, fortunately, to have done much damage. The stone walkway must look terrible though.

Getting out of her parents' house had become an absolute necessity.

"I saw Adrian this morning," Sally continued. "He looked terrible!"

"Did everything go well at the Peters' house?"

Sally had been staying with Adrian's parents since there hadn't been enough room at Zoey's. The guest room at the Westwood residence was being renovated and Fran had refused to accelerate the completion schedule in time for the party. Zoey suspected that they had purposely prolonged the project so they wouldn't have to host Nana.

"It was perfect," Sally replied. "They are a charming couple. I slept in a bedroom covered in Laura Ashley wallpaper. Adrian played the piano this morning. He's crazy talented."

"Yes," mumbled Zoey, who had no desire to get stuck on the subject of Adrian. "Let's say goodbye to my parents and Dalton, and get out of here, okay?"

Sally smiled a little.

"Ha - you don't want to face them alone."

"Definitely not."

When they went into the house, Fran and Joe Westwood were sitting in the living room. From the beige couch, Fran was sitting perfectly straight and dressed in an impeccable blue silk blouse and gray slacks. She was watching the news on the huge television next to the chimney, the dog asleep at her feet. Joe was reading the newspaper but his heavy eyelids indicated he was fighting sleep.

He jumped when Zoey announced that she was about to leave.

"It was perfect, my Zoey," he said. "Thank you again." He stood up to embrace her. Zoey held back the desire to cling to him in a desperate hug.

Then, she walked around the coffee table and bent down toward her mother. Fran icily returned her hug.

"Don't forget to call your grandmother, please."

"I call her every week," Zoey replied.

"And be careful on the roads," her father added. "Are you driving, Sally?"

Sally nodded and thanked them for their hospitality.

Dalton came down the stairs right then, most likely because he had heard his sister leaving. He'd showered, shaved, changed his shirt and had even take the extra effort to comb the hair on the back of his head.

This one was dark blue and brought out his eyes.

"Suck up," whispered Zoey as she gave him a noisy kiss on the cheek.

Dalton winced and approached Sally. During what seemed to be an eternity to Zoey, they stood face to face, obviously uncomfortable, and then made an awkward movement toward each other.

They didn't exchange one word. Zoey glanced at them, exasperated, before leaving the room, saying a last goodbye, Sally at her heels.

When they were finally settled in the pickup, they let out a sigh in unison.

"That was a tough evening," Sally said, starting up the sound system.

The sounds of the first song on the Moriarty album filled the cab while she turned the key.

"Did you get to sleep okay?" she asked.

"Yup," Zoey asserted. "A good night's sleep, in my bed. My own little bed."

"Great," Sally replied, digging around in the glove compartment to find her sunglasses. "Another quiet night!"

Zoey didn't appreciate the joke, but Sally didn't insist.

The pickup turned into the alley. Sally stopped in front of the Peters' house. Behind the white wood fence, Ludwig, Adrian's parents' lab, looked at them with undisguised joy.

"Did you forget something?"

"No. Adrian asked me if we could give him a ride back to New York."

"What?"

Zoey hadn't meant to shriek. Sally stared at her, surprised.

"It's not the first time there will be three of us in the cab," she objected.

"That's true. No problem," she sputtered, praying that she wasn't turning red.

Adrian came out of the house right then. He had also showered and even found a clean sweatshirt in the depths of his old closet. Their high school logo, white on navy blue, was still visible, even if the shirt had seen better days. He came down the outside stairs, carrying himself just as he had fifteen years earlier when Zoey would wait for him on her bike so they could go riding together. Their eyes met and he jumped over the last step. He still had the same unique way of moving his body, as if nothing mattered and literally nothing could touch him. Nonetheless, the events and margaritas of the day before had made their mark. The circles under his eyes drooped down to his cheeks, testifying that he still had more alcohol in his veins than blood. But that was nothing next to the pallor of his skin and his unkempt hair.

He patted Ludwig's nose and shut the gate behind him, after waving to his mother who was watching him leave from the living room window.

Zoey slid over to the middle spot.

"Is your butt getting bigger?" he teased, pushing her aside and taking her place.

He clicked the seatbelt. Zoey wanted to respond with a good comeback like normal, but nothing came out. She simply looked at him and she must have appeared dumbfounded, because Adrian frowned, amused.

He then turned the subject to the music playing and frowned again when Sally informed him that Dalton had suggested it. Their musical tastes had never been remotely the same.

Finally, they fell into a silence that Zoey felt was extremely awkward. She concentrated on the road that she'd known by heart, having taken it every day of her childhood and adolescence. She wasn't able to breathe normally until the vehicle left the neighborhood. At every street corner, she saw herself with Adrian, first as kids, playing outside, then as teenagers, when they'd spend hours sitting on the sidewalk talking, until one of their parents would come home from work and asked them to stop acting like homeless people.

On top of these images of Adrian in a Superman t-shirt and Adrian dressed in black from head to toe were superimposed those from this morning: Adrian naked in her bed, then standing in his boxers in front of her, mocking and haughty.

When they came upon the low wall protected by trees where they'd often hid during their freshman year of high school, she smiled. They had discovered the perfect place to escape their mothers' eagle eyes. Stella and Fran had heard there were drugs in the neighborhood, and, obviously, had immediately thought that their children would be at risk, because that was the Zoey and Adrian that they thought they knew.

Which was completely ironic considering all that Dalton had smoked in college.

Their hideout had lost its luster after the incident with Jon Garibaldi and Adrian's stupid behavior. In his teenage years, his behavior had been bizarre and unpredictable.

This led to their only quarrel and it lasted two weeks, the time it took for the bruise on Jon's face to heal—the same amount of time that he was "going out with" Zoey.

Passing the wall, stuck between Sally and Adrian, Zoey realized that they had never discussed what had happened. They had simply starting talking again, avoiding any mention of that particular incident, and then life went on.

Thinking back on it now, she remembered the exact moment when she was going up the street with Jon, holding hands, like teenagers do. Adrian's foot had suddenly appeared from behind the branches and landed on her boyfriend's nose with a swift kick.

Adrian hadn't said one word, given any warning, and didn't even try to make it seem like an accident. He gave no excuse for this act of violence that was totally out of character.

Just his foot and a black stare and then Zoey saw Jon's nose bleed all over and began screaming.

The pickup turned left, definitively taking them away from this wall where neither of them had dared return since.

Sally talked about the music and the road. Zoey felt Adrian's arm against hers and kept trying to discretely move as far away as possible, pushing up against Sally, who, in turn, pushed her away, gently but firmly.

"I can't drive if you're pushing me, Zoey," she finally said.

"Adrian's the one that's taking up all the space."

She bit the inside of her cheek. For a few seconds, she'd forgotten that she wasn't supposed to talk to Adrian—or even about him, until they were able to discuss what happened yesterday.

"Me?" Adrian said indignantly. "I know girls who'd pay to be in your place."

"That'd be an interesting way to make money."

Adrian put his arms around Zoey's shoulders and hugged her to him. She suppressed a gag. Their proximity felt embarrassing and strange. Adrian's hand was touching her bare arm and the contact with his skin made her shiver.

"There, do you have enough space now?" he said in his most serious tone.

She felt the tips of his fingers slide softly over her skin. When she turned to look at him, furious, he raised his eyebrows.

She asked him twice to remove his hand, but he acted like he hadn't heard her.

"I do not think this is funny," Zoey enunciated.

"Yeah, I can see that—apparently I'm not good at making you laugh lately."

She held back an exasperated sigh and gave him a sharp elbow in the ribs. He yelped in pain, but otherwise, did not move an inch. Zoey hit him again, and Adrian responded by pinching the extra skin on her biceps, which enraged her further. They fought for several seconds in silence.

"Could you please stop wiggling around?" complained Sally. "You are going to make us have an accident."

"Adrian is going to make us have an accident."

"What is going on with you two? You can't stop moving around today!"

Zoey seethed with rage. That was so Adrian, to pinch her where it hurt. He would keep teasing, mocking and making grotesque allusions, without directly addressing the subject. Worse, he would keep at it until she became hysterical.

"What do you want me to say," Zoey said, grabbing her friend's hand as hard as she could to force him to let go. "Sometimes, Adrian, you drive like crap."

"Both of you are terrible drivers," Sally retorted. "Both of you seem to be having a hard time getting over your hangovers."

"Zoey isn't a terrible driver," Adrian stated, while he tried in vain to stop Zoey's fingernails from digging into him, while holding onto her tight. Zoey's thing is to make others drive like crap, and then complain about it afterward. You know, like she makes you break your neck on a ladder and then complains that you fell on top of her.

Sally looked from the road to Adrian. Zoey noticed that her eyes widen quickly, as if she had just understood something that had been under nose the entire time. Zoey started to panic. Turning to Adrian with the intention of putting her hand over his mouth, she saw that he was returning Sally's gaze with a mocking look on his face. The pickup deviated slightly from its course and clipped the median.

"Sally, look where you're going! And you, calm down or we are going to drop you off on the side of the highway. You can hitchhike, if anyone will pick you up—you've got a serial killer vibe and look like death warmed over. And, with your luck, it'll be a truck driver."

"Who knows? I might meet up with one of your exes."

"Hurry up and get this trip over with," Zoey ordered her friend. "Otherwise, you may have to report a murder."

"The trunk is already full, Thelma," smiled Sally.

"We'll find room. Now, remove your hand from my shoulder, Adrian, or, I swear, I will never speak to you again."

Adrian narrowed his eyes, searching Zoey's face to find out if she was joking, and then removed his hand, without a word. The trip seemed to go on forever.

Adrian locked down into a silent pout. Once they were in New York, he only spoke to Sally, to ask her to drop him at the subway. He avoided hugging them goodbye, under the pretext that the truck was blocking traffic, and disappeared into the crowd. Shutting the door behind him, Zoey sighed with relief.

"What was that? What game were you playing with Adrian?" asked Sally nervously. "Did you have an argument?"

Zoey was dying to tell her friend everything, but thinking about how it might hit Sally as hilarious, or worse, sad, stopped her. She was already ashamed enough as it was.

"He was acting very weird," Sally continued. "It seemed like he was settling scores. He was acting like ...OH. MY. GOD."

She turned toward Zoey, like a vulture toward its prey.

"You slept with him," she said flatly.

"I certainly did not!"

"Don't lie to me. I can see it on your face."

Zoey wished she could just disappear. Sally looked at her evenly, she wasn't laughing and she didn't seem shocked. She looked serious and curious.

"I'm not sure, actually," Zoey admitted. "I was drunk. I woke up next to Adrian. I don't know what happened."

"Do you think he's the one that started it?"

50

"I told you, I don't remember anything about it! And Adrian doesn't either!"

Sally whistled.

"Yeah, sure!"

This assertion gave rise to doubt in Zoey's mind, but she firmly rejected it. If Adrian had remembered something, he would have been as embarrassed as she was. And when he was embarrassed, which happened very rarely, he usually took off. He would have taken the train, which he hated, back to the city, rather than be stuck with her in the truck on the highway.

"You don't know Adrian like I do. He likes to act like he knows stuff, just to make people mad. When we were teenagers, he convinced me that he'd read my diary. So, I burned it."

"You burned your diary?"

"Well, I couldn't burn Adrian, so - ha! Afterward, I realized that he couldn't have read it because it was written in French. I had done so Dalton couldn't read it."

"You wrote your diary in French?" Sally burst out laughing.

"I've always been good at languages," Zoey mumbled. "I was a good student, if you want to know. Adrian was terrible at French, just like he was terrible at everything, except music. As for Dalton, he was really bad. He couldn't even tell the difference between French and Spanish. In any case, it doesn't matter. I'm not planning on seeing Adrian again for a long time."

"You'll see him next Saturday, at the reception at the Brazilian consulate."

"Oh, no!"

Adrian had pulled strings for her to get this client. The reception at the Brazilian consulate, along with her parents' thirty-fifth wedding anniversary, had taken up all of her time and had caused her a lot of stress over the past few weeks. Adrian had to be there. He was playing the piano, accompanying a singer coming from Rio.

"He'll be chained to his piano and me, to the kitchen," Zoey responded. "Neither of us will have any free time."

"If I were you, I'd let it go. It seems like things aren't clear between the two of you."

Zoey gasped, indignantly.

"Adrian is my best friend. My only male friend, in fact. We are practically brother and sister. Everything is fine, okay?"

"I get it! Calm down!"

"I am calm!" screamed Zoey.

They had arrived at the store. Above the roll-up metal door, the name *Zoey's Kitchen*, freshly painted, was written out in yellow on the shop's navy blue background. Her apartment building was next to the building that housed her storefront. It seemed to have been dropped by mistake into the tiny space between the two large, imposing buildings. Zoey loved it. With its tall windows, brick that had yellowed over time, and faded roof, it looked like an old-fashioned Christmas lantern, forgotten in an antique dealer's window display. Sally parked in the delivery spot and turned off the motor.

"I have to unload the boxes before I park the truck in the garage."

"I'll help," Zoey promised, even as her stomach was violently protesting the idea of being squished in between plastic boxes.

"No worries. You don't look like you're up to it."

Zoey thanked her friend and got out of the vehicle, moving toward the red, peeling door of her apartment building.

"Zoey? " Sally called, through the open truck window. "Don't worry too much about it."

"Why does everyone keep telling me that?"

Sally's smile said a lot, but she wisely avoided the question.

"If something happened between you and Adrian, he will need time to figure out what that means."

Zoey shrugged her shoulders. She didn't have the energy to think about her friend's vague statement.

"Let's not talk about it anymore, okay? See you tomorrow?"

"Yes, tomorrow, Zoey," Sally sighed.

She looked at Zoey as if she had wanted to add something but then changed her mind. Zoey entered her building.

She climbed the three flights to her apartment and opened her door carefully. The last thing she wanted was to see Karen's door open and be forced to have a long conversation with her talkative neighbor. She was helpful and cheerful and Zoey liked her, but with this hangover, she didn't feel like she could stand her blathering on, telling jokes.

When she arrived, a ball of black and white fur threw itself at her and furiously rubbed against her calves. Sushi was the only cat she knew that acted like a dog when welcoming her home: hyper and clumsy. I'm sure it's because of her name, Adrian had said once. A cat named after food, and after fish no less! That would make anyone crazy!

She stamped her feet, annoyed. She did not want to think about Adrian, even if, she realized, the good thing about it was that she'd forgotten about Spencer.

Obviously, then, that made her think about Spencer again and the awful scene that had ended with her throwing the curry on Laurie's dress. She took Sushi in her arms. The chat purred with delight, snuggling up against her chest, and Zoey crossed the nine feet over to the couch.

She lowered herself onto it, the springs squeaking.

"It may be true that I've gained some weight," she said to Sushi.

She automatically reached out her hand to grab the land line and pushed the playback button.

"I shouldn't really be checking work messages on a Sunday, should I, my lovely? In fact, it's pathetic. I've only been gone three days. But, you missed me, didn't you?"

While scratching under the cat's chin, she absent-mindedly began listening to the four messages.

"Hello, Ms. Westwood, this is Jenny Hawkins. I received the suggestions you sent for the menu at our wedding. My fiancé and I were wondering if we could have chocolate fondue at each table, mini fondue pots, actually, instead of having one big one in the buffet line."

"Of course you can!" Zoey sighed That's only the third time you've changed your minds, both of you. She hit "delete," making a mental note to call this client back tomorrow morning to tell her, like she had before, that anything was possible if the budget was right. Zoey was a caterer, not a magician.

"Zoey? It's Orlando. Do you have an extra key to the back door? It's Friday night and Gabriella lost hers."

Zoey frowned. She hoped that, in the meantime, Orlando and Gabriella, the managers of the Italian restaurant next to her kitchen, had found a solution. She worried about them. If they hadn't been able to find their key, Gabriella, who waited on customers, would have had to pass through the front door, tiring her out. She was in the sixth month of her first pregnancy and Zoey knew it was a difficult one, even though the mother-to-be refused to let her husband take care of the restaurant without her.

"Zoey? It's your mother. I hope you haven't left yet. I wanted to check and make sure that you knew to put the vegetarian dishes on a separate table, away from the rest of the food. Do you have labels? Dalton is already here. He's made a mess of our CDs. Your father is very upset. See you soon. I'm going to try your cell phone."

"Delete," Zoey grumbled, pushing the button again.

There was one more bleep.

"Ms. Westwood, this is Matthew Ziegler."

Zoey trembled. A short silence followed, as if the caller was giving her some time to digest the information.

"Last night, I really enjoyed the buffet you prepared. I'd be very interested in having another opportunity to taste your cuisine, perhaps in a less conventional setting. I would like to know if you offer tastings. Don't worry about making any curry though. You can call me at my office..."

Another silence, longer this time, told her that he'd just realized it was Sunday.

"...tomorrow. I look forward to speaking with you."

He left his office number twice and repeated "I look forward to speaking with you" in a firm tone, that didn't leave her any choice. Zoey lifted the cat off her chest so she could pick up a notebook to jot it down.

"Don't worry about making any curry though."

Laurie's face, almost in tears and her robe smeared with curry came to mind, and then an image of Matthew Ziegler's amused expression took front and center. Adrian and she had made a spectacle of themselves.

She put the phone back in its cradle and sank into the sofa, her head on the cushions. Sushi pushed up against her, reclaiming her spot and mewing loudly. As she hugged the cat and took instant comfort in its soft fur, she did what she always did after a wild evening: swore she'd never touch another drop of alcohol or a man again, as long as she lived.

6
EGG YOLKS

"You can't keep changing the menu up till the last minute," complained Sally, looking at the doodles Zoey had made on her notebook.

She was sitting on a metal bar stool at the counter in the shop, one leg tucked under her. Her auburn hair fell onto her bare shoulders. Mondays were always the most laid back day of the week at Zoey's test kitchen, allowing Sally and Zoey a chance to relax in comfortable clothes after the busy weekends of the past few months. Sally was wearing a blindingly bright yellow t-shirt, jean shorts and a pair of red plastic flip-flops. Open notebooks were spread out in front of her along with empty mugs on which cold coffee had left a sticky ring, countless dirty plates, and a plate of creampuffs—a testament to the creativity that had forced Zoey out of bed at an early hour.

"You need to make up your mind and stop changing even the smallest details. Really, Zoey, your petit-fours were perfect."

"Taste this!" was all Zoey said in response.

She held out the plate and reveled in the expression on Sally's face as she bit into one of the creampuffs.

"Lemon, and...sugar, of course....and, wow, Zoey! You filled them with caipirinha cream!"

"Nana gave me the idea. Well, sort of. I adapted one of her suggestions. I wasn't sure how it would turn out, because of the cachaça."

"They are delectable - and light too! The texture is anyway." She finished the creampuff off with a look of ecstasy on her face.

"You have to serve these Saturday!"

"See, it was worth it for me to keep reworking the details!"

Sally laughed. "You're right! I've made a note of it. One thing to cross off the list. They were truly excellent! Is your list ready for me to order?"

Even though Sally was a reliable source of encouragement for Zoey, she never forgot about the logistics. Zoey appreciated her professionalism that made it possible for them to work together without it negatively affecting their friendship.

She had never regretted hiring her. She had hesitated, though, after Sally's first interview. She was gorgeous and didn't look the part, this girl who'd given her a resume that read like she was going to be a CEO someday: MBA from an Ivy League school, internships at top companies, management experience and multilingual. In addition—a detail that had made an impression on Zoey—she had been a star athlete in high school.

She felt like Sally had been miscast and called her after the interview to ask a question that she hadn't thought of at the time: "Why?"

Sally had responded very seriously that she wanted to create her own role and not just be passive.

There may not be a word for "falling in love" with a friend, but that is exactly what Zoey experienced at that moment.

For the past four years, they had shared the daily experience of running the business together, perfectly merging work and friendship without ever stepping over the limits that they had implicitly set. Everything came naturally with Sally, even when her friend had to rein in Zoey's exuberant creativity and her tendency to jump from one thing to another, ignoring what was realistic or not. And she had to do that often, actually.

"I just need to finish up the passion fruit cheesecakes," Zoey said. "It'll take me at least half a day."

Sally's put on her schoolmistress face.

"Zoey, the Richardson-Welleba wedding is in one month. You promised the bride a cake that looks like the Statue of Liberty and you still haven't looked at Elena's samples. She sent you several photos."

Elena was Gabriella's sister, from the restaurant next door. She was a cake decorator. Talented but young, she worked on the side, to pay for school. She made special desserts for the restaurant, when customers would order a birthday cake or when Orlando couldn't make a custom order.

"Oh," sighed Zoey, raising her eyebrows. "I'm overwhelmed."

"Okay. I know that you have high expectations for the party at the consulate."

"Yes. I do. Mr. Delacruz is pleasant to work with and encouraging."

The Brazilian consul had given her *carte blanche*. The only requirement was that the food should be inspired from both Brazilian and American cuisine.

"I know that you'll do a fabulous job," he'd said when contacting her. "I have already tasted your food, at Amandina's wedding. I like to use different vendors, to spread the wealth, as it were. Your friend Adrian told me that you're very creative. I'm open to anything."

The consul had, in any case, participated in a private tasting event that Sally and Zoey had quickly put together. Afterward, he had confirmed that he wanted her to cater an "intimate" evening event for 50 to 60 people. It was the unofficial kick-off to a festival that would include a friendly soccer match and several concerts. Then, there would be a large party for more than two hundred people.

It was just a "simple" welcome reception.

"This is such a wonderful opportunity for you to be able to show what you can do!" Sally said excitedly. "Weddings are so constraining. I never would have thought the consul would be so open and, actually, looking at what you've come up with, he's given you more freedom than any New Yorker under thirty-five years old."

She said this without irony. Sally was a native New Yorker, born and raised. She strolled around the city with a natural confidence, like it was her back yard, but could also fall prey to sudden fits snobbery that made Zoey smile.

"I find that a bit unfair. You like our brides and grooms as much as I do, even if their total lack of realistic expectations is exasperating."

"That's not what I mean," frowned Sally, revealing her opinion of other New Yorkers. "I only meant that it's about time that you receive some recognition and that it's time for Zoey's Kitchen to take off. Having seen Mr. Delacruz once, I agree that he's someone who really appreciates creativity. He likes discovering new talent."

Zoey made a dismissive gesture. Truth be told, she couldn't care less about being "discovered." She wasn't in it for the money,

even if she wouldn't mind having a little more. She wasn't in it for the glory either. She just wanted to be able to use her skills to do what she wanted, adding a bit of passion and originality to everything she produced.

"It's an opportunity to get some more visibility, Zoey," Sally insisted.

"Do you think we need more exposure?"

Her friend hesitated.

"I think we could use social media more and that we are behind in how we communicate. When I see what some others have been able to accomplish with less than we have, I'd really like to…"

She stopped in mid-sentence and looked at Zoey, biting her lower lip.

"Do you feel too confined?" Zoey asked.

Her tone was harsher than she'd intended. She knew very well that she often failed to take the initiative and this bothered her. Perhaps the only negative consequence of hiring Sally was that Zoey sometimes felt that her tasks weren't challenging enough and this caused some Sally some tension.

"No," Sally said, with an exaggerated smile. "However, if I had more money to spend and more freedom, I'd use everything available to us to get the word out about Zoey's Kitchen."

"Sally, we already have too much work," Zoey said in an bossy tone. "We can't take on any more."

"Well then, maybe we should expand our offerings, raise our prices and..."

"Absolutely not!" Zoey interrupted. Sally sighed.

"I get it...Call Elena back at least, about the cake."

Zoey nodded. She couldn't help being stubborn about it. If they did everything their customers wanted, they'd need to hire a full-time commis chef and some part-time staff. This approach was too risky for a business which, according to Zoey, needed to stay small to be able to maintain its high standards.

She quickly disappeared into the test kitchen in case Sally brought the subject up again. The kitchen was a disaster. She could be very meticulous, sometimes to the point of excess, but when she was in the middle of a creative spurt, she needed to let her herself be taken over by whatever came to mind when she was creating a new recipe.

She took the crusts out of the oven and placed the four golden circles on the cooking rack.

Sally's head popped in through the half-open doorway.

"I just listened to the messages. Matthew Ziegler called. The message was saved, so you heard it too, right? Have you called him back?"

"Not yet," she responded distractedly. She avoided Sally's pointed look and took a stainless steel bowl out of the refrigerator. She knew her friend well.

She wasn't going to let it go.

"Should I set the tasting up for next week? Do you want me to call him back?"

"No."

Sally's facial expression was worth a peek. It had changed from authoritative to resigned but Zoey knew it was all an act from past experience—she's seen this many times.

"What does that mean? 'No, I'll do it,' or 'No, do not set up the tasting?' Because if it's the second, Zoey, I'm going to be very upset. Disappointed, really."

Any tactic was fair game, even emotional blackmail. Zoey smiled.

"Sally, you imitate my mother perfectly. Yes, I am going to call him back, but no, do not set up a tasting. And don't give me your speech about communicating. I refuse to waste my time preparing private lunches for journalists, food critics and bloggers."

"That's how things are done now," Zoey.

"You're probably right," Zoey said quietly, in a more conciliatory tone.

"Of course I am! Oh, I know that tone—stop that right now! You did have a tasting for Delacruz!"

"That's not the same. Delacruz wanted a traditional evening event. Most of the what we offer requires us to take the decor and people's vision into account. Without that, everything is out of context and could work against us. And, also, I don't want to."

"You might by the least ambitious person I know," sighed Sally, rolling her eyes.

Zoey's face took on a disappointed air.

"It's just that my ambitions are different than most people's."

"I know."

As Sally left, Zoey focused on her springform pan. She knew that Sally was right. Bloggers and food critics had enormous influence on the reputation of those in the restaurant business. Several bloggers had already contacted her about writing an article on her after another blogger had posted about the "A Thousand and One Nights" she had experienced at one of Zoey's wedding receptions. She'd loved what she saw. Zoey hadn't been against it, but she liked the idea better of them attending a real event where they could taste her cuisine.

As she lined the cheesecake pans with passion fruit coulis, she went back to her discussion with Sally. Her friend always tried to describe her food in the most flattering terms possible and to bring attention to her work. Zoey sometimes felt that she was being unfair to Sally, even though she continued to stubbornly reject all of Sally's suggestions. Sally's ambitions scared her.

The phone in the kitchen rang just as she had set down the pitcher full of coulis.

"I'm transferring Matthew Ziegler to you," Sally announced, in an exaggerated sing-song voice.

She was going to tell her not to transfer the call when a brief "hello" told her that the call had already been sent.

Cursing her friend, she cleared her throat and replied:

"Zoey Westwood."

"I am thrilled to finally have you on the phone," Matthew Ziegler replied professionally.

"It's still Monday," Zoey said defensively. "I was going to return your call."

"You just did."

Zoey gave her friend a silent but deadly stare as Sally looked smug sitting in front of her open order book.

"I was intrigued by what I tasted on Saturday," Matthew continued. "Would it be possible to participate in a tasting?"

"I'd like to be helpful, but I don't do private tastings."

"Oh!" exclaimed Matthew. "That's too bad. Where could I have the opportunity to experience your cuisine again?"

His voice suggested that he wasn't only talking about her food. Typical for this type of man, confident, seductive, even when they were in a professional setting.

"Ah, well, at the reception at the Brazilian Consulate next Saturday, if you are on the guest list, or at your own wedding, I guess."

"Not yet," Matthew laughed. "But that's funny, because I do have acquaintances from Brazil...as well as being well acquainted with caipirinha."

"I thought you were a margarita guy."

Zoey punctuated her words with a little laugh, that sounded idiotic and totally inappropriate, and then started banging her head against the wall.

Matthew Ziegler responded with a stiff laugh of his own.

"I'll see you Saturday then?"

"Wait, I...Hello? Hello?" He had already hung up the phone.

"What a pretentious jerk!" Zoey hissed, the phone still at her ear.

"Sorry, I dropped the phone," said Matthew's voice on the other end. "You were saying?"

"I was saying, yes, see you Saturday, perfect," muttered Zoey, feeling her cheeks getting hot.

"I'm looking forward to it. Goodbye!"

She stammered a quick goodbye and cut the communication, checking twice to make sure that the phone was actually disconnected. Sally ran into the room, jumping up and down.

"So?" she said.

"So, he's coming to the Brazilian Consulate event on Saturday."

"I thought we couldn't invite anyone...?"

"I didn't invite him. He invited himself and I'm not sure how."

Sally laughed silently. Zoey couldn't be mad at her though. Sally acted the same way that Adrian, Dalton and Zoey herself did: she did exactly as she pleased. They couldn't stop themselves from always trying to get the upper hand.

"He's quite attractive, that Matthew Ziegler."

"Sally, stop making everything about sex. I'd like to remind you that he was with my cousin Tina. I think they're together.

You don't bring someone to that type of family event if you're not in a serious relationship, right? I don't like Tina, but not to the point of stealing her fiancé, understand?"

"They're engaged now?"

"For her sake, I hope so. Seeing how motivated she is to find someone,

60

let's hope it moves along quickly."

"Clearly, she's the only person in your family who's motivated to find a partner."

"Don't start. I'm doing just fine on my own."

"Really?"

Sally looked at her suspiciously. She looked so funny with that expression on her face that Zoey finally smiled.

"I was thinking about Dalton, actually," she specified.

"Dalton is immune to pressure," Zoey replied. "Really, you're becoming more and more like my mother. A little nicer perhaps, and without the blow-dried hair."

Sally smiled at her.

"I'll take that as a backhanded compliment. In any case, I'm happy that you've decided to value your own talent."

"Sure. I decided...Sally, the next time you take the initiative to call someone, let me know beforehand. I had passion fruit coulis all over my hands."

"When you say it like that, it sounds kind of dirty."

Her friends insinuation made her roll her eyes.

"You are terrible. Go finish working on the orders, would you? Maybe that will calm you down."

"Yeah, sure," Sally answered, with a sigh.

She left the room.

Zoey was alone now, in the middle of the mess that she'd made in the test kitchen. She wasn't able to bring herself to be angry with Sally. She actually felt oddly relaxed. Maybe she really did need a little push.

She had spent the last two years avoiding any publicity except for word of mouth.

The truth *is that you are terrified of the idea of playing with the big boys. But not only that...*

Until now, she had not used her relationship with her grandmother to her advantage. No one new she was the granddaughter of Angelina Pinallo, the author of cookbooks that could be found in every home and had inspired thousands of housewives in the previous generation. In addition, curiously, she had become fashionable again about five years ago. The popularity of all things retro were in her favor and most of Nana's books had been reissued.

No one could deny the important role that blogs had played in her resurgence. Endorsed by a community that had grown up eating their grandmothers' recipes, her books had been extensively cited and shared on the Internet.

Zoey didn't want to be associated with "everyday" cuisine and she also didn't want to be compared to her grandmother.

"Make your own choices," her grandmother had told her.

That would be difficult if someone decided that her own expertise was simply an echo of the elder woman's great talent. Of course, Nana had taught her what she knew, spending hours with Zoey in the kitchen when her mother was working. But Zoey felt that she had added her own personal touch to family recipes, freeing herself from her legacy, which could also be a burden.

Or maybe she *hadn't, and perhaps that was what worried her...*

She doubted that any blogger would be able to make the link between Nana and her. Matthew Ziegler, however, with his network and connections in the food world, might.

Or maybe simply because dear Tina just couldn't *stop herself from telling him.*

He had to know already. Also, she suspected that he was a snob and would hate the family-style cooking that Nana's recipes offered.

What was his game? To test her? To kill two birds with one stone, and have fun destroying her and the very popular cookbooks by Angelina Pinallo at the same time? Use her to promote the newest culinary trends?

She wanted to call him back to convince him not to come to the consulate event. She wouldn't be able to convince him, obviously, and she'd be humiliated.

However, the fear she felt was more disagreeable than begging him to cancel.

'Make your own choices,' she heard her grandmother say again.

She was right. She had always made her own choices and, now, she had to defend them.

She decided to confront Matthew Ziegler.

"And to do so with class," she told herself. She glanced at her disaster of a kitchen.

"There's a lot of work to do," she added, picking up a bowl from her the counter.

The mirror on the wall did not reflect a glamorous image back.

"On many levels, but let's start with what's easiest," she sighed.

She started cleaning up her test kitchen.

7
MILK CHOCOLATE

"What about the cake?" The young woman asked in a neutral tone, while her smile indicated that she had already been on edge for a while.

Between them, on a blue metal table, an a dazzling array of samples was on display, showing what Zoey's Kitchen could provide. Too preoccupied making sure that her expectations were being met, Jenna Welleba had not touched any of the samples Zoey offered. Her fiancé had already eaten four. Zoey flipped through the folder that Sally handed her and pulled out the photos. A mini-Statue of Liberty reigned over three layers of white buttercream.

"This is what it would look like. The pastry chef would like to know if you'd like something written on the cake."

Jenna Welleba looked at the photograph carefully. Her eyes narrowed.

"I would have liked to talk to the person making the cake myself."

"Everything will be fine. I work with her a lot. Is something bothering you?"

"I thought the statue would be bigger."

Zoey stopped herself from laughing, purposefully avoiding looking at Sally. They'd already used up all their jokes on the subject, but even the mention of the size of a cake made them hysterical.

"It's almost 6 inches," Zoey said.

"And so it is," confirmed Sean Richardson, the future groom, who hadn't said anything until now.

"For a man, 6 inches is always enough," Jenna Welleba replied, her eyes flashing.

Her fiancé wanted to say something, but apparently, decided to keep quiet. He was easily ten years older than Jenna—balding, with tortoiseshell glasses and a jacket that perfected the English professor look.

Zoey bent over the folder. The last think she needed was for the couple to start fighting in front of her. Unfortunately, this had already happened several times since she started in this business. From past experience, she classified engaged couples into several categories: the always-agree types (but that was often for appearances only because the bride would often call back with instructions contrary to those that had been decided upon), the never-agree types (where one of them would always give in) and the you- -don't-know-anything types.

This couple was firmly in the "you-don't-know-anything" group. Jenna Welleba broke her fiancé's gaze and reached out a hand adorned with a stunning diamond solitaire to tap the second photo, a close up of the cake.

"I didn't see this part. Just the statue."

"It's very difficult to make," Zoey told her. Jenna pursed her lips.

"You don't understand how important this is to me."

"I understand perfectly."

"Everyone things we are getting married so that I can get my green card, the young woman continued. Because I'm an immigrant and I'm Indian."

Her perfect British accent indicated that she'd never seen the Taj Mahal. Unless, of course, it was visible from Big Ben. She shook her pretty head back and forth, making her earrings jingle, in a disapproving motion. Her impassioned discussion had reddened her bronzed skin.

"When I arrived from the UK, Sean asked me to marry him right away, and I said no."

She emphasized the last word.

"I am marrying him as an American citizen. I want a wedding cake that symbolizes that. He is marrying me without any strings attached, and I am doing the same."

"I understand," Zoey said quietly. "Please understand that I respect your commitment within the context of generations of women who were not able to choose whom to marry."

Jenna stared at her. Right then, Sally clearly but discretely shook her head *no*. Too late.

"What are you insinuating?" huffed her client.

"Nothing. I wanted to say that I respect your commitment to the feminist cause."

"My parents were never even married, the young woman pointed out. Only my father is Indian. I don't have anything to prove to my family, if that's what you mean."

Zoey smiled, despite herself. She knew this type of anger, the type that fed off the slightest awkward word or expression. Still behind the counter, Sally was making a strangling gesture, to order Zoey to be quiet.

"I understand, Zoey said in a soothing tone. However, I don't think it's going to be possible. Considering your budget. Only if we cut back on the cocktail hour."

She'd made her point. Jenna sat on the edge of her chair and sighed.

"In addition, I don't think it would meet your expectations."

"You think it's kitsch, right?"

— "Yes, Zoey admitted."

"I can't stand kitsch. Because I'm half Indian, people think I love glitz, but I actually can't stand it."

Zoey stopped herself from saying that the Statue of Liberty in sugar would be considered extremely kitsch by most of the guests. She preferred to focus on the menu.

"We are staying, then, with the lunchtime buffet, option A, London Garden Party. Here's the invoice for the wine."

She held out the bill to the couple, purposely sliding it between them, so that each of them could view it. Jenna placed her hand on it and pulled it toward her, ignoring her companion's obvious efforts to read the amount.

"Why are there two names on this invoice?" she asked, raising an eyebrow.

"It's your wedding," Zoey replied, not daring to look at the future husband.

"I'm the one who's paying," specified Jenna sharply. "Right, Sean?"

Sean stammered in vague agreement.

"That means it should be in my name. I make a point to never be dependent on anyone. And why is Sean's name listed before mine? That's so American."

Zoey was starting to feel annoyed. She was also embarrassed to see Sean Richardson shrink behind the table while his future wife continued her tirade of criticism.

"We always list the names alphabetically," Zoey lied, even though she knew it was her error.

"Oh, obviously, like at school," Jenna smiled, winking at her fiancé.

This woman seemed to switch from seething rage to friendly joking within a few seconds. Zoey took advantage of the moment to divert her attention.

"Have you decided about the flowers? I need to know if there will be any arrangements on the buffet table or smaller tables."

"Both. My mother-in-law loves flowers. I wanted to make her happy. Also, the wedding dress I will be wearing was hers."

Zoey laughed to herself. *The bride's paradox.*

Most of the time, brides made it known that they didn't have to depend on anyone and wouldn't accept other people's suggestions, but, in the end, they would give in to old-fashioned traditions. All brides, no matter what category they fit into, were conventional enough that they were able to anchor their wedding ceremony within family tradition and accepted practice.

"My mother never married...," Jenna began, with a dangerous look on her face.

"I've noted down the flower arrangements," Zoey interrupted to avoid hearing Jenna's opinion on her parents' living arrangement. "Even if you will be the one paying, I need both signatures on the invoice. It's your promise to pay."

Money obviously talked to Jenna Welleba. She pushed the paper toward her fiancé after signing the bottom, and watched him sign.

"Perfect," said Zoey, taking the document. "I'll send you a copy."

The door to Zoey's Kitchen opened. Dalton walked in, a sports bag nonchalantly slung across one shoulder, his hair disheveled. When he saw that Zoey was in a discussion, he went directly to the counter and sat done on one of the bar stools and, in a low voice, began talking to Sally.

"Do you think this will be enough food?" Jenna asked, indicating the long list of selections that she had just approved ten minutes before.

"Definitely. But, if you'd like some advice, make sure the servers bring the alcohol in a little at a time. The problem with cocktails is that people drink too quickly in relation to what they eat. By the middle of the evening, some guests will be more than tipsy."

"I'm not worried about that," replied Jenna. "Remember, I'm British. Half of the guests are British too and there'll be beer on tap."

"On my side, the guests aren't big drinkers, Sean objected. You should listen to what..."

The young woman took her fiancé's arm and smiled.

"Maybe it's time all you Americans relaxed a bit."

Behind them, Sally burst out laughing. Zoey realized that this was not related to the conversation she was having. Her friend's pale skin had turned crimson, as had been happening frequently lately, while Dalton was leaning over the counter to whisper something in her ear.

"I think we're finished here," Zoey announced.

"Yes, I agree. I still have many details to attend address, but I'm happy that this has been taken care of."

Jenna stood up and held her hand to Zoey.

"We'll see you in a month and a half."

"Call me if you have any questions."

Jenna nodded and left, her fiancé in tow, his mouth full of the last of the samples he'd snagged during their visit.

Zoey looked at this strange couple, who didn't seem like a good match at all, take each other's hand on the sidewalk and disappear into the street. Then she turned toward her brother and her assistant.

"Would it bother you to be more discreet, or even mature, when I'm receiving clients?"

"Hi, big sister," Dalton responded, jumping down from his stool, hugging her warmly. "I've brought you some stuff you forget at Mom and Dad's. Call Mom and let her know I did it, okay?"

"Oh God, I don't want to talk to her this week."

"You are correct that she's furious with you."

"She thinks I made a big scene, right?"

"Well, that and...," Dalton said, a mischievous smile on his lips. "After a half-gallon of margaritas…"

"Don't even mention that! I still feel sick."

She climbed up onto the bar stool and held out the folder to Sally. Miraculously, a hint of gloss had appeared on her friend's full lips. Sally was like a magician where makeup was concerned: no one ever saw her touch it up, but she was always perfectly put together. Feeling like a traitor to women, Zoey also suspected that there had been times when she had resorted to fake tears. Her eyes always looked dewy and bright, which made her look just adorable.

If Sally hadn't been her friend, Zoey probably would have hated her.

"I thought Jenna Welleba was never going to stop talking," Sally said.

"I thought she was going to tell me about the role that cake decorating played in the women's liberation movement."

"Are brides always that annoying?" Dalton asked.

"They aren't annoying. They're just very particular. This one will walk up the church aisle in her mother-in-law's dress and will cry when the rings are exchanged."

"Having seen her, that's hard to believe."

"Believe it. You don't claim your independence with such passion when you've decided to get married. It's called convincing yourself. Someone who is truly independent would never even consider getting married."

"Who are you talking to?" Zoey tousled her brother's hair, in an exaggerated gesture of tenderness.

"You know I hate that," he complained.

"Weddings?"

"When you touch my hair. Weddings too."

"We'll see, the day you bring home the perfect blond wife with rosy cheeks."

"Why blond?"

Zoey stole a look at Sally.

"Or Irish. That would make Mom so happy."

"Oh, yeah, that's right. Italians dream of their children marrying someone who's Irish, cackled Dalton. Dad would be thrilled that we'd be

67

preserving his Celtic blood."

"I don't think Dad cares if we get married or not, as long as we're happy."

Dalton laughed.

"You're forgetting that our dear old dad has lived with Mom for thirty-five years. Never underestimate the influence of the woman who gave birth to you. In any case, Mom would be happiest if we married someone she knows."

He licked his lips and smiled again.

"So, any news from Adrian?"

One of these days, I am going to kill you, Dalton, Zoey thought.

She tried to kick him undetected but missed his shin and smashed her big toe against the metal stool.

"No, no news," she said, frowning in pain. "We just saw him three days ago."

"That's true, we just saw him," Dalton said, with exaggerated seriousness.

Zoey look at Sally, imploringly. Her assistant was reading the Richardson-Welleba file, taking notes. This was her preferred approach when was didn't want to participate in a conversation. Zoey noticed that she was biting her bottom lip.

"We just saw him," Dalton repeated, encouraged by the fact that his sister had turned her head away. At sunset and sun up. It was like he was part of the family

"Dalton, I..."

"And so?" Sally murmured, but

it sounded she was hissing. Dalton rested his arms on the counter, with an expression on this face that was both cynical and attentive.

"And so what if Zoey saw him at sunset and sun up? They're adults, aren't they? They can do whatever they want."

"Far from me to tell them how to be," Dalton retorted, irritated by the Sally's tone.

"The only person that should be told how to behave here is you, Dalton," Sally countered.

She lifted her head.

"Zoey knows exactly what she's doing," she added.

"That would be a first," Dalton noted.

"I'd suggest you take care of yourself, before you stick your nose in other people's business."

"You're not going to get into a fight every time you see each other, are you?!" Zoey interrupted, conscious that her role was now the one that Sally had been playing for her and Adrian.

"That would be a shame," responded Dalton. "I wanted to invite you both out the evening."

"You're paying? What's the occasion?"

"No reason, just to help you relax a bit before your big evening. Last week, Josh started working as a bartender at Raines Law Room. He's be glad to see us. Their cocktail menu is worth it."

Josh was Dalton's best friend. He'd graduated from college the same year as Dalton, but unlike him, had decided to take a year off before getting hired by a law firm. He was very smart and also had a certain charm. Zoey immediately saw an opportunity to introduce Sally to him, to distract her from her brother who didn't seem to be interested in her. Maybe they'd be able to have a normal conversation. She was not interested in her best friend and her brother bickering every time they met.

"Is Josh still single?" she asked.

"He's as free as air. He had his heart broken by that Spanish girl, you know."

"A broken heart," said Zoey, raising her eyebrows.

"Broken into a thousand pieces," replied Dalton. "Obviously, to understand how that works, one of you would have to have one."

"What do you mean by that?" Sally cried.

"That's enough!" exclaimed Zoey. "I've had more than enough of seeing you both laugh like hyenas and then seeing you fight like dogs a minute later!"

She turned toward her brother.

"Remember that you're the one who invited us."

"No worries, big sister sweetie. After the third glass, it's usually you who forgets what's happened."

Before Zoey could respond—or hit him again—he jumped off the stool and added:

"Tonight at the Raines Law Room. 9 p.m.?"

"That's in Chelsea, right?" Sally asked.

"Yes."

"8:30," she said in a bossy tone.

Zoey shrugged her shoulders. She didn't understand what was going on between the two of them. And, truth be told, right now, she didn't really care. She regretted having agreed to go out. She was tired and worried about the big event on Saturday. With Dalton out the door, Sally arranged the file with the others under the counter and mechanically ran her fingers through her hair.

"Is Josh nice?" she asked.

"He's cute. But he's Dalton's friend."

Zoey realized that she was doing a poor job of selling the guy she planned to introduce to her friend. She thought for a moment how she could transform Josh, Dalton's best friend and partner in crime, into someone desirable to Sally.

"Yes, but he's better than Dalton. He's more mature. Not the same make and model at all. And he's very smart!"

"I see...Do you like him?"

Zoey let out an exasperated sigh.

"I don't only date guys that have a connection to my family, okay"

"No?" Sally responded, with a strange look on her face, one that showed both malice and disapproval. "No, really."

"He's my brother's best friend. The first time that Dalton had brought him home from college, they'd competed to see who could drink the most beer before taking a breath."

"Charming. I can't wait to meet him!"

"But that was a long time ago," Zoey pointed out.

"Josh has changed a lot since then."

"Yes, now he bartends for a living. What an amazing progression!" Sally laughed out loud. "Should we meet there?"

"Yes, that sounds good. I'm not sure I can get there on time," Zoey replied.

She wasn't even sure that she'd be able to extricate herself from her seat to shut the front door and go upstairs to take a shower.

"No joke?" Sally replied, before wisely slipping out the door.

Zoey got down from the stool, rubbing her neck. It was sore after she'd spent the morning looking at her notes and the various open orders.

Sally was aware of the effort it would take Zoey to get out the door once she was comfortable on her couch, as was her habit, with Sushi snuggled up against her. It was also be a big effort to act happy and fun for Josh and Dalton.

She couldn't remember the last time that Sally, Dalton and she had gone out together. For the last two years, she'd preferred to stay home.

She liked being *a loner.*

Sally, on the other hand, went out a lot. For reasons she had never explained, the enthusiastic redhead had never had the same interest in sharing her private life as her professional life. She met men, that Zoey never saw, but asserted that she wanted to stay single. The way she conducted her love life fascinated Zoey. Sally was not held back by social constraints or self-doubt, while Zoey, on the other hand, had regretted the rare hook ups—often one-night stands—that she'd had since Spencer.

Sally and Dalton were very alike on this point. They both kept people at a distance and were wild in their own way. They had the perfect relationship to party together, not ever having developed a friendship outside the rare moments they shared with Zoey.

She felt, however, that Sally had changed recently. The way her assistant looked at her brother as well as Sally's refusal to discuss her love life, that she said was at a standstill when Zoey insisted, worried Zoey.

She seemed more disillusioned and less enthusiastic.

More secretive, she thought, looking at Sally's strawberry curls bouncing on her shoulders as she was leaving to get ready.

Knowing that she'd be doing something nice for her gave Zoey the energy to clean up her work space before climbing the stairs to her apartment.

It could be that Sally and Josh experienced love at first sight. That would be the perfect scenario, except where Dalton's ego was concerned.

Which would be good for him, Zoey was sure, pushing her front door open. She didn't have time anyway to think too much about her adorable younger brother's raging ego and it had already received too much attention. A different problem was now the focus of her attention—she had nothing to wear, of course.

8
DARK CHOCOLATE

Zoey arrived at the entrance to the bar a good twenty minutes late. She had taken the effort to put on some cute flats, to dress up her jeans, along with her black, low-cut top, showing off her generous chest. She hadn't been out in such a long time that she felt very out of place and old compared to the trendy young women she saw.

"They're Instagram-ready," Sally would have said.

She'd touched up her hair, pinning two loose ends at the nape of her neck. Her hair was already coming undone. Her large leather bag contained her notebook, which she was never without, her phone, and her wallet that had seen better days.

She was familiar with the Raines Law Room: when they'd been together, Spencer and she had been here several times to listen to jazz. It was not, however, with him but with

Adrian that she'd come here the most frequently.

She pulled back the curtain on the bar door. She loved the decor here—the spacious couches, the leather chairs, the expansive library full of both books and bottles. At this time of night, in the middle of the week, there weren't many people: two couples were comfortably installed in an alcove, there was a man alone at the bar, and small group of young professionals who had obviously just left the office, still in their suits and white shirts.

Looking for Dalton and Sally, Zoey saw Josh emerging from the back room. She hadn't seen him in a year and was glad she'd trusted her intuition. He had matured. The party boy with his ridiculous haircut and t-shirts that were as bad as her brother's (one said *hugs* on the front and *Thank me, babe* on the back), had been transformed into a clean-shaven man, with close-cut brown hair. He was wearing a dark green shirt that perfectly matched the dark wood found throughout the bar.

He smiled at her. His face had also matured. Behind his glasses, his gray eyes were intense and thoughtful. They made him seem serious and a bit melancholy. His smile was, on the other hand, as appealing as ever.

She leaned over the counter to give him a kiss on the cheek.

"Hey, Zoey!" he said cheerfully. "Hanging out with the night shift?"

"Yeah, that was how Dalton convinced me to leave my house," she responded. "How's it been going?"

"Great. I am experiencing "real life" before selling my soul to the devil, as you can see."

"I'm not sure that serving liquor in a bar will guarantee that you get into heaven, Josh."

"No, but it's like a taste of heaven.

What can I get you?"

"What do you suggest? Dalton's paying."

"Oh, okay," said Josh, amused. "He must have done something bad. Would you like something off the official menu or one of my own creations? Be forewarned, mine are still in the experimental stage."

"I like experiments."

"You like lemon, right?"

She suppressed a smile. Josh was someone who was particularly attentive to others, able to retain the smallest details about people he liked, which he didn't always. When he didn't like someone, he would totally shut them out.

Now, Zoey understood why he'd chosen this demanding job, where interacting with others was as important as speed or creativity. He must have known that this type of approach would not have worked in the harsh, competitive legal world.

In that way, he was the exact opposite of Dalton who was very at ease socially. Their mother had raised them both this way, though Zoey had eventually rebelled, refusing point blank to be forced to be nice to people she couldn't stand. In social interactions, her brother's sense of humor was irresistible, both subtle and accessible. In contrast to Zoey, he also knew when to keep quiet.

Josh disappeared into the back room. When he returned, he set a luscious looking concoction in front of her.

"Aged rum, lemon, ginger, candied cherry zest, chartreuse."

"Candied cherry zest?" Zoey exclaimed, lifting the glass to her lips. "Josh! This is fabulous!"

"I would have also added a dash of paprika, like I normally do, but I remembered that you're not a big fan. I think I recall that you prefer curry, right?"

"News travels fast," winced Zoey.

"Dalton loves to tell family stories, as you know. Don't ever change—I love the way you do things. I'd like to throw some barbecue sauce on the jerk that my ex took off with."

"Barbecue sauce?"

"The industrial kind. I'm middle class, you know."

A customer had discretely signaled Josh from the end of the bar. Josh excused himself and seemed sincerely sorry to have to interrupt their conversation.

"No worries," she assured him. "I'll go look for the others."

"They're over there, near the wall."

Zoey took her glass and went to look for Dalton and Sally. She crossed the main bar area and found them sitting on a blue couch, in an alcove covered with heavy curtains, sitting next to each other.

When she approached, Sally gave her a tense smile.

Adrian was across from them, just a few inches away from a stunning woman whose black hair was pulled back, emphasizing her olive skin and fine features.

Zoey put her glass on the table. She had no desire to talk to Adrian and even less to see him flirt with a girl who was almost perfect just to provoke her, which he was totally capable of doing. She noted, with a touch of cynicism, that he had placed his arm on the back of the couch, just behind the unknown woman.

"I see that you've already been served," Dalton said.

He slid over on the couch, next to Sally, to make room for Zoey. Zoey squeezed in, trying to sit as far away from the edge as possible, to avoid spilling her glass into the walkway.

An awkward silence fell as she sank into the cushions. Dalton was focused on downing his elaborate drink. It was a pretty amber color with small black flecks floating in it. Sally, who always had had very simple tastes where alcohol was concerned, was sticking her nose in her pint of beer. She was dressed to the nines in an ocher-colored mini-dress that looked gorgeous on her, and matching sandals with leather heels. She was the only one who would dare wear these colors with the mass of fiery hair that was falling on her bare shoulders.

"I put it on your bill," Zoey replied to her brother.

She shot Adrian a smile and examined his companion, who was checking her out too, impassive.

"Hi. I'm Zoey."

The statue allowed herself a little smile and held out her hand to Zoey, murmuring a sweet *hello*. Her slight accent was the perfect complement to her appearance. Worse, it made her even more sexy. Adrian removed his arm from the back of couch to pick up his drink in a quick motion as if he'd been hit in the funny bone.

"I'm Marianita. I've heard a lot about you."

Marianita gave Adrian a conspiratorial wink.

"Me too," Zoey lied, dazzling Marianita with her most phony smile.

Dalton jumped in, "You must know then that Marianita will be at the Brazilian consulate Saturday," as disingenuous as always in this type of scenario.

Zoey didn't reply.

"You're a caterer, right?" Marianita inquired.

"Yes, and you're...?"

She stopped herself from saying, "the trophy date that Adrian is going to show off on his piano."

"I'll be the one singing that evening," the young woman responded.

"Marianita and I worked together in Rio," Adrian explained nervously.

Zoey suddenly realized that he had never mentioned the name of the singer who he'd be accompanying. He had just said that she was a Brazilian expat living in New York and that her voice "went well with" the type of music he played. Zoey had been careful not to ask any more questions about her, mainly because she simply wasn't interested and because Adrian was always discrete about his conquests. And, anyway, he'd always sworn that he avoided relationships with women he knew professionally. This seemed wise, considering the ease with which he cut ties with all the women he had had any type of liaison with.

"What a coincidence seeing you here!" Zoey muttered.

"It's not a coincidence that we're here," Adrian retorted. "Dalton invited us, actually. He must have something to announce, don't you think?"

"You've always been psychic!" smiled Dalton. "Yes, you're right. This morning, I signed a contract to work for Mansfield, Hanson & Wurd."

"Congratulations, little brother!" Zoey exclaimed, lifting her glass while wondering what Marianita had to do with this particular event. "I'm not surprised, but you should be proud!"

"Thank you," Dalton replied seriously.

"Congratulations," breathed Marianita in turn.

She leaned over to give Dalton a kiss on the cheek, revealing her plunging neckline that made

Zoey's outfit seem like she was a retired nun.

As she sat back down, Zoey and Sally exchanged a long, meaningful look.

"I won't stay long," Marianita said. "I won't intrude on your celebration. I was just stopping by."

"I gave Marianita the bar address because she was looking for a place where the first Brazilian guests to arrive could get a drink," Adrian explained. "It was a great opportunity to see each other before the rehearsal to go over our piece."

The image of Adrian and the Brazilian beauty entwined together in the alcove gave Zoey a glimpse into what he meant by "the details."

Whatever the singer was supposed to bring to this professional meeting, she could have least have worn a bra.

"I see that some of my friends have arrived, cooed Marianita as she stood up. It was a pleasure to meet you."

She threw kisses to the group and, as elegantly as possible considering her outfit, made her way to the back of the room. Adrian watched her walk away, an appreciative smile on his lips.

"She was nice," commented Zoey.

"That's not the first word that comes to mind," Adrian replied. "She's also very talented."

Dalton smiled but didn't say anything, which surprised Zoey. He was carefully observing Adrian, with a serious look on his face, as if he were trying to figure out what their long-time friend was feeling at this exact moment.

"Another drink?" he said abruptly.

They nodded and he got up to place an order with Josh.

"Is everything going okay, Zoey?" Adrian asked.

"Yes, why?"

Her tone was much too aggressive. In any case, if Adrian was sleeping with one of his singers, it wasn't her problem. It didn't affect her in the least, even though she'd prefer that he inform her of this type of thing in advance and not here.

"You seem nervous. Anxious about Saturday?"

His voice was calm and gentle. To her, he came across as he normally did—thoughtful and considerate.

"A little," Zoey admitted, lowering her eyes.

"I'm sure it will be a great success. After all, if they like my music, they will really like your food."

She smiled.

"If needed, Marianita can always give the guests a dance lesson", she retorted.

Adrian frowned, but Zoey didn't understand why—they always made up these kinds of stupid jokes.

"Marianita is a singer, he pointed out. Not a cabaret dancer."

"I was joking."

"Your joke was sexist and uncalled for."

Zoey felt her face getting hot.

"You? You have the nerve to call a joke uncalled for?"

"And sexist," Adrian insisted.

"This is the first time you've been offended by a joke like this. You normally love them."

"Maybe people change."

Zoey wanted to call Sally as a witness, but the redhead made a show of turning her face toward the wall, lost in her thoughts.

"Maybe I've realized that I, myself, was sexist in the past," Adrian continued.

"And don't forget, uncalled for," Zoey added, with a sarcastic smile.

"It might even be that the behavior of certain individuals has made me realize this recently."

They stared at each other in silence for a moment until Dalton interrupted them, sitting back down

between Sally and his sister.

"Perhaps you should talk to these people about it then," Zoey replied.

"Maybe I don't want to discuss this with them," Adrian shot back. "That is something that you could understand, I think. You, the Queen of the Unsaid."

This was completely unfair. The nickname her ex-boyfriend from college had given her had no place in this discussion. Adrian must really feel cornered to be so petty and underhanded.

Maybe some people would rather say nothing than to continuously state the opposite of what they really think, hissed Zoey.

"Maybe some people would say what they really felt if they felt they were being listened to. For example, if they were not bound by a stupid contract."

Zoey stared at her friend. What was he talking about? Adrian had a unique take on his relationships with the opposite sex, but in practice, it was similar to Dalton and Sally's approach.

He never stayed long in any one relationship. He was even more cautious than his two friends. Even as Dalton and Sally rejected the pleasures of being an established couple, Adrian couldn't even imagine it.

To Zoey's knowledge, he'd never even been in love. He was happy enough to make humorous and off-color jokes about girls that he found attractive or wanted to sleep with, without bothering with the details.

Of the four friends, he had always been the most self-possessed, the most secretive and the least sure of himself. Hearing him talk about a contract was confusing. However, the word reminded her of something. They must have talked it about it at one time or another.

The non-relationship contract!

Of course!

The memory came back to her, clear as day.

When she and Adrian were in college, things had spiraled out of control one evening when they had come home to their parents' houses tipsy, during a particularly festive reunion weekend. They had decided to draw up a contract: no matter what happened, they would never have get into an intimate relationship with each other, even if they were pushing thirty.

"We'd just end up ruining our friendship, Adrian had said.

At the time, Zoey couldn't have agreed more.

"Any anyway, none of us will be single at thirty! And in any case, times have changed!" Now, that she was going to turn thirty-one soon, she knew that this was not totally true. Most of her friends and acquaintances were part of a couple. Sally and she were often invited to parties were they had to put their diplomatic skills to work to avoid being stuck in long, boring conversations about how to set a holiday table or choose the perfect dress. They were also often forcibly paired up with the two single males in attendance.

"A contract?" she continued.

Adrian was annoying. This discussion should be taking place somewhere else, and in private.

He was incapable of conducting himself with the minimum discretion you'd expect from a friend, or a boyfriend. Or, from a lover—whatever you called the person you had a contract with, who still acted like a teenager, and with whom you probably slept three days ago.

"What a great way to deal with love, Adrian," she added, in response to his silence. What type of contract should be used to formalize a relationship?

Even in her exasperation, she sensed that he'd call out her bad faith and that she'd lose this round.

"Technically, there are many types of contracts," Dalton interjected. "Any relationship is based on a contract."

She should have known that the counterattack would come from Dalton; he loved pontificating on semantics.

"Is this the attorney talking, or the guy who's never been able to eat breakfast two times with the same person?" she shot back.

No longer smiling, he sank into the couch with a scowl.

"Okay, calm down," he murmured. "I was only trying to help."

"This conversation is getting really annoying," Sally whined. She'd been pulled from her reverie by her friends' sharp tone. "Could we just have a nice evening?"

"If I'm bothering someone here, I can just go sit with the Brazilians," Adrian said.

"No, you're not bothering anyone," Zoey sighed. "Sally's right. We're here to celebrate the beginning of my little brother's brilliant career. Is that where the Brazilians are sitting?"

Sally must have seen the same thing because a big smile spread across her face. Four men had entered the bar. Zoey was barely able to restrain herself from smacking her lips.

"If I had done that, I would have been lectured about how we should treat people," cackled Dalton. "They are not pieces of meat, girls."

"If you'd done that, I would have been busy calling Mom to tell her about your coming out," Zoey replied, without looking away from the group that was walking toward the back of the room.

"Oh, who, what...," Sally murmured, poking her in the ribs with her elbow.

Matthew Ziegler had just come through the door, behind the group of men. Squinting, he pulled a case out of his pocket and put on an elegant pair of tortoiseshell glasses to look around.

"He is so sexy," Sally murmured.

"Or just nearsighted," Zoey replied.

She had to admit that there was something very attractive about this man with impeccable style, hesitantly donning his specs.

"I wonder what he's doing here. It's a coincidence, I'm sure," she said sarcastically.

Sally shrugged her shoulders.

"I swear I didn't have anything to do with it! Didn't he tell you that he knew a lot of people at the consulate?"

"That doesn't mean he knows every Brazilian in New York."

They stopped talking as Matthew Ziegler, walking toward the alcove, noticed them. He approached their table and extended his hand to Dalton.

"Hello, Dalton. How's it going?"

"Great, Matthew. It's nice to see you. What are you doing here?"

"I came to get a drink with my musician friends. The Cariocas group I had mentioned to you earlier."

Zoey stared at her brother; she was once again amazed at the facility he had for expanding his social network. He must have talked to Matthew during their parents' anniversary party.

Matthew then said hello to her, without extending his hand. She wanted to say something but remained seated in front of him, lifting her head in an exaggerated motion to look at him, mute and stupid.

"Hell, Sally," he continued, without appearing to have been offended by Zoey's rudeness.

Sally responded with tinkling laughter and ran her fingers through her hair. Zoey received a certain satisfaction at seeing her act as idiotically as she had, and doing so loudly, too.

"Hello, Matthew. I really liked your last critique."

Zoey tried hard not to laugh. Her friend had to be aware of the cliché that just came out of her mouth, beaming and blushing. Matthew Ziegler, however, seemed to appreciate her remark.

"You did?" he responded.

"I feel like you—Vietnamese cuisine is the current big trend, but, sometimes, it needs to focus on the basics."

Zoey's mouth was gaping. Matthew Ziegler wrote such banalities?

"That's not exactly what I said," he said, in a tone that was a bit condescending. "But, that was the idea. That's the problem with food trends. The desire to innovate overtakes the desire to create well-balanced fare. This does not prevent some deviation from the basics."

Sally laughed again. A sarcastic smile spread across Adrian's face.

"You explained it better than I did," Sally simpered.

Zoey gave her a disapproving look. Was she also going to ask him if she could shine his shoes or carry his bag?

"Everyone has their own area of expertise," Matthew Ziegler said, with an amused tone in his voice. "You create, I critique."

"That's the easier job, in any case," added Zoey.

Had she really just said that to the guy who was going to taste her creations three days from now? Had she just signed her professional death warrant?

"If being hated half the time is easy, sure."

"You don't have to say things that make people hate you," she added.

"That's true. That said, I don't often write about restaurants that are not at a certain level. Maybe I should. It's because critics like myself pick apart the culinary darlings that flourish in a city like New York that smaller companies are able to exist."

He interrupted himself for a second, revealing white teeth and an ironic smile.

"I'd imagine that you are okay with all that."

Zoey controlled the wave of anger that was slowly rising from her stomach and responded with her own ironic glare.

"Smaller companies have done just fine without help from the critics. But, I applaud your commitment."

"That's one of my strengths."

His voice took on more of an edge. Zoey picked up on a harsh quality to it, almost cold.

"My friends are waiting for me. It was a pleasure to see you again," he said, taking on a ceremonious tone. "See you next time, Dalton. See you Saturday, Sally and Zoey."

When Matthew had left, Adrian let out a groan.

"He's as stiff as a board and he borders on rude."

"I don't know if you remember from the party on Saturday, but you were quite rude to Tina," Dalton replied.

"And? What's new?"

"Tina is the one that brought him."

"Thanks, Tina," Zoey mumbled, rolling her eyes.

Sally said nothing, but gave Zoey an angry look.

"What?!" barked Zoey. "I talked to him!"

"Yes, you did," retorted Sally, still grinding her teeth.

I wasn't sweet enough, I guess?

Sally's green eyes darted to her friend, her face contracted in frustration.

"I'd like to remind you that I put a lot of effort into getting the word out about Zoey's Kitchen and you risked ruining all that in just three sentences. Really, Zoey!"

Sally's lecturing tone was getting on her nerves. She was tired of her giving her advice and criticizing how she conducted her life and ran her business. Everyone talked to her like she never did anything right. Her mother, Dalton, Sally…

"I'd like to remind you that I am the one who started Zoey's Kitchen, and I don't need your little lectures."

The damage was done. Sally eyes widened. Zoey immediately regretted what she'd said. She had never spoken to Sally like that before. She had never made her feel like she was her actual assistant before. She didn't even know why she was so angry or if her fury was directed at Adrian or Matthew Ziegler. Or at Sally. Or at herself for being so rude and irrationally vindictive.

"I think it's time for me to leave," Sally said coldly. "I have to start early tomorrow."

Before Zoey could reply, or act on the internal voice that was begging her to stop her friend from leaving and ask for forgiveness, Sally had disappeared.

Dalton let out an admiring whistle.

"That was perfect, Zoey. Just wonderful."

"Don't you start now."

"Or what? You're going to humiliate me in public?"

He took a drink and frowned.

"I don't know what your problem is lately, Zoey, but you are becoming a real pain."

"Leave her alone, Dalton," Adrian chimed in. "Everyone is stressed out."

"The role of peacemaker doesn't fit you, my friend," retorted Dalton.

Zoey noticed that his eyelid was quivering, a nervous tic he had when he was angry, which wasn't very often.

"Don't shoot the civilians," Adrian growled. "All of this has nothing to do with me."

"Really? That's the way it always is, right? You're never responsible. Like when we were kids and you two would keep pushing each other further and further?"

"Are you going to hold something against me that I did when I was 12 years old, Dalton? Do you really want to get into who does what to who?"

"You know very well what I'm talking about." They looked at each other defiantly, without saying a word.

"And what are you talking about?" Zoey asked.

She immediately regretted having asked the question. Dalton's jaw tightened but he kept his eyes locked on Adrian's.

"I'm just saying that Adrian needs to choose his playgrounds…less close to home if he can't take responsibility."

Zoey couldn't believe her ears. Her brother was playing the macho. He was the one who had laughed like a crazy person when she had asked him for help.

"Trust me, I don't need you to tell me how to live my life," snapped Adrian, a nasty gleam in his eye.

"Yeah, mind your own business, Dalton," Zoey added.

"I would like to do just that," Dalton replied. "The problem is, you're the ones that involve everyone in your drama. You both need to grow up. Even though it hurts me to admit it, Mom is right sometimes."

Zoey's jaw tightened. That was a low blow, beneath even Dalton.

"Really," she hissed sharply. "We are the ones who need to grow up, Adrian and me? You should think about what that means for you, since you've been following us around all these years. On that point, I'll be leaving as well. It's way past my curfew."

She stood up and grabbed her bag.

"I'm used to you being a more worthy opponent," Dalton spat.

"I'm sure, but, like you said," Mom's right. "I'm just a disappointment."

She crossed the room, her hands in tight fists around the strap on her bag, and left the bar.

Once on the street, the warm wind on this stifling hot summer night stuck in her throat. She had to stop on the sidewalk.

How could she have spoken like that to her brother?

To her best friends?

Things were not going well. Her intuition rarely betrayed her and, in general, anger showed its face at the same as doubt. She was upset with them, but why?

Over the past two years, they'd all grown apart. She had become so used to being alone that, sometimes, she felt strange when she was in a group.

"Poor stupid me," she mumbled to herself.

"Poor—I don't know about that," an amused voice behind her said.

She turned around to find herself nose to nose with Matthew Ziegler. He took off his glasses and meticulously arranged them in their case.

"And, stupid, I didn't get that impression. Can I walk with you?"

"I'm not in that great of a mood," Zoey asserted.

"You do seem a bit overwhelmed."

"You seem to have a talent for seeing me when I'm like that."

"I hope you aren't as drunk as you were the other day! In any case, even if you insist, I'm not going to ask for just one last drink. I've learned my lesson."

Zoey hesitated. The thought of going home alone and dwelling on this horrible evening did not sound appealing.

"I don't really feel like talking," she heard herself say in a hoarse voice.

"I'll do the talking. Does that work for you?"

As he approached her and offered her his arm, gallantly, she felt oddly better. He emanated a feeling of safety and control.

More specifically, he gave off the vibe of someone who was successful, despite his nearsightedness and wry smile. He was definitely a grown up. That was exactly what she needed right now —her brother's harsh words still resonated in her head and she felt stupid at having made such a dramatic exit.

"I love walking in New York at night."

"I live fairly far, she noted."

"I know where you live." He shook his head and continued:

"Not because I'm a serial killer who's been stalking you for a month in my car."

"I don't think you have a car."

"That's correct. How did you know?"

"You're a real New Yorker."

"No. I'm a transplant, like most people. I just can't stand being stuck in a confined space."

"Claustrophobic?"

"Traffic-phobic, rather. I don't like wasting my time."

"So, you are a real New Yorker. How did you know my address?"

"Your home address and your professional addresses are in the same building."

"And how do you know that?" she simpered, while hating herself for it.

He looked at her, perplexed.

"I am interested in your food," he replied, with a surprised expression. "I did my research. In any case, I have the Internet, like everybody else."

She was almost disappointed with his response.

"Let's keep going, okay?" he added. "If it's too far, I'll hail a cab for you. Rest assured that I know you're not afraid of walking by yourself."

"Why would you call a cab then?"

"I don't want you to get too tired on the way home. Considering how you react when someone talks about your feet, I'm the one that's scared of you."

The smile he gave her was both irresistible and annoying.

Nevertheless, she turned and followed him.

9
VANILLA EXTRACT

First, they walked along in silence. The artificial illumination from the street lamps bathed the asphalt in a sterile, flat light. The evening was host to the random tourist or New Yorker on the way home. They passed busy people walking alone, dour couples, happy couples who were holding hands and groups having fun.

"You didn't stay very long, she said after a few minutes."

"I never stay out late."

"I see."

"What do you mean by 'I see?'" he fretted. "I see, 'you are more of a morning person,' or I see, 'you are really boring'?"

"I never stay out late either."

"I had you pegged as someone who liked to party," he objected.

"If partying means drinking a gallon of margaritas and humiliating yourself in front of your entire family, then, yes, you are correct."

"There were extenuating circumstances. Just so you know, I thought you showed a lot of class, even after the curry episode."

Zoey moaned in shame despite herself.

"If I understood correctly, you were engaged to Spencer?" Matthew continued.

"Not engaged, but we were together, yes, whatever that means. We were seeing each other," she specified.

"I love that phrase. It means everything and nothing. Then Laurie came on the scene?"

"Laurie was always there, I believe. Early on, I introduced Spencer to my parents and he attended one of their barbecues. Looking back, I think that's when he fell in love with her. It took him six months to break up with me."

The memory of it hurt her heart. Spencer went to Europe for three weeks. He called her every day. At her parents' house, Zoey had seen Laurie's mother. She had informed Zoey that her daughter was on vacation in Paris with a friend and had met up with Spencer. Spencer had not mentioned her even once. Three days later, he sent an email saying that he wanted to "take a break." The day after that, he informed her, also through email, that he was breaking up with her.

Even though he had seen Laurie a few times with her, always at her parents' house, never during her relationship with Spencer had she ever imagined that her childhood enemy would be her romantic rival. Her famous intuition had failed her.

"I was totally blindsided," she continued, following her train of thought. "Now, it's your turn to talk. As I understand it, you were introduced to my lovely family through Tina."

"Yes, that's right."

"And…have you been seeing each other long?"

"We do see each other," he said seriously, before retreating into silence.

She didn't push further even if though she was dying to know the details of their relationship. Walking with him, she felt flustered, her arm in his, seeing in other couples that they passed the reflection of what they must look like to others.

"You don't like Tina that much, do you?" he said suddenly.

"No, it's not that," she stuttered. "It's complicated."

"I noticed, during the little show the other night, that you and Adrian have a long history of verbally jousting with her."

"I'm sorry about that. Sometimes, cousins have difficult relationships. My mother has always been competitive with her sister. Actually, she's competitive with the entire world. When we were kids, Tina and I were constantly being compared to each other."

"But you're nothing alike."

She wondered how she should take his comment. If he was seeing Tina, like he said, he must think highly of her. Which put Zoey in a bad light.

"Yes, that's true. In my mother's eyes, I never measured up to Tina and Laurie. They, well, they were what she thought a girl should be. Me, on the other hand, I was always running wild, with skinned knees, hanging out with Adrian and Dalton."

"You and Adrian seem very close."

His tone was light, but it seemed to Zoey that Matthew had suddenly become tense, before returning to the conversation and his role as the conventional, experienced man that he seemed to be.

"We've been close since we were kids. Adrian wouldn't talk to anyone but me. They thought he was autistic until he was 10. In fact, his parents had him tested. It was just that Adrian waited to speak until he could defend himself. It was a sort of defense, I think. He's a musical genius."

"Like you with food."

"No, he's something special. We can't compare Adrian's talent with my skill. He creates art and I'm an artisan."

"Would I look stupid if said that you make music in the mouth?" Matthew laughed. "I hate definitions."

"Me too. Getting back to Tina, I think that she suffered as much as I did from the constant comparisons, and even more so because Nana never paid her much attention."

"Your grandmother?"

"Yes. My grandmother is an extraordinary woman, but I can't say that she is fair. She can be harsh, even with those she loves. I think that she always thought Tina was too soft."

She stopped suddenly and looked at him. She should really not be talking about either Tina or her grandmother with him. Matthew looked at her, his head cocked to one side, and he seemed genuinely interested. His chestnut-colored eyes reflected the light. She hadn't noticed the gold flecks in them before.

"You're making me talk!" she said.

It was true that he'd succeeded in delving into her family life without revealing anything about himself. She knew this trick, though. The technique was in all the business communication handbooks and her mother had used it for years: Don't talk too much. Ask questions. She couldn't be too mad at Matthew, however. If he was interested in Tina, he was also interested in learning more about her. She fought against the urge to share the worst stories from when they were kids and teenagers. It was true that she and Tina had never developed the idyllic relationship that had been expected of them, but the last thing she wanted was to be seen as catty. She didn't know Matthew or what his intentions were with regard to her cousin.

It wasn't her place to influence him.

Nobody liked a gossip. Worst case scenario, he'd judge her and would eventually mention it to her cousin, creating a new scandal.

"Zoey, the bitter old maid who despises those who have been able to find someone worthy."

She smiled. Or, better yet, "Zoey, the alcoholic who sleeps with her best friend, gets into a fight with him, causing general chaos during which she spits on her most loyal allies."

"What would you like to know?" Matthew asked.

"It doesn't work like that. I'm not going to interrogate you."

"You could always wait till you get home and do an Internet search."

"What does your official biography say?"

"That I've been a food critic for eight years. I was born in Chicago, my mother was French and my father was American, with German roots. My given name is actually *Matthieu*, but since my mother died, no one calls me that. My father always called me *Matthew*."

"Your biography says all that?"

"No. In any case, what's online is always useless. Oh yes, getting back to what I do for a living, you may find some insults flung my way, on certain restaurant sites."

"Favorite food?"

"I've never liked Twenty Questions."

"Brazilian acquaintances?

He sucked in his lips, embarrassed.

"My biography doesn't mention that. Too personal."

"Really? A deep secret?"

"So secret that I'm not sure I know it."

She burst out laughing. That was an answer that she could have given. As she was laughing, he leaned his head toward hers, suddenly serious. The gleam in his eye surprised her.

"Not many women laugh at my jokes," he said.

"That doesn't say much about me."

She had used her most cheerful voice, but an alarm was ringing in her head. She had to move away from him as quickly as possible. Or get closer. Or move away.

"Yes, it does," he exhaled. "It says a lot about you, actually."

He stopped walking, forcing her to stop as well and to turn toward him. She found herself face to face with him, her face just an inch from his. Some students bumped into them, laughing.

"Control yourselves," the young man cried gleefully, pulling along his mirthful companion.

"That's what we're doing," Matthew murmured.

Zoey stared at him, shocked. A desire to laugh was tickling her nose, but Matthew was not laughing. He looked at her, frowning, serious, then he leaned toward her slowly, until she could feel his breath on her skin. She trembled.

"You've been drinking—it smells like whiskey," she said.

She felt her heart beating, not knowing if it was excitement or total panic. She had already looked foolish a good number of times in the past, but this was the first time she had talked to someone who was about to kiss her about his breath.

The alarm wouldn't stop. He was going to kiss her. He was dating her cousin Tina. To do so would be totally disloyal and even indecent.

"Yes," he responded.

"I can't stand whiskey."

She looked at the street, suddenly wondering if she should throw herself under a bus.

"That's too bad for you," he whispered.

His arms were around her and she found herself up against him when he put his lips on hers.

In contrast to what she'd been expecting–if she'd really been expecting anything at all–the kiss was particularly passionate and had an aftertaste of cinnamon rather than whiskey.

She immediately felt their strong mutual attraction, a sensation that she had only felt once before in her life. She knew it would be difficult to separate herself from him, even if he was a perfect stranger and things were going too fast.

As their lips drifted apart, she went up on her tippy toes to prolong the moment.

She had miscalculated her momentum, energized by the kiss that had electrified her from head to toe. He took a half step back, lost his balance and bumped into the wall behind him. Regaining his balance, he gently placed his hands on her hips. Then, he slid them under her shirt to firmly place them on her skin.

Zoey pushed him backed up against the wall. Their mouths were still joined as Matthew's hands went up her back to pull her closer to him. A wave of heat went through her chest and down through her stomach as she pushed her hips against Matthew's. He seemed to be having a very difficult time controlling himself; she felt his fingers fluttering on her skin while he brushed them across her back. Without warning, he pulled her toward him with a certain fierceness.

They were as close as they could be. Again, he slid his hands along her spine, under her shirt, from the top to the bottom and then from bottom to top, in a controlled but efficient caress.

"You are undressing me on the street," she murmured into his ear.

"I've been wanting to do this from the moment I saw you," he replied, breathing hard. "Barefoot and wild in the garden."

"I was not wild."

"Yes, you were. Like you are now."

He ran his hand through her hair, tugging at the unruly strands that were projecting out from her almost-chignon. She closed her eyes as he leaned into her.

She felt his hot lips softly tickle her lips for a second. As she surrendered herself to him, he pushed her away slightly, to be able to wrap his hands around her waist and place them on her stomach. She trembled.

"I think we need to stop here," he said without conviction. "It's a real possibility that I will undress you and make love to you up against this wall.

"You're the one against the wall," she commented.

He didn't reply. His fingers had reached the curve of her breast and were outlining it with a gentle movement, following its contour, reaching under her bra. He seemed in control of his movements, as if he had known her for years, as if he had caressed her a thousand times before and knew exactly what he needed to do to arouse her. However, there were moments when he hesitated, his fingers in the air, immobilized by an irrepressible thrill.

Alternating between these moments, when Matthew seemed to be fighting a battle between his head and his desire, made her crazy.

She wanted him so badly that it was almost painful.

"Get a room!" another voice cried from the sidewalk.

Bursts of laughter followed the inebriated exclamation. Matthew seemed to come to his senses, removed his hand and then readjusted Zoey's top. She moved slightly to the side to separate herself from him.

She had never regretted something so much as she did at that moment. Where he had touched her, her skin was still quivering, sending tingling waves down to her groin. She caught her breath with difficulty and then braved a look at him.

He raised his eyebrows. His lips were parted and unsmiling.

"Should I walk you back?"

"I'm warning you," Zoey frowned. "I'm still not going to offer you that last drink."

"I'm not that thirsty, so no worries."

He took her by the hand and drew her to the edge of the sidewalk to hail a cab.

Gallantly, he let her get in first and then walked around to the other side to take his seat.

As far away as possible, Zoey pleaded.

She was thankful for that. She wasn't sure that she would be able to resist the slightest contact and didn't think the driver would appreciate seeing them breathlessly making out in the backseat.

Though he's probably *seen worse*, she thought. Matthew tapped the window with his index finger.

"The best Indian restaurant in New York is on this street," he said.

Zoey giggled nervously. She actually chuckled.

He turned toward her.

"You couldn't care less, right?"

"Exactly," she murmured.

He remained motionless for a moment, enthralled by the movements of her lips, and then she added:

"But, I'm listening."

She moved her hand along the seat toward his. She saw his knuckles tense up and then relax.

"It's a very good restaurant," he repeated.

She started playing with his fingers, stroking each one in turn. The tautness of his forearm showed her that it was taking a lot of effort to ignore her caresses.

"Do you mean that everything there is good?" she smiled.

"Not at first glance, no. The decor is pleasant, but the staff..."

"Less pleasant, perhaps?"

"They were out of control...But, I was really touched by the..." (he hesitated) "...decor."

He smiled his sardonic smile again, the one she had detested. But now, she thought it was incredibly sexy. She had the impression that he wanted to devour her.

"It's important to be touched," she commented, very seriously. "But, you can't judge by appearance only."

She felt quite sure of herself. Her hand climbed up to Matthew's rigid wrist. This contact with his skin, even softer at this point, made her tremble.

"You are correct. We need to use all of our senses to come up with an objective critique."

He freed his hand and brushed it against her cheek.

"Touch."

He plunged his nose into her neck.

"Smell."

His mouth quivered behind Zoey's ear.

"Taste."

And, moving around gently to her face, he added:

"Sound is optional."

"Then you should be quiet now."

He placed his lips on her forehead, exploring the hair framing her face down to that sensual spot just behind the earlobe, where the jaw begins.

"That would be a shame. You wouldn't be able to hear how much I want you."

She didn't say what she was thinking: that she didn't need to hear it, or to say it. It took a superhuman effort for her to pull away from the kiss of this man who was presently burying himself in her neck, and to stop herself from running one hand through his thick hair that was tickling her chin, while kissing his open mouth with her tongue, and with the other, unbuttoning his pants.

A discreet cough came from the front seat and brought them back to reality. The taxi was stopped in front of her building and had probably been there a while. The driver was peering at them through the rearview mirror. She lifted her head at the same time that Matthew did. They were looking directly into each other's eyes, their faces only separated by half an inch.

Matthew's mouth immediately found hers. While he tenderly opened her lips with his tongue, she saw him remove a bill from the back pocket of his jeans and hand it to the driver, then open her car door. He held on to her while she slipped backward, still attached to his mouth. She especially liked the pressure from his arm that kept her from falling and the smile on his face as he continued to kiss her, but then she cried out in surprise. She freed her legs and placed both feet on the sidewalk, exiting the taxi backside first.

If someone had passed by at that moment, they would have found this image quite amusing.

She let go of Matthew, regretfully, so that he could also get out.

Once she was out of the car, after smoothing his shirt with a practiced hand, he lifted his head toward her.

She didn't know what to do. Separated from him, she felt less sure than she had in the taxi where she would have murdered anyone who had dared to get between them.

"You've made it home safe and sound," he said.

Her stomach tightened. She had not been expecting that. Across from her, Matthew seemed to have regained his control and composure. He quickly fixed his hair, running his fingers through it, exactly as she had dreamed of doing just a few minutes earlier.

She had to extricate herself from this situation immediately, before he started laughing, or worse, before he thanked her. She desperately needed to regain the upper hand, and her dignity.

"Thank you for accompanying me home," she asserted, as politely as she could. "See you soon."

She turned toward the door of her apartment building, her heart beating hard. He had simply dropped her there, at the doorstep.

She should have acted firm, regal, haughty, and told him, first, that this wasn't anything serious.

Now, it definitely wasn't anything serious.

She punched in the building code but after pushing the last number on the pad, she felt hands around her waist. She spun around. Matthew didn't wait for her to speak before his mouth was on hers again, with an intensity that she herself had trouble containing.

She must have pushed him away to catch her breath.

He stepped back, letting out a deep sigh, taking one of her errant tresses between his fingers.

"I wouldn't want to be thought of as inconsiderate," he murmured, as if he were speaking to himself.

He took one step back, his face frozen in a smile that was set in an upward turn, both full of doubt but also serious.

"See you Saturday, Zoey," he said suddenly.

Before she could say another word, he moved away from her.

See you Saturday, Zoey?

She watched him walk away, unable to miss the elegant way he held himself, but doing so unconsciously.

Was she the type of girl that men kissed in a taxi because they couldn't resist and then ditched afterward?

Had she been giving him signals?

Absolutely not! screamed an indignant voice in her head.

He had insisted on accompanying her, he had kissed *her*, she'd said goodnight, then he had come up behind her as she was entering her building. All that she had done, according to her, was to respond to his kisses, because...

What an idiot*!*

She had been wrong to let herself get swept away. It went too far. She had not been in control at all. She should have gently sent him home, before he kissed her in the street. After that, it had been too late.

Why am I always attracted *to guys like that?* she wondered.

A psychologist could have given her a complicated and detailed explanation, but she knew what Sally would say: "You make life too complicated, Zoey. Have fun. Live life to the fullest."

Sally, however, would not have allowed herself to be discarded like that, for the sole reason that she would not have played this game. She would have kissed him too, of course, but, once she had arrived home, she would have told him: Thank you so much, but I think that this is a good place to stop for tonight.

Sally would have understood what kind of a man he was.

A man who was capable of cheating on the women he was dating–who he was seeing– with her own cousin!

Her cousin *who was an awful person.*

She could already hear what Tina would say when she learned what had happened: Zoey is such an idiot. She threw herself at Matthew, obviously just to get at me! He made it very clear to her that he was not interested!

Not that she cared that much about what Tina thought, but this would completely destroy what was left of her reputation within the family—well, any *good* reputation that is. He mother would never forgive her and Nana would be even less accommodating.

Do it with style, Zoey! her grandmother would often tell her when she'd been punished–often after she and Adrian had taken well-deserved but sometimes cruel revenge on Tina and Laurie. Give as good as you get, but always be fair. Always. Only cowards need to cheat. Cowards and people who aren't very smart.

She entered her code, this time completing it, and climbed the stairs, not being able to stop herself from thinking about what an idiot she had been and replaying the scene in the taxi with alternate endings.

It was, no contest, the worst evening of her life.

Though there *had been several that were a close second!*

Like that time last year when she spent two hours consoling her date who had just gone through a difficult break up; their first evening out together reminded him of his first date with his ex.

Or the time that she realized that the guy– Andrew, blond, good-looking– who had taken her out for a drink had lied about his age and was still in college.

She undressed quickly, still smelling Matthew's scent which made her crazy and furiously angry at the same time, and jumped under the shower.

As the water flowed, she tried to convince herself that she wasn't really interested in him and promised herself to do what she always did in situations like this: dive into work and forget it had ever happened.

At least until next Saturday.

10
CREAM OF TARTAR

Zoey crossed the room to the imposing piano on which the florist was placing a bouquet of roses. Mia, the consul's assistant, was supervising the final preparations with an apprehensive expression on her face, an open folder in her hand.

"I've been looking for you," said Zoey.

In her haute-couture suite, Mia's whole body tensed up on cue. She inspected Zoey as if she was the cause of all her problems, or, at the least, an aggravating annoyance.

"What can I do for you?" she articulated, with visible effort.

"I need someone to move the table in front of the main window," Zoey said, without taking her eyes off the florist arranging the flowers on the piano. "If I could make a suggestion, you shouldn't put that vase there."

"Why?"

"Adrian Peters will have them removed."

"Really?"

His tone challenged anyone who would get near his roses.

"He will also tell you that your bouquet of roses will hamper the piano's sound. Believe me."

Mia shrugged her shoulders. The expression on her face gave Zoey a brief glimpse into what she thought of artists at this very moment.

"We'll put the roses on the gueridon table next to the blue chair, over there," she said to the florist. "Is that true?"

"What?" Zoey asked.

"That a bouquet would hamper a piano's sound."

"I have no idea."

She suspected that her friend used this pretext because he simply didn't like superfluous details.

"Do you need anything else?" asked Mia, whose stilettos were already making dents in the thick rug laid out in the reception hall.

"No, everything's fine."

"Wonderful. You can go talk to Jorge about the correct protocol".

"Protocol?"

"Mr. Delacruz would like you to present the dessert yourself. I mentioned that to you."

Her tone left no room for argument.

"Yes, of course. But going forward, I'm not going to have much time. I only have a few minutes before the event starts."

"You will need to be able to remember how to pronounce certain names. Jorge will assist you."

Zoey headed toward the young man with short brown hair, slicked back, wearing a white shirt and gray pants. He was reviewing some papers in front of a dark wooden cabinet. He gave her a friendly smile and held out his hand.

"You must be Zoey, our chef this evening."

"You're very observant."

"You're wearing a chef's jacket," noted Jorge, without an inkling of humor. "I'd like to introduce you to the three people with whom you will being unveiling the dessert."

Unveiling the dessert.

Zoey smiled, in spite of herself.

"Gilberto Da Costa is the soccer team coach. Rafael Branco is here representing the Minister of Culture and you will also meet Sofia Alves, who I think you know. Will you be able to handle that?"

Zoey repeated the names, pronouncing them almost perfectly.

Jorge wasn't listening to her. His eyes widened as he looked toward the reception area and suddenly tightened his hands into a fist. He seemed ready to attack someone just behind Zoey.

"Wait two seconds!" he exclaimed.

He thrust the guest list into her hands and began running and shouting:

"What are you doing with that banner? This is not some college party!"

She burst out laughing. This is exactly the type of thing she would say in a similar situation. She lowered her eyes to the list so she could successfully memorize the names.

She couldn't stop herself from looking for Matthew's, just like she hadn't been able to stop herself from Googling him and lingering on photos and articles about him, which were, for the most part, quite flattering.

She found his name: "Matthew Ziegler + 1."

Plus one? He's coming with a date? Was he really going to come with another woman to see her? With Tina?

The mental image that she created of Tina making an entrance on Matthew Ziegler's arm could have been a painting entitled *The Triumph*.

"Zoey?" Sally's voice behind her said.

The jump she executed would have instantly qualified her for the Olympics. Her friend gave her an impassive look.

Zoey wanted to show her the list so she could commiserate. Sally would have found the right words to make her laugh about it all and make it seem less dramatic. Since that evening at the Rains Law Room, they had only talked about work. Several times, Zoey had wanted to approach her friend and apologize. The scowl on her face had dissuaded her from doing so.

"We have a problem. Hakeem had a car accident."

"Is he okay?"

"Yes, but he cracked a rib. He can't make it this evening."

Zoey moaned. Hakeem was her assistant cook, the most talented student from the hospitality program where she hired students to help with receptions. Once she was sure he hadn't been hurt badly, she understood the gravity of the situation. She took her phone out of her pants pocket. The look on Sally's face did not make her feel better.

"I called all the students we've worked with before and none of them are available."

"We'll have to do without."

She used her most professional voice but wasn't sure what to do next. Every person in the team was important to pull of an event like this. Hakeem was used to dealing with hectic orders, often reduced to a single word. Without his speed and skill, the success of the reception was in jeopardy. Worse, his absence would cause delays.

She breathed in deeply to regain her composure, and started prioritizing.

"We only focus on what has to be done, one thing at a time. Put Phil and Becca on hot prep, start the appetizers, and I will take care of the dessert soufflés."

Sally nodded her head curtly, like a soldier ready to take action, and disappeared into the kitchen. Zoey was going to follow her until she saw that Adrian was arriving.

He looked magnificent in his gray dress pants, no tie adorning his white shirt, his hair a bit crazy as always, with his jacket over his arm. Marianita entered the room just behind him, wearing a tight but simple black dress, perched on four-inch heels. She sat down a leather weekend bag and caught up with him.

Zoey descended on Adrian.

"Adrian! You have to save me."

"And hello to you too! I'm sorry, but I don't think I have time for that right now."

She grabbed his arm, ignoring Marianita's astonished expression, and dragged him toward the reception room.

"I swear, if I survive this weekend, we will have that talk. But, in the meantime, and in the name of twenty-five years of friendship, you have to help me make up for lost time."

"Lost time? Is something wrong?"

"Not enough staff. Do whatever you have to do, but you've got to mesmerize them at the beginning of the evening. They have to be so enthralled with you that they don't think about eating, okay?"

"I'm always mesmerizing."

"Stop joking around. I know how it works for these types of events. You start out playing softly so that people are able to hear themselves when they talk to each other."

"Please, Adrian, I've never ask you for anything!" she implored.

"You ask me to do stuff for you all the time. I can't change my program at the last minute, Zoey."

"Adrian, my life depends on it!"

"Don't exaggerate."

"I'm not exaggerating."

"You could simply switch the order of the first two selections," Marianita interrupted.

Zoey hadn't seen her walk up. The young woman smiled. She took Adrian's free arm.

"Come on, Adrian, you can't refuse to help a woman in distress," she added, cajoling him.

She put her head on his shoulder, taking her turn to implore him.

"You don't even need to change the order of the individual pieces within each section. All we have to do is start a half hour earlier, she continued."

"Because you're ganging up on me," grumbled Adrian. "I'll do it, Zoey. But you owe me a big one. You know I hate last minute changes."

"Thank you, thank you, thank you!"

She would have thrown her arms around him but didn't want to risk finding herself nose to nose with Marianita who'd had the same idea. The gorgeous Brazilian removed her arm from Adrian's and planted a kiss on his cheek. Adrian smiled, embarrassed.

"I have to go," Zoey mumbled.

She definitely hated the intimacy between them that reminded her of she and Adrian had together. Marianita acted like she had known him for years.

Irritated, she left them, crossing the room, quickly and with determination. When she was sure that she was no longer in view, she broke into a sprint toward the kitchen.

Becca and Phil were already at the stove while Sally was lining up the serving cups on a tray. She glanced around, evaluating with one quick look what still needed to be done. Sally had set up at the work table, across from Zoey, near the ovens. She felt a knot of panic forming in her stomach. The hot soufflés, to be topped with cold ice cream, were unforgiving and had to be timed to the very second. Without Hakeem backing her up, she wasn't not sure she could make it work. Sally or Becca could help, but she'd have to explain every step and didn't have the time to train someone on the job. It would be faster if she just did it herself, even if she knew that her chances of success were slim. If the dessert were ruined, she'd only have herself to blame. Even if she Hakeem hadn't been out of commission, the head chef was ultimately responsible.

She had a bizarre urge to laugh. It wasn't only the soufflés that were on the line.

No.

It wasn't only the soufflés that were on the line. Her desire that everything be perfect, her reputation, and the trust that Adrian had placed in her by recommending her was all at stake. All of these were reason enough for her to make it to the finish line.

Her assistants were all looking at her, waiting for her to say something or issue an order, as they were accustomed to doing. Each of them was keenly aware of the precariousness of situation.

She was suddenly filled with gratitude. They had confidence in her, whatever happened.

"Okay! I'm counting on each one of you to do your part. We'll do without Hakeem this time. And we will execute it all perfectly."

The terrified look Phil wore and Becca's worried look told her that her speech hadn't totally convinced them.

"Or, at least, we'll do our best," she added, sighing. "It's really important that each one of you give it your all. Becca, keep a close eye on the sliders. Phil, the fish feijoada has to simmer twenty-five minutes, and not one minute more. While that's simmering, you can sauté the vegetables in sesame oil. Sally?"

Her assistant blinked her eyes.

"Be careful not to overfill the glasses—they should only be two-thirds full."

"Got it."

She immediately started in on her own task.

She had already filled three-fourths of the soufflé ramekins when the servers arrived to carry out the first trays. She stopped one of them on his way out to the reception hall.

"Is everything going well out there?"

"The guests have arrived. But, I think there has been a mix up in the evening's program."

"What do you mean?" Zoey responded, trying to stop her voice from cracking.

"This is the first time I've ever been at an event like this that started with a real concert. So, no one is that interested in eating."

Zoey sighed, relieved. "Thank you."

"Those who are eating seem to be enjoying it," the server said reassuringly, having picked up on her anxiety.

Then, he disappeared with his tray.

Zoey went back to focus on her work. When she put the soufflés in the oven, it was 8:30 p.m. The guests had arrived at least an hour and a half ago. She noticed that the server's dance was getting more hectic and that they were coming and going more quickly. Adrian had kept his word.

Jorge's peeked through the double doors.

"Ms. Westwood? Mr. Delacruz is asking for you."

Oh God, no, Zoey thought, panicked.

Two ideas were floating around in her head at the same time: the fear that she'd be dismissed on the spot and that she wouldn't be able to finish the soufflés that had taken so much time and energy.

"Phil, please take the soufflés out of the oven in one minute. Please listen carefully. Add the glaze just around the rims, definitely not directly on top, and send them out immediately. You, over there—" (the server she had stopped who hadn't seem surprised) "you wait, and then grab one of your coworkers when the soufflés are ready, take them directly to the reception hall."

She removed her uniform, combed her hair with her fingers and hurried after Jorge who was making urgent motions.

"Why does he want to see me?" she asked once they were in the grand hall.

"He wanted to congratulate you personally."

"It's a bit early for that," Zoey moaned. "There's still work to do."

"Do you want me to tell him that? In front of the guests?"

Jorge's friendly smile suddenly became worried and tense.

"No, that's not necessary," stammered Zoey, realizing that she would never have been able to work in a position like his.

She would have told off the first diplomat who tried to tell her what to do, and, eventually, she would have committed countless faux pas. Or, more realistically, she would have been fired after committing the first one.

The room was crowded with guests, the purpose for which it was made. The lights had been dimmed, making the it feel warm and friendly. From his platform, Adrian was playing a soulful jazz piece, sitting alone at the piano. She had seen him play hundreds of times, but was always impressed at how striking and perfect he looked when he performed—removed from how she knew him in everyday life, but also exactly as he should be. She gave him a smile straight from their past that she had only used with him since childhood. He didn't see it and she continued to make her way toward the back of the room.

A group of men dressed in dark suits gathered around the seating area. They appeared to be from the teams that were going to play a friendly soccer match the day after tomorrow. In one corner of the room, she recognized the musicians she had seen at the Raines Law Room a few days earlier.

They were laughing uproariously, surrounded by Marianita who was obviously in heaven, simpering more than ever.

Jorge led Zoey to the buffet, where Luis Delacruz, a glass in hand, was having an engaging discussion with an imposing man with gray hair, and a more stern man with a military-style haircut. He must have been the team coach, Gilberto Da Costa. The former was most likely the attaché from the Ministry of Culture. Matthew Ziegler stood next to them, listening interestedly to their conversation, a serious expression on his face.

Seeing him like that, leaning against a chair, with such a nonchalant stance, Zoey thought her heart was going to burst. She prayed to the heavens that she wouldn't blush, stutter or look at him longingly, all of which she felt capable of, considering the attraction he held for her. She had to control herself! She was still humiliated from the way he had left her at the door of her building, casting her off like an old pair of shoes.

When she reached the group, the consul smiled at her and with an elegant gesture, opened up the circle for her to join.

"Ms. Westwood, Mr. Branco wanted to meet you and you should be honored."

"I hope I'm not interrupting," the silver-haired man said, with almost no trace of an accent.

"No, not at all," Zoey smiled nervously. "It is a pleasure to meet you."

"And for me as well. Your feijoada was quite interesting."

"Oh?"

She hated this expression; it was often tainted with sarcasm. Interesting. This is what you said to a someone when you were bored out of your skull. In fact, she'd been told that many times when she had passionately shared her love of food with someone who, unbeknownst to her, had never set foot in a kitchen. And then she'd seen their eyes glaze over. When someone applied it to a dish they had just tasted, it meant that the person had almost vomited and had bent over backward to avoid doing so.

Her eyes met Matthew's, who was looking at her right then.

"I thought it was fabulous," Rafael Branco added, who, despite his excellent level of English, did not master irony with as much ease as she thought. "It's my mother's favorite dish. Your version is exceptional."

"I used the spices that we often see in gumbo," Zoey replied. "That is

101

also a food with slave origins."

She immediately felt uncomfortable, remembering that some Brazilians didn't like to be reminded of their country's slave past.

Matthew raised an eyebrow.

"These dishes seem simple, but aren't," added Rafael Branco, without seeming to have noticed any slight. "It's not just the spices, however. Again, congratulations."

"Thank you."

"Mr. Delacruz told me about the goal for this menu, to represent both cultures. I wasn't expecting that, however. What's next?"

His expression made plain his obvious love of good food.

"Rafael is a real foodie," Luis Delacruz asserted. "Mr. Ziegler was just talking about his last trip to Brazil and how refined Mr. Branco's own cooking is."

"I only dabble," Rafael Branco replied modestly. "And what's next on the menu?"

"Soufflés," Zoey responded. Both hot and cold, together.

"Rio in summer, New York in winter."

Now that she had expressed it out loud, her idea sounded stupid and simplistic to her.

"Fabulous!" Luis Delacruz explained, encouragingly.

She wanted to die. He was congratulating her like a child who was showing off her Play-Doh flower pot.

"Yes, that does sound interesting," Matthew added. He seriousness was getting on her nerves.

"Matthew, my glass is empty," a feminine voice sang out, interrupting them.

A hand, followed by a gold and diamond bracelet, held out her glass over the folder the critic was holding. The woman, who had been hidden till then, stood up from her chair. She had to be around fifty, and except for the tiny wrinkles at the corner of her eyes, she was the spitting image of the younger woman that Zoey had seen surrounded by musicians on the other side of the room—Marianita.

"I'll take care of it in a second, Sofia," Matthew replied.

It seemed to Zoey that his voice had softened. He took the empty glass with one hand, and the woman's arm with the other, to help her join them. She wore a long, white dress that accentuated her figure perfectly. Her black hair was pulled into a tight chignon. A simple, flat gold necklace emphasized her fine neck. She was, in fact, even more beautiful than her daughter.

"I enjoyed the food you prepared," she said, unsmiling. "But, soufflés…" (She shook her finger, like it was an orchestra conductor's baton.) "They require a delicate touch. My own chef in São Paulo says that one can't claim to be a chef before making a successful soufflé but that then you have to throw out the recipe. It's very...how do you say that, Matthew?"

"Retro," Matthew stated, avoiding Zoey's gaze.

When he finally looked her way, he had a regretful grimace on his face.

"You must know of Sofia Alves. She doesn't need an introduction within the food world. Sofia, I'd like to introduce you to Zoey Westwood, a promising young chef."

Zoey noticed the obvious difference that he made between the one who didn't need any introduction and herself, whose role in all of this had to be specified. Nevertheless, she tried to act like she recognized her. Her name did seem familiar. She'd have to ask Sally. She could already hear her exasperated response: "Sofia Alves?! Zoey, I hope you behaved."

"I'm sorry to be so direct," Sofia said. "But, I'm used to working with chefs. I know how they like to be spoken to."

"Well then, you must also know that it's better to taste a chef's creations before announcing your opinion about her choices."

Matthew looked like he wanted to crawl into a cave. Zoey saw his hand, which had not left the woman's arm, press down slightly, as if he were commanding her to remain calm. This intimate gesture put her over the edge. This was not a simple discussion. It was a rival declaring war.

"Matthew told me that you have a true chef's temperament," Sofia added.

"I thank you for having tested me," Zoey retorted. "Since you didn't do so for my soufflés."

Sofia's nose quivered and her black eyes sent daggers Zoey's way. However, unexpectedly, she bowed her head and replied, laughing:

"You are correct. Matthew often tells me that I lack tact."

"A quality that he possesses in spades," Zoey snapped.

"I don't agree," Rafael Branco laughed suddenly. "I remember this one time in Rio when…"

"I beg you, dear Rafael," Matthew interrupted. "You are not going to share this embarrassing memory, are you?"

"I have worse ones," added Sofia.

She ran her fingers through Matthew's hair in a tender gesture that left it tousled.

What is this, this habit of touching each other in public? Zoey frowned to herself, suppressing the image of her and Matthew entwined in the middle of the street.

"Remember that time in Bahia?" she continued.

Rafael Branco let out a laugh, his eyes shining in complicity. Matthew offered a feeble smile.

Zoey nodded her head as politely as she could, to give the impression that she was interested in the conversation. However, internally, she wanted to scream in frustration. Not only had he had the poor taste to come accompanied by his lover, who was clearly his exact opposite, but she was bent on emphasizing to what degree they were intimately involved.

Soon, she was no longer listening. Out of the corner of her eye, she was watching the servers pass by carrying the soufflés in their molds, mentally calculating how much time she needed before prepping the creampuffs and presenting them for dessert. She had lost the thread of the conversation when Matthew's voice could be heard above the others.

"We don't want to keep Ms. Westwood any longer," he said. I'm sure she has a lot to do. That's how it is when you're the chef.

"I've kept you too long," Rafael Branco apologized. I let myself get carried away by my enthusiasm. Thank you for time, Ms. Westwood, and I can hardly wait for the sequel.

Sofia Alves was satisfied to simply nod, accepting defeat. Zoey stammered a thank you and escaped as quickly as she could.

Just as she was about to enter the kitchen hallway, a hand stopped her. Marianita put herself in her path.

"I saw you speaking to my mother."

"That was your mother?" Zoey said, unconvincingly, her mind already preoccupied with what was to come next.

"Yes. I'm not thrilled that she showed up. In the beginning, she didn't want to. But Matthew Ziegler convinced her."

The way she said his name conveyed what she thought about him. With interest, Zoey noted that the pretty Brazilian was more reserved than the other times she'd met her.

"I don't know what she said to you, but I'd like to apologize in advance. I saw your face. My mother can be extremely rude and impulsive. I can't believe that she still has a relationship with him."

She had spit out the word "relationship," not leaving any doubt as to the type of association that her mother had with Matthew.

"It must really bother her that her mother is dating someone who is just a little older than she is," Zoey thought, forgetting for a moment that Marianita was talking about the man she'd been obsessed with for three days, with a mixture of anger and attraction, both as irrepressible as the other.

Then the absurdity of the situation hit her. She was discussing Matthew with Marianita, who it appeared was Adrian's lover, with whom Zoey had…

"I really have other things to think about right now!" she yelled inside her head.

"When I think how he hurt…that he…" Marianita continued. "In any case, I'm so sorry."

"Really, it's no problem," Zoey replied, bursting with annoyance. "I'm not upset at all and I need to return to the kitchen. We'll have a chance to talk again soon."

"I hope so, yes," the Brazilian replied, with a charming smile. "There is another subject that I wanted to discuss with you."

"Another time, okay?"

She felt like she was going to explode. Without saying goodbye, she left Marianita there and ran toward the kitchen.

Sally also seemed close to despair. Becca and Phil were busy barking orders, exactly like Zoey would have done, if she'd been there.

"It's a total catastrophe," whispered Sally. "Where were you?"

Zoey had to stop herself from screaming in Sally's face. At least she had stopped acting like the injured employee and had turned back into herself, the Sally that Zoey knew.

"I was fighting off an Brazilian attack," she responded.

"I'm back now."

"We should have prepped more in advance. We should have planned better," Sally whimpered.

"Planned for a car accident? That would take more than planning, that would require being clairvoyant! Let's get going! Are the rest of the desserts ready?"

"If I help Becca and Phil, it should be fine. Can you prep the creampuffs by yourself?"

"Of course!"

She was perhaps overestimating her ability to make up lost time, but she was sure that no one could blame her for a bit of forced enthusiasm.

11
PREHEAT THE OVEN

A half an hour later, she realized that she'd been too optimistic. The oven that she had tested earlier in the week had never been transported to this location before. The move had affected it and the differences in temperature were problematic, despite all of the precautions she had taken. The texture of the cream was too smooth, and it prevented her from going as quickly as she wanted. At this pace, she'd never have enough time to assemble the pièce de résistance, a French-style *croque-en-bouche*, a towering cone of cream puffs, set with spun caramel. She should have started an hour earlier.

The servers were taking out the last trays of the Brazilian-American fusion hors d'oeuvres, including pão de queijo with a pesto twist. From the insistent looks on their faces, she measured the extent of the damage. Some of them seemed panicked while others expressed mocking disapproval.

After the hundredth cream puff, she leaned over her work space. Nothing had gone as planned.

She had expected there to be little snags—there always were—but not such a disaster in both the kitchen and the reception area, where she had been doubly humiliated.

Sensing someone next to her, she turned her head and saw Matthew rolling up his shirt sleeves in a perfectly natural gesture, as if he were already part of the team. Sally looked at her quizzically from the back of the kitchen, and Zoey replied by a guarded shrug of her shoulders.

"Could you please tell me what you think you are doing?" she demanded.

"Obviously, I am going to fill the cream puffs," he replied, amused. "We put you behind."

"So you came to help me as compensation?"

He picked up a pastry bag and started working, concentrating.

"No, I came to apologize for the way Sofia acted."

"Okay, that's very nice of you, but I don't allow amateurs in my kitchen," Zoey retorted, in her most contemptuous voice.

He let out a laugh.

"If you knew who Sofia Alves was—which wasn't the case, I know, even though you tried to make us think that you did—you would have known that she is the owner of four of the best restaurants in Brazil. I apprenticed in her restaurants."

"You went to cooking school?" Zoey replied, shocked.

"Yes, but I was never able to make a soufflé. I learned to cook because a good critic must be able to talk about his subject in a concrete fashion, don't you think? Look, I'm not doing such a bad job. So now, be quiet and get to work. We're losing precious time."

Zoey opened her mouth to reply but noticed that he was indeed doing more than fine.

Almost as good *as Hakeem,* she had to admit. For the next half hour, they exchanged only a few words. Zoey gave orders, forgetting who she was giving them to. Matthew followed them and, sometimes, anticipated them.

Zoey watched as the caipirinha-flavored croque-en-bouche left the kitchen, carried out by three servers. She had never felt so tired and so wound up at the same time. She wasn't able to feel even the slightest relief, even when Becca, Phil and Sally noisily expressed their enthusiasm at being done, when they brought in the trays of mignardises and placed them on the side table for the servers to pick them up.

Next to her, Matthew was leaning on the work space, his arms crossed.

"I have to go present the dessert," she said with exhaustion in her voice.

"I release you from this responsibility. They wanted to see and they saw you. I think that you need to take a little break, have some fresh air and a glass of champagne. Shall we?"

Without waiting for a reply, he steered her toward the refrigerators, taking out a bottle, grabbing two glasses from a nearby crate.

"Let's go," he said, gently pushing her toward the door. "You deserve it."

"Yes, go for it," Sally added happily, winking. "We'll take care of the rest."

Zoey let herself be persuaded. She needed to drink something and to get out of this overheated kitchen. She felt the sweat sticking to her hair, at the edge of her temples.

The cool air felt good. She leaned against the outside wall. At least that is what she wanted to do, but slumped instead, completely exhausted.

"Take off your uniform—you must be burning up," Matthew said, pouring champagne into the glasses.

He held one out to her, and she let the uniform fall to her hips.

"Bravo. You won them over. And that's despite Rafael Branco being quite difficult where the culinary arts are concerned."

"That wasn't my main goal for the evening," Zoey noted.

"No, but it helped. For the others, I don't know, but it was important to the people you met. That, and your friend's concert."

He emphasized the word "friend."

"It was impressive," he added.

Zoey emptied her glass as if it had been filled with water and handed it to Matthew. He smiled, before giving her seconds.

"And to think that I had been looking forward to seeing you sober..."

"And to think that I had been looking forward to seeing you be truthful," she said, tit for tat.

He glanced at her, surprised.

"I always tell the truth," he retorted, with a hurt look on his face. "I really appreciated his music. Almost as much as sparring with you."

She bit her lip to avoid replying. So close to him, she wanted to slap him, jump on him and throw her glass in his face, while spitting out the word *Sofia*.

But that would only have revealed how much he had been on her mind these past few days. He was smug enough already.

"I really enjoyed the evening," he repeated.

Seeing him study her like that, so intensely that she could feel the air between them thicken, her confidence began to slip away.

"Especially when you almost got into it with Sofia Alves," he insisted.

"I wasn't 'getting into it' with anyone," she replied, unable to take her eyes off his lips as they moved.

"If I had been you, I would have. In the end, you are the more restrained of the two of us. It wasn't worth it."

She sighed and looked straight at him.

"Could you possibly, for once, be clear about what you mean? I don't understand anything you are saying. I am really grateful for your help and your encouragement about my social life, but I would like it if..."

She didn't have time to finish her sentence. He grabbed her by the arms and pulled her toward him. A second later, he was kissing her. She let herself be overcome. He gently spun her around and pressed her up against the wall. The contact with the stone brought her back to her senses and, with it, her sense of pride. She used both hands to push him away.

"That is not going to happen again!" Zoey exclaimed. "We've been there, done that."

He looked distressed.

"Done what?"

"You kiss me without asking permission and push me up against a wall."

"I was the one that was up against the wall last time. As for asking permission, would you like to sign a release form? That can be arranged," he concluded.

He seemed quite amused by this way of looking at it.

"I don't think this is funny!" she snapped. "For the past week, I've been had some ridiculous experiences and you played a large part. It may well turn you on to make out with women that you hardly even know and then dump them to the curb without explanation, but that's not going to happen this time."

"That's really not what turns me on," Matthew growled in reply. "Normally, I don't make out with women that I hardly know."

"Oh, I see. The other women, you 'see' them. That's the right word, right?"

"If you mean your cousin, I'm..."

"Do not mention my cousin! Definitely not her!"

"...not seeing her anymore."

That took Zoey off guard, and then she felt a wave of satisfaction, followed by resentful anger. She must look totally ridiculous and comic, because Matthew seemed to be holding back a grin.

"What do you mean by, 'I'm not seeing her anymore?'"

"I met her through a common acquaintance, but I quickly understood that it wasn't going to work for me. Your cousin is charming, very pretty and obviously from a nice family, but that isn't the type of woman that I see myself in a relationship with."

"You met her family!"

"Just as her date for the evening, which I was. She asked me to accompany her and I accepted."

"Do you often attend family functions as just a date?"

He lowered his head, visibly embarrassed.

"I had other reasons for wanting to attend. Reasons I'd rather not talk about now."

"You are just full of mystery, aren't you? And Sofia Alves?"

"What about Sofia Alves?"

"Were you 'seeing' her?"

Suddenly, his face tensed in anger.

"Is this an interrogation? My relationship with Sofia is personal!" he asserted, obviously offended.

She forced herself to laugh.

"Just one minute ago, you had your tongue down my throat, but that's not at all personal."

"First, I didn't have my tongue down your throat, and, as we keep going down this path, believe me, I'm regretting it. Second, this is the first time a woman I have not slept with has caused such a scene."

"That's not uprising, since there aren't many of those in New York. Now I understand why you travel so much."

"You're going too far," he replied, his jaw tight.

"I could say the same about you." She dashed toward the door.

"Thank you for showing me all of your many talents," she said cuttingly. "For now, I'm good with just your culinary skills."

As regally as she could, she left him there, pale with rage and speechless.

As soon as she entered, Sally came toward her cheerfully.

"I came to find you, they are asking for you in the reception area. It was a success. From the beginning to the end. We can all be proud."

Sally was wearing a mischievous smirk.

"When I left, I couldn't find you," she continued, a teasing look in her eye.

All I could see was Matthew Ziegler's back. I'd never noticed that he had four arms.

Behind her, the two assistant chefs commis chef stifled their laughter into the sauce pans they were holding.

12
GREASE THE RAMEKINS

"An inventive cuisine that doesn't hesitate to veer away from the classics to reconstruct them at a higher level, a perfect mixture of Brazilian sensuality and American spontaneity."

Sally's voice exploded in thrilled exclamations.

"Are you sure he's talking about your cuisine, Zoey?" Zoey rolled her eyes.

"Leave me alone about that stupid Matthew Ziegler article," please.

"A promising beginning though Zoey Westwood has much to learn about the subtleties of the pleasures of the palate."

"He wrote that?!" howled Zoey, ripping the newspaper out of friends' hands.

"Of course not," Sally replied laughing. "You realize that you go totally crazy whenever Matthew Ziegler is mentioned, right?"

"You've been torturing me with this for a week, whined Zoey. Can we move on?"

"No. We'll move on when I say we move on." Sally took the newspaper back and turned toward her friend.

"Would you have preferred the one he wrote about the Stan? 'It's often a nice touch when the chef makes rounds in the front of the house, but not when he spends more time getting his hair fixed than taking care of his clients who've been waiting a half an hour for ceviche de gambas with ginger and cranberries. Reality television has not been good to the restaurant business—and vice versa—but, in contrast to my dinner, at least it was a wrap.' You should write him a note to thank him."

Zoey hit her head against the counter.

"I'd rather die," she groaned.

"It's your professional duty. Critics are very sensitive."

"Sally, I told him to go to hell. We're past being 'sensitive.'"

The assistant stood up and filled the espresso machine with water.

"I don't think so, Zoey. I saw the way you were both looking at each other when he came into the kitchen. It was hot."

"I almost slapped him. I'm not joking, Sally. This type of guy is the lowest form of womanizer. He dumped Tina."

"That's just shows that he has taste. You are way sexier than Tina."

This thought gave Zoey a deep satisfaction.

"He's having a relationship with a woman who is around the same age as his mother," she added.

"And? Nobody is asking you to marry him! How long has it been since you slept with someone exactly?"

Zoey lifted her head. Exactly one year and two months. And "sleep with" was saying a lot.

"Are you telling me I should do it with someone in our professional circle?"

"I'm asking you to get over it so that you can sleep with someone you're attracted to."

"You are seriously telling me to get over the fact that he is, and I quote, 'the man who can make or break my career'? Exactly how long have been on drugs?"

Sally burst out laughing, setting down a cup of coffee in front of her friend.

"That's my only drug. Admit that you want to sleep with him and I'll let it go."

"No, I have no desire to sleep with him," Zoey lied.

The idea brought to mind unbearable images. She saw Matthew's mouth, his hands, and the moment when he had lifted her top to caress her, in the middle of the street. She shivered on her chair, hoping that Sally didn't notice.

"If that's that case, then I won't try to convince you," her friend said. "We're going out tonight and we're going to find you a nice guy. Just what you need. Or, we go meet up with Josh at the Raines Law Room. You both have broken hearts, so you can probably work something out."

"That sounds really appealing, thanks, no thanks. Aside from the fact that I would not sleep with my brother's best friend, I'm going to Nana's birthday celebration tonight."

"Oh, sorry about that. I totally forgot. Everyone will be there, I suppose. Adrian too?"

"No, just the family."

They always went to a restaurant for Nana's birthday and it inevitably kicked off the vacation season for the Westwoods. Fran Westwood considered this event her last obligation, after having packed her luggage and finished her spring cleaning. The next day, the Westwoods would take a plane to Florida to see Joe's family. When they were younger, she and Dalton would accompany them, but, now, they always had a professional excuse ready to avoid this chore. It wasn't that they didn't love their aunt and uncle on their dad's side, but the prospect of spending three weeks on vacation with their mother at the home of in-laws that she had never really liked was beyond what they could tolerate.

"Even so, Zoey," Sally added, turning her cup around in her hands. "Even if it's difficult, you need to thank Matthew Ziegler. It was a really flattering article and it's even more impressive if it ended badly when you were together. He's a true professional. Show that you're one too. But, I don't want to lecture you, of course."

"If you didn't lecture me, I'd think that you needed an MRI."

"It really is important. It's called "communicating" and I know you're not the only one in the world who has a hard time with it, except, of course, when you're telling people off. Please, Zoey, don't ruin all our efforts."

She sighed.

Zoey had stopped counting the number of times that she'd finished by saying, "Okay, I'll do it," in that same voice, part weary, part exasperated.

"Are you going to do it?" Sally asked, digging around behind the counter to find the cards they used for such a task.

"I don't know," Zoey responded, needling her.

Sally authoritatively placed a card and a pen in front of her.

"Zoey, you're not funny."

"It makes me feel guilty, you know? We're cutting down forests to produce paper. I don't want to participate in such destruction just to satisfy Matthew Ziegler's ego." (She brought her cup to her lips.) "I'll send him an email."

She dodged the pen that her friend threw in her face and savored her coffee.

"You know, I'm glad that we made up," she said quietly after a while.

Sally let out an exaggerated sigh.

"Me too! Being mad at you was the worst thing that's happened to me lately, well, except for the…"

She stopped suddenly and blushed.

"The…?"

"The reception at the consulate."

Zoey raised her eyebrows. She knew when Sally wasn't telling her the truth. It wasn't that hard when she had the creamy skin of a redhead that reddened at the slightest bit of emotion.

"Is there something you're not telling me?" she demanded suspiciously.

"Nothing that's important," Sally replied.

Then, she quickly took her leave. Zoey booted up the computer. Just because, and mainly because she couldn't stop herself, she typed Matthew's name in the search engine. When his face appeared, her heart went to her throat, and she felt an annoying hot sensation in her thighs. In all the photos, he had that same smile— professional and charming. She noticed, with a certain satisfaction, that someone else with his same name was a bald, dim looking fifty-year old who appeared to have spent time in prison. She then clicked on one of his critiques posted online.

"No Limit could have conjured up a futuristic *food concept in the style of Blade Runner, if the owner had not decided to follow the repulsive concept restaurant trend where everything is thrown together—and, note, I said 'thrown together,' not 'fusion.' Baroque-style couches, industrial shelving, fake 19th century lamps—nothing could save us in this former garage, a space much too small to not constantly bring the decorator's lack of talent to mind. The food itself, far from pushing any boundaries, while providing satisfactory enough family restaurant-style fare, does so without any charm or authenticity and little warmth. I could make the same comments about the cocktails offered by Steve Serder, but I think I've made my point. The dull menu, combined with the bloated, almost fungal feel of the space itself, will guide you, depressed and feeling a bit heavy, into that well-defined rectangle that is your bed, because, at No Limit, it takes a very long time to get seated. This is a direct result of the interminable wait during which the only place you can rest your gaze without recoiling in horror is a white wall that Beyoncé reportedly touched, most likely after she succumbed to starvation and decor-induced dizziness."*

She couldn't help laughing.

He was caustic, amusing and arrogant in just the right dose, just as she had imagined him to be. His reviews matched his personality. It was actually annoying. He had been caustic and arrogant with her, without showing much, if any, common sense, but still had that irritating self-confidence of men whose job it is to judge others.

With an infuriated click, she opened her email inbox.

Dear Matthew? Too informal. Dear Mr. Ziegler? Stupid when she thought about what had happened...

She remembered the scene from the taxi. The way he'd pushed her against the seat, while looking for money in his pocket with one hand, while crushing her against him with the other.

She shook her head.

Hello. Well, okay.

She interrupted herself to think about it. The message should be short, polite and aloof, while still expressing her gratitude.

I would like to thank you for your article. Too curt. I was pleased to... oh no, I wasn't pleased.

She let out an exasperated groan, and then, propelled by rage, began to type furiously on the keyboard.

116

"Hello. I would like to thank you for your flattering article. I would have also appreciated it if you hadn't acted like a total ass the last two times we met. You may be an expert on food, but let me tell you, you have a lot to learn about getting along with others. You took what you wanted, without even considering whether I actually liked you or not. I'm not going to deny it—I do want you, even if, right now, I would rather punch you in the face for having humiliated me in both public and private, and leaving me high and dry. I was in such a state that I had to take a cold shower when I got home and then spent my week Googling your name while throwing insults your way. Too bad the Internet doesn't chew liars up and spit them out."

She stopped writing and started giggling. Obviously, she'd never send this email, but getting it all out made her feel much better. She was sorry that Sally wasn't around to both laugh and be annoyed with her, before suggesting other, more refined approaches.

"Just know that I didn't find your approach particularly *creative or* novel *and that the way you kissed was certainly not 'classic' and didn't make me want more. Zoey."* She reviewed what she'd written and felt lighter. She selected the text to delete it. The door to Zoey's Kitchen opened.

She quickly closed the computer.

It was Gabriella, not Sally. The young woman's enormous belly protruded under a tray that was just as large what she was carrying out in front of her.

Zoey hurried over to relieve her of it.

"These *agnolotti* are for your grandmother," Gabriella specified.

"Gabriella, you are so sweet!" Zoey exclaimed, placing the tray on the counter. "You never forget Nana's birthday!"

"I never forget that it's thanks to your grandmother that we were able to open our restaurant."

"You're exaggerating! All Nana did was share her recipes."

"Let me repay my debts," the young woman replied, laughing. "While I still can. Once the baby arrives, I'll have less time."

Zoey glanced at her bulge. It looked like she was ready to give birth, but she was only six months along.

"Are you sure you're not having twins?"

Sit down for a minute.

Gabriella look at the stool regretfully, then sat in one of the chairs reserved for clients that was more accessible to her.

"Believe me, if I hadn't seen this baby in the monogram, I'd think it was triplets!"

Before she was with child, Gabriella had been slender and energetic, a talkative woman who was social and lively.

Now, her face was lined with exhaustion, and both the heat and her pregnancy weighed her down significantly. Even her hair, which had previously been a deep brilliant auburn, now seemed dull and flat.

"Don't get pregnant," she recommended. "I'm so ugly I could cry. If one more person tells me it's a blessing...! I hate everyone, but especially other pregnant women I meet who glow. I'm never doing this again!"

Zoey gave her a glass of water.

"I don't even recognize myself. I'm always arguing with Orlando. He feels like he has to constantly tell me I'm gorgeous and he goes overboard about everything. It's terrible. I've been wondering if I'll hate the baby too."

"Of course not! I'm sure you'll forget all this once he or she makes an appearance."

Gabriella gave her a weak smile.

"That's what my mother says too. But she also told me that getting dental work done is fun. How about you? How is everything?"

"It's going well. I've been working a lot." Gabriella sighed.

"Please! Tell me something a little more exciting! I'm pregnant, not dead! I'd like to believe that your life as a single girl is more exciting than mine."

"I hate to say it, but it's not. Sorry about that."

Gabriella looked dubious then stood up by pushing on the back of the chair.

"Well, I'm off since you don't have anything interesting to share with me. I'm sorry I'm being so obnoxious. I'm awful! Give Nana a hug for me."

"I'd be happy to," smiled Zoey. "Be careful going back to the restaurant."

Gabriella raised an eyebrow.

"I'm just going next door," she noted. "But, you're right. I don't want to get kidnapped by the garbage man. He might confuse me with a garbage can."

She waved and went out, leaving Zoey alone.

Zoey stretched. She had one hour to shower, get dressed and make it to the restaurant where the family was meeting to celebrate her grandmother's birthday. She liked attending these types of events, mostly because they were associated with pleasant memories. The meal was always a fun event. Nana knew how to throw a party. For birthday dinners, even Tina and Fran behaved themselves, to create a vision of the perfect family.

Zoey needed a truly relaxing evening.

She left her computer on and her documents open, locking the front door, making sure all the lights had been turned off.

13
DISH WITH SUGAR

The restaurant that Nana had chosen this year fulfilled the same requirements that the previous ones had: pleasant decor, an excellent menu, and a just as excellent wine list.

Zoey stopped at the entrance to enjoy the view that she had of the well-sized main room. It was neither too big or too small. The round and oval tables, covered with white table cloths, were arranged around a rectangular table on which were proudly displayed five enormous vases filled with white flowers.

Simple yet chic.

As the maître d' welcomed guests, he seamlessly took the red scarf she'd worn for how it looked, not because she was cold, since the evening was sweltering. Nana was drawn to elegance out of personal affinity rather than social convention, and to honor her, Zoey had purchased a light gray linen suit for the occasion, on which were intertwined cherry blossoms in silk thread of the same color. She had slipped her feet into matching sandals whose straps delicately wrapped her ankles. She had left her hair down, but pulled away from her face by a thin, gray silk band. A silver necklace at her throat was decorated with two blue feathers that brought a joyful touch to the ensemble.

The maître d' escorted her to the table that Fran and Joe had reserved. As was usually the case, Nana was seated in the middle between her two daughters who were, in turn, flanked by their husbands. Dalton was to Joe's left. He looked stunning in his gray suite accented by a blue dress shirt that had been a "suggestion" offered by Fran. He waved to his sister to indicate the empty spot next to him.

Zoey sat down next to Tina, who had swapped her every day attire and pony tail for a little white and green dress and a side braid that emphasized how delicate the nape of her neck was.

In her head, she could hear Matthew Ziegler's voice saying, "Your cousin is charming and very pretty,"

The fake smile she bestowed on Zoey as she sat down was less so. There was another empty spot, meant for Great Aunt Vicki.

"My heir has finally arrived!" Nana said, beaming.

"If your mind is already made up, I don't see why I have to sit through yet another dinner with you," Dalton replied cheerfully.

"Dalton!" Fran, who took everything literally, exclaimed. Joe smiled.

"You're not very much fun to be around since you became an attorney, Dalton," Nana replied, deadpan. "Don't worry. When I'm dead, I won't leave you with nothing. You'll have the memory of all the love I gave you."

"Can we buy a Porsche with love?" Dalton continued in the same vein.

"Yes, but in that case, you'd need to choose a different career, I think, replied his grandmother," before having a good laugh.

"Mother!" Fran and her sister Babeth cried together.

"Don't act like you aren't familiar with my sense of humor."

"No, we know it all too well," frowned Fran. "You passed it on to your grandchildren. Could we avoid making a scene?"

"What's the point of spending all this money if we can't make a scene?" huffed Zoey.

She caught her grandmother's eye and saw amused approval in her regard. Aunt Vicki showed up just then, in a dress that had been stylish in a different era, covered in sparkling sequins. She hugged Zoey warmly.

"I was in the restroom," she explained.

Fran Westwood rolled her eyes. She acted like she was being tortured.

"You never change."

"Your great-grandfather taught us that you can judge a restaurant by its toilets."

"And what's your verdict?"

"It's acceptable," laughed the elderly woman before turning to Zoey. "How are you? Did you come alone?"

"With whom would you like me to come, Aunt Vicki?"

"Sit down, Victoria," growled Nana, in a bossy tone.

Victoria obeyed, just as she had been doing for 75 years when she received an order from her sister. She took her place between Tina and Malcolm and started chatting with her nephew by marriage.

Zoey focused her attention on the menu the server had brought her.

Dalton hadn't spoken to her yet and was being careful to avoid doing so, turned toward their father, speaking quietly, involved in a discussion that was drowned out by the more animated discussion Fran was having with her sister and mother. Uncle Malcolm already looked like he was going to die of boredom. That is to say, everything was normal.

Earlier, Zoey had been satisfied to quickly greet Tina.

Now, her cousin suddenly asked, "So, the reception at the consulate, how did it go?"

Zoey knew Tina's method of operation when it came to conversations during Nana's birthday parties. To avoid directly provoking a new conflict in the cold war that they have been fighting for thirty years, she'd always begin by asking Zoey if she had any news, before finding an opportunity to underhandedly insult her about her choice of careers.

She felt justified in looking down on her cousin when it came to business. Tina worked in her father's large corporation where the main focus was buying companies and getting them in shape to be either sold or liquidated. She was the director of purchasing in one of the subsidiaries.

Zoey thought this type of job was deathly boring and felt strongly that it was morally suspect.

However, Tina had had less luck in love. Zoey was convinced that she was holding out for the perfect husband and rejecting suitors for ridiculous reasons, such as their name or the color of their socks. She remembered one of Tina's boyfriends in college that she'd dumped because he liked rugby and she thought it was a low class sport.

"Everything was perfect, Zoey replied. And how about you? What's popping?" She like to have fun with Tina by using trendy expressions to annoy her.

"Everything is fine, her cousin replied. I've been working a lot. I go out a lot too. Summer's a busy time. I'll be going on vacation in September this year. I'm hoping for an Indian summer. What about you?"

"I never go on vacation in the summer—it's wedding season."

"Oh, that's right. You don't find that depressing?"

"No, I love New York in the summer."

"No, I mean to cater all these weddings when you aren't even engaged."

First shot. The attack lacked finesse and could prove to be dangerous to the attacker herself. Tina was on edge.

"It's not anymore depressing than always being a bridesmaid and never a bride," she replied with a meaningful smile.

"How funny that you mention that! Just yesterday, Laurie asked me to be her bridesmaid!"

Second shot. She'd arrived at her destination. She had been impatient to get there. Normally, she waited for the entrée to arrive before she got serious. Zoey kept smiling, but her hands were tightening on the menu she was holding.

"That's fabulous!" she responded, sweetly. "A new bridesmaid's dress! Do you know what color it will be this time? Pink? Pale green?"

"Blue. We are going to try them on at Dior. It's going to be a large wedding. I think that even you may be invited."

Zoey stopped herself from hurling a particularly creative insult.

"I don't know why they brought us menus!" Nana suddenly exclaimed.

Her grandmother was looking at her. She must have been following their exchange from afar. Fran and Babeth were talking amongst themselves. From their expressions, Zoey knew that they were criticizing something from where they were sitting, and it was probably Nana's choice of restaurant.

"I requested the same meal for everyone. You'll have to trust my judgment. I didn't want us to spend hours making up our minds. You know I'm not that patient."

"You know what you want, you mean, interjected Uncle Malcolm. Just like Tina does. She also has your eyes. She's the one that looks the most like you, Angelina."

Third shot. Inevitably, Uncle Malcolm tried to make Tina seem more important, since he felt that her grandmother had wronged her, from many angles. He must not have appreciated that she had called her Zoey her "heir" in front of everyone.

"Yes, Tina does resemble me some," Nana said in a soothing voice. Zoey inherited my love for cooking. But the grandchild who is the most like me is that little spoiled brat bouncing around in his chair because he doesn't have anything to drink.

Dalton lifted his head and gave his grandmother a smile.

"All of this reminds me of birthday celebrations in Naples," Aunt Vicki added, "Except, this time, nobody is saying that it has to end. Isn't that wonderful?"

"Yes," Nana murmured, her eyes shining. "My parents always celebrated our birthdays like we were the Virgin Mary incarnate. The restaurant was filled with flowers. Our Aunt Tilla would make her orange blossom cake. I've never been able to find that recipe."

"And the birthday girl was allowed to sit at the head of the table," Aunt Vicki added. "Papa still kept the restaurant open for regular customers and everyone would drink to our health. Once, I even got to taste some white wine!"

She laughed mischievously at this memory. Nana's eyes misted over as she looked at her sister.

"Even a little thing like you was allowed," Nana said tenderly. "I would give anything to relive just one of those minutes. The parents would dance—very poorly actually, and we'd fall asleep on the chairs, our stomachs hurting from too much eating and too much dancing. And Papa..."

She stopped suddenly.

"Could you order the wine, please, Malcolm," she continued with a slight tremble in her voice. "I know you are all going to like it."

"Your husband kept the tradition going," Aunt Vicki added. "The birthday parties that you've had! They were always so wonderful! Unique!"

"He was one of a kind too," Nana replied.

Zoey had always regretted that she'd never known her grandfather. He'd died of a heart attack right before she'd been born.

"Zoey is so much like Dad," Fran interrupted. "Not good with money at all and never able to dress herself correctly."

"And the same sense of humor," Nana shot back, the tone of her voice noticeably less kind now. "She has his forehead too, and that same special way of tripping over the rug, even when there is no rug."

Zoey laughed. Nana's comments about her were always couched in tenderness.

"I really don't like it that you are painting a negative image of your father, Francesca," Nana added, addressing her daughter. "He adored you. Again, I ask myself why when I hear you talk about him this way."

Fran gritted her teeth.

"So," Babeth mumbled, stealing an uncomfortable look at the servers who had walked up. "I think that we are at least ready to order the wine."

Malcolm perused the wine list, making pretentious comments, as usual.

The conversations were going along nicely. Zoey responded to her father's questions about the reception at the consulate, then listened to Aunt Vicki treat Tina to a story about a day when she'd volunteered for a youth center.

When a plate of langoustines in a sherry sauce was set down in front of her she savored its fragrance. Then, Dalton poked her with his elbow and almost made her drop her fork.

—— "What's your problem?" she snapped, furious.

In the wake of the maître d', Adrian and Marianita cleared a path to the back of the room.

Nana gestured to them.

"Oh, you're here too?" said Adrian with a friendly lilt to his voice.

"It's true, New York is a small town," hissed Zoey.

He had to have known where Nana's birthday celebration was taking place. Fran told his mother everything, especially when it made her look good.

"Come sit with us," Nana invited them.

"You've already started. And it's a family affair."

"Look here," chuckled Aunt Vicki. "You're practically family!"

Adrian shyly lowered his eyes and his smile made Zoey want to murder him. She read between the lines and saw what he was trying to do. This made her both furious and sad. He didn't need to act like a lover who wanted to dot all his *i*'s.

Nana motioned to the server to bring two chairs and indicated where he should set them, between Dalton and Zoey. For an entire minute, everyone moved their plates, in a racket of chairs scraping across the floor and clinking cutlery. The maître d' hurried over.

"I'm sure this won't be a problem for Frédéric," Nana told him calmly.

At the mention of the name of the restaurant's prestigious French chef, the maître d' immediately relaxed and then hurried the server along, for no reason.

"Marianita, sit next to me," Zoey exclaimed with an engaging smile.

She didn't want to be next to Adrian or she'd be tempted to stick a fork in his hand, like at her eleventh birthday part–after a fight over a piece of cake. Adrian quickly sat in the chair that Zoey had shown to the young woman, before announcing with a bossy flair:

"And deprive you of my presence? I'd rather die!"

"That could be arranged," she mumbled tilting her head toward him.

"Don't be mean, Zoey." He looked at her with a mocking expression on his face.

"What the hell are you both doing here?" she asked in a low voice.

"It's just a coincidence."

"I don't believe you. You hate this kind of restaurant."

He shrugged his shoulders. Next to Zoey, Tina admiringly and enviously eyed Marianita. The young woman had it all. She was wearing a summer dress with a vintage fifties cut, knee-high and tight at the waist. It was a shade of green that flattered her golden skin tone and black hair. Dalton had a sly look on his face but was having a most polite conversation with her. On the other side of the table, Fran watched them out of the corner of her eye, expressionless.

Suddenly remembering where she was and that Tina's eager ears were close by, Zoey decided to silence the rude remark that she had been preparing for Adrian.

"We'll settle this another time," she said through clenched teeth.

—— "I don't doubt that for one second."

Zoey sighed. She knew him too well. She also knew herself. Neither of them would lower their guard.

And her langoustines were now cold.

She spent the rest of this course listening to the others, sullen. Only the questions that Aunt Vicki was asking Tina provided her with some amusement. Her cousin defended herself against the older woman's curiosity as well as she could—at least as politely as she could, without realizing that Zoey could hear their conversation.

"And the young man that you brought to your aunt and uncle's house?" Aunt Vicki asked. "He's not here?"

"This is a family dinner," Tina commented, lowering her voice, probably in the hope that her great aunt would do the same.

"Have you been seeing him a long time?"

"For a few weeks."

"His name is Matthew, right?"

Zoey shook. Before his name was said out loud, the possibility of a relationship between Matthew and Tina didn't seem quite real, even if, according to what the critic had said, it was nothing more than a few dates.

"Will you see him again?" wondered Aunt Vicki.

Tina pouted pensively to show that she didn't attach much importance to Matthew Ziegler.

"I'm sure I will. We're supposed to go to dinner together next week."

"Aunt Vicki!" Uncle Malcolm suddenly exclaimed. "You haven't told me about your evening at the country club!"

While Aunt Vicki was turning toward him, thrilled and ready to gab, Uncle Malcolm gave Zoey a long glance. She didn't like what she saw there. He had seen her listening to the conversation. For some reason or another, he was angry about it.

Or maybe it's because he doesn't want my dear cousin to reveal that she brought someone *to a family function who isn't really interested in her, and* she *acted like they were a thing, as simple as that.*

That didn't matter. Matthew and Tina were supposed to see each other next week. Why? To break up perhaps, like he told her.

"I'm not seeing her anymore."

Who took the time to break off a relationship that had only consisted of a few dinners together?

Maybe not everyone *is like Spencer,* she thought bitterly. *Or maybe you don't break up with a girl like Tina via email. But with me, you do.*

The main course had arrived. As the server set a dinner of sole with pistachios and almonds in front of her, Zoey continued to reflect. Adrian leaned toward her. His face was particularly welcoming.

"You're calm," he remarked.

"Yes, I'm calm quite often." He rolled his eyes.

"When you're sleeping. And then some!"

"I'm enjoying my dinner. Isn't this amazing? Have you been here before with Marianita?"

"I don't go out with Marianita that often."

"Oh, I see.

They probably preferred to stay shut up in a room."

"That's not exactly what I'd call it, having seen you together a lot this week," Zoey insisted.

"We work together. Marianita is going through a difficult time. What's your deal? Since when are you so curious? You could pass for your Great Aunt Vicki," he added, lowering his voice.

"I'm worried about you."

"Everything's good with me."

"No, because you seem anxious too," she said, absentmindedly picking up her glass of chardonnay.

"I'm good, Zoey. Let's just say that I'm at period in my life where I need to come to terms with a few things."

Zoey felt part of her resistance melt away. She was now seeing the Adrian she recognized, as he often was in private, considerate and almost chatty. This reminder of their long friendship, which until recently had only experienced little bumps along the road, made her feel better as much as it worried her. If Adrian needed to talk to someone, it must be serious. But she was still a little mad at him. But, mostly, she didn't know what to think.

"I see what you mean," she murmured before drinking another sip of wine.

The wine was excellent and made her smile briefly.

"Really?" asked Adrian.

"Really. I've had a lot of trouble following my dreams. I thought I was very liberated but now I see that I've been restricted in so many ways. Maybe I had to find myself in this situation to realize it."

"That's it exactly. Following your dreams."

He gave her a sweet smile, Adrian's true smile, the one that, since they were kids, he hardly ever used anymore, and put his hand on her forearm.

His fingers brushed against her skin, making her shiver.

"I'm afraid that, if I follow my dreams, I'll lose something precious to me."

Zoey felt the color slowly rising in her face. What exactly was he doing? She put her glass down, embarrassed, and took the opportunity to remove her arm from under his hand. When she raised her eyes, she met Nana's searching hers.

Her heart beat faster. Was she understanding what he was trying to say? Maybe Marianita being there was just a way to make her jealous?

She was not ready to have this discussion with Adrian. She should probably have felt bashful or emotional, in a good way, or even flattered, but she didn't know how to untangle the thoughts and feelings that were mixed up in her brain and were making her stomach tight.

Between the entrée and the dessert, the main topic of conversation was work that Nana needed to do at her house. Fran was trying to convince her that, as she aged, she needed to install an elevator to access the second floor.

"And make a hole in my bedroom floor?" the older woman said, indignant.

"Since you refuse to consider a retirement home. You'll need to be able to get to your bed somehow."

"We'll put my bed in the living room. That's where I spend most of my time anyway. No one is going to touch my house! If you don't agree with that, Fran, you could always invite me to live with you."

Fran did not hear the sarcasm in her mother's voice.

"In the meantime, since you won't listen to reason, Babeth and I have to make a lot of round trips to help you."

Nana's eyes narrowed.

"I'm really sorry that in my old, old age, which isn't here yet, by the way, is going to crimp you and your sister's style. I should have thought of that when you were children and I spent my life driving you around to music lessons, dance class and riding lessons. I think this is an inappropriate conversation to have the day of my birthday. Zoey, would you please accompany me to the restroom?"

Zoey stood up, deeply relieved to get away from Adrian and, at the same time, take a break from the table that was starting to feel suffocating.

She took her grandmother's arm.

"Don't let Mom drive you crazy," she whispered in her ear, as they walked away. "She's truly worried about your future."

"My future? You're so cute. I know that, honey. It's just that, if I end up like your mother says I will, my "old age," as she calls it, will be a literal nightmare. I love my daughters, Zoey. Since you don't have children yourself, you don't know what we are capable of doing for them. That being said, the last thing that I want is to have them around me for the last years of my life. I'd hire someone to help me and threaten your mother that I'd leave them everything."

She smiled, obviously pleased with the idea.

In the restroom, Nana made an elegant movement, fixing her hair in the mirror.

Zoey admired how delicate her wrists and fingers were. Nana had always had beautiful hands. As Nana looked at her reflection, her grandmother stared back at herself with hostility, as if she were asking herself who this old woman was, and where had she come from.

Zoey was overwhelmed by tenderness. She'd often heard her say that getting older didn't bother her. The closeness of the mirror revealed this lie, which had been a ruse.

"I didn't need to use the facilities," Nana said.

"I thought that was probably the case," Zoey replied.

"I have to put on a good face. My goodness, at this point, I need to paste on one of those collagen smiles, like they do at the funeral home! But it has to be done. I can't always be grumpy. They're all making an effort, even your father who hates fish and has to pretend that he enjoys himself at each one of my birthday parties. They are going to give me my presents. How much do you want to bet that there's a shawl? All that because, one

127

year, I said that I thought they were charming and practical."

She paused, to pin a lock of hair into her chignon.

"Your mother brought up the subject of my age before dessert. Your Uncle Malcolm will wait until the coffee has been served before he attacks, like a good businessman."

"Attacks? What for?" Zoey asked, leaning toward the mirror too, to check her makeup.

"He wants me to write a new cookbook. I don't know what his game is. But he is very insistent, and not very subtle, actually."

"Maybe he thinks that you need something to do."

"I think it's more that he wants to make sure we continue to make money. Zoey?"

Nana looked at her closely.

"Yes, Nana?"

"What do you really think of Tina?"

"You know very well what I think of her."

"I'm being serious. I'm not asking you what twelve-year old Zoey thinks. What does adult Zoey, today, think? Do you know what her life is like? Who her friends are?"

"Not particularly," Zoey mumbled.

She held back from saying that she only knew Matthew Ziegler and that she sincerely felt that he was way too sexy and intelligent for her cousin.

"I think that she's having a hard time," Zoey continued. "She is smart and beautiful. She's trying too hard to please her parents."

"That's what children do. Look at your mother and your aunt. They can't stand me sometimes, but they do everything they can to make me happy."

Nana tucked in a last loose lock, picked her handbag up and turned toward her granddaughter.

"It's funny that Adrian is here too, isn't it?" she stated neutrally, keeping her gaze on Zoey through the mirror. "I really like this boy."

Zoey pushed back against the wall.

"He likes you very much. He is very attached to our family."

Nana did not lower her eyes, her happiest smile tugging at her lipstick-free mouth.

"What's the boy's name in *Little Women* again?"

"Nana, I can assure you that Adrian is not my Teddy."

"Are you sure? I was watching you, at the table."

"Of course you were! Is that all you have to do, on your birthday?" Zoey said accusingly. "Adrian is a friend. You're not going to start in like Aunt Vicki!"

"I'm not starting anything," Nana snapped, annoyed at being compared to her sister. "I only meant to say that you should be careful not to give him false hope."

"I haven't given Adrian false hope and, in any case, he doesn't have any hope. Male-female friendships are complicated sometimes, that's all."

"I don't believe in male-female friendships."

"Probably because it didn't exist when you were young."

"You really think that?" Nana retorted with a mocking tone.

"Whether it existed or not, you don't believe in it, period," Zoey continued, not ready to lose the battle. "Adrian and I have always been friends. We always will be."

"Okay, Zoey. Know, however, that you have a lot of influence over this boy. Ever since you were children, he's followed everything you do. Don't..."

Nana hesitated.

"Don't what?" Zoey inquired.

"Don't use him as a substitute. I don't believe in male-female friendships and you are probably right that it was less common when I was young. However, I want to make one point clear: we cannot simply use people to fill voids in our lives. Please do the right think, okay?"

"I don't know why I have to be subjected to this, actually," Zoey muttered, lifting her head.

She caught her grandmother's eye, and there was no criticism or disapproval there.

"I'll be a good girl, okay?" she said quietly.

"Because you are a good girl!" Nana gushed joyfully. "That's what matters, that we do the right thing, according to our own conscience and by others. This is a tenant that I have always tried to follow."

Her mouth turned into a mischievous grin.

"But not this evening. This evening, it's my birthday, and with age comes certain privileges. Like being able to torment those you love."

She put her arm in Zoey's and navigated toward the door.

The dessert had arrived. Nana hated birthday cakes. That meant that Zoey was able to enjoy a lychee-flavored mousse, taking note of its subtle flavors, from basil to balsamic vinegar, that the chef had layered in between the crust and dark chocolate.

Adrian was turned toward Marianita and was listening to the enthusiastic conversation Joe and Dalton were having. Joe, a passionate lover of music, was talking to Dalton about Brazilian groups he liked. Marianita mentioned the newest ones on the scene and Zoey's father made notes on his smartphone as she talked. Dalton interrupted them at times to make a comment. When he did, Marianita was silent, tilting her head, as if he were the expert.

Zoey noticed that her brother looked like a rooster in a hen house when the pretty Brazilian bent her head down (most likely to hear him better); any objective observer would have thought he looked silly. She took a mental note of this moment, that she'd place in her Dalton file, since she couldn't use it this evening due it being Nana's birthday and their ongoing dispute.

When everyone had brought out their gifts, Nana looked thrilled and opened the first package—which contained a shawl. She exchanged a private look with Zoey.

It's made of silk, thank you so much! she exclaimed, hugging Fran. You spoil me.

Fran Westwood seemed to be satisfied, noting that the texture and design of the fabric were elegant. Nana proceeded to open the other gifts: a new handbag from Babeth, a vintage brooch from Tina (that Zoey studied, envious and feeling particularly generous for admitting that this showed good taste on the part of her cousin) and an e-reader from Dalton. He explained to her how it worked and promised to go to her house to show her how to use it, without being very convincing, however.

Finally, Uncle Malcolm held out a small package covered in white paper and topped with a pale, yellow ribbon.

"Now what could this be," Nana murmured, playfully. "A rocking chair, perhaps?"

The contents of the box were revealed to be an exquisite gold-tipped pen that glided across the wrapping paper Nana tested it on.

"Thank you very much, Malcolm," she said warmly.

Zoey noticed a cold look pass over her face, that she was able to hide behind her carefully constructed mask.

"I will put it to good use. I understand your reference," she added, pointing her figure in his direction.

"It's all up to you now!" her son-in-law added, pleased with himself.

Zoey stood up to offer her gift. She set it in front of her grandmother, and when she tried to sit back down, Nana held her back by the wrist.

"Stay, won't you? Let's see what you've brought."

She removed the decorative string around the Japanese washi paper and laid the gift on the table.

Nana raised her head toward Zoey, holding in her hand the mother-of-pearl handled silver spoon, worn by time, that her granddaughter has just given her.

"Where did you find it?"

"It's almost the same."

"My dear Zoey."

Tears appeared at the corners of her eyes. There was silence in the room. The old woman was not known for crying easily.

"A spoon?" Fran exclaimed, laughing. "You're going to have to explain it to us. It's an original gift, that's for sure!"

Not able to stop smiling, Nana tenderly turned the spoon over in her fingers

"When Zoey was little, with me in the kitchen, she never wanted to use a wooden spoon, Nana explained. I had to tell her over and over again that we don't make food with a silver spoon. She wanted to use one that was just like this one, but, of course, I didn't give it to her. It was the last piece of tableware from my father's restaurant in Naples. All the rest of it was sold off to pay for passage to the United States, or his debts, perhaps. In any case, one day, this young lady decided that she had had to have that spoon, no matter what. She must have been what, three years old? She came into my kitchen, took the spoon and went outside behind the house to play in in the lot that is now the Glousters' house, but was under construction at the time. When she came back in, she was covered in dirt. I asked her where my spoon was. She replied that she had buried it—if she couldn't have it, no one could. We never saw it again."

Zoey frowned, uncomfortable being the center of attention. Her entire family was looking at her intensely, except for Fran who was looking at the spoon, furrowing her brow, and Dalton, who was whispering something in Marianita's ear.

"The story doesn't end there, Nana continued, becoming emotional. Each time that Zoey would ask me something that I didn't want—or couldn't—give her, I would reply: 'When I've found my silver spoon.'"

"I had so much guilt over that spoon, Zoey mused. I'd see your face when you talked about it: 'my father's spoon'—I was so sorry, Nana. And you used it to your advantage."

"I've never heard this story before," frowned Fran, obviously annoyed. "But that is exactly something Zoey would do."

Zoey's jaw tightened. Fran had the gift of ruining emotional moments, especially when she wasn't directly involved.

"Maybe that's because, back then, I spent more time at Nana's house than at my own, and you weren't really interested in what I was doing."

She spoke too loudly and too quickly. Fran's mouth stiffened. Joe frowned in his daughter's direction. A man who spoke little, he detested big public revelations.

Zoey's eyes began to fill. Her father had never looked at her with such disapproval.

"This is not the time," Nana whispered, pulling Zoey to her to speak directly into her ear.

She discreetly squeezed her hand.

"Don't be mad at her, Fran," Nana continued, without paying any attention to the expression on her daughter's face that was becoming more and more tense. "There's no reason for you to be upset. We are all in agreement that I am the one that did a poor job of raising this child. That is what I did with the spoon. She had to be taught a few principles. At least

131

those that are the easiest to follow. Your debt has been paid, Zoey! You can now ask me for whatever you wish. Whatever you wish!"

Zoey looked at her grandmother—her lined face, her white hair, how perceptive she was and her youthful spirit. She noticed the delicate nature of her shoulders and the slight tremble in her beautiful hands. For the first, time, she saw her as someone fragile. A small voice inside her, surely the one that she had had as a child, murmured: *I don't want you to die.*

The entire table was waiting.

Zoey smiled at Nana and replied:

"I would like your silver spoon!"

Everyone burst out laughing and, Nana, laughing louder than all of them, opened her arms to Zoey.

"I brought you candy," said Aunt Vicki, holding out a huge box with a ribbon around it to her sister. "I think it is silly to give presents to older people. As if we were going to be able to use them for an extended period of time!"

"I won't be able to use my teeth that long, eating all that candy, Victoria," Nana replied happily. "You never liked presents anyway. But, I love them."

She wrapped herself in the shawl that her daughter had given her. She seemed even smaller, draped in all that silk.

Then, she regally lifted her head, announcing:

"I am going to have you all buried with me, like a Pharaoh!"

Zoey laughed, despite herself. Her heart was heavy with the vision she had seen, of this tiny woman who had held her family up, raised her daughters, and then her grandchildren. She had delighted those around her with her food, and almost the entire world with her recipes. She had lived her life and it had made her who she was.

14
MELT THE CHOCOLATE

The next day went by slowly. The evening of the dinner, after it was over, Zoey had declined Adrian and Marianita's invitation to have one last drink with Dalton who they had convinced to accompany them. Her father had convinced her to let her parents take her home. Fran kept her teeth clenched the entire trip. For the first time, Zoey felt ashamed for what she had said to her mother, even if she did think it was true, and was, to some degree, perfectly justified. She waved goodbye from her doorstep and Fran did not respond.

Feeling depressed, Zoey briefly recounted the evening to Sally, without mentioning that Adrian had been there. She didn't particularly feel like dissecting what she thought about the incident and she didn't want to explain to Sally why she didn't want to talk about it either.

Sally left earlier than usual to meet with a supplier. Zoey closed up shop by herself, after spending an exaggerated amount of time on an estimate that she had promised Sally she'd work on to appease her. The truth was that she had been coddling Sally since they'd made up, and this had made her realize the monstrous amount of work the young woman was up against.

All the work that Zoey had passed off to her, bit by bit, with great relief and without even realizing the extent of it—all the administrative tasks, put end to end.

Around 9:30 p.m., she turned her computer off, stretched her shoulders, tight from having spent so much time hovering over the keys. She decided to go home, make a salad and mindlessly watch TV. She lowered the roll-up metal door and walked toward her apartment building door. She almost regretted living so close. She would have liked to walk a bit in the evening to enjoy the more reasonable temperatures after four days of blistering heat. However, she didn't feel like walking alone at this time of night.

She'd often gone walking when she'd been heartbroken, just after the break up with Spencer. Her memories of this period were of a terrible sadness, mixed with others that were more upbeat; she appreciated and understood New York better having gotten to know it after night fall.

Sometimes, on her way back home, she'd stop to drink a glass of chianti at Orlando and Gabriella's. This was how she'd become friends with Gabriella.

Until that point, they had only had the banal conversations that neighbors have or exchanged compliments about each other's cuisine.

Gabriella had picked up on Zoey's sorrow and, without ever calling it out, tried hard to make her life easier. She'd send Orlando over to help her when she needed it or regale her with anecdotes about the restaurant's customers.

This evening, Zoey needed to be cheered up. But it was too early. She would be bothering them while they were servicing their customers, unless their diners weren't in a hurry.

She glanced over at the restaurant. Orlando had put two tables outside, as he did in the summer. A couple was sitting at one of them. At the other, she saw Matthew Ziegler.

When he saw her, he acknowledged her with a move of his head, and then with one of his hands.

After such a lethargic and exhausting day, she shook with anger.

She confidently marched up to him.

"At this point, I'd call this harassment, and I would think you'd realize that too!" she scolded, standing in front of him.

He stood up and invited her to sit down, which she pretended not notice.

"Harassment? I've been waiting for you for two hours."

On the polka dot table cloth, a half-empty bottle of wine confirmed this information.

"Did we have an appointment?"

"No, actually," Matthew admitted. "However, I'd say that you owe me an explanation."

"You'd say?"

"Please take a seat."

"Do not tell me what to do!"

Gabriella came out of the restaurant, a plate in each hand. Her belly put her a bit off balance and she was grimacing. When she saw Zoey, her mouth turned up in an elated smile.

"I was right when I told you that she'd eventually come out of her lair! she said to Matthew. I'll bring a second glass."

"Don't bother," Zoey replied. "Mr. Ziegler is not staying."

"Really?"

Gabriella seemed to think that was a shame.

"A man who has waited for two hours deserves to be listened to for a few minutes," she asserted. "Sit down, Zoey, and I'll bring you a glass, okay?"

"Gabriella, I can assure you that…"

"You are not going to kick one of my customer's out of my own restaurant, are you?"

Her tone was kind, but Zoey recognized the authority in her voice that she sometimes used with Orlando. The only option would have been to leave, but she didn't want to cause a scene, especially now that the diners at the next table over had turned their heads to follow the exchange. She would be ashamed to act up in Gabriella's restaurant. Gabriella wouldn't tolerate it anyway, as she had made clear.

"You have five minutes," Zoey said, sitting across from Matthew. "Not one minute more."

"I'm listening."

"*You're* listening to *me*?"

"Yes, I am waiting for your explanation, I'd like to remind you."

Was he trying to say "we have to have the talk"? What was he going on about? He was the one that had jumped all over her and he was the one that had lied to her twice.

Matthew calmly put his hand on the table, with the attitude of a manager who had summoned an employee to be disciplined.

"What do you think 'Too bad the Internet doesn't chew liars up and spit them out'" means?

Zoey held back a gasp.

"I don't know what you're talking about. I never said that!"

"No. You wrote it."

He removed his glasses, took his phone out of the pocket of his jacket and touched the screen.

"Would you like me to quote?" he asked, raising an eyebrow. "'I'm not going to deny it—I do want you, even if, right now, I would rather punch you in the face for having humiliated me in both public and private, and leaving me high and dry. I was in such a state that I had to take a cold shower when I got home and then spent my week Googling your name while throwing insults your way. Too bad that the Internet doesn't chew liars up and spit them out.'"

"How did you get this email?"

She was more than furious. She was beyond even that.

"You sent it to me."

"I never sent that email!"

"Well, I received it."

"I erased it!"

"You admit having written it then? I particularly liked the conclusion: 'Just know that I didn't find your way of being creative particularly novel and that the way you kissed was certainly not "classic" and it didn't make me want more.' If we ignore the questionable style, this is not exactly what you appeared to be feeling."

"Give me that!"

She grabbed the device out of his hands. Without believing what she was seeing, she saw the words scroll by, the words that she had written the day before, before going to Nana's party.

"I think that you owe me more than five minutes," Matthew specified.

He drank a sip of wine, totally at ease. Zoey stared at him, speechless.

"I don't like being called a liar. If I had seduced you, if I had promised you something, well...It seems to me, however, that we didn't take the time to really discuss what our expectations were."

Zoey's eyes returned, riveted, to the screen. She just couldn't believe she had sent this email. She could see herself selecting the text to erase it...and then shutting her laptop. She must have hit "send" by accident. The other explanation was that her computer had a mind of its own and had decided to ruin her life.

"You can re-read it," Matthew continued. "It won't teach you anything that we don't already know."

"You are so full of yourself," Zoey retorted, before throwing his phone on the table.

Gabriella reappeared to place a glass in front of her and quickly left, without a word.

The interruption calmed her somewhat and Zoey looked on as Matthew served her some wine.

So. We are going to have this conversation. She breathed deeply.

"You lied to me about Tina."

"No."

The firmness of his tone surprised her.

"You deny that you are going to see her next week?"

"No, I don't."

"Stop playing games!" she chastised. "You lied to me then!"

"Absolutely not. I told you I wasn't dating her anymore. I didn't say that I didn't see her anymore."

"You're playing with words."

"I do that sometimes. That's my job. But not in this case. I clearly told Tina that were no longer seeing each other in a personal capacity."

"How would you see each other then?"

That silenced him for a few seconds and that allowed Zoey to realize how stupid her question was.

"Professionally," Matthew replied.

"I understood, thank you," Zoey replied before picking up a glass to give her some confidence.

Now she knew why she got drunk so quickly, considering the number of glasses that she held in her hands so that she appeared to be aloof. At this rate, she'd end up being an alcoholic.

"And I'd like you to understand that I have nothing more to say on this topic. That's the end of it."

She wanted to know, though. She was wondering what Uncle Malcolm's company would need from a food critic. And vice versa.

"And Sofia? You did come with her to the reception at the consulate, right?"

"Yes," he said, in a voice that was half hesitant, half amused.

"And?"

"Again, you are bringing up a topic that I don't want to discuss."

"Ah ha!" Zoey said triumphantly.

"In addition, I didn't lie to you about Sofia, being that I had never even mentioned her to you. Are we in agreement that your accusation was baseless?"

"Maybe."

He gave her a meaningful look that instantly relaxed his face.

"Still, I am surprised at your ability to look for excuses."

"Look for excuses?"

"Yes. Let's look at another part of your email." Zoey drank another sip of wine, more quickly than she would have wanted.

"We don't need to."

"And deny me the pleasure of reading your own words back to you again? 'I'm not going to deny it—I do want you…' I like this sentence very much."

"Wait one second! Your insincerity is so disrespectful! You clearly said that you wanted me."

"I don't deny it."

"That's so kind of you! You threw me aside."

"I never 'threw you aside,' as you call it."

"You took off and said—and now it's my turn to quote—you didn't want to be 'inconsiderate.'"

"That was clumsy, I agree. Sometimes, I express my thoughts out loud when I shouldn't. So. I'll explain it to you. At that moment, I was still 'seeing' your cousin Tina, because I had not yet told her that I no longer wished to continuing seeing her in that way. Opposite of what you think, I am scrupulously honest. To continue the relationship would not have been honest and would have risked putting you in a difficult position."

137

He smiled.

"Since we are having this type of conversation, know that I also want you. Right now, at this very moment even, while you are looking at me angrily and you have spilled chianti on your t-shirt, I only have one desire: to take you to your apartment and take your clothes off. Now, I don't believe that you are the type of woman who asks for guarantees when it comes to this type of thing. In any case, I can't assure you that we will have a relationship."

— "I haven't asked you for anything."

Zoey had to admit that he had earned a point there. She had always been surprised by women who—beginning with Tina—wanted to be sure of their partner's feelings before allowing themselves to be seduced. She's always enjoyed the urge in the moment, at these junctures when she let go, even if she sometimes regretted it later. Truthfully, she had always preferred to be with men who respected this sort of contract and, even if she hated contracts, she had to admit that all relationships had one.

A contract of respect or of honesty, or, often, a contract of mutual freedom.

Finally, the only time that she had respected the various stages of a relationship—seduction within the bounds of propriety—she had fallen in love with Spencer and had been hurt.

"You do recognize that the beginning of our relationship was a bit unconventional?" she continued.

Matthew leaned toward her. His hands were almost touching hers. He placed his elbows on the table, pouring all his powers of persuasion into this gesture.

"The beginning of our relationship was physical. I want you. I already said that, right?"

Each time he said, "I want you," part of her believed that she was agile enough to jump over the table and kiss him straight on the mouth, while the other part, more realistic, was satisfied to simply giggle nervously.

"I don't know why," Matthew added.

"Charming."

"Stop that. You know very well what I mean."

She did know, actually. Even if he irritated her with his upper crust confidence, and even if she had been able to resist his advances at least once, she knew, at this very moment, that she would never have the will—and certainly not the pride—to reject feeling this exquisite sensation. Matthew continued speaking while she imagined him getting up, taking her by the hand and making love to her under the first porch they found—probably hers.

"How many times does that happen? A connection like this? I'm not the wild type, where my love life is concerned. I've always been the type that people set up on blind dates, ever since I was a teenager. I don't normally jump on 'women that I hardly know,' as you put it. And I don't normally go to the other side of New York for an explanation about an email. But, I'm not going to say that it was that difficult for me."

He looked at her for a moment.

"Even though you make me feel like I am interviewing for a job, which I hate," he added.

Zoey didn't know what to say.

"Are you doing anything tonight?" he added.

"Not really," she mumbled. "As you can see."

For the past year, she had resigned herself to not getting close to anyone and certainly not hooking up. She was surprised at the shyness she felt. It was unlike her, but the paradox between control he displayed and the gentle way he looked at her encouraged her to not refuse the invitation.

"Would it inconvenience you to spend the evening with me?"

"Would it inconvenience you to spend the evening with me?" Who talked like this? *Except him?*

"Not really," she said finally. "If you promise to stop mentioning that email. I am so embarrassed. I swear that I really didn't mean to say all of that to you. It was just a way to, to..."

"Blow off steam? I get it. If you knew the number of emails I've written and then erased! Thank god, I've never accidentally sent one."

"Thank you," Zoey murmured, smiling. "Insulting and awkward... That describes me well lately."

"And funny. And obviously intelligent enough to see your mistakes in a self-deprecating light. That shows a real thoughtfulness."

"That's the first time that someone told me I was thoughtful."

Her tone was light, but she was stating a fact that had often been painful to her.

Matthew slid his fingers across the table, till they were next to hers.

"That's the first time that someone told me I was insulting."

"I have a real talent for bringing out the best in people."

Matthew's caressed the tips of her fingers with his. Their contact gave her a delicious, gentle shiver, far from what she had experienced the other times he had touched her. Simple and comforting.

"You promised to keep your hands off me," she breathed.

"My hands. Not my fingers."

She laughed. And then wondered if Gabriella would be angry if the they threw the table to the sidewalk.

"Only those on my left hand," Matthew continued. "Did I tell you that my favorite expression is, 'The left hand doesn't know what the right hand is doing?' I can assure you that my right hand would be outraged to know that my left hand doesn't honor its promises. Or it's just jealous."

"Your self-confidence is astounding."

"I was brought up that way."

"I'm surprised you're still single, then. You must be hard to get along with otherwise."

"Do you think that self-confidence is really the only quality needed for a successful love life? Actually, it's true that we put men in categories—those who have courage and those who don't. I wasn't always like this. Having self-confidence doesn't mean taking risks. Especially when it's more social than personal. Let's say that, in recent years, I've learned that life really is too short to pass up interesting opportunities."

He stopped for several seconds, lost in his thoughts. He continued to use his fingers to play with Zoey's.

"I absolutely refuse to live a lackluster life," he added.

"How did you come to this conclusion? As it relates to relationships, I mean."

"Ah, wonderful. Now we've come to the point where we have to talk about our past. So. Let's pull our notes out. I'm warning you, it's pretty dull."

To her regret, he let go of her fingers. She followed the movement of his hand, now well-behaved and terribly far away, as it moved to the edge of the table. She would have given anything to have it over resting on hers.

"I'll risk it," Zoey replied very seriously. "I'll have taken at least one risk then, in my own boring life."

"Your life will seem much more interesting after my monologue, I think. I've only had one long relationship, assuming that you can judge what someone's worth by how many years they have been able to put up with another human being. We broke up five years ago. More specifically, it was Kat who broke it off. She finally came to the conclusion that all the qualities that had made her fall in love with me were faults. Classic, right? One day, she just picked up and left, leaving everything behind. I had to send her things to her new address. She never thanked me. Do you know most love stories end? In boxes. Then I put anything that reminded me of that period in boxes, and threw it in the trash. It felt both unbearable and exhilarating at the same time—what we'd had ended up in the garbage."

"Is that the feeling that pushed you to refuse to have colorless relationships?"

"Not at all. It was that feeling that caused me to act like a total ass during the year that followed. When you get to the point where you see the woman that you loved as a piece of garbage to be tossed out, it's not a good thing. And because humans are a proud sort, they continue down the same path, to prove themselves right. The incident that caused me to open my eyes does not concern me directly and I can't reveal secrets that involve other people. Do you understand?"

140

"Of course," Zoey lied.

She was dying to know more.

"I had a few short relationships, that often ended because I realized I had made a mistake—or she did, as well as four or five one-night stands, but always sober."

"Too bad—alcohol is an excellent excuse for living in denial."

"I never deny anything. In any case, it's not really worth it if you leave before coffee."

"So, you're that type of guy."

"Because women never do that?"

"Perhaps they do it less," Zoey stated, but without great conviction.

"Only because, most of the time, the man goes to the woman's apartment, and not the other way around, so the women can control the situation. I can assure you that three-fifths of the time, I've been made to feel like it was time for me to go."

"I admit that I've done that."

Only twice.

"Have I passed the interview?" Matthew asked.

"Absolutely not. You failed at the only real relationship you've ever had and three out of five women made you feel like you weren't up to their standards, after having spent the night with you."

"If you know someone who is, without fail, good in bed, please share. I'd like to know."

She burst out laughing. When she stopped, she realized that he was observing her with a serious look on his face. In his eyes, she noticed an eagerness that she'd seen before, when he had pushed her up against the wall and kissed her. His hands were slightly tense, on the edge of the table. She didn't doubt for one second that he only had one wish too: to lead her out of here and throw himself at her.

"Do you feel okay?" she asked, aware that this was totally disingenuous.

"Where did you learn to laugh like that?" he murmured.

"Do you have something against my laugh?"

"It's torture."

"That was nice, thanks."

She couldn't help but smile.

"I can assure you that if you do not suggest that we go to your apartment right now, we are going to attack these good people's sensibilities and the two of us will end up in jail."

She licked her lips.

"I am tempted by the idea of seeing you in handcuffs."

The look her gave her was indecipherable—at least it would have been if he'd been trying to communicate a message that was even vaguely civilized. He was giving off an animalistic aura.

141

"I was just going to suggest that we go to my place," she added, forcing her voice to stay calm.

He was silent for a moment.

"I have to feed, Sushi, my cat. Don't say anything about my terrible sense of humor."

"I wasn't going to say anything, except for that that's the worse excuse I've ever heard."

"I promise you, it's not an excuse. I could just leave you here, but I'd be afraid that you'd auto-combust if I ditched you."

He laughed.

"You are a cruel woman. You crush your adversary, not even letting him maintain a shred of dignity."

"I think the question has been settled."

Matthew cocked his head to one side.

"Are you really inviting me to go up with you?"

"To feed the cat, and take this wine-stained t-shirt off."

She smiled mischievously.

"I'm sure I can do it without any help."

"This really is the worst excuse you could offer to get me to go with you."

I'll find another one to keep you from leaving."

Matthew's knuckles were white, from gripping the table. His self-confidence seemed to have melted in the heat the candles were giving off, as had the dignity that he'd mentioned. Zoey was thinking how hers had taken the first flight to Timbuktu the first minute he had laid eyes on her.

She stood up and Matthew followed. After waving to Gabriella, she started toward her door, and then turned around.

"Don't worry! I'm keeping my distance," Matthew said, being overly cautious.

"I just wanted to make sure that you were still there."

"You never forget, do you?" he murmured.

She opened the door.

"Never, she replied, as he walked into the hallway. See? It's not so bad."

"You can't hold it against me that I hesitated to follow a perfect stranger to her apartment. Using the excuse that she had to 'feed her cat.'"

"I'm not sure I can follow the metaphor anymore, she laughed. That's more Adrian's style, when he's on a roll."

Again, she firmly rejected the image that came to mind. It was Adrian leaning toward her.

She continued to climb the steps without a word. Matthew was silent too. Only the creaking of the steps accompanied them to the third floor.

When Zoey opened the door, Sushi leapt between her legs, growling furiously.

142

"It was true! I'm almost disappointed," Matthew said, bending down to pet the cat.

The animal welcomed his attentions by swatting Matthew with his paw, claws exposed.

"And, he looks like you!" Matthew smiled, before bringing his hand to his mouth.

15
STIR THE VANILLA

"Your apartment is exactly as I expected," Matthew noted.

She didn't know what he meant by that or if it was a compliment. Her tiny living room had been invaded by total chaos. A heap of—fortunately clean—clothes was in a basket behind the door. Magazines and books were strewn all over the coffee table. One of her running shoes was lying in the middle of the room and the other one was peeking out from under the curtain. The cat was to blame for much of the mess. She suspected that, in an angry frenzy, he had pushed over the pile of papers and cup of pencils that were now scattered all over the office floor.

The kitchen was the only room that was not a mess. She left the cat there after Sushi approached her aggressively--the animal was impatient as Zoey filled the bowl with cat food.

She offered Matthew a glass of water and sat next to him on the couch. She didn't have an armchair and, in any case, wasn't going to sit far away from him on one of the kitchen chairs. In the midst of all that disorder, her arm on the armrest, he aroused urges in her that she had no desire to suppress.

"That's you, right?"

He indicated a photo on the wall. Dalton and she were posing in front of their treehouse. The photo of Dalton conveyed the good-naturedness that he had retained into manhood. Next to him, Zoey, who was eight or nine, was hanging on to the tree with one hand, raising the other to the sky. She was wearing Bermuda shorts and a belt decorated with blue stars. Her knees were scraped. Her hair was already showing itself to be unmanageable, defying the law of gravity and the ability of most barrettes to subdue it.

145

"You're very observant," she replied.

Also framed was a press clipping that showed her with Sally, sitting at the counter in her workspace, three years before. Underneath that, there was another frame showing her and Adrian as teenagers, pensively hanging over the edge of a boat. Adrian had a serious look about him, that, has he had gotten older, had given way to laid back teasing.

"Are these the only people who are important to you?" Matthew asked.

"For the most part, yes."

"You do seem, however, to be quite attached to your family."

"'Attached' is the word. If you mean that I love them, yes, that's true. It's just that, my friends are precious to me."

She sighed.

"I'd like to be able to say that I had a difficult childhood. I'm sure that would make me more interesting to you, but, really, it was pretty idyllic."

"Why do you think that a difficult past would make you more interesting to me?"

His tone was teasing.

"Isn't that what people do normally? Make themselves seem profound with a terrible secret?" she asked.

He grimaced.

"True secrets aren't revealed so easily, on a couch, after having offered up one's romantic credentials, especially when they are terrible."

"Well..." Zoey smiled. "My mother did smack me once."

"Really?"

"I deserved it. I burned sugar in her favorite tea set. She'd found it at an antique shop and it was from the 18th century."

"The cups exploded, right?"

"Only after I put cold water in them, thinking that would help remove the caramel color. That's the day I learned it's not a good idea to play with hot and cold."

"You've learned nothing of the sort," Matthew remarked. "You're still playing that game, and you're good at it too."

She moved closer to him.

"That's the pot calling the kettle black. How is your hand?"

He moved his fingers around, showing her the scratched knuckle.

"Your cat has good aim. Fortunately, it's the right one."

"You promised to keep your hands to yourself."

"But you didn't, did you?"

"My hands can also have a mind of their own, but, for now, they are still doing what I tell them."

She took a glass from the table to emphasize her joke. He narrowed his eyes and Sushi jumped in between them, aloof.

"Perfectly fine with me," Matthew murmured, putting his legs on the coffee table and his hands behind his head, totally at ease. "Logically, if you drink, you're going to lose control."

"It's water," she remarked.

The way he put his feet up on the table, his body relaxed, as if he were offering himself to her, sent a delicious shudder through her.

"Ah ha," he replied. "Let's see what it does to you, if you're not used to it. Was there something particular you had in mind for us this evening?"

"Watch a TV show, on my couch, totally naked," she replied in a neutral tone.

It sounded like he gasped and choked at the same time, but he was smiling.

His smirk was predatory, revealing his teeth.

"Can I help you?" he asked, also in a detached tone.

She wanted to pin him up against the back of the couch. She grabbed his wrists, spreading his arms and sliding onto his knees.

Literally.

She then pivoted toward him.

He let out a stifled moan, a bit surprised, but bent one of his legs on the couch so that she could put her legs on either side of his thighs.

The upper part of Zoey's body was sliding over Matthew's shirt, making a delicious rustling noise that she could hear over her rapid breathing. The skin above their waist bands touched. Their contact brought her to a frenzy, even more frenzied than she'd been on top of him, the bulge of his jeans against her own groin.

She danced her fingers across Matthew's forearm up to his elbow and reached to caress the area where his skin was softest. With her other hand, she pushed herself against the couch, next to his hips. His face was so close to Matthew's that she felt his breath on her chin. Matthew opened his mouth, but it was obvious he wanted to say something.

Alas.

"I know exactly what you are going to say," Zoey said.

"I can assure you that you do not."

He squirmed under her, with an embarrassed look on his face.

"Your cat is digging its claws into my ribs."

Zoey pushed Sushi off the cushion where he'd fallen asleep, waking the cat with a start.

It gave a disgruntled growl and jumped off the couch.

She placed her hands on Matthew's shoulders and slid them to the back of his neck, crossing her fingers. Taking her time, her eyes fixed on his face—he was smiling, probably relieved the animal was no longer at digging its claws into his side—she got closer and closer until her lips touched his. He opened his mouth slightly. She caressed it softly while pushing her hips against his.

Her hands went to his shirt collar and she undid a button.

She smelled his cologne and the scent of his skin, hot, giving off waves of salty musk. The heat and their proximity had caused a light layer of sweat to form on his torso, which she discovered when she unfastened two more buttons.

Her fingers brushed against it, down to his belt. She slid her finger under the top of his jeans. With her other hand, she passed the belt through the loops. She felt Matthew's body pull back and his stomach push forward, to help her. It seemed like he was fighting the urge to use his arms, but she thought that he was resisting more out of pleasure than to respect a silly promise. She took her time unbuttoning his jeans.

Matthew's eyes were closed and she was thrilled to see several emotions passing over his face, from lust—mouth open and neck bent toward her, to a feverish exasperation—lips turned down and quivering nostrils.

A pleasurable urge—free of malice but with a penchant for this game that he seemed to appreciate—drove her to slow down even further.

Her hand moved off the last button and suspended in the air for a moment. Matthew opened his eyes. The voraciousness that she read in them scared as much as it excited her. His mouth closed onto hers and Matthew's hands encircled her waist to pull her toward him. The contact was electrifying.

A new wave of his scent, with no trace of the cologne, filled the air, his shirt partly open, as he lay across the back of the couch.

This made Zoey shiver. He responded by a sensual movement that placed her underneath him.

She felt each muscle against her shoulders and chest as he took her in his arms while his tongue followed a path between her lips. With one leg, he opened her thighs. Then, with quiet authority, he lifted his body, letting his fingers play on her stomach, following the hollow of her waist, climbing back up to her breasts. Lifting himself halfway, he undid the clasp her bra so easily that it made Zoey smile.

He smiled back, then as an accent to his kiss, his tongue circled her breast. He began unbuttoning her jeans, letting them fall to her ankles. Zoey helped him by rocking her hips. He swept them aside and removed his mouth from hers for a moment, as he removed her shirt and bra, throwing them over the back of the couch.

"You're practically naked," he breathed. "Do you want the remote?"

"Don't underestimate yourself."

A flash of amusement could be seen in Matthew's eyes. Serious once again, he buried his face in her neck.

His tongue made a groove behind her year, then along the back of her neck and shoulder, down to her breast, turning around its pink center. She let out a moan that was almost a plea. Her stomach contracted deliciously while his lips surrounded her nipple with a gentleness that aroused a wave of heat throughout her entire body.

He continued along his path, tongue flickering along her skin, slowing down at her stomach, and then at her pubic area.

"I was sure you'd have ripped underwear," he said.

Elle suppressed an embarrassed groan. Was he actually talking, with his face in her panties? Did he never stop talking?

"Good Lord, be quiet for just two minutes!" she growled, breathing hard.

"A bit longer than two minutes, if that's okay with you."

The undergarment found its place with the other clothes on the floor.

Zoey's breathing quickened. He did, in fact, keep quiet for more than two minutes. Long enough for Zoey's heart to feel ready to burst, until her orgasm made her forget about the possibility of having a heart attack.

It was as if a galaxy had formed in her belly, as if she mastered all the secrets of the universe and that, in the end, all this knowledge didn't really matter. The Big Bang, on a human scale, and beyond.

Far from thinking about science, Matthew climbed her slowly, kissing her stomach and then her breasts, eyes closed.

"We'll have to stop here," he said with a smile.

Zoey propped herself up on an elbow.

"You don't have a condom, then?"

"I was trying to be more subtle about it," he said.

She stood up, bathed in the living room light that they had left on. In her nudity, she was free of any self-consciousness as she dug around in her bag. Triumphant, she pulled out a condom. Matthew didn't laugh nor did he seem embarrassed. He opened his arms to her and she laid down next to him, which, due to the small size of the couch, was a precarious balancing act. He took the condom from her, having definitively decided that he'd take care of this step himself.

To Zoey, it seemed to take an eternity and she thought she heard him swear a few times, before he came toward her, his eyebrows crinkled in annoyance.

"Are you going to do it again?" she whispered.

"Do what?"

"Stop right in the middle."

His expression softened. Zoey's heart began beating more quickly, but this time it wasn't due to excitement. She glimpsed a brief moment of confusion on Matthew's face which she didn't understand, but that she found touching. A second later, the look resembling lust had returned to his face—the one that she had found so appealing.

"I was just thinking that I didn't see your face when you had your orgasm."

"Good Lord, no," Zoey replied.

"I was also thinking that the first time is always when..."

As he was talking, her penetrated her gently. This was a man who definitely never stopped talking.

"...when we fit together perfectly with another body..."

She moaned and heard her own breath make a path through her tight throat. Instinctively, she wrapped her legs around Matthew's waist.

"...the way you folded your legs around my waist just when I was going to ask you..."

A shiver went through the warm spot between her legs, up through her belly and chest as he pushed further into her.

She let out another groan, this time deeper, more animal like. On top of her, Matthew shook.

"Please, don't moan like that," he panted.

She couldn't help laughing. In reply, she arched up, inviting him to slide more deeply into her. Now, it was his turn to moan.

"I promise you, I'm trying to contain myself," she breathed, guiding his hips with her hands.

"I promise you that I am too," he groaned.

She followed his rhythm, his movement restrained at great effort, exciting him even more than was evident on his face. Her soft box, still shaking from the waves of orgasm, tightened around his shaft.

He suppressed a hoarse protest.

"Perhaps this position isn't working for you," she said, without being able to stop herself from teasing him.

In reply, he separated from her slightly, and taking hold of her waist, pivoted together with her, until they were sitting on the couch, she on him, and him in her. She congratulated him silently for his quick thinking and also for his agile strength that had saved them from an embarrassing fall.

She began to move on top of him. The couch had a low back and he had either the good taste or survival instinct to not put his head back or close his eyes. He watched her with a delicious stubbornness, following the waves of pleasure on her face, now between his hands.

Zoey tried to bring her rate of breathing back to a more normal rhythm.

This time, the heat that had passed through her belly was, to her great annoyance, now moving to her thighs. She cursed herself for not having been more into sports. Everyone had always said that one day they would come in handy, which she had been too happy to ignore.

The position awakened muscles that she had gladly forgotten some time ago.

He realized that she was in a difficult position and let out the beginnings of a harsh laugh, that she stopped immediately with a furious cluck of her tongue.

It was he who gracefully regulated the movement of their two bodies together, going faster and faster, his face in her hair, until his own climax. It was so powerful that she had to hold onto the back of the couch to keep from falling.

Then, unexpectedly, he started to laugh.

It look Zoey a few seconds to realize what he was doing. Matthew's entire body shook. She couldn't figure out if he was expressing his remaining pleasure or simply unable to suppress his mirth.

She stood up, freeing herself from his strong grip with difficulty. Their torsos came apart with an embarrassing noise.

What she was hearing was indeed an outright laugh, almost a roar.

Never had a man burst out laughing after making love to her. Once, one of her exes in college had cried, but she preferred to forget that unfortunate moment.

Matthew's laughter subsided until she heard only his irregular breathing.

"Is something funny?" she demanded, disconcerted.

Matthew caught his breath as well as he could.

"I'm sorry, I should have warned you. I always laugh when...when I have an orgasm. It's very unsettling, I agree."

"That's for sure!"

She sat up straight. It would have made sense for her to be upset, get up and put her clothes back on. But her clothes were on the other side of the couch and Matthew didn't seem to want to let her go.

"You don't believe me?" he exclaimed. "If you give me some time, I promise I'll can prove that I'm not lying. It might take a little while. I'm the first one to be embarrassed by it, believe me."

He didn't seem especially embarrassed. He had the same teasing look that he'd had that first evening.

Satisfied.

She was seriously considering smacking him when he kissed the tip of her nose. She cooled off a bit.

"My thighs are really sore," she remarked.

"I forbid you from moving," he said.

She obeyed, pushing on him a bit more, her buttocks against his upper thighs.

He suddenly frowned.

"Actually, it would be a good idea if you could get up for a few seconds."

"The condom..."

"The joys of modern sex," he apologized.

"Stop laughing like that. It seems to me that you could have at least minimum of consideration since this situation involves you too."

The scene that followed was a cringe worthy fiasco. She went into contortions to be able to stand up, almost fell, without any help from him since his hands were occupied. She was able to regain her balance but it was very unflattering. Finally, she landed on the couch which creaked under her weight, ruthless. Then Matthew disappeared into the kitchen. As he walked, she noticed that, no matter what the circumstance, he always had a certain level of nobility. She also noticed that his butt was very muscular.

She suppressed a new urge that would have been awkward if she were to mention it, considering the context. At least, not right away, as he had suggested.

Matthew came back to the living room and sat next to her, elegantly crossing his legs, still totally naked. He put his arm across the back of the couch, so she could cuddle into it, exactly as if they were getting ready to do what they'd initially said—watch TV. He was able to alternate between the most conventional and unconventional situations without any transition or apparent discomfort.

She was clearly less at ease. She knew that this position made her stomach stick out, even though she didn't dare lower her eyes to check. She would have liked him to turn the ceiling light off, but asking him now would require her to admit to her insecurities.

But also for him to get up, she thought, aroused at the thought of seeing him standing again, from the back, and in motion.

"It's the first time that you've been able to be quiet for more than five seconds," she said after a minute.

"It's the first time you've been able to be next to me and keep your hands to yourself." (She let out a furious gasp.) "Could you take them off your stomach, for the love of God? It makes it seem like you're sick to your stomach, which doesn't reflect well on me. Do you have any coffee?"

"You're planning to stay for coffee? Really?" she replied, teasing.

"It's not even 10 p.m."

He kissed the top of her head and then her forehead. His fingers, which had captured Zoey's and stopped her vain attempt to conceal herself, spread hers so that they were palm to palm.

"If it's okay with you, I would like to stay a bit longer."

It was, even if she was incapable of stating that right then.

"On the other hand, sorry to be annoying, but I really need a coffee," he added.

"I understand. You get tired easily."

The tightness of his mouth made her understand that he didn't appreciate that particular joke.

"You can be tedious, I have to say," he responded acidly. "But, I'm sure that if I fall asleep, you'll have a bed to offer me, if only to be polite."

She laughed, but it was a laugh that sounded so stupid that she wanted to give herself a lobotomy, if she hadn't already had one.

16
COMBINE YOLKS

While sipping her espresso, Zoey watched Matthew Ziegler on the phone, pacing up and down in her work space, in the same clothes as the day before, which made him seem scrumptiously scruffy.

They had woken up quite late, caressed by the sun falling on the bed, twisted up in the sheets that the heat had made unnecessary. Matthew stretched like a feline—well, any feline except Sushi who normally woke up by jumping on Zoey's head begging for food. Matthew smiled at her. He drew her close, his stomach against her back, his arm around her breast to hold her tight, moving his mouth from her neck to her ear, murmuring:

"Do you have a printer?"

This was followed by an exchange about the best way to say hello and they decided on something that worked for them both.

Twice.

Now, he was speaking firmly to an administrative assistant about an invitation he wasn't able to download. Zoey half listened while fixing her eyes on how, with each step, his jeans tightened around his buttocks.

"It's unbelievable that they use the Internet but are incapable of figuring out the QR code! he exclaimed, hanging up. You really don't know how your printer works?"

He stared at her, brow furrowed. Normally, Zoey would have thought this was annoying and bossy, but, at this very moment, she would have put up with any type of conversation, even about something as dull as the limits of modern technology, as long as he continued to pace around the room like this.

She wouldn't even have minded hearing about boring paperwork if he decided to come toward her and sit her on the counter top.

She realized her fantasies were the result of an overdose of hormones, and she was content to drink her coffee while casting interested looks his way.

"You don't know what I'm talking about, do you?" he asked.

"Of course I do. I have a smartphone too!"

"And you use it to play Candy Crush?"

She held her tongue.

"What level are you?" he continued with a satisfied smile.

"Forty-seven," she mumbled. "I have the right to be like the Amish if I want to, don't I?"

"Yes, you can have the right to do anything you want," he replied seriously. "As long as you leave me some rights too, in very specific circumstances.

She wondered if it would bother passers-by if he were to push her up against a stool to kiss her.

It would embarrass Sally, in any case. She had just entered the shop, stopped, gazing at Matthew Ziegler's wrinkled shirt. She smiled slightly and belted out a jovial "hello."

Zoey let out a nervous laugh—to be included in the list of her stupidest laughs ever— which Sally, a true friend, ignored.

She simply put down her bag and raised an eyebrow toward the illuminated printer.

"You need to connect it to the Wi-Fi for it to work," she noted. "Wait."

It took her two minutes to fix it, during which time Zoey poured herself another coffee without saying a word, praying that her stupid-sounding laugh was gone, leaving her with at least a shred of dignity. Sally pulled out the sheet of paper and handed it to Matthew.

"Thank you," he said, quickly perusing the information it contained.

"Are you going to Wonderful Lunch?" Sally asked.

Of course, she seemed to know exactly what it was about, and even seemed a little envious.

"What's 'Wonderful Lunch?'" Zoey chimed in nonchalantly.

"It's where food bloggers meet with three chefs, to taste samples."

"And why is it 'wonderful?'"

Sally stared at her, her eyes wide. She held back in front of Matthew, but her entire face expressed deep indignation.

"The most popular bloggers will be there. It's an excellent PR opportunity."

"Do chefs really need to do that to make a name for themselves?"

"Yes, Zoey."

Sally wore a dangerous smile. Matthew came to her rescue:

"Your friend is right. Without the blogosphere, today, it's difficult to get established."

154

"I'm not convinced."

Matthew sat at the counter, in front of the coffee that she had just served. Even when he was serious and professional, he was hot. His tone was professional too, though, normally, she would have thought it was slightly condescending, especially in front of Sally who was gloating in silence.

"You act like some of my colleagues, other critics. They're old school. They scream that their precious paper is being replaced by the Internet."

"Thank you, but I'm not old-fashioned."

"The blogging community has a lot of influence, is very active and takes initiative. They are curious and anxious to learn. I firmly believe that our two camps can work together—the traditional critics and their enthusiastic group. They have experts in their ranks as well. Certain chefs have become extremely popular, more than they deserve, thanks to the bloggers."

"It seems like you've forgotten that I mainly cater wedding receptions."

He shook his head. Matthew was not the type that forgot anything. With the smile that he gave her, she wondered if he were really trying to convince her that his strategy was a good one, or, if he too was distracted by the same images that had been bombarding her since earlier this morning. As he spoke using a serious tone, she could clearly see the little wrinkle that appeared when he crinkled his eyes. She'd seen it earlier when he'd kissed her.

"There's a whole network to be explored in this field as well. Wedding planners, and especially food stylists, can use photos to show what they have to offer. You already have a good sense of how to set the stage and you could be a lot more visible on the web. It's the first place that the generation who is getting married right now looks."

Zoey rolled her eyes.

"Thank you," Sally sighed in Matthew's direction.

"No problem," he replied with a smile.

"Would you like to go with me, Zoey?"

Sally let out a somewhat hysterical squeal. Zoey had never seen herself in the role of official groupie. She wasn't the fashionista type who'd show up in Manolo Blahnik boots. The last time she'd been this thrilled is when the mayor of New York had announced new bike parking in Manhattan.

"I would be out of place. Sally, however..." She smiled at Sally, in what she'd meant to be a kind way, but ended up being somewhat sarcastic. Sally shrugged her shoulders, apparently peeved by her lack of tact.

"That's a good idea," Matthew approved. "I could introduce you to Cybil Green."

"I love her—she's such a wonderful food stylist!" Sally exclaimed. "If Zoey could free up some of the budget for her, we'd finally have photos worthy of being called that!"

"I didn't want to say anything," Matthew replied.

"What's wrong with our photos?" Zoey asked, offended, even though she hadn't had anything to do with the photos or their website.

Sally seemed contrite and began to play with a lock of hair, which she often did when she found herself in an embarrassing situation.

"They are wedding photos."

"They are photos of wedding buffets," Zoey corrected.

"We could use more professional photos."

"And that would show off your excellent work," Matthew repeated. Sally gave him her most grateful smile.

They were able to convince Zoey to think about it and to decide when Sally and Matthew would meet up. Sally waited until the conversation wound down to make an exit, leaving them face to face, in an embarrassing silence.

"Well," Matthew said suddenly, picking up the cup in front of him. "Thank you so much for the coffee."

Zoey rolled her eyes. They'd returned to their starting point. They were going to be polite, distant and thank each other.

Or, he could say something like: "Would it be okay if I call you?"

Or worse: "Would it be okay if we act like nothing happened?"

He probably wouldn't say that. He would just not call and she knew that that would make her furious. She would refuse to call him herself, not because women couldn't call men, but because it was out of the question that she show the slightest bit of interest under the circumstances.

"Since we are talking about work...," he begin.

Nothing was off limits.

"My friend Rafael Branco, the cultural attaché, loved your food, as he told you directly, and asked me to ask you if it would be possible for you to cook a dinner for him and some of his friends."

Zoey hesitated. She'd stopped doing private dinners years ago. Though she had liked the challenge of working in non-professional kitchens, she had, on the other hand, hated the impression she'd had of being a simple underling for rich foodies.

"I will understand–and he will too–if you don't have time. However, the experience could be interesting and a way to diversify your offering."

She was stung. Her catering business was going well. Sally and Matthew gave her the impression that she continually needed new opportunities.

"If you want my advice, you should accept," he continued. "He's been thinking about opening a restaurant in New York for a while."

"Would that help you out if I accepted?" Zoey asked, sharply.

"I'm sorry—is something wrong?"

"Would it be advantageous for you if I were to accept?"

"Yes, in a way, because Rafael is a friend and I like to help my friends out. From a professional point of view, no," he added with a teasing smile.

"So. Here's my proposition. I do this dinner for your friend, and, in exchange, you help Sally negotiate a good price for photos by that Cybil Green that she admires so much."

"You keep your eye on the ball," Matthew said. "Next Tuesday?"

"That's a bit soon, but it's a deal. An agreement is an agreement."

He finished his coffee, satisfied, and put his glass in the sink next to the machine. Turning back around, he seemed to be in deep thought and then looked at her, smiling. She felt like throwing herself at him, the same way she felt every time he wore this expression. It was both charming and slightly sarcastic.

"Fortunately, you are not such a hard negotiator in more intimate matters, or I'd still be in my boxer shorts right now, he murmured."

She held back a laugh.

"You overestimate what you have to offer."

"I'm sure," he retorted. "If you're already getting a sarcastic reply ready, I'd like you to know that I enjoyed last night."

"Your total lack of pride upsets me," she replied, hiding her own smile.

"Pride and sex don't go well together. I think I made that point last night, waiting for you for two hours on a restaurant patio, to be yelled at in public."

He seemed to be hesitating to move toward her and then changed his mind.

"I suppose that I should kiss you goodbye."

Oh, Good *Lord*, she thought.

Did he always have to comment on what he was about to do?

"You certainly don't have to," she said a bit too sharply.

She was dying for him to kiss her. And to not say goodbye, in all honesty.

"Perfect, he said. I hate these kinds of public displays."

He took several steps toward the door and then turned around.

"However, I give you permission to call me," he specified.

She hadn't had time to digest what he'd said when Sally, who, she hoped, had not been listening their conversation from the test kitchen, burst through the door.

"You slept with Matthew Ziegler," she blushed, gleefully.

"Your powers of deduction will never cease to amaze me, Sally," Zoey replied, taking out the order book.

"What was it like? Is he just as sexy in private? Are you going to see each other again?"

Zoey thought about it for a moment. The ball was in her court. Part of her was dying to see Matthew again, and the other part had no idea what to do. He'd talked about sex, not a relationship. She had nothing against the idea of having a friend with benefits, especially with someone like Matthew, but they weren't actually friends and she had no intention of getting involved in something that would inevitably be disappointing once the bloom wore off.

Specifically, with a man who was capable of saying: "I really enjoyed last night," which seemed to be his maximum degree of spontaneousness.

Without even mentioning, "I suppose that I should kiss you goodbye."

In somewhat of a frenzy, Sally followed her thought process.

"No details," Zoey announced, opening her order book with snap.

"You really are a terrible friend."

"Really? Do you I ask you about the details of your many sexual encounters?"

"All the time."

"Only because I know you love talking about them. That's what it means to be a real friend, get it?"

Sally laughed.

"So, at least tell me if you are going to see each other again."

"I don't know yet," Zoey lied.

She wasn't going to mention the dinner that she'd agreed to prepare for Rafael Branco or what she had negotiated with Matthew. She wanted the victory to be entirely Sally's if Cybil Green agreed to work for them. She owed her that much.

"Not next week in any case, she continued. We have the Hawkins-Lopez wedding on Saturday and Cass's party Friday night."

"The more things continue like this, the more it seems like you and I are a couple," grumbled Sally, blowing on a lock of red hair. "If this continues, we should just live together—that would save commuting costs."

"It's up to you if you choose to be with someone else," Zoey retorted critically.

Sally stared at her.

"Why did you say that?"

"You have to want it," said Zoey shrugging her shoulders.

At this moment, her friend had the same strange look on her face as the day before. Almost like she was being followed. Zoey was now sure Sally was hiding something from her.

An alarm went off in her head. Sally had clearly expressed her thoughts on the lack of vision at Zoey's Kitchen and Zoey's lack of initiative. She was constantly trying to develop new ways to get the message out but Zoey hadn't attached much significant to it, just as she had done earlier today when Matthew talked about it. The way she had jumped at the chance to attend the luncheon and the interest she had shown in the food stylist proved once again that she must be bored being the assistant for such a small, risk-averse company.

158

"Sally, if something were bothering you, you'd tell me, right?"

"Yes, of course!"

Sally seemed to relax slightly, even if her expression remained anxious.

"We tell each everything, right?" Zoey added, a knot in her stomach.

"Not where your love life is concerned," apparently, Sally tried to joke.

Her tone failed in that regard. Zoey didn't know what to say. She didn't want to pester Sally with questions or be the type of boss who micromanaged. For the first time, Sally's role as both her friend and her assistant seemed difficult to manage. Sally had to feel the same way.

Sally, however, hopped nimbly onto the stool next to Zoey and gave her attention to the order book.

"Let's get to work!" she said happily.

"Yes, let's get to work," Zoey agreed, less happily.

She felt that things were not quite right and she'd known for a while that things were not going well.

Nevertheless, she smiled at Sally and both of them focused on the upcoming orders.

17
BEAT EGGS WHITES

Rafael Branco's rented apartment in New York was beyond Zoey's wildest dreams. The kitchen was a technological jewel and the numerous marble counters provided enough space for her to spread out as much as she wished.

She had been at the oven since the early afternoon when the cultural attaché stuck his head in the door to welcome her. She hadn't seen him yet. A cold, distant employee had greeted her and guided her through a maze of hallways to the kitchen.

"Do you have everything you need?" Rafael Branco asked, after saying hello.

"Your kitchen is a dream," Zoey replied spontaneously. "Would you like to see what I..."

"No, no!" the Brazilian exclaimed. "I want it to be a surprise! My guests will be arriving any time now. If you need anything, I'll be in the living room."

Zoey was unable to identify where the living was, or even the dining room, even though she'd had a tour earlier.

"Everything will be ready," she confirmed in her most professional voice.

She was not lying. The only thing left was to prepare the plates for the first course—giant prawns with avocado puree and fresh cilantro. She still needed to grate the Parmesan shavings for the salad and put the duck, fig, truffles selection in the oven at just the right time. Nana's special lemon tarts were waiting to be decorated with white chocolate and candied lemon rind, a two-minute task.

The sommelier had brought out the wine and was decanting his selections in the pantry and the attaché's personal employee provided wait service. It was, as Branco had emphasized, a truly intimate dinner.

When she received the signal, Zoey made sure the first course was served with perfect timing. The rest of the dinner proceeded in the same fashion. Twenty minutes after having sent out the dessert, several beeps sounded on her phone, indicating she had a message.

She sat at the edge of the table to look at it. It was from Matthew.

"It was absolutely magnificent."

She touched the "reply" button. Another beep interrupted her.

"I'm talking about your tarts."

Obviously, he was in the dining room. She should have known that he was going to be attending this dinner. He'd set it up and was a friend of Rafael Branco's. She had not thought about the people eating her food as people that she might know. That was part of the difficult game involved in cooking at someone's home when the client was someone as unpredictable as Rafael Branco. Most other clients had a clear idea of what they wanted at their table. She had come up with what she would need to seduce or appeal to total strangers.

Fortunately, Matthew had been thoughtful enough to not come see her before the dinner started.

She was going to reply when the assistant, whose name she still didn't know, entered the kitchen to ask her to go to the living room, before directing her to the coffee maker, indicating with a cold look that she was making things difficult.

Zoey removed her uniform and ran her hand through her hair. She had succeeded in pulling all her hair together in a very tight bun at the nape of her neck. This style kept it under control, but, in general, she avoided it because she thought it was too severe and made her think of her mother as well as giving her a terrible headache.

It took her a few minutes to find the living room, and, in the process, she randomly opened the doors to several bedrooms and a closet. The apartment's luxurious and elegant atmosphere made an impression on her, now that she had left the kitchen, always the most informal place within a house.

She finally found the living room. The gray walls opened onto several multi-paned windows that looked out onto a terrace. On a white fabric couch, Rafael Branco was speaking with a bohemian couple about his age. The man was dressed in light linen and the woman, despite the heat, was draped in a long dress made of red silk. Together, they were almost blinding, in contrast with the filtered light from the candles placed around the room. Across from them on the couch, Matthew was stretching out his long legs under the coffee table. He displayed the nonchalant attitude that she knew to be his normal countenance. The guests were drinking champagne and cognac as well as coffee, which had been brought to them before she arrived. There were voices on the terrace.

Rafael Branco welcomed her warmly and introduced her to the couple–Brazilian musicians–and had her sit across from them, next to Matthew. They congratulated her enthusiastically, asked her questions and answered hers about the cuisine of their country. Like Branco, they were amateur gourmets.

"I've been looking for a chef like you for years," Rafael Branco suddenly said, taking advantage of a brief pause in the conversation." It's been my dream to open a restaurant here."

"There are lots of opportunities," Zoey responded. "New Yorkers are always on the lookout for new places to go."

Rafael Branco eyes narrowed.

"I don't want to have one of those trendy restaurants that lasts a year. I want a sophisticated menu, focused on several dishes, and refined decor. Innovative but also authentic."

"I'm sure that a restaurant like that would be successful," Zoey replied politely.

"Think about it," Rafael added, looking at her kindly.

Matthew remained silent, his thigh touching Zoey's. Their proximity was getting more and more difficult for her to handle. His hand was nonchalantly resting on the back of the couch and he used it to discretely caress her back with his fingertips.

At least, she hoped it was discrete.

This simple contact excited her more than it should have, making her tingle from her head to her toes, slowly transforming her polite laugh into a sort of hysterical titter. She wondered how Matthew was able to keep an impassive face while he drew designs on the fabric of her shirt.

When his fingers ventured down toward her waist, to the top of her skirt, she took advantage of a new silence in the conversation to ask to see the terrace.

The view was gorgeous. So was Sofia Alves. She was having a discussion with Luis Delacruz as they both leaned against the railing. She wore a backless top and flowing, high waisted pants–the type of pants Zoey dreamed about but couldn't wear since they would make her look like a chubby sailor from ads in the 1930s. Sofia Alves turned and noticed Zoey and Matthew behind her, and walked toward them, smiling.

"It was delicious, dear Zoey," she said in a tone that immediately Zoey assessed as fake.

Then she recalled that both Marianita and Matthew had attested to her lack of sincerity. She was on her guard. She didn't want to be humiliated in front of Matthew, although he had made clear that it was up to her to make the next move. And also that they didn't really have a relationship. She'd always refused to participate in the games of the upper class, but she was Fran Westwood's daughter: rejecting them didn't mean that she couldn't win them.

"Thank you. Coming from you, that means a lot to me."

"I'm always looking for new talent," Sofia continued. "Would you be interested in visiting one of my restaurants?"

The question took Zoey by surprise. She had never imagined she'd have to respond so directly to a barely disguised offer of employment. She had always dreamed of traveling and had even thought about living overseas. Obviously, Zoey's Kitchen had taken most of her time and energy for the last four years, but the real reason she'd never pursued going abroad was that the idea of leaving her friends and family had stopped her. Next to her, Matthew chimed in.

"That's an excellent idea," he said.

The idea that she might leave for Brazil didn't seem to bother him. She was almost disappointed.

"I'd be happy to," she replied.

"Matthew, love, could you go get my bag for me?" Sofia asked.

The "love" made Zoey feel very annoyed. This intimacy, emphasized by a cooing that Zoey thought was ridiculous for a woman of Sofia's age, even though she knew full well that was not the case, made her want to say something excessively sarcastic.

She held her tongue, however.

She did note that Matthew obeyed. She was curious as to what expression she'd see on his face if *she* were to call him "love" and order him around, even if the idea also brought to mind a totally different type of request.

When he brought the bag, she purposely gave him a contemptuous smile to which he did not respond. Sofia pulled out her business card.

"My assistant will call you, but you can also contact me directly if you have any questions."

Zoey would have liked to reply in the same manner, but she'd never before uttered the words, "my assistant will call you," even if that was Sally's official title. And her business cards said *Zoey's Kitchen*, not her own name.

"Your lemon tarts were amazing," Sofia added. "What special ingredient did you use?"

"It's a secret," Zoey replied.

"Indeed," Matthew interrupted. "It was too subtle for any of us to figure it out. Can you give us a clue?"

"I don't reveal what's in my recipes," Zoey answered laughing. "Not even to Sally."

"You aren't as generous as your grandmother," Sofia remarked.

Zoey raised her eyebrows. She hadn't been expecting this, or that the imposing Brazilian would so directly broach this subject. She had become accustomed to everyone ignoring this detail of her background.

"I'm not sure that Zoey appreciates such a direct comparison, Sofia," Matthew murmured.

She was grateful to him for coming to her assistance, even if she didn't feel she needed it.

"My grandmother is a cookbook author. I'm a chef. I am sure you understand the difference."

"Yes. I didn't mean to be rude. I like your grandmother's books very much. I think you are her worthy heir on several points."

Her voice had softened. The fact that her apology was half-hearted made her more sympathetic in Zoey's opinion. Sofia simply didn't know how to keep her thoughts to herself. She wondered how this woman had been able to build such an empire, without the diplomacy required of all successful leaders.

"You remind me of me at your age. I know I shouldn't say that to a younger woman who is far more attractive as well," Sofia continued.

This remark threw Zoey off balance.

"You have immense talent and I am sure that you have mapped out a good career path. Having a specific goal is important."

"It seems like it would have taken a lot of work to create a network of such exceptional restaurants in a country like Brazil, especially being a woman."

"You know, I know how to leverage other people's talents," Sofia murmured, suddenly modest.

"Sofia is an excellent strategist," Matthew said.

"Not in everything, unfortunately," Sofia replied.

Her eyes clouded over suddenly, as her gaze fell on Matthew. A sad expression crossed her face. It was brief but intense. Zoey observed Matthew. He was also looking at Sofia and made a gesture toward her. She felt excluded from their exchange and quite ill at ease.

"Excuse me, but I have to go," she stammered.

Sofia sat up abruptly, as if she realized that she had exposed a bit too much of herself.

"It was wonderful talking to you."

Zoey slipped away. She crossed the living room, meeting up the employee whose name she didn't know and asked where the restroom was. She indicated where they were with a vague gesture. She was clearly indicating that Zoey was out of her league.

Zoey chose a hallway covered in blue wallpaper with a hand-drawn silver pattern. She followed it until she recognized the intersection she'd taken from the kitchen. She went right, pushed open a door, then another, until she happened upon a bedroom where the light had been left on. At the foot of the unmade bed, she saw women's shoes and a wrinkled dress. She went in, hoping to find a bathroom.

The first door opened into a huge walk-in closet, where only one rod was being used. Just when she closed it, a footstep, muted by the thick rug, made her turn. Matthew was standing in front of her.

"I got lost," she stammered.

She had no desire for him to think that she was an idiot who couldn't find her way out of a paper bag, but she couldn't think of anything else to say.

"I came to save you," he replied, looking amused.

He was less than three feet from her now and seemed bent on reducing the proper social distance between them.

"It's true that I was in great danger here," Zoey said. "They might have found me in the morning, wandering around in the walk-in closet, totally dehydrated."

"You don't understand the risks you're taking, actually, walking around alone in this apartment."

"Sofia must be wondering where you are."

He shrugged his shoulders and stopped smiling.

"Are you jealous of a woman who was gracious enough to offer you a position that most chefs in the world could only dream about?"

"I am not jealous."

"That's good to know. I hate jealous women."

He had a talent for being annoying at the moment when he should have simply been attractive and funny.

"Time to go back," Zoey commanded, more for herself than for him. Everyone must be wondering what our relationship is, and even more so if they saw you caressing my back when I was in the middle of having a professional conversation.

Matthew nodded.

"You loved it when I was caressing your back. You trembled like a schoolgirl. It was adorable."

"You really have a gift for making me look ridiculous," Zoey murmured.

If he came one step closer, she felt certain that she would no longer be able to control herself.

"I said you were adorable," he insisted.

He came a bit closer. She smelled his cologne and the arousing scent of his skin. Matthew leaned toward her.

"You have so little self-confidence that you think any interest in you must be condescending."

"Spare me your psychoanalysis," she snapped, surprised.

His hands were getting dangerously close to her hips.

166

"You are so proud that you would rather die than call me."

"I am not proud!"

"Yes, you are."

The tips of his fingers caressed the fabric of her top where it met her skirt. and skimmed her skin. She experienced a delicious shiver.

"Admit it or I will make love to you right here and make you scream so loud that no one in this house will have any doubt about what kind of relationship we have."

"How dare you!" she said, breathing hard. "I never screamed."

"Exactly," he replied. "I took it as a personal affront."

"I promise you that if you make me scream, it will be out of frustration."

She was being totally dishonest. And he gave her a dangerous reply:

"I promise to not lose control even though I'm dying to let go."

"What makes you think that..."

Matthew didn't let her finish and pulled her against him.

His mouth searched for hers, found it and kissed her with a ferocity that almost made her cry out. He put his hands under her shirt, without worrying about waiting the officially prescribed amount of time before moving to this step. They were past that anyway.

She was suspended from his neck and kissed him back with the same passion. Her tongue insinuated itself into his mouth. Encouraged by her initiative, he pressed on the small of her back to arch it, pressing his hips against hers.

She had forgotten where she was and what she was doing. She had only one desire, to rip off his shirt and pants and push him down onto the carpet, where some other person's belongings were to be found, in this anonymous room.

He straightened his head to catch his breath, his fingers sliding over her skin with a soft, faintly feverish touch.

"You mentioned a walk-in closet?" he asked.

She looked for the handle and opened the door. She was focused on unfastening the buttons on his shirt as he followed her into the closet, his mouth again attached to hers and his hands on her hips. He left the task to her but offered assistance her when she fought with the buttons on his cuffs. With a will of their own, Zoey's hands attacked his belt and slid it out of its loops, then the buttons on his pants which fell to his ankles. She lifted her head toward him, triumphant.

He narrowed his chestnut-colored eyes and, now more than ever, the golden flecks within gave him the look of a wolf ready to jump on its prey. He turned her around. She found herself facing the clothes rod. Instinctively, she put her hands on the bar to prevent her from falling. In any other circumstances, she would have found this gesture to be out of place, and even somewhat humiliating, but Matthew attached his mouth to her neck, and with immense tenderness, danced his hands along her thighs, lifting her skirt, a little at a time.

His right hand stroked her buttocks through the fabric of her panties. She heard the noise of a package being torn and smiled at the idea that he'd planned to make love to her this time. He placed his hands on her buttocks and slid her panties off. She kicked them aside with a quick flick of the ankle. With an eager firmness, he spread her thighs, positioning her legs on either side of his, forcing her into a full arch. When he penetrated her, he let out a muffled moan that was amplified by the echo inside the empty closet.

His hands climbed back up to her stomach and then her chest as he rocked his pelvis back and forth. She spread her legs wider to receive him. He pushed the cups of her bra under her breasts, caressing her nipples, with a gentleness that had an undercurrent of savagery that was obviously difficult to contain as he pushed even further into her.

Zoey held onto the clothing rod. Later, she'd wonder how it didn't break under their weight and the force with which Matthew had made love to her, moaning into her back. For the moment, however, she didn't give it a thought. Her mind was somewhere between her the soft spot between her legs and her throat. She stopped herself from screaming with pleasure.

Out of pride, she had to admit, but also because she knew that Matthew couldn't resist her moans.

He abruptly stopped moving, his hands on her breasts, throbbing inside her. His hand went down to between her legs. She moved forward a bit to let his fingers reach her sweet spot. His other hand was suspended above her chest, stroking it, causing her to move toward it. Her gesture was in vain, because his fingers moved slowly away as she straightened.

As Matthew masterfully caressed her, his teeth delicately sank into her neck. She felt his breath quicken as he nibbled her, his body shaken by a panting that betrayed his impatience.

Their hips moved together in a succession of slow, tense waves, leading her up to a level of pleasure that she could sense was going to be violent.

He murmured something to her that she couldn't hear, focused solely on the sensation that was rising through her body, as he increased the pressure from his fingers.

Finally, she climaxed with such violence that the closet rod trembled in her hands.

Convulsing with pleasure, she couldn't contain a luxurious groan, to which he responded with an expletive before penetrating her again in a feverish motion. Several minutes later, he grabbed her by the hips and brutally pulled her toward him. She heard the burst of laughter that had so disturbed her the first time and that continued to surprise her.

"I'm so sorry," he whispered in her neck. "I got carried away, I think."

"You didn't get carried away," she replied, her voice hoarse.

"Stop using that voice right now," he scolded. "Or I will lock us in here until the end of our days."

She shifted her hips to separate from him.

"You are a wild romantic. We'd eventually be discovered."

She turned around. The light from the bedroom filtered into the walk-in closet and lit Matthew's face. He took her in his arms and pulled her close, with a gentleness that was somewhat disconcerting.

"I'll say that you took advantage of me," he declared.

"I'll deny it."

"No one will trust a woman who puts tequila in lemon tarts."

"You figured it out."

Her smile was interrupted by Matthew's mouth engaging hers. His kiss brought a new wave of warmth from her stomach through her chest. He tenderly pushed her away.

"I'll let you get dressed," he murmured before traveling across her face with his lips, to the top of her head.

Considerate. Polite. Efficient.

She didn't stop herself from rolling her eyes as he pulled up his pants, groped around for his shirt and left the closet.

She leaned against the wall, her heart beating. She wasn't sure she could get used to this type of relationship, but, on the other hand, she knew that she had never before experienced such pleasure or desire. She had already had sexual encounters in several interesting places and was proud of not being uptight. She had even shocked Spencer at times, though that was not difficult. During their time together, Spencer had shown himself to be more of a traditionalist where sex was concerned, which had caused her to call her own moral values into question.

Matthew could convince her to make love anywhere, anytime—which he had basically just proved to her. He was able to act like a perfect gentleman one minute and a total barbarian the next.

She heard the bedroom door open and then shut and began looking for her panties. She finally found them, sadly hanging from one of the walk-in shelves.

Once in the bedroom, she saw her own reflection in the mirror across from the bed. Her hair was threatening to come out of the tight bun at the nape of her neck. Her eyes were shining, her cheeks flushed and the mark made by Matthew's teeth showed on her neck.

She couldn't show her face looking like this, at least not right away. She had to go back to the kitchen to pack her equipment and then figure out how to say goodbye as quickly as possible.

It took her twenty minutes to get ready. When she looked at herself in the one of the hallway mirrors, her skin had returned to its normal color and Matthew's bite was now only an imperceptible red spot that could have been caused by anything. She chose not to believe Dalton's big theory that, after having an orgasm, people emitted a specific odor, so full of hormones that it awakened the most primitive instincts.

She wound her way through the maze of hallways and found the living room. Empty glasses filled the table and most of the guests were on the terrace.

Not all, however. She stopped suddenly.

Matthew was sitting on the couch, the flickering light from the candles dancing on the shirt that she had ripped off him a half an hour earlier.

Her head resting on his shoulder, her knees bent gracefully, Sofia Alves was moving her mouth towards his ear.

He didn't move and didn't seem to have any desire to push her away, his legs stretched out under the table in his favorite position. Worse, his face showed an emotion that she had not yet seen there.

Without a word, she took a step back, did an about-face and left the apartment.

18
MIX CREAM OF TARTAR

Cass's party was always the second Friday in July. It took place in her top-floor apartment in a building that always seemed like it was about to collapse. Like her parents' annual barbecue or Nana's birthday, this event made a mark on the month of July and definitely provided more alcohol and more fun.

Zoey almost canceled at the last minute. She had just suffered through two days of total depression. When she was alone, she'd vacillated between expressing raw anger or giving into tears.

Matthew had sent her three messages the day after the dinner. In the last one, he had asked what was wrong. He was not aware that she had happened upon him and Sofia. She'd been able to make herself delete his texts to avoid any temptation to respond with outrage. She wanted to have no such interaction with him, even if it meant letting off steam. Her work had once again allowed her to be distracted during the day, but, in the evenings, alone in her bed, she had all the time in the world to revisit what occurred that evening and the violent emotions she still felt.

She needed to talk with Sally, but both of them were so busy preparing for the Hawkins-Lopez wedding that she preferred to postpone that conversation to a later time.

When she arrived at Cass's building, she only had one wish and that was to find her friend, tell her every detail, and cry on her shoulder. Sally would find the words to comfort her as she did often and so well.

She could hear the noise from the party in the stairwell.

Cass's parties were always exceptionally eclectic, combing a formidable sense of logistics with a mass meet-up. Cass was of the opinion that the ideal party was made up of thirty-three percent close friends, thirty-three percent acquaintances— including some die-hard partiers—and thirty-three percent of what she called "spontaneous guests." By that, she meant people she was interested in at the moment who she wanted to get to know better. The one percent that remained were the "last minute unknowns" and they were, according to her, the risk required to make the evening a success.

At first, Zoey had been one of the spontaneous guests. She met Cass in a yoga class when she had first moved to New York.

This was when she'd still been under the illusion that she liked sports– and yoga was definitely a sport, as she had concluded after how sore she was the first time. She'd originally had the vague impression that you just laid down on a mat and focused on breathing. To her horror, she'd had to do sit-ups.

After the third session, she'd been waiting in the hallway and Cass came up and asked her if she'd like to get a coffee, instead of "dying of boredom on a mat that smelled like death." She had gratefully accepted.

Cass was funny, somewhat crazy and perfectly comfortable with the idea that wearing workout clothes to buy a cappuccino was the same as working out. Zoey had liked this long-limbed brunette right away. She dressed like a rocker and worked at a news outlet. She had been invited to the July party, a bit surprised that it was scheduled for a specific date, since, until then, she'd only seen her parents and their friends organize parties for a set date.

"Tradition is cool," Cass had explained. So is meeting up every year. Hipsters don't understand what's really cool.

Out of anybody else's mouth, this would have made Zoey smile sarcastically. But Cass had a self-assurance and a nose for the next trend that could have convinced Fran Westwood to wear leopard skin if she had told her too.

Adrian and Dalton had made integrated themselves into the parties as well. In the beginning, Zoey had asked Adrian to go with her since, she admitted, she was a bit overwhelmed by her new friend. Then Cass and Adrian had hit it off–and Zoey had often wondered how close they actually were. And Dalton, who never missed a chance to live it up, had also been able to insert himself into the mix, in his role of the little brother that he'd always been. Then, Zoey had asked Cass if she could bring Sally.

When she reached the top floor, the floor under her feet was vibrating from the music. This had never been a problem for Cass—her neighbors, artists or partiers like she was— were all in her apartment anyway.

She didn't need to ring. The door was open and the hallway was full of people talking, drinks in hand. She greeted the ones she knew and then weaved her way into the apartment, looking for Cass and Sally. Her hostess burst into the hallway, followed by her best friend, Morgan, who was whispering something in her ear. Cass was wearing a ruffled pastel yellow silk top and an extra-short miniskirt, the color of pink grapefruit. A gold headband was buried in her brown hair hanging loose to her shoulders.

"I'm so happy to see you!" she exclaimed, hugging Zoey. "You look gorgeous!"

Zoey let out a doubtful grunt.

"You do!" Cass insisted.

"I think so too," Morgan added enthusiastically from the sidelines.

Zoey preferred avoiding the subject, which seemed both interesting and fraught. She didn't want to go into detail about her problems, and especially not with Cass and Morgan who were exuding such cheerfulness - and alcohol.

"And how are *you*?"

"Great!" Cass said in a high-pitched voice. "Do you need something to drink? Morgan will get you something."

He nodded. Cass continued to make the rounds, as a busy hostess, after nodding back.

As Zoey moved toward the living room, Morgan stopped her.

"Not that way," he said, pushing her toward the hallway that lead to Cass's huge, haphazard kitchen. "They're already drunk. Your brother is the worst of all of them this evening. You'd think he wasn't even twenty. Physically, too, actually. And how are you doing?"

"I'm a bit older and I feel it."

He let out an alcohol-fueled laugh. With his recent haircut and his soft, fine features, he looked like he had only recently left his teenage years behind.

They cleared a path to the kitchen, saying hello to people Zoey knew and who greeted her noisily. They reached a counter overflowing with all different types of bottles that guests had brought. Zoey grabbed a glass of what seemed to be an Italian wine.

"You are not going to drink a bottle that we've been trying to pass off on someone for three nights!" Morgan exclaimed.

"I'm not going to drink the entire bottle!" Zoey laughed.

Morgan went to the freezer and took out a drink and put it under Zoey's nose. It was light amber in color and the homemade look of it was not a good sign, or more specifically, brought to mind inebriated memories that had ended in a pounding head and a day in bed.

"Don't be scared," Morgan said, seeing her doubtful expression. "It's just vodka and honey."

"In a lemonade glass," Zoey noted as he poured her a generous portion. "Have you seen Sally?"

Morgan straightened up the glasses as if he were an accessory to a crime.

"You two are inseparable. I think I saw her on the terrace talking with a super-hot, totally hetero guy."

Suddenly, she no longer heard his voice. Adrian had come into the kitchen, an empty glass in hand and his head turned back toward the open door, replying to someone in the living room. Zoey couldn't understand what he was saying, his words drowned out by the music, the laughter, and the hubbub of the party. He turned toward her. When he saw her, his eyes darkened slightly. He looked pretty drunk too, his hair mussed, and like he was in a bad mood.

"Hey, Morgan," he said tapping the other man's shoulder. "Do you still have any of that awesome vodka, so we can finish it off?"

His enthusiasm attested to the fact that he'd already imbibed quite a bit.

He opened his arms and hugged Zoey against him.

"I've missed you!" he breathed, reeking of alcohol.

"We just saw each other last week."

At work and my parents' party.

"I'd love to be invited to your parents' party," Morgan gushed, serving Adrian and himself. "I'm serious. I'm polite, have good manners and am an exceptional listener. Old people love me. It's a shame I've never had in-laws. You had them once, Zoey. Tell us what they're like."

The only "in-laws" that she had ever had were Spencer's parents. From their very first meeting, his mother had made clear to her that she was not worthy of her son, and his father had tried to say as little as possible to her, under the circumstances. Both of them had flipped out about her choice of professions and the way she dressed. They must love Laurie.

"In general, parents don't like me," she said flatly.

"Mine like you," Adrian specified.

"You two are adorable," Morgan said. "You'd be the perfect couple, if it weren't incest. "

Adrian spit the vodka he'd be drinking into his glass.

He face briefly changed color.

"In any case," Adrian, Morgan continued without acknowledging any change in the Adrian's expression, "the day you bring home a serious girlfriend, you'll have to get Zoey's approval. Seeing how you're joined at the hip, she'll be worse than your mother."

"There's no threat of that," Adrian murmured.

"Anyway, Zoey, how's it going?"

"Great."

"You made a big impression at the consulate the other evening."

The consulate made her think of Matthew and his appalling behavior. Again, she decided to postpone the conversation that she needed to have with her best friend. The only person who could console her and who she wanted to talk with was somewhere else in the apartment, talking to a man who was "super-hot."

"Do you know where Sally is?"

"Five minutes ago, some jackass was coming on to her. Another mama's boy who wants to look cool by..."

"...getting drunk on honey-infused vodka," Zoey interrupted.

"...by acting like he's a feminist," Adrian finished. "I've heard him give the same speech three times. Using his hair to make his points. Because he has long hair—obviously."

"I'll send Dalton to take care of it," Zoey said, before remembering that she wasn't talking to her brother.

"Leave Dalton out of it," he replied, turning around. "He's busy. And the problem has been taken care of, apparently."

He casually gestured toward the living room that could be seen through the half-open door. Zoey could see her brother, leaning against the wall, talking to Marianita and Sally, who'd dumped the pick-up artist. Dalton was recounting what was surely a thrilling anecdote because the two women were listening intently and laughing uproariously at times.

"You had to bring Marianita?" she sighed.

"Why would you care?"

His gloomy face did not bode well for the rest of the evening. Morgan seemed to tire of the conversation and started crawling toward another group of people. She found herself alone with Adrian.

"Why would I care?" she said, grinding her teeth. "After all, she just shows up in our lives, she's everywhere and she even asked me to have coffee with her. Like I was her friend or something."

"Why don't you like her, exactly?"

She clearly remembered what the other woman had said about Matthew. Right now, that was irritating her, even if Matthew didn't deserve her concern, and everything to do with him should be left in the past, in the recent and painful past.

"Marianita is a nice, friendly person," Adrian continued. "That must be a change for you to have branched out a bit from the closed circle of Sally, Dalton and me."

"Because I don't have other friends, you mean?"

"What are we talking about?"

Things were heating up, bit by bit. Zoey had already grown tired of fighting with Adrian, but anger pushed her on, despite herself. She had been so angry with Matthew that she was ready to take on any man.

"Acquaintances, yes," Adrian conceded. "Morgan is right. You are so attached to your friends..."

"I'm the one? What about you, Adrian? Do you want me to psycho-analyze you? You are incapable of expressing your true feelings."

At that moment, she didn't know if she was talking about Adrian or herself, but since he had hit the nail on the head, she didn't feel like being accommodating.

She didn't need him to tell her she was high-maintenance. She already knew that about herself. Several times throughout her life, and even when she was a child, people had complained about how all-encompassing her relationships with people she liked were. She'd been like that with Adrian, keeping him from hanging out with other kids, using the excuse that she was protecting him. She'd been like that with Spencer.

She would have been like that with Matthew Ziegler if he'd given her the chance, meaning if he hadn't been so hot and cold with her, and additionally, cuddled on a couch with his official mistress when he'd just made love to her.

"You always push away the women that put up with your constant sarcasm and mean jokes that you use to protect yourself," she concluded, with such malicious satisfaction that Adrian blanched.

Her high-pitched voice attracted the attention of a group who'd been immersed in a lively discussion next to them. Adrian took her arm and pulled her toward the sink, in the back of the kitchen.

"Are you planning to drown me?" Zoey demanded, leaning precariously over the dirty dishes.

It was no longer anger that she felt in her stomach, but rage. She tapped Adrian's forearm to loosen his grip.

"Understood, Zoey," he growled, "you're an awesome listener who never says anything mean to anyone."

"Me? Have I said mean things to you? You are crazy!"

"Obviously," spit Adrian. "You say things and then you forget."

"I do not know what you are taking about," Zoey enunciated, as if she were talking to a child.

"The night of your parents' party, when you…"

An energetic shadow was blasting toward them. Sally's tousled, jubilant head appeared next to Adrian's shoulder.

"Zoey! Do you know what Dalton just told me?"

Dalton appeared next, yelling like he was possessed, obviously as smashed as the others.

"I swear, you're going to regret it!" he cried.

He grabbed Sally by the waist and pulled her away from Adrian's back where she was trying to hang on. Then, he wrapped her in his arms, lost his balance and they fell together on the counter, causing a clatter of bottles.

Zoey returned her gaze to Adrian. He was staring at her with a dark, veiled expression.

Behind him, Sally and Dalton were making a racket, yelling loudly. Marianita joined in, no longer elegant or sophisticated, her eyes glazed over with alcohol and laughter, jumping on Dalton, ordering him to let her friend alone.

Her friend.

Zoey let out an angry grunt. She hated Marianita.

The first measure of "Go All the Way" by the Raspberries reverberated throughout the room, followed by several hoots and applause.

"*Baby, please, go all the way,*" Dalton sang, in his best crooner voice, preventing Sally from getting up, laughing, sitting on the counter.

Her brother was bombed. With one hand, he grabbed Marianita and pulled her against him, as he kept on singing.

"*It* feels *so right being with you here tonight,*" he continued, burying his nose in Marianita's neck, who defended herself weakly, and then in Sally's neck. She encircled him in her arms.

"Dalton, stop it!" Adrian groaned with clenched teeth.

"Relax, dude!" Dalton replied, laughing hysterically. "*Go all the way !* So? Who's going to be first? Sally? I've dreamed about sliding an ice cube down your cleavage."

"You're not in college anymore, dude!"

Dalton totally ignored his childhood friend.

"Marianita?"

He tightened his hold on her. Her head back, the Brazilian giggled and pleaded at the same time.

"Dalton! Stop right now or I swear, you'll regret it."

"You're pissing us off, Adrian!" Dalton yelled, looking over his shoulder mockingly. "It's not because you missed your chance that..."

Then, something shocking happened.

Adrian leapt toward them like a crazy person, landing in front of Dalton, grabbing him by the shoulder, force him to turn around, punching him straight in the face. Dalton's head was thrown back, as if it were on a rubber band, and then bounced back forward, right as Adrian jumped on his childhood friend and tackled him to the ground.

Sally started screaming and so did Marianita. The guests, seeing the scene, backed up several feet.

Zoey threw herself on them, trying to stop Dalton who was trying to free his arm to strike Adrian. Morgan appeared next to them as Zoey was pulling at her brother's collar, grabbing him around the waist and forcing him to get up.

Dalton was flailing wildly, and just missed hitting her in the nose with his elbow.

"Don't kill the reinforcements!" whined Morgan, getting Dalton under control.

Adrian jumped up. Before he made another move, Marianita put herself between them and implored them to get control of themselves. Zoey had time to grab Adrian by the wrist and pull him toward the door.

"Calm down! You've gone completely crazy!"

Zoey pushed him against the wall. Out of the corner of her eye, she saw Cass in front of her brother who was surrounded by Morgan and Marianita.

"I swear that next time, I'll smash your smug face in!" Adrian barked in Dalton's direction as Dalton charged forward in reply, but was held back by his friends.

A trickle of blood was flowing from his right nostril and his eyes flashed.

"You've all gone totally insane!" bellowed Zoey.

Her cheeks flushed, Sally suddenly appeared in the hallway.

"Your behavior is unacceptable!" she shouted at Adrian.

"Is that all you've got?" Adrian countered. Zoey froze. This wasn't one of Adrian's usual retorts when he was attacked.

There was a desire to wound, she thought.

Like when he'd been picked on at school due to his inability to understand social interactions, or when she and Dalton had let themselves get carried away by the sometimes cruel collusion that was the prerogative of siblings.

Sally was paralyzed and looked at her, dripping with sweat.

"That was idiotic!"

"You are right, Sally, it was totally idiotic," Adrian replied, in a detached tone with an underlying belligerency.

"Listen, Adrian," Zoey interrupted. "They're all drunk and you know how Dalton likes to push the limits, but I'm sure that he didn't mean anything by it."

"Always ready to defend your dear brother, Zoey," her friend hissed. "You are both the same. Spoiled children who have absolutely no understanding about how others feel."

Then he pulled away from her and disappeared down the hall, leaving her alone in her incomprehension.

Not totally alone. Sally was watching her, her lips tight. Dalton walked toward them, his t-shirt stained with blood. Zoey looked at her little brother's nose. It's probably not broken–Adrian lacked experience and fighting skills.

"Are you going to explain this to me?" she demanded.

"Explain what?" Dalton spit defensively. "That your friend is a jackass?"

"Adrian is not a jackass," Zoey murmured. Dalton's bright eyes darted around her face.

"I'm going to explain something to you, Zoey. The world hasn't revolved around you and Adrian Peters since elementary school. You've tried to make yourselves the center of the universe, but other people have lives too. You feed off each other's feelings and you wallow in them. It's been like that for a long time."

"Wonderful. You talk like he does," Zoey replied, feeling the blood gradually leave her face. "Excuse me, I didn't know that rubbing up against Sally and Marianita was how you expressed yourself."

"My poor Zoey."

He put as much disdain in his voice as he could. He knew she hated that. He'd often used that trick when they were teenagers.

"You know what? I'm tired of being the one who has to spell it out for you. In the end, it's none of my business."

He gave her one last look and she could see that he was still angry, but he also hesitated, as he went toward the door. Zoey leaned against the wall, void of all her energy. Around her, the party had returned to normal and everyone seemed to have forgotten the incident.

"When did we all stop listening to each other?" she asked Sally.

She felt dazed and lost. She had never imagined that they would disagree so violently. She had never imagined that Adrian would hit Dalton, or anyone else for that matter.

"If you want my advice, it was when...," Sally hesitated.

"I'm listening," Zoey said softly.

"Don't take this the wrong way, but I think it's been since your break up with Spencer. You became so..."

"So what, Sally?"

Now, her voice was clearly aggressive.

"A bit harsh," Sally suggested. "Less thoughtful."

"You all seem to agree on that 'fact. Wonderful. So, if Adrian punched my brother in the nose, it's my fault?"

"That's not what I said, but the situation would be easier if you..."

"What situation?"

Sally took a long breath.

"We should take some time to discuss this. I have lots of other things to tell you, Zoey. About that and about Matthew Ziegler and..."

"What, Matthew Ziegler?" barked Zoey, worked up.

"You see—it's impossible to..."

"To what, Sally?"

"To talk to you!" she said without any hesitation.

"And, really, I can't do this anymore!"

It was her turn to disappear and Zoey was really alone this time, in the hallway full of music and laughing guests.

19
INCORPORATE THE SUGAR

Zoey collapsed into the wrought iron chair across from Gabriella and her sister Elena. They were both taking advantage of the afternoon sun. She had just returned from wandering around the neighborhood. On her way back, she didn't have the heart to face the solitude of Sunday alone in her apartment. She felt as deprived and empty as she had during the break up with Spencer.

Gabriella was wearing a pretty blue cotton dress. Next to her, Elena looked like her twin—thinner and not pregnant, of course, and also quite a bit younger. She'd gathered her black hair together under a red scarf and was sipping orange juice through a straw. With her cropped pants and sleeveless shirt showing a tattoo on her bicep, she looked like she'd just stepped out of *Grease*.

"So, if I understand correctly," Gabriella continued, "in two weeks, you've lost a phenomenal lover, fought with your brother and your best friend…"

"They picked fights with me!" Zoey corrected. Gabriella smiled.

"It always takes two. When I argue with Orlando, I always come up against an adversary who has sharpened his knives and who's waiting for the first shot across the bow. I often cause the argument because, in my heart, I know I've done something that he won't like."

"Once, we had a fight too," Elena interrupted.

"Once?!" Zoey exclaimed. "I should have had a sister! Dalton and I have had too many fights to count."

"It's just because I'm an excellent big sister," Gabriella stated.

"And also because we're five years apart," Elena added. "You and Dalton are very close in age. I noticed that when that's the case, brothers and sisters are very close and that makes it hard for them to communicate normally."

Zoey had to concede that her analysis had some truth to it. She and Dalton had developed a relationship that Nana sometimes called twin-like. The fact that Elena was studying psychology seemed useful to her for once.

"I also had a falling out with Sally, I think."

"You think?"

"We worked together the day after Cass's party and that's it. She hasn't called me the whole week."

"She didn't come to work?"

"She always takes a few days off in July. After the first two weeks, things always calm down until the end of August. She'll be back for the Welleba-Richardson wedding. I'm not sure that I'm ready to see her again considering the circumstances. It's been twice in two weeks that we've been cool to each other. And I swear, I'm making an effort!"

"Do you think that maybe you should call her?" Gabriella asked. "A best friend is easier to call than an inconsiderate lover. I also think that you should ask Matthew for an explanation."

"Never!" Zoey exclaimed fiercely.

"What I've seen of him does not correspond to what you describe."

"You saw him for five minutes on the patio."

"I saw him wait for you for two hours, Zoey! And I saw how he looked at you. He acted like someone in love."

This perspective gave her a fleeting satisfaction, but she decided that this positive thought was too hard to hold onto against the torrent of anger that's Matthew's behavior had provoked.

"He acted like a guy who was on the make," she glowered.

The two sisters exchanged a knowing look that reminded her, a bit cruelly perhaps, of the connection that she shared with brother.

"A guy who's only on the make does not humiliate himself in public, especially when he is as attractive as this Matthew is," Gabriella said.

"You can take it or leave it, Zoey, but here's my advice," Elena intervened. "If I were you, I'd call everyone and try to clear up what seems like a series of misunderstandings. Maybe, actually, Adrian is in love with you, and maybe Matthew was simply consoling a woman that he obviously left for you."

"By letting her put her tongue in his ear? Very kind of him, actually!"

Elena started laughing.

"Did you really see her put her tongue in his ear?"

Zoey wasn't sure, but she had every intention of believing it, to support the scenario that she'd been focusing on for a week.

"Adrian is not in love with me. How do you explain that he went crazy with rage when he saw Dalton flirting with Marianita?"

"I think that he and Dalton were settling an old score," Elena said. "When someone becomes violent, especially if, like you say, Adrian has never done that before, it means that they've exhausted all other means of communication. Maybe Dalton is a sort of brake against what Adrian feels for you. The brother, you know, that Adrian always was for you, don't you think?"

Zoey bit her lip.

"Actually, he was violent one other time, with Jon, one of my first boyfriends."

Elena made a satisfied sound.

"And you say that everything's been resolved between you two? The first boyfriend, the brother... It's all very ambiguous."

"Do you mean that Dalton is a surrogate?

In Adrian's mind?" Zoey continued.

Gabriella burst out laughing.

"You're taking your analysis a bit too far, Elena. Sometimes, things are less complicated than what we find in a psychology book. Dalton and Adrian are also very good friends, right?"

"Yes," Zoey replied. "They're not as close as Adrian and I are, but they are close."

"Call your brother—that's even easier."

And then, depending on what he says, call Adrian.

"Adrian is very attractive," Elena noted, playing dreamily with her straw. "You've never considered it?"

"Oh God no!" Zoey shrieked, making the two sisters laugh more.

"He seems like a good catch to me," Gabriella replied. "I've always liked the silent type."

"Silent—Adrian? He hasn't been like that for years!"

"When I saw him the other day..."

Gabriella stopped suddenly and stared at Zoey, open-mouthed.

"When did you see him? What?"

"I promised him I wouldn't say anything," Gabriella murmured, blushing violently.

"You've already said too much. Where did you see him and why did you promise not to tell me?"

"Do you promise me that you won't repeat it?" Gabriella asked pleading.

"I promise. So?"

"The night when you left with Matthew, Adrian came to the restaurant. Well, he walked by and asked us if we'd seen you. I said you had just left with a friend. I didn't tell him about Matthew, I swear! But, he looked up at your apartment and he saw the light. He seemed very disappointed. He asked me not to mention it you and he didn't even say goodbye."

183

Zoey sighed.

"A missed opportunity," added Elena to relieve some of the awkwardness that had descended on the table. "Call him."

"I don't know," Zoey said. "He's become so distant. He doesn't tell me anything anymore."

"And what about you?" asked Gabriella kindly. "Have you told him about Matthew?"

"No."

Actually, she was the one who had started pulling away from him. Even if it wasn't totally her fault. She hadn't been able to talk to him since they woke up together in her bed the day after her parents' anniversary party.

"And have you told Dalton?"

"Dalton? I don't talk to my brother about who I sleep with!"

"I tell Gabriella everything," Elena pointed out.

"She certainly does!" Gabriella agreed. "Most of the time, I have to stop myself from sending her off to the crazy house!"

Zoey and Elena laughed at her sincere outrage.

Then Zoey felt her phone vibrate at the bottom of her bag. She looked to see who was calling.

"It's Dalton," she announced to the two sisters.

"You see!" Elena declared triumphantly. "Pick it up!"

She stood up to move a few feet away.

"I'm happy to hear your voice, Dalton," she said, greeting him. "I'm sorry."

"Zoey?"

The way her brother's voice sounded set off a loud alarm in her brain.

"Zoey, I'm on the road. I'm coming to get you.

Are you at your place?"

"What's going on?"

"We have to go home."

The alarm became a siren, painful and harsh. Nana. She had seemed so fragile at her birthday party. Zoey let out an internal scream.

Anything but that!

The last thing that her grandmother had said at the dinner came back to her and, now, it seemed to have been prophetic:

"I am going to have you all buried with me, like a Pharaoh!"

"Is it Nana?" she stammered.

Dalton's sigh made her want to let out the scream that was coming up her throat. He wasn't able to reply. A muffled sob reverberated over the phone.

"No, Zoey, it's Mom."

20
FOLD INTO THE BASE

Dalton was sobbing when he arrived in front of Zoey's building and it took him a few minutes to be able to formulate a coherent sentence. Zoey had never seen her brother in such a state. When he had stopped crying in her arms and they had climbed into the car, he tried to explain to her what was going on, his explanation interrupted by sobs.

"They came home from Florida yesterday. Mom said she was tired. Mom, tired! She went to bed before Dad did. During the night, he heard her get up. He thinks she was going to the bathroom. She collapsed in the hallway. It was a stroke. She's in observation. She regained consciousness but can't talk and the doctors say we have to wait. Dad is devastated. He called me from the hospital. Fortunately, Adrian's dad is a doctor. He knew what to do right away."

"Is Nana there?"

"Yes, Dad waited to see what the doctors had to say before he called her at noon."

"She must be sick with worry."

Dalton gave her an indecipherable look. Zoey was naturally very anxious about the idea that her mother might not recover from something as serious as a stroke, but her thoughts were always focused on Nana, above everything else. She couldn't help thinking of the older woman as a mother, more than her own had been, really.

"Yes, she's is sick with worry. But it's Nana.
She's strong. Much stronger than Mom is."

Zoey placed a comforting hand on the back of her brother's neck.

"Mom is invincible, Dalton." She wanted to believe that. She did believe it.

"She's not as strong as you think she is," Dalton murmured. "It seems like she wants to control everything but she often had to be like that with Dad. He doesn't understand anything about what it takes to run a household and he hates being constrained. It wasn't always easy for her to work, take care of two kids, and a husband who was focused on his career."

"Nana helped out a lot."

As soon as the words were out of her mouth, she regretted it. Now was not the time to settle scores.

"You are so wrong," Dalton asserted, but without being unkind. "Obviously, in your opinion, Nana is the most important person in the world. But not to me. I don't share your love of cooking. I have totally different memories than you do, Zoey. It wasn't Nana that nagged me to do my homework, it wasn't Nana that drove me to tennis, it wasn't Nana that helped me get ready for tests in high school. It sure wasn't Nana that stayed up with me and brought me coffee when I studied for the bar. That was Mom. Truthfully, you were shut up in the kitchen with Nana and you didn't see any of that. Or the Sundays she spent helping Dad with the accounting—because you weren't there. You were with Adrian or Nana."

Zoey bent her head down, overcome with emotion. Her brother had never spoken to her like this about their mother or their childhood. Like her, he had been happy to use humor to highlight her faults, but rarely in front of her. Now, as he was confiding in her, images of Fran and Dalton came rushing back.

Fran and Dalton sitting together at the table, when she'd suddenly hear her mother's laugh as she bent over the book her son was reading. She could also see Fran in her tennis outfit, totally "Country Club," waiting for Dalton at the gate, as he dragged his feet to join her. The very specific way he would kiss her jumped to mind—hugging her and kissing her very gently on her forehead, protectively, and tenderly. It was true that they had always had a certain closeness that she'd never been able to share with her mother and that she had developed with her grandmother instead.

Because Mom never knew how to talk to me, she thought.

"Do you want me to drive?" she asked her brother after her rested his head on his hands as he gripped the wheel.

"I'll be fine. We don't want to waste any time."

The trip was a nightmare. Dalton never unclenched his jaw except when, from time to time, he let out a silent sob. They had to stop for coffee and switched drivers since he was having so much trouble focusing on the road.

Zoey was upset with herself for not being as affected as her brother. Her heart was heavy, but she had a certain detachment that allowed her to finish the trip without being too stressed. It was as if she had become someone else. Someone who was calmer and more mature.

186

When they arrived at the hospital, Dalton stopped at the front door.

"I can't do it," he said, putting his hands over his mouth.

"Of course you can, Dalton."

She wrapped her arm around his shoulder and hugged him to her.

"Think about all the times that Mom has been there for you. You're going to do the same for her, okay? She needs you. I'm here for you."

He seemed to recoup a bit and agreed to enter the hospital. A dejected Joe Westwood was sitting in the waiting room on a chair next to his mother-in-law. From what her grandchildren could see, her face was grim. Zoey flung herself into her grandmother's open arms and Dalton hugged his father.

"How is she doing?" Zoey asked.

Her father's mouth trembled as he told them that he had been waiting ever since the Peters had dropped him off at the hospital after calling the ambulance. Adrian had called twice and sent his love.

This moved Zoey. Normally, Adrian would have called her directly.

"Thank you," said Nana's voice, addressing someone behind her.

Zoey turned around. Matthew was standing in front of her, an embarrassed expression on his face and a cup in each hand. He looked at her for a long moment and then held out one cup of coffee to Nana and the other to Joe. She suppressed her surprise. She had other things to do and think about than why Matthew Ziegler was in the waiting room in the same hospital in New Jersey as her mother.

She turned toward her grandmother.

"Dad needs to go home," she said. "He looks exhausted."

"I'll be fine," Joe replied.

"Dad, you're as white as a sheet. Mom needs you. You won't be able to help in this condition. Go back with Nana, please. Dalton and I will take over."

Dalton took up the argument and, five minutes later, they had convinced him. Matthew Ziegler suggested that he accompany them home, and Nana accepted eagerly accepted. She was aware that her son-in-law was too tired to drive.

Zoey and Dalton stayed back, side-by-side on the uncomfortable plastic waiting room chairs. Zoey broke down.

"I spoke to Mom in such a mean way at Nana's birthday party," she said, feeling tears pooling in the corner of her eyes. "If she dies…"

"She is not going to die!" Dalton exclaimed desperately. "Zoey, you weren't any worse than you usually are with Mom. She knows what's important. She'll be happy to see you when she wakes up and I'm sure that you'll be able to tell her how much you love her."

"Do you really think I was being unfair?"

"I never said you were unfair. I just said that, sometimes, you have a hard time imagining that the way you see things is not always the truth. You've always been like that, Zoey."

"I know."

She knew it too well. Her life was like a battle field. In two weeks, she had lost those that she loved the most in the world, and, now, she was going to lose her mother with whom she'd only ever been able to bicker.

"And, could you please explain to me what Tina's boyfriend was doing here?" Dalton asked suddenly.

"He's not Tina's boyfriend."

"Then that makes his presence even weirder."

"I don't know what he was doing here or how he knew about Mom. I slept with him."

Dalton let out a whistle, and for a brief instant, he was once again the rowdy, carefree little brother he'd always been.

"You slept with Tina's boyfriend?"

"I just told you that he's not Tina's boyfriend."

"Was that the same week as Adrian?"

"Dalton. That's not funny and I don't feel like laughing right now." Her brother's face darkened.

"I need to. Since we're spilling our secrets, I'm sleeping with Marianita."

Zoey stared at her brother.

"Since when?"

"Since the evening when I signed my contract."

"That's why Adrian punched you."

"Not exactly. In any case, to be honest, I'm not just sleeping with Marianita. We're a thing. And, it's hard because…"

He looked at her. For a second, he looked exactly as he had when he was four, when something had happened and he came to her for comfort. Zoey couldn't help but notice how handsome her brother was and, aside from the young attorney's arrogance, how sensitive and affectionate he was.

"Because I think she's going to go back to Brazil in two weeks."

He sighed.

"I'm in love with her. If you laugh, I swear I'll make you pay."

"I'm not going to laugh," Zoey said kindly. "I'm so sorry for you."

"Not just for me," Dalton said frowning.

"Doesn't she want to stay here?"

"She can't. She doesn't want to be so far away from her mother. She says she's too fragile. There was some guy who took advantage of her, according to the few things that Marianita told me about it."

Now it was Zoey's turn to frown.

"What about you? Would you join her?"

"In Brazil? I don't even speak Portuguese."

"You can always learn."

"You know how bad I am at languages. In any case, now, it's a moot point. I'm the one who can't leave his mother now. Except..."

He interrupted himself with an unexpected sob. Zoey held him tight. He put his head on her shoulder and cried his eyes out. Strangely enough, her brother's tears soothed her. They stayed like that for a long moment, until his sobs slowly subsided and then stopped.

Matthew came into the waiting room just as Dalton was lifting his head, taking the Kleenex offered by his sister.

"Your father asked me to bring his car back, in case one of you wants to go home, he said, handing the Mercedes keys to Zoey."

She thanked him, begrudgingly.

"Can I help you with anything else?" he asked.

"I'm going to get us some coffee," Dalton said.

"Stay here with Zoey."

"Really, there's no need," Zoey mumbled.

"Yes, there is," Dalton insisted. "I don't want you to be alone if the doctors show up. Thank you, Matthew."

He walked across the room, to the hallway that lead to the elevator. Matthew sat down next to her.

"May I?"

"You already have."

A long silence followed. Zoey was boiling, again. The last person she wanted to see now, in this place was the man who had manipulated and humiliated her.

"I think that, under the circumstances, you should have the decency to leave," she finally exploded.

"Your brother asked me to watch out for you."

"My brother would be better off taking care of himself," Zoey retorted. "Can you tell me exactly what you are doing here?"

Matthew sat up straight in his chair.

"I do not think that this is the time to have that conversation," he replied in that polite way he had.

"Then get out!"

He jumped at her raised voice. His hands tensed, but he was able to stay calm and turn toward her.

"I'll stay till Dalton returns and then I'll leave."

She nodded. Yet again tears were threatening to make their way down her cheeks, flushed from the violent exchange with Matthew and all she was going through. A young doctor with black hair and a sympathetic but angular face appeared in the hallway and approached them.

"Are you Francesca Westwood's children?"

"I am her daughter," Zoey confirmed. "How is she doing?"

"She has fully regained consciousness and she's talking. She's asking for

189

you—for you and your brother."

"Can I see her?"

The young doctor looked truly sorry. This was probably a well-practiced expression he used several times a day, in an almost a tic-like fashion.

"Not now, I'm afraid. She's still at risk and needs to rest quietly. Too much excitement could add more stress."

"Is she out of danger?"

"It's too early to tell, but let's say that we see encouraging signs. Her stroke was transient. You'll be able to see her tomorrow."

"We'd like to stay here overnight if we can."

"There's no reason to do that. If there's any problem, we'll call you. Are you the husband?"

"I'm just a friend," Matthew replied neutrally.

Zoey huffed and moved closer to the doctor to purposely exclude him from the conversation.

"I can assure you that it is fine to go home," the doctor insisted. "The waiting room chairs are uncomfortable. Your mother will need you to be in good shape tomorrow and not too tired. You don't want her to see how worried you've been."

The doctor's words made sense. Zoey had said almost the exact same thing to her father. Dalton came back right then and heard what the doctor was saying. He more easily accepted the doctor's suggestions.

"Can I drop you off at the train station?" Dalton asked Matthew as all three of them left the hospital.

Night had fallen a while ago. It had to be close to midnight.

"I'd like Zoey to take me. We have some things to talk about."

"I'd rather not," Zoey retorted.

"Wait just a second," Dalton said, grabbing his sister by the arm, pulling her aside. "Listen, Zoey. I know absolutely nothing about why you are giving Matthew the cold shoulder or about exactly what's going on between you two. What I do know is that he stayed with Dad and Nana before we got there, and for this, you need to give him the benefit of the doubt."

"So, you're giving me a lecture?" Zoey hissed.

"Yes, I am. It won't hurt you this once. I don't know much about what's happened in your love life since Spencer and I'm glad about that. I have my own problems and don't need to listen to your hysterical complaining."

"Hysterical?"

"You get into a real rage when you want to. In any case, from what I know about you and your...relationship management, you are too quick to blame people. Without listening to what they have to say. That's what you did with Adrian and something tells me that is also at the root of your problems with Sally lately. So, you are going to listen to him until the rail station, and, after that, do what you think is right. Got it?"

"I…"

"Got it?" her brother insisted unsmilingly.

"Yes, I understand," she mumbled.

He hugged her.

"You are a good girl," he said, half mockingly, half affectionately. "And, if you need to get rid of the body, you can count on me."

After thanking Matthew and shaking his hand, he went on his way.

"So," Zoey said, turning toward Matthew.

"I'll drop you off at the rail station."

They climbed into Joe's car.

"I would like to tell you why I was here," he said. "I can assure you up front that it has nothing to do with you. I came to see your grandmother."

"My grandmother?"

"We are working on a project together."

"You are working with my grandmother?" She was flummoxed.

"It was your cousin's idea. I couldn't mention it to you because this type of project requires a certain level of confidentiality. But, under the circumstances…It's better to be able to explain, in this case."

She looked at the almost-empty parking lot, and feeling and suddenly exhausted. She needed air. Joe's car smelled like new leather and she'd always hated that odor. And Matthew's cologne was wafting throughout the car, reminding her how much she had loved breathing it in. She lowered her window.

"I'm helping her select recipes and write the book preface," Matthew continued. "I was having lunch with her, at her house, when your father called. I rode with her in the taxi to the hospital and stayed with them until you and your brother arrived. They were in shock. Your grandmother is an exceptional woman."

"I know, thank you," Zoey replied, her voice tight.

"You are like her. You have her sense of humor and her strength. You are lucky to have both her and your parents. Your mother will recover quickly."

"Are you a doctor?"

He sighed.

"No, I am not a doctor. Zoey, the other evening…"

"This is definitely not the time." She started the car.

"It's never the right time, right?" he murmured.

"If you think that my mother's stroke is not a good enough reason, I don't know what else I can say."

"It's exactly the right time."

"Are you going to give me your speech again about how life is precious, because we could die at any moment? Seriously? You, who just does whatever you want—you are going to pick the day my mother is possibly dying to spill your guts?"

"I don't just do whatever I want," Matthew replied, hurt. "I should have been more open the other night. I understand that my attitude shocked you."

She turned to give him a sharp look.

"It takes more than that to shock me."

"So, explain why you've refused to talk to me."

She was longing to talk to him about Sofia and tell him about all the resentment that she'd built up over the week, but she was also weary from the difficult night she had just had. At the moment, all of this seemed futile and useless.

"You left without saying goodbye to anyone. I thought that with what had happened in the walk-in..."

"It has nothing to do with what happened there," she said flatly. "Well, yes it does. I can't handle this type of relationship."

"Could I ask exactly what type of relationship you mean, exactly?"

"The type you have with Sofia Alves."

He bent his head down, toward his hands, murmuring softly. When he lifted it back up, his expression was one of fatigue and he looked almost lost.

"Yes, that's true—you and I do not have that type of relationship."

"You admit it. Perfect."

Her hands tightened on the steering wheel in a cold rage.

"What else could I do? I'm not sure what you are thinking."

"Please explain it to me."

"I already told you that that's impossible. It's not my place."

"Because you took advantage of her, right?"

"Because I what?"

He grunted in anger.

"Marianita told my brother that there was a man who'd taken advantage of her."

Matthew gritted his teeth.

"Marianita needs to learn to ask for forgiveness. I simply cannot talk to you about it. I'm asking you to trust me."

Zoey cackled cruelly.

"Trust you? Why should I? "

"Because you have continually pushed me away and I have come back each time."

"That's your problem, not mine."

His nostrils flared and Zoey couldn't tell if he was angry or disgusted. In any case, she'd never seen him do that before. In a quick motion, he opened the car door and got out.

"I'll figure out how to get back. I do not want to subject you to my presence any longer."

"Don't be ridiculous. It's past midnight and you'll never find a taxi at this hour in this town."

"That's my problem, not yours."

He slammed the door. Apparently, he did have feelings sometimes and didn't always do what he wanted.

21
COMBINE VERY GENTLY

Zoey slept very little. At six o'clock in the morning, after going back to bed but failing to shut her eyes, she went down to the kitchen and found Dalton there, looking haggard and drinking cold coffee. He had given his bed to his grandmother and had spent the night as restlessly as Zoey, on the living room coach.

"Do you want me to make you another one?" she asked, taking the cup from her brother.

"Just put it in the microwave," Dalton replied.

Even if Mom would kill us if she found out.

She realized that he'd been thinking about their mother all night and felt ashamed. In her insomnia, she kept thinking about her discussion with Matthew. It had played on a loop in her head, adding in the things she hadn't had the presence of mind to say to him.

"The hospital had not called. She's getting better, I'm sure of it," she said, tossing the coffee in the sink, moving toward the espresso machine. "Were you able to sleep?"

"No. I was on the phone till four in the morning with Marianita and I couldn't fall asleep afterward."

"Oh?"

Dalton smiled weakly.

"I think she's in love too."

"That's wonderful," Zoey replied, feeling emotional.

"You know, she freaked out when I said that Matthew was there. I think she was implying that Matthew is the guy who'd led her mother on."

"I know," Zoey sighed.

She focused on replacing the filter so that Dalton couldn't see her face.

"I don't believe it," Dalton replied. "She wasn't very clear about it. She seemed overwhelmed and was speaking in Portuguese half the time. But did you talk about it?"

"Yes, we talked about it. But nothing was resolved."

"Do you like this guy, Zoey?"

She positioned the cup and turned the machine on, giving her some time to decide how to reply. It would have been easy to lie to Dalton, which she did anyway when her romantic liaisons were involved.

She'd told enough lies.

She had enough of all these stories, misunderstandings, friends who weren't talking and who were growing farther apart. But, mainly, she was done hiding her feelings under the disguise of being "free" when that had really only been a way to protect herself. What she had criticized about Adrian also applied to her. She missed him terribly. If he'd been here, she could have put her head on this shoulder and listened to him talk nonsense to distract her.

She suppressed an exhausted sigh. It wasn't Adrian's shoulder that she missed, it was Matthew's. She didn't want to laugh or think about anything else. At this exact moment, she needed someone to take her in their arms and tell her that everything would be all right.

"Yes," she exhaled. "Yes, I like him."

She put the full cup in front of her brother and looked him in the eye.

"I really like him," she repeated, close to tears.

Dalton smiled at her.

"So, you really don't care if he's been with other women. Tell him."

"You told me to be good, right? I wouldn't be. Good girls like honest men."

"You know the expression, Zoey, right? Good girls go to heaven and bad girls go where they want."

"About that, if I talk to Matthew, will you ask Marianita to stay?"

Dalton drank a sip of coffee as he thought about it. She felt a surge of tenderness toward him. They were so alike.

"It's a deal!" he replied. "I tell Marianita that she's the woman of my dreams and you tell her stepfather that you have feelings for him."

"He's not her stepfather, Dalton."

"Technically, almost."

"Technically, you are a creep."

Dalton laughed.

"Then, in this new spirit of getting your relationships back on track, call Sally and apologize."

"And will you call Adrian?"

Dalton cleared his throat.

"It's more complicated than that."

"Because you had a fight? Is there some macho thing stopping you from making the first move?"

"I can't say any more about it."

Zoey walked over to pick up her coffee and sat back down, skeptical.

"It's crazy the number of people who can't give me the information that would help us resolve our differences."

"It's a secret, that's all."

"You have secrets with Adrian that you keep from me? Great."

Dalton laughed again, silently this time.

"Here's what I suggest," he said, setting the cup down. "You call Sally, then you call Adrian, and then I'll call him. If I'm still alive."

"What do you mean, if you're still alive?"

"Because, when you know the rest of the story, I'm sure you are going to shoot me," he replied, grimacing.

He seemed so impish, like when they were kids, and it made her feel so sentimental that she forgot her troubles and smiled back at him.

22

SMOOTH TOP

Zoey was the last one to go into her mother's room. Dalton was already in Fran's arms, crying hot tears even though the doctor had said to avoid exciting her. Pale but with every hair in place, propped up on pillows, Fran Westwood didn't seem too stressed out by the noisy demonstration her son was putting on. In fact, it seemed to Zoey that she reveled in it.

"I see you're on your second wind," Nana teased, accepting the chair that her son-in-law pulled close to the bed for her.

Fran didn't say anything but smiled wanly at her mother. Zoey hugged her and stood behind her grandmother. She answered their questions, and after a while, Fran asked Joe and Dalton to leave.

"I need to talk to Zoey and Nana," she said, very politely, which caused some dismay from her husband and son.

But, they left together, a worried silence hanging over them.

"Well," Nana said. "The reckoning is nigh."

"Don't start, Mother. Zoey, the evening of your grandmother's birthday, you were very hard on me. More than usual, actually. I was shocked and I am pretty sure that my accident last night was a result of that evening."

"I caused the stroke?!" Zoey gasped, turning pale.

"In part, yes."

Zoey's hands gripped the back of the chair, so hard that her knuckles turned white and it was painful.

"I refuse to listen to this."

"You are going to listen to me, however. Once again, you resented me for not having taken care of you when you were little and you're convinced that that's the reason we are not as close as you'd like."

"I'm very happy with the relationship we have," Zoey said, her jaw tight.

"We couldn't do any better, considering how different we are."

"What differences?" Fran demanded. "You are stubborn and incapable of expressing your feelings. Just two of the things you have in common with me."

She had obviously tried to soften her tone, but in vain.

"Uh huh. I thought I was a carbon copy of my grandfather."

"I'm like him too. Last night, when I had the stroke, I was able to see what was really important to me. Since then, all alone in this awful room, I've been thinking. Do you know what I saw, Zoey, just before I passed out?"

"No."

"I saw you and your brother."

"I think I'll leave you two," Nana commented as she pushed on the armrest to stand.

"No, Mother, you stay. I have things to say to you too."

"Is that an order?"

The challenge made her voice tremble. This made Zoey cringe, like any time Nana lost her temper, but Fran, took no heed.

"Yes. You won't live forever either. I don't plan on dying tomorrow and you are probably going to leave this earth before I do. And that's not going to happen before you listen to everything that's in my heart."

Against expectations and despite her testy countenance, Nana sat back down.

"I also need you to confirm some things as well. Zoey, I had you very young, and, even though you father and I were very happy, it wasn't the right time. Your father had just started his career and I hadn't had time to experience life with him. Your birth was very difficult. Your brother was less problematic on that front."

"Obviously," Zoey commented, rolling her eyes.

"Your brother didn't weigh 10 pounds," Fran continued. "I'll skip all the details about this joyous occasion—you'll discover it on your own you decide to have children one day. In any case, I was not at all ready to be a mother and even less to be a mother like I'd had, always there to serve her husband and children. Nana was thrilled to have a granddaughter and started to take care of you like she had done for us. Better, even. Am I wrong, Mother?"

"No, you're not wrong, Nana said quietly. I was in love with Zoey from the beginning. More than Tina or even Dalton."

"You really have a talent for remembering what you want to remember," Fran laughed, but with some bitterness. "You were not only motivated by love, believe me. Everything that you hadn't been able to give us, you gave it to Zoey on a silver platter."

"You and your sister never wanted for anything," Nana retorted.

"Yes, that's true. We had the best teachers, the most beautiful clothes, but, Zoey, you got the rest. If you messed up, or did something silly, Nana was there to encourage you or forgive you."

"What exactly are you trying to say, Francesca?" Nana asked, an unwavering eye focused on her daughter.

"I want to tell Zoey that if I didn't live up to my responsibilities as her mother, it's because she didn't need me. Love, teaching her what was right or wrong, providing comfort—everything a mother should give her children, she always got from you."

"I don't understand why you are angry with Nana," Zoey interrupted.

Fran suddenly seemed sad.

Zoey didn't know whether she should be worried or happy to see something other than indignation on her mother's face.

"I'm not angry with Nana," she replied gently. "For a longtime, I blamed myself for many things. For not having spent more time with you, for not having just had babysitters instead, which would have preserved my place in your eyes as more important than the person who took care of you during the day."

She fell silent. Zoey moved closer to her grandmother. Nana looked at her daughter coldly. Then the harshness slowly disappeared and she didn't fight the tiny tears making an appearance.

"I'm overwhelmed, Francesca," she replied, in a voice cracking with emotion. "You are right. In one way, I stole Zoey from you."

She broke off, but Zoey didn't dare intervene—trying to defend her grandmother would only make things worse.

"I had to make up for lost time," Nana continued. "I know that I was hard on your sister and you. But I wanted to make sure you were successful. When my books were a hit, I realized what a wonderful opportunity they had brought me. Independence. Not that your father was a tyrant—no, he was the opposite. But he was of a different generation than you and Joe. He would never have allowed me to work outside the home, and he provided well for us. At the time, I never felt that I was giving you up: I was able to offer you the life I'd never had. I made things easier for you."

Zoey watched her mother. Tears were running down her cheeks and trickling into her ear.

"You did," Fran murmured..

"Yes, but it made you rigid and hungry for freedom. When Zoey was born, I was selfish. I had another chance. It wasn't difficult. Zoey was an easy child."

"An easy child?" Zoey murmured. "I thought I was a terrible devil."

"You were only a little devil with your mother," Nana said. "Because I spoiled you. You liked what I liked, and, it's true, I liked making your mom mad. She was cold toward me, unlike her sister who was always more

201

malleable. With Dalton, things evened out a bit, because I didn't know how to take care of him. He had way more energy than you and he could never make anything but mud in the kitchen. But you—you had talent! I've made a real mess."

A flicker of admiration passed furtively over her eyes filling with tears.

"No!" Fran asserted in her most authoritative voice. "You did a wonderful job with Zoey."

Zoey looked at her mother intently. It was the first time her mother had complimented her, and so spontaneously.

"I don't want to place blame," Fran added. "Not now. I was so scared. Zoey, you are a funny and pretty young woman, despite your eccentric hairstyles and your poor taste in athletic shoes. You are talented, like your grandmother said, and you run your business better than your grandmother or I could have done. And it's thanks to Nana. I'm just sorry that I was not able to see all that before."

"It's also thanks to you," Nana said. "You didn't give up fighting against the terrible ego that I created in this child."

She laughed thinly.

"I do not have a big ego!" Zoey cried.

"Yes, you do!" Fran and Nana replied in unison.

They had the same tone in their voice and, for just a moment, the same amused grin. They were also very alike. Obviously, such humor and authority had been passed down from generation to generation.

"I don't have any self-confidence," Zoey said defensively.

"Don't confuse ego and self-confidence," Nana said. "Without your mother's influence, you would be a bossy little person, in love with herself, because I wasn't strict enough and was too taken with your talent."

"You're ganging up on me!" Zoey complained.

She took a certain satisfaction from that. Seeing her mother and her grandmother getting a long for once lifted a weight from her chest. She had to have suffered from their implicit disagreements as a child, and may have even felt conflicted in her loyalty.

"I'm happy that we were able to address all of this," Fran said. "Zoey, now go find your father and brother. I'm sure that they think we've killed each other. I need to talk to Nana a bit still."

Zoey smiled at her mother. Without warning, she bent down and hugged her.

"Don't mess up my hair!" her mother cried, pushing her away.

She smiled too.

"I don't want to look like a sick person. You know your father—this has been very hard on him."

Zoey nodded and, after hugging Nana, went to find Joe and Dalton in the waiting room.

Seeing their terrified expressions, she knew her mother had been right. They'd imagined the worst. She sat between them.

"Were you nice to your mother, Zoey?" Joe asked.

"As nice as Nana was," she replied.

He grimaced.

"I'm kidding, Dad," she added. "It was Mom who was nice to me."

Joe let out a surprised gasp.

"She must have really had a shock," Dalton murmured.

"I think we all have," Zoey whispered. "I'm not sure I'll be able to get over it."

"You're a good girl," Joe said, putting his arm around her neck. "You've always been a good girl."

"I keep telling her that," Dalton added. Then, he leaned down toward his sister's ear.

"But you know where bad girls go, right, Zoey?

"Dalton!

"Yes?"

"You are a good person too! But…"

"But?"

"You can be extremely annoying."

She punched him in the bicep and, for once, he didn't respond.

23
ADJUST THE HEAT

Zoey decided to stay at her parents' house until her mother returned from the hospital. Her effort was commendable, but the result was less successful than she'd imagined. Her lack of housekeeping skills prevented her from keeping up the house like Fran would have liked. Fortunately, Dalton's efficiency compensated for the ease with which Joe and Zoey never put things where they belonged or simply lost them.

Fran Westwood was able to come home to a clean, welcoming house. In her wheelchair, she seemed like the queen mother visiting her subjects, a role that Nana did not give up without a fight, commenting that Fran should think about how to make the house handicap accessible. Zoey noticed that her mother had returned to full form with the zinging responses she gave to her own mother.

Everything was back to normal.

She tried to pay specific but discrete attention to Fran, even preparing balanced meals for her with the steamer, without adding any personal touches.

When she brought her some tea on the veranda next to the living room, Fran held her back.

"I'd like to hire a landscaper to update the garden a bit," she told her. "What do you think, Zoey?"

Zoey appreciated that her mother was involving her in the project, even if it was more for the principle than for her actual thoughts on it.

"As long as they don't touch the treehouse, that seems like a good idea," Zoey replied.

She could see part of the infamous treehouse where she had so often taken refuge.

"That treehouse," Fran murmured, "you got into so much mischief there."

"Not that much," Zoey countered.

"If you think that I don't know what you all were doing in there when you were teenagers! Not to mention Dalton. I am not naive, Zoey. Teenagers around the world hide in their childhood treehouses to kiss each other. And they continue to do so later."

"What do you mean?"

"Nothing," Fran replied mysteriously. "I'm happy that your brother is in a relationship."

"You know about that?"

Fran lifted her perfectly made-up face toward her daughter.

"Dalton tells me many things," she commented, evenly. "I'm his mother. Really, a Brazilian. I was wondering if she was your assistant. She's very pretty, even if she does share your penchant for wild hair."

"Sally and Dalton..."

"There's no future in that, I know."

"Excuse me?"

Fran sighed dramatically.

"One day, I'll die of shame from all your brother's antics."

Zoey noted with a certain satisfaction that the dear Dalton had lost his place as the favorite child, probably because he would one day leave to live in Brazil, depriving Fran of access to the precious grandchildren that she coveted, according to her.

"The night of our wedding anniversary party. With Sally, in the treehouse! I don't know where he got the womanizer gene from. Fortunately, your father didn't know what was going on! You know he's old school."

"Sally and Dalton?"

Zoey was completely blindsided.

"They just kissed. Thank God that you and Adrian interrupted them."

She didn't remember seeing Dalton and Sally in the treehouse, kissing or not. She just remembered trying to climb the ladder.

"How do you know all this? Did Dalton tell you?"

"Zoey, my bedroom looks directly into the treehouse window. You all really take me for an imbecile." Zoey didn't reply. Sally and Dalton. And she and Adrian had interrupted them. Adrian.

"What an idiot!" she exclaimed.

"Excuse me?" Fran replied sharply.

"Not you, Mom! Me! It was there, right in front me! Thank you!"

She jumped up to hug her mother.

"Don't mess up my hair," Fran frowned. "Where are you going like that? And why are you thanking me?"

"To the Peters' house! Tell Dalton to get his butt over there when he gets back."

"Zoey, your language!"

"Sorry, Mom! I'll explain later! She ran out of the house."

24
BAKE

Sally was dancing from one foot to another in the Westwood's living room. She was watching Zoey and Fran Westwood like she didn't know what to say or do. She had made an effort to dress nicely to come to the her friend's parents' house, even if, for Fran's taste, her pale green sweater contrasted too harshly with the citrus pink dress she was wearing. Fran simply raised an eyebrow and gave her most polite smile.

They exchanged banalities about Fran's health and recovery till they saw Dalton walk past the patio door and gave the thumbs up sign.

"Come with me," Zoey said, taking Sally's hand and leading her toward the front door.

"Can you explain what's going on?"

"No. You have to trust me, Sally.

I'm your best friend, you know."

"Sometimes, I wonder," Sally whined. "You have been pretty difficult lately. You hurt me."

"I'm so sorry. I didn't mean to do that. But, I have some good news for you. I received the quote from Cybil Green that you did a brilliant job of negotiating, and I totally agree that we need these new photos. When we get back to work, I'll set up a tasting for the blogging community. We could call it 'Marvelous Lunch.'"

Sally's expression told her that she would not be put in charge of coming up with a name or promoting the event. Sally's face broke out in a happy smile.

"Can I promote it on social media?"

"Obviously."

"Okay! You're still my best friend and not a bad boss."

Zoey laughed.

"In exchange, I need you to do me a favor."

"Yes?" Sally replied distrustfully.

"Follow me without asking any questions."

Sally nodded. She did follow her, to the treehouse and up the ladder. Zoey smiled, satisfied as she saw the results of her work. She had cleaned the treehouse and, with some regret, thrown out the old sofa that had always been there. With Dalton's help, she had added a fresh coat of paint to the walls. The white lanterns from her parents' party added a Bohemian elegance. Sitting on a new sofa of an exquisite sky blue, Adrian was waiting, and he seemed as suspicious as Sally had a few minutes earlier.

"Sally, I'd like you to meet Adrian."

Sally's cheeks flushed when she saw him, and he coughed, embarrassed.

"He's my best guy friend," Zoey added. "Sometimes, he's a bit too sarcastic, but I don't know anyone who is more concerned about others than he is."

"This is not funny, Zoey," Adrian interrupted.

"Adrian, make an effort."

"It was unfair to go through my mother to make me come here."

"It's clear that he doesn't want to be here," Sally said, in a small voice.

Zoey ignored them.

"Adrian, I'd like you to meet Sally. She is also my best friend. We have many things in common, and one of these is a certain mistrust of men. That being said, I don't think she's as bad as I am."

"What's your game?" Adrian demanded, without daring to look at Sally.

"I'm not playing," Zoey asserted. "I'm putting things back where they belong and I'm fixing my mistakes. Sally, I think Adrian has a thing for you."

Adrian unclenched his teeth to let out an ironic whistle.

"We are not in elementary school," he said. "Does the word "intrusive" mean anything to you?"

Without listening, Zoey replied, "Sally, Adrian deserves a chance and also that you see him as more than a good friend to party with."

"You are the most hideous fairy godmother that I have ever seen in my life," Adrian retorted.

Sally didn't say a word, watching them, back and forth, self-conscious.

"It would be good for both of you to get to know each other. Sally, please, just one date?"

Her friend made a strangled sound. She looked like a mouse caught in a trap by a mad scientist.

"It's an interesting idea," Adrian added, a smile on his lips. "It's true, Sally, maybe we should go to a restaurant together."

The tone of his voice was dangerously mocking. Zoey wanted to stop him, but it was too late. Adrian eyes flashed with derision.

"Afterward, I could, how do you say it again? Do the nasty?"

"Oh my God," Sally gasped, raising her eyebrows.

"Oh my God!" Zoey repeated. Adrian! That is definitely not..."

"Definitely not what?" he growled, maliciously. "Romantic? Appropriate? Do you know what your friend's idea of romantic is? Sending a text when she wants me to come over."

"You have a funny way of rewriting history," Sally interrupted.

"You've been sleeping together?" Zoey exclaimed. They looked at her with pity.

"From time to time," Sally whispered in a very small voice.

"For how long?" Her voice had become shrill. She couldn't believe that they had lied to her, or, more precisely, that they had not informed her of such an unexpected turn of events.

"Several months," Adrian said. "Ask Sally, she's the one that keeps the schedule."

"Of course," Sally retorted. "The cruel, heartless Sally who uses men for sex. You're forgetting part of the story, Adrian. The part where we couldn't tell Zoey that we were sleeping together because you were too afraid of her reaction. When did you ask me to do that, again? After the first time, right? How did you think that would make me feel?"

"I don't see how being up front was problematic for us," Adrian murmured guiltily.

"But the fact that you are in love with my best friend, that's a problem," Sally replied.

Adrian stared at her for a second, his face tense.

"I am not in love with Zoey."

"I can confirm that," Zoey added.

"We really couldn't care less about your thoughts on this," he hissed. "If I were in love with Zoey, Sally, forgive me, but I would not have not slept with you."

"Are you staying it was a mistake?"

"That is absolutely not what I said. But, think what you want."

He turned away and retreated into a sulky silence.

"This is completely ridiculous," Zoey said. "Sally, if you still have doubts, tell me why Adrian reacted like that after surprising you and Dalton in the treehouse."

"Because you know about that?" Sally yelled looking at Adrian, ready to blame him.

"Adrian had nothing to do with that. My mother told me."

"Oh, perfect," Sally moaned.

She was dying of shame.

"Adrian was jealous," Zoey said, before turning toward him. "That's

211

why you punched, Dalton, isn't it? Because you saw them in the treehouse."

Adrian shrugged his shoulders, obviously indifferent to her desperate efforts.

"Best night of my life. First, you tell me that crap in the kitchen and then I witness a passionate kiss between Sally and your brother."

"What crap?"

"Nothing worth repeating," Sally urgently whispered.

"No, wait, Sally. I need to know," Zoey said, interrupting her. "What did I say?"

"You said that you would never speak to us again if something was going on between us."

"What? I said it like that?"

"No," Adrian admitted. "There was a specific context. Not very smart, considering the context and our blood alcohol levels. But you did say it and Sally took you at your word."

"I wasn't sure how I felt about Adrian," Sally stammered, frowning.

"You believed me?" Zoey cried. "I was drunk."

They turned toward each other, embarrassed, each waiting for the other to have the courage to say something.

"You were both that scared of me?" Zoey asked.

She regretted the question—she could see the response in their eyes.

"Forget that. I will still speak to you if you are together. Truthfully, I'd be happy about it, unless you make out in front of me."

"There's no worries there," Adrian said, standing up.

"Adrian, please. I know you don't like the idea of being part of a couple but…"

He lifted his head and stared at her, defiant.

"I'm not the one who had a problem with that, Zoey. In the beginning, maybe a bit. But not afterward. It's that Sally did everything she could to push me away, telling me over and over that I was just a friend with benefits. And, you were wrong, Sally. You meant to say I was your sex toy. Even though it might be hard for you to put both me and Dalton side by side in your dresser drawer. "

"Don't be so mean," Sally murmured.

She seemed close to tears. Zoey, on the other hand, was picturing Adrian and her brother, next to each other in a huge dresser drawer, like two dolls. She would have preferred to keep her mind focused on the conversation.

"I did not sleep with Dalton," she continued. "Zoey's comment bugged me and you were laughing like crazy. You seemed so close. I was jealous and Dalton, well, he's Dalton."

"No need to go into all the details," Zoey muttered as she kept trying to push this disturbing image out of her head.

"Let's just say that I spent the evening hoping to have a moment alone with you," Adrian said.

It was exceedingly difficult for him to say just these few words. Sally let out an exasperated gasp.

"You spent the evening drinking with Zoey," she countered, her cheeks flushed. "I had no idea that you wanted to do anything else."

"You were the one who kept talking about the contract," Adrian cried.

The contract. The night when they were drinking at the Rain Law Room and he had mentioned that ridiculous contract, he was talking about the contract with Sally, not the one from when they were teenagers, which wasn't bad in and of itself. She felt stupid. She had believed that Adrian had had feelings for her. She hadn't been able to see the signals that he was sending to someone else, her best friend. In front of her, Adrian and Sally continued to bicker.

She tried to move discretely toward the treehouse trap door.

Adrian held his arm out in her direction, without looking her way.

"You stay here. With you in the room, maybe Sally won't take off."

"I'm not taking off."

"I'd really like to," Zoey sighed.

But, she stayed there, standing, as they looked at her defiantly, facing off against each other. It was the worst dumpster fire relationship counseling session she'd ever seen in her life and she wondered if she had discovered a new reality TV concept. She'd call it "The Treehouse" even if the treehouse made her think more of that creepy scene from *The Blair Witch Project* than a TV show for suburban housewives.

Sally crossed her arms across her chest.

"So. I did mention a contract."

Adrian let out triumphant cry.

"A contract stating that we were non-exclusive and which I was ready to accept. Except that, you had to go and kiss my best friend from childhood."

"My brother," incidentally, added Zoey.

"I was worried there for a moment!" Sally cried.

"Nice excuse!" spat Adrian. "I also feel that way—when I panic, I also have an irresistible urge to stick my tongue in someone else's mouth."

"I don't want to hear this part of the conversation," Zoey mumbled. Adrian turned toward her.

"Is there a specific word that is causing a problem for you, Zoey? Have you suddenly become pure and innocent?"

"Adrian is not wrong," Sally sighed. "You don't like that I kissed your brother, but, if I recall correctly, you slept with my guy."

Adrian and Zoey both turned to look at her.

"Because, then, I was your guy?" Adrian blushed.

"Yes," she asserted, evenly.

213

Zoey couldn't believe her ears. She was wrinkling her nose and frowning, as if she were trying to suppress hysterical laughter.

"You are the most complicated person on earth!" Adrian roared. "You are even more annoying than Zoey! And she sets the bar high!"

"Hey, stop dumping on me! I'm not involved at all, for once."

"Well, yes, you are. You should know that we didn't sleep together that night at your parents' house. Are you happy, Sally?"

"You are free to do whatever you want," Sally asserted, her arms still crossed.

Adrian threw up his hands, exasperated.

"You could have told me before," Zoey murmured.

"Really, Zoey, if you were me, you would have planted a doubt just to drive me crazy too. And, of course, it made Sally uncomfortable too, I think."

"You used me to make her jealous. That is disgusting, Adrian," Zoey cried, thinking back to the scene in the pickup.

She remembered how poised Sally had been when Adrian went off with his vulgar allusions, and specifically when just she and Sally had talked about it, right before they had arrived at the shop. Her friend hadn't shown the least bit of discomfort, no emotion at all, actually.

"You did the same thing to me to get Stan Meyer's attention," Adrian objected.

"We were six years old!"

"It was still hurt," Adrian emphasized.

"Well," Sally huffed. "I would love to stay and listen to your walk down memory lane but I think that I've had my fill of revelations for the day."

"Look, she's ready to run off again," Adrian spit out.

Now he crossed his arms across his chest and jutted out his chin, in a motion that was both angry and disdainful.

"This is enough!" Zoey cried. "Sally, you are going to tell me the truth. Are you in love with Adrian, yes or no?"

"Don't answer that," Adrian interjected.

"That would be interesting to know," Sally responded, with a mocking smile. "First of all, I don't even know what that means. Secondly, I can't stand the jealous type and I hate the violent type even more. Or guys who are incapable of expressing their feelings. Or their non-feelings. Really, it's easy to say that all of this is my fault! Adrian has never shown the slightest interest in me outside the bedroom. The only thing that was important to him was what you would think about it."

"You already said that," Zoey murmured.

"Maybe because it is important? For him to even speak to me, you had to bring him here."

"I had to bring you here, too," Zoey replied.

"That's different. I don't want a man who can't tell me his opinion on anything without first asking his best friend."

Now it was Zoey's turn to roll her eyes. Sally didn't make any decision of her own without first talking to Zoey.

"That's what friends are for," she remarked. "Adrian never talks to me about his personal life."

"Nothing to talk about!" Sally said sarcastically. "He's happy to just do what you say on everything."

"I have had enough!" Adrian explained, offended. "I certainly do not need Zoey to tell me what I think about you."

"I'm just dying to know," Sally frowned and said bitterly.

Adrian regarded her intensely then took a long breath.

"First of all, it's true that I didn't really want to have to define what we had between us. Contracts and definitions—that's not my thing, it's yours."

Sally didn't reply.

"I'm also not as easy going and self-confidence as Dalton. Before I saw you kiss him, I didn't even know if I was in love with you, if you want to know the truth."

Zoey looked at Sally. It seemed to her that her friend let the facade slip for a moment. She'd been using so much energy to keep up.

"It's actually the last thing I wanted to be, considering the way you were treating me."

"I never mistreated you."

"Only if we consider that you never let me stay the night at your house, though that never kept you from falling asleep in my arms."

"All this is getting embarrassing," Zoey said frowning.

Adrian ignored her and continued his onslaught:

"Do you know what you do when you sleep, Sally? You can't stand having any hair touch your neck and you put your hand behind your ear, like a cat primping."

"I do not do that," Sally said softly.

"Yes, you do. You may not want a man who doesn't know how to make a decision on his own, but I certainly don't want a woman who does the most adorable thing on earth when she's in my arms and then pushes me aside like a piece of garbage the rest of the time."

"Nobody wants anybody then," Sally concluded.

Her eyes filled with tears.

"That's correct," Adrian confirmed.

His face took on his usual expression, mocking and detached.

"I do want you—if you'd let me stay the night with you."

"Another contract? I thought you didn't like that sort of thing."

"Take it or leave it." Sally lowered her head.

"No one says 'I want you,'" she murmured. "It's condescending. I am not begging you."

"I can do that if you'd like," Adrian replied. "Even in front of Zoey."

"Please, no," Zoey groaned, having reached her maximum level of embarrassment.

"If I want you, do you promise to stop hiding your feelings from me?" Sally asked gently.

"I will try."

"Is it that hard?"

Adrian let out a bitter laugh.

"I'd like to you remind you that the only woman I have had longer than a two-hour relationship with is your idiot friend. Not the best role model to teach me how to express my feelings."

"You have a point," Sally admitted, winking at Zoey who was now about to scream. "It's a contract then."

"An addendum, I'd say."

They exchanged a knowing smile that told Zoey it was time for her to leave. She tiptoed to the trap door and slipped through the opening.

She'd settle her own scores later.

No one tried to stop her this time.

Dalton was waiting for her at the bottom of the tree, curious.

"Watch out you don't fall on your butt, he said when she jumped to the ground, not without difficulty."

"Leave my butt out of it," she mumbled.

They could hear that Sally and Adrian's shouting had morphed into a murmur that was just audible in the peaceful summer afternoon.

"Let's stop spying on them, okay?" Zoey suggested.

She and Dalton moved to the middle of the garden where the chaise lounges were waiting for them.

"Especially since Mom's the one that does that," Dalton replied sourly.

"That keeps you from being a jerk. Do you have anything else to share with me now that we're on that topic?"

Dalton let out the same fake, embarrassed laugh he had when he was ashamed.

"I slept with your friend Cass last year. Once."

"Do I have a friend that you haven't tried to get into bed, Dalton?"

"No, there's no one I haven't been able to get into bed, well, except Sally. But only because I didn't have enough time. That's a moot point now anyway. Oh, and since we are spilling our guts, Josh has fantasized about you for years. I really don't understand why and it's kind of annoying."

"Do you know what, Dalton? Sally and Adrian are a thing now and you and Marianita are too."

"That's definitely not a done deal," Dalton replied, sucking in his lips.

"Yes, it is. I'm going to stay single. Actually, I could see myself with

Josh."

"I forbid you to use my best friend as your rebound guy."

Zoey raised one eyebrow in disbelief.

"Do you really want to talk about who can do what with someone else's friends? I'm kidding anyway."

"I know. There's Matthew Ziegler. How do plan on resolving that problem?"

"I have no idea."

"Maybe you should send him an email."

She burst out laughing. Dalton didn't understand why. However, she didn't really feel like laughing. She truly didn't know what to do or if she even wanted to resolve things. Matthew had to be furious with her and think she was fickle.

Paranoid, too, she thought.

"What do you do when you want to seduce someone? Send an email?"

"Me?" Dalton said. "No."

He put his hands behind his head and closed his eyes.

"Baby, I got style."

She smiled. He was right.

25
UNTIL PUFFED

Late that night after Zoey had climbed into bed, she heard tapping on the window pane. It took her a good minute to realize that someone was throwing rocks. She got up. Adrian was in her parents' yard, wearing only his pajamas. She smiled at him. It felt like she was back in the past.

"Wait," she whispered.

She noiselessly left her room and walked through Dalton's. He lay diagonal across his bed, sleeping like a rock. A lock of hair fell over his forehead. He only needed his Batman PJs to once again become the little boy she had recently glimpsed.

She carefully opened his window and descended using the trellis, praying that it didn't collapse under her weight.

It was a cool August night. She shivered as she hopped around on the grass that was already damp with dew. Dawn was near.

Adrian was waiting for her at the corner of the house.

"Sally's not with you?" she asked.

"She's asleep in my room," he replied. "My parents are going to have a surprise at breakfast."

"That's a huge deal, apparently. Do you have some other problem other than the fact that you finally brought a girl home and your mother is probably going to announce it to the world first thing in the morning?"

"I wanted to thank you."

"For what? For being your girlfriend's stupid friend?"

Adrian frowned.

"I don't like that word. Girlfriend. It's ridiculous."

"Because 'stupid friend' works for you?"

"Zoey, please. You know I don't think that. Well, not all the time anyway. If you'll let me talk…"

She sat on the bank next to the garden path, ready to listen to what he had to say. He plopped down next to her.

"I really want to thank you," he continued. "I know what it cost you to take such a risk. Last night, I knew you'd always be my friend."

"Did you ever doubt it?"

"Sometimes, yes. I'm sorry that I kept secrets from you. It was difficult to look you in the face. We usually have such a good time together. I thought you wouldn't like it if you knew the truth."

"It's true I might not have been happy with Sally," Zoey confirmed. "But, I'm happy for you both, you know."

"You're still going to keep bossing us around."

"I'll control myself," she said smiling. "Something is bothering me, though. How did we end up together naked in my bed?"

"You undressed me with the clear intention of taking advantage of me."

A brief smile indicated that he was joking.

"What really happened, Adrian?"

"The truth is, I don't know what really happened," he admitted. "I think that I just couldn't sleep in the same house as Sally after I saw her kissing Dalton. I went to sleep where I was."

"Naked?"

"I always sleep naked and you were in no state to put your pajamas on. How were you even able to take your clothes off?"

"Are you totally sure nothing happened?"

"Zoey, with the amount of alcohol I had, I wouldn't even have been able to have an erection. And it was you, so…"

"Lovely."

"Really," he confirmed. "If I'd had a thing for you, we both would have known. I'm not saying that never crossed my mind when we were teenagers. But you know how it is at that age—all those hormones."

"I see what you mean. "

She hugged him, a gesture familiar to both of them.

"I'm so happy we made up," she murmured. "You have the most comfortable shoulders in the world."

"Wait till I develop a belly like my dad," he replied.

Zoey sat up straight.

"Do you think that will bother Sally? I can't even imagine having to act differently in front of her or even feel guilty."

Adrian laughed a little and pulled her to him, assertively but tenderly. She let him. She badly needed someone to take her in their arms.

"If that bothers her, too bad. I never even considered going out with a girl who wouldn't accept you. Sally will understand anyway, better than someone else would. She already feels pretty guilty about the secret we kept from you, no matter what she says, and maybe more than I do."

"Why more than you?"

"Because it's not the first secret I've kept to myself. Like you have—I'm sure you've had some from me."

"Maybe. Let's just say that we haven't had the chance to talk lately. That was hard too. About Marianita and what she may have told you."

The shock that she read on his face reassured her, for a short moment.

"What does Marianita have to do with it?"

"Well, not her directly," she stammered. "But, Matthew, on the other hand…I slept with him, I was awful, and now, I don't know what to do."

"You were awful in bed?"

"Don't say stupid things like that," she retorted, aggravated. "I was awful afterward."

He tapped her on the head affectionately.

"You were Zoey, that's what."

"Do you really want me to bring up how you acted with Sally?"

"No thanks. I think we've covered that. And what about him? What does he think?"

"I don't know. The last time I spoke with him, he got out of my dad's car and slammed the door."

"He's tougher than he looks."

Zoey shrugged which almost made her fall off the bench and forced Adrian to tighten his arms around her.

"Anything can be fixed," he said. "If Sally and I were able to figure things out, you can too. I'm sure you'll trip over yourself doing it, but without needing anyone's help. Maybe he's the not-so-perfect guy you've been waiting for."

"You don't like him that much," Zoey noted.

Adrian lifted her head up slightly so that he could look her in the eyes.

"My opinion is not the one that matters, Zoey. You know," he added, clearing his throat. "It's actually possible that I was a bit jealous of him."

"Don't be stupid. I can't see why you'd be jealous of Matthew."

He looked at her intensely and got close to her face on which the moon was casting a pale glow. A flicker of annoyance passed over his face.

"You and Sally were fawning over him like he was a rooster in a hen house. Now, seriously, Zoey, if you really have feelings for this Matthew, who is way more awkward than I am, I suggest you do everything you can to get him back. If you have to grovel, do it. I can give you lessons."

She laughed.

"Dalton told me the same thing."

"Dalton as a relationship counselor," Adrian grimaced. "Even if I admit that, in this case, he was right."

Zoey thought about it for a moment. That was it—she would explain everything to Matthew.

"I have to go," Adrian said suddenly. "I don't want Sally to wake up alone in my teenage bedroom. My mother wasn't able to wallpaper it over with a Laura Ashley design, but, still, it might give her a scare."

"I understand."

However, she stayed on the bench, not letting go.

"What's wrong?" he asked worriedly. "I'm sorry to leave you like this , when you are unhappy, Zoey, but…"

"I'm so humiliated," she stammered. He looked at her, taken aback.

"Humiliated? Did I say something wrong? "

"No, it's not that."

She lowered her head, her mouth twisted in a grin.

"I don't know how to climb back up the trellis," she confessed.

"Of course you don't," Adrian burst out laughing.

26
TAKE OUT QUICKLY

Once she was sure that her mother was doing better and back to running her husband's life, Zoey gave herself permission to go back to her own apartment. Her neighbor had been feeding Sushi. She was glad to see him again even though he'd torn up part of the living room, enraged at having been abandoned.

She had two days of relative calm before her next deadline. Sally and Adrian were still getting to know each other again at Sally's house. She refrained from calling them but had sent Sally a text to tell her that she didn't need her at work and that she could take a few more days off. When she received the return text, she laughed. Adrian was the one that replied and he said that everything was good between them. Now there was just Dalton. He was still vacillating between his usual cheerfulness and when she sensed that he felt totally lost or particularly sad.

She had to do something. After all, as the oldest, it was her job to help and protect him. And maybe because she felt guilty. Thinking about others prevented her from feeling the full weight of the void in her life and the regret that she felt at the idea of losing Matthew.

Helping others made her feel important, more than she ever had in her career. It gave her an ego boost.

Once she had decided to take control of Dalton's situation (he was always disorganized anyway), she picked up the phone and called Marianita's number to invite her to coffee.

The Brazilian had probably arrived on time, since she had scattered all the sugar packets around her cup by the time Zoey showed up, living up to her reputation for always being late. She apologized repeatedly.

"So," Zoey said after the usual small talk, "I suppose you know why I asked you here."

"To talk about Matthew Ziegler? I feel really badly about that, Zoey. Dalton told me all about it."

"No. I'm here to talk to you about Dalton, actually."

The young woman suddenly seemed terrified.

"Do I really have that effect on people?" Zoey asked. "Do I scare the people who hang out with my brother and my friends?"

Marianita swallowed and for a moment, staring intently at the mess she had made with the sugar packets.

"Yes," she stammered. "Dalton values your opinion immensely."

"I value his opinion immensely too. I'd like to know what you are planning to do."

"I don't know."

"Can I ask you a personal question?" Zoey asked, without waiting for a response. "Are you in love with my brother?"

Marianita did not hesitate for one second, nodding her head.

"Well then, can you stay?"

"No. My mother is going through a difficult time. I can't abandon her. I'm very close to her. She raised me by herself, you see. My father left her before I was born. She's never been lucky with men."

"Apparently not."

Marianita's eyes flashed and her nostrils flared.

"This Ziegler person! For years, years!"

What came next was drowned out in a cascade of Portuguese that Zoey thought were swear words.

"Listen, Marianita. I have decided I don't want to be stuck in the past. I don't want to hear anything about Matthew."

Marianita shook her head, indicating her violent disapproval.

"Every time she sees him, she gets in such a state," the young woman cried, carried away by her anger. "She knows it, but keeps going back. Like an addict! And afterward, she takes out letters, photos, and she talks about Chicago and Paris and the house in Bahia. It's not enough that he ruined part of my childhood!"

"Your childhood? But, wait. Matthew Ziegler is only a few years older than you are."

Her fury was evident. Dalton was going to have negotiate his life with this passionate woman and something told Zoey that he wasn't always going to get away with fancy footwork, a wink, and his famous charisma.

"What—Matthew Ziegler? Matthew is only...he's just the constant reminder! I am talking about Richard Ziegler, his father!"

"His father?"

"Of course, his father! This disgusting human being who made her think he loved her but he never did. He never left his wife! Even after she died and he was free. And now he's dead too, but he continues to have a hold on her. Every time she sees Matthew, they talk about him. She obsesses about all she never had, and, instead of cutting ties, he encourages her."

Zoey wanted to reply, but nothing came out of her mouth. A nervous laugh was rising up in her throat as the Brazilian railed more intensely against Matthew's father and her own mother until she started swearing in Portuguese again.

"Calm down," she commanded, as firmly as she could. "Listen, I totally understand how you feel, but don't you think that your mother wants something else for you? Dalton is crazy about you and he's a wonderful person. Your mother doesn't need you. He does."

Marianita shook her head.

"Please. Think about it. I haven't seen Dalton like this since that awful Iva."

"Awful Iva? The girl who broke his heart?"

Zoey smiled, not even surprised that her brother had told the story—the scandal, he'd call it—about the woman he'd loved. He had to be even more in love this time around.

"Yes, her. The year he turned sixteen was a nightmare for the whole family. Underneath all his suave, carefree behavior, my little brother is a real softy. He's just, well, he's just Dalton. He never does anything unless he's all in. He is not the person who would be stuck in a bad relationship just to avoid being alone. He refuses to put himself in difficult situations."

Marianita eyes filled with tears. Zoey frowned. She decided to play her last card.

"I like your mother very much, Marianita. She's a strong, direct woman. She'll be able to make it. You know, when my own mother had the stroke, she told me something that really made an impression on me. Something that was very true."

"Yes?"

"She told me that loving your children means that you don't want them to make the same mistakes you did. You want them to reach higher. Wider."

Obviously, Zoey was lying. Nana was the one who had said that. But in her own way, Fran had expressed the same idea.

"Maybe there is some way that your mother can stay here."

"How?"

"I'll see what I can do," Zoey replied with a mysterious smile. With a definitive gesture, she swept away the sugary disaster that Marianita had created on the table.

When she got home, she turned on her computer, looking for the emails from Rafael Branco and Sofia Alves, praying to Sally's god of communication that she'd find just the right words.

Then she took the most logical approach out of all the possibilities available to her, to resolve the situation she was in, now convinced that it was partly her fault.

She opened a new message window and started writing a long email to Matthew.

What she lacked in style, she would make up for in brutal honesty.

27
SERVE

Zoey open the gate to Nana's yard. She had so many memories of this spot lined with forget-me-nots that she couldn't help but smile. Looking up, she saw her grandmother waiting for her from behind the window, like when she used to come home from school. Going back to her grandmother's house soothed her, even if she was wondering why she'd been invited. More precisely, she'd been summoned.

She only hoped that she could avoid another conversation about her big ego.

She pushed the door open.

"Come in, my dear Zoey," Nana cried from the hall. She found her and gave her a hug.

"Did you have a good trip?"

"Yes, thank you, Nana. How's everything going?"

"Everything is going very well. I would like you to meet someone."

Nana led her into the living room. Matthew was sitting on one of Nana's arm chairs with his legs crossed. When he saw Zoey, a flash of surprise passed over his chestnut-colored eyes before he composed himself.

"Matthew, I would like to introduce you to my granddaughter, Zoey. She is a very talented chef. But maybe you know each other already? I am pretty sure Dalton mentioned that. One is so forgetful at my age."

Zoey cursed her grandmother and brother. He should have held his tongue.

"We do know each other," Matthew replied, formally. "I don't want to infringe on your time together, so I'll be going."

"Absolutely not," Nana purred in her most pleasant voice. "The three of us need to talk some business. I'm going to make some tea. Sit in my spot, Zoey, I'll be back."

She left the room, carrying herself proudly, smiling in a way that Zoey would describe as gleeful.

"How are you doing?" Matthew asked.

Polite. Like he always was.

"I've been working a lot. And you?"

"I've been working a lot too."

For a moment, they stared at each other.

"I sent you messages," Zoey said.

"I received them," Matthew said coldly.

"Great."

Matthew's right foot began nervously tapping to an inaudible beat.

"I particularly liked the one where you told me that you were sorry for having suspected, and I quote, that I was 'having an affair with, I'm still quoting, 'a much older woman' who was actually my father's mistress."

"I'm not good at expressing myself," Zoey stammered.

"Oh, yes, yes," Matthew contradicted her, frowning, "you are. I'm happy that you no longer think I'm a garden variety womanizer, and I would like to quote you again, 'as the way I acted might make you think.'"

He stared at her intensely and then suddenly jumped up, pacing energetically around the room.

"You are particularly good at making excuses. But, as you can understand, I'm afraid that won't be enough. Since I've met you, you've screamed at me, humiliated me, insulted me numerous times, without even mentioning the times you made fun of me, and made me be as mean as you."

"I didn't make fun of you," Zoey stuttered.

"Is that what you think is the worst thing on this list?" Matthew groaned.

He was losing his cool. She had never seen him angry. He had the same moody eyes, shining with flecks of gold, that he'd had when he'd desired her. She had a hard time meeting his gaze but did succeed.

"I'm so very sorry. I acted like an idiot. An idiot with an oversized ego."

"And the grace of a bull in a china shop."

"Of a bull in a china shop," she repeated with difficulty. "I couldn't possibly have known that your relationship to Sofia was so dramatic. You have to admit that appearances can be deceiving."

"That's so you!" he exclaimed, on the verge of a cold rage. "You make excuses for yourself and then you wait for others to take responsibility for the blame you assign them. Sit down. Now, *you* are going to listen to *me*."

She sat down, in silence. He froze in astonishment, realizing she had obeyed. His face softened.

"My father is not the bastard that Marianita wishes he were. Please note that I do not hold that against her. She saw her mother suffer alone, while I was lucky enough to have both my parents. My father loved my mother. But, if the truth be told, that was nothing compared to what he felt for

Sofia, from the minute he saw her. But, I was only ten years old and my father refused to make me a child of divorce. In addition, he had a deep affection for my mother and realized that she was not responsible for how he felt about Sofia. He wasn't searching elsewhere for something he didn't have at home. It was an instant attraction, that's all. For years, he tried to end the relationship. He felt guilty where my mother was concerned, where Sofia was concerned, and toward me as well. I learned all of this when my mother died. I was twenty-seven years old and Kat had just left me. It must be said that I was angry, hurt and bitter. I already knew Sofia, because I had done my apprenticeship with her. At the time, I hadn't realized that, in part, she was interested in me because of my father, even though I think she ended up actually liking me. When they could have finally been happy, fate dealt them a bad hand. After my mother, it was my father who was diagnosed with cancer. Of the pancreas. When he learned that, he broke it off with Sofia for good, telling her that he no longer loved her and that he had always seen her as just a mistress, so that she'd hate him. Unspeakably cruel. In reality, it was a gesture of love, a desperate gesture by a man who didn't want the woman he loved to see him wither away."

He stopped suddenly, breathing hard, with a painful grimace on his face.

"I'm the one who contacted Sofia after his funeral. I couldn't stand the idea that she thought that he had stopped loving her."

"That's what made you realize that you had to live life to the fullest."

He looked at her for a long moment. His lower lip was trembling slightly. She wanted to take him in her arms, but, for the first time, to console him.

"That was what made me realize that I had to find the woman that I loved enough to not let her watch me die."

She made a motion toward him but then changed her mind.

"I ended up meeting you. When I saw you in your parents' garden, so passionate, bare feet, wild hair, I thought that you might be that woman."

Zoey's heart jumped in her chest.

"Even when you screamed at me hysterically."

"I was not hysterical."

"Even when and your buddy Adrian made that ridiculous scene."

She didn't reply. She could not deny that they had been ridiculous.

"I envied the idiot who had made you suffer. I still wonder what you saw in that guy—he's as boring as sin."

She had to admit, however, that he did have some things in common with Spencer. He was polite. He was (usually) in control. Except in bed, of course. She pushed away the images that this memory brought to mind.

"And then I kissed you in the street. That night, I wanted to go up to your apartment. Truthfully, making love on the porch of your building wouldn't have bothered me either. However, I needed to be totally unattached and even if nothing physical had ever happened between me and your cousin..."

"You were seeing her at the time," murmured Zoey.

"Yes, I was seeing her. What did you think?"

"That you were just in it for the fun."

"Oh, it was a lot fun to walk away from a woman I was desperate to make love to so that I could go home by myself," he exclaimed.

"My grandmother is right next door," Zoey stuttered.

Matthew smiled roguishly.

"If you want my opinion, your grandmother left the house at the right moment. Do not try to get out of this conversation. I am not done with you. I received your email. Normally, I would never have spoken to someone again if they sent me such an insulting email."

"Please," Zoey begged, "don't remind me about that email."

"Oh, yes, I will! So, I waited for you for two hours on the patio of your friend Gabriella's restaurant and to add to my humiliation, she followed all of this with passionate interest. We spent the night together. One night that I..."

"...that you appreciated very much, I know."

"Stop interrupting me!" Zoey closed her mouth.

"What did you want me to say? I had no desire to see you gloat! After that, there was the party at Rafael's. It was hell sitting on that couch with you, just a few inches away from me—the way you were trembling. I probably shouldn't have followed you. But, how can I explain it? It was like I was starving. So, yes, I followed you into that bedroom. And you know what happened next."

"We made love," Zoey murmured.

"Thank you, I know that part. I can no longer walk into my own closet without getting an erection. This makes me late every morning."

"Then you just abandoned me."

"You are right about that."

She let out a satisfied exclamation, but, stopped cold when she saw that his expression was still furious.

"I was embarrassed," he continued. "I got carried away in the minute. Perhaps a bit too much. As opposed to what you think, I am not as comfortable as you think with, with this type of thing."

"Spontaneity?"

"Impulse," he specified. "Good Lord, Zoey, I threw myself at you in the guest room at the house of one of my father's oldest friends!"

"In the closet," Zoey corrected.

"Stop smiling like that."

He approached her. She recognized the hungry look that she'd seen on his face previously.

"Otherwise, I'm going to have to get into macho mode and I don't want to go there again. I hate it when you always have the upper hand."

He was so close that she could have lifted her arm to touch him, which she was dying to do.

"Well, I don't always have the upper hand," she objected. "You've been arguing with me for at least fifteen minutes."

"I'm not arguing with you. I'm explaining things to you. Could you finally tell me, please, why you left Rafael's apartment, if it wasn't remorse?"

"I saw Sofia in your arms. I thought, I believed..."

"That I had simply gone back to be with my official mistress."

"Yes."

"That is absolutely ridiculous!" he declared, moving away from her. "I came back to Sofia in tears. If you want the truth, and God knows that it's hard for me to admit it, but when she saw how I looked at you, it reminded her of my father. She was humiliated at having broken down in front of everyone. I was consoling her. Then I went to look for you. What did you think was going on?"

"That she was licking your ear."

His eyes widened, horrified.

"You have an unbelievably perverted way of looking at things. And you have no self-confidence!"

"That's true," she mumbled. "You've already told me that. Don't act like you don't know that already."

She took a long breath.

"I'm sorry. I get it. It's clear that you didn't respond to my messages and that you never want to see me again."

"Correct, I actually didn't want to see you ever again. These have been the worst weeks of my life. It was torture, waiting by the phone. I, I..."

He swallowed and gave her a long look, full of resentment.

"I Googled you every day. Did you know that your official photo is extremely hot?"

"The one where I'm wearing the toque?" Zoey exclaimed.

"Yes, that one."

"Now, you're the perverted one."

"Honestly, I have never met anyone as complicated, or as twisted as you."

She got up.

"Well. Again, I'm very sorry. You can tell Nana that I had to leave for a work emergency."

"Which I don't think she's going to believe since you're not a heart surgeon or anything," he said sarcastically.

She was standing right in front of him and had no idea what to do. He had accomplished the incredible feat of uttering the most beautiful declaration of love she'd ever heard in her life while shouting at her and telling her everything that was wrong with her.

And he had brought up the scene in the closet.

"Now that we've gone over all of that, I have one more thing to take care of."

In several steps, he was next to her, the look of outrage still on his face. She was ready to hear another round of criticism. Her heart was beating a mile a minute and she was gripped by excitement and a desire so violent it was paralyzing.

He leaned toward her and stared her straight in the eyes.

"Do you see any problem with me kissing you?" he asked in a hoarse voice. She shook her head.

28
GRAB A SPOON

"I've accepted Uncle Malcolm's offer," Nana announced, holding out glasses to them. She was not at all embarrassed by the fact that she had left to make tea and returned a half hour later with a pitcher of her famous lemonade and three cut crystal glasses, to find them kissing each other on the mouth in her living room.

Matthew had regained his composure and was now serious and professional, and Zoey was sitting quietly in the arm chair next to him, avoiding her grandmother's amused expression. Nana had always been impossible and, for the first time in her life, she was dreading when they'd be alone and she'd have to listen to the teasing.

"I don't understand Uncle Malcolm and Tina's role in this story," she said.

"They purchased the publishing house that had previously published your grandmother," Matthew informed her. "That is what I couldn't tell you."

"One more thing," she said with hint of cruelty aimed at Matthew. "Nana, I don't understand! You're going to be at Uncle Malcolm's mercy. That's unacceptable!"

"Don't worry about it," Nana said, with a sly look on her face. "I have excellent attorneys and no self-important little businessman is going to take advantage of me."

Zoey chuckled. Only Nan would call Uncle Malcolm "little."

"I'm not a fool," the old woman added. "He maneuvered it so that Tina was involved in managing what will be your inheritance. I don't have a problem with that. You have your own career to manage. Dalton doesn't care about money, or at least that's what he says, and he spends it all. Tina has a good head on her shoulders and even if we are not close, I admire that quality."

Zoey mumbled her disapproval.

"Zoey, you aren't twelve anymore," Nana exclaimed. "Your cousin is not the monster that you think."

"I never said she was a monster. It's just that she's boring and she is not a generous person."

"You could say that about yourself too. You've always been a bit harsh when it comes to giving affection, don't you think? We've already established that it was my fault. Tina is kind of boring, but being boring doesn't mean you can't be successful. What does your brother call it? He says to dazzle them with style. How stupid, especially where business is concerned. Tina will take care of all that. I owe her that much. I've never been that close to her. Now, we need to figure out what we want to do."

"We?" Zoey said, shocked.

Nana burst out laughing.

"Well, what do you think? That I'm going to give Uncle Malcolm my recipes from a different era? I want this book to be successful! You're going to be in charge, with Mr. Ziegler. And I'll write the preface. This is what he and I have agreed on."

"Thanks for asking me in advance!" Zoey said indignantly.

"You'd refuse the last request of the woman that raised you, Zoey?" Nana groaned, her sharp gaze fixed on her granddaughter.

Zoey sighed.

"You don't have to resort to emotional blackmail. I'll think about it. But, I've just started a new...venture and I'll need to delegate my work at Zoey's Kitchen to Sally."

"A new venture?" Matthew asked abruptly, leaving his usual politeness at the door.

"I've accepted Sofia's offer," Zoey whispered.

Matthew's mouth dropped open and then tensed up.

"In Brazil? Is this a joke?"

"Not at all," Zoey said with a broad smile. "But I accepted her offer with the condition that she open her restaurant in New York, with funding and artistic direction from Rafael Branco."

Matthew's mouth opened and closed, before forming a satisfied grin.

"That's why Rafael invited me over for dinner tonight! What was the deciding factor?"

"I'm a romantic at heart."

"Romantic as a young virgin," Nana muttered, sarcastically.

"Nana!"

"I'm only calling it like I see it," laughed the old woman. "So, you've decided to be a chef. Well, well. And what's the reason if it isn't driving ambition?"

"Dalton. Sofia will have to stay in New York to launch the restaurant. So Marianita won't have any reason not to stay."

"You're a good sister, Zoey," Nana replied, her expression full of joy.

"You can say that again!" Zoey answered. "This will also let Sally run Zoey's Kitchen and manage it like she wants. She's always been too constrained in the role of assistant. I'm sure that she'll do a better job than I would."

She stood up.

"You'll have the time to perfect your recipes and we could even work with Sofia Alves, Nana suggested. Or whoever you think would be good, Matthew. I trust you. Your advice to work with my son-in-law impressed me."

"What do you mean?" Zoey asked.

"Matthew is the one who told me about your uncle buying the publisher, when we first met. He didn't want me to sign the contract without being aware of the exact situation. Can you help me carry all this back to the kitchen?"

Zoey nodded.

As they were entering the kitchen where she had spent her childhood learning the fundamentals that lead her to where she was today, her grandmother leaned toward her.

"Matthew is going to be quite a challenge, you know?" she said. "He has fire in his eyes."

"I've noticed that too," Zoey agreed, pursing her lips.

"And you really are a good, sweet girl. But what does your brother say about good girls?"

"They go to heaven. He's not the one that said that, Nana. He found it on the Internet."

"Whatever. It's true: bad girls go where they want."

She took her granddaughter's arm, hugged her tenderly and whispered, mischievously:

"Be a bad girl, sweetheart." So Marianita won't have any reason not to stay."

"You're a good sister, Zoey," Nana replied, her expression full of joy.

"You can say that again!" Zoey answered. "This will also let Sally run Zoey's Kitchen and manage it like she wants. She's always been too constrained in the role of assistant. I'm sure that she'll do a better job than I would."

She stood up.

"You'll have the time to perfect your recipes and we could even work with Sofia Alves, Nana suggested. Or whoever you think would be good,

Matthew. I trust you. Your advice to work with my son-in-law impressed me."

"What do you mean?" Zoey asked.

"Matthew is the one who told me about your uncle buying the publisher, when we first met. He didn't want me to sign the contract without being aware of the exact situation. Can you help me carry all this back to the kitchen?"

Zoey nodded.

As they were entering the kitchen where she had spent her childhood learning the fundamentals that lead her to where she was today, her grandmother leaned toward her.

"Matthew is going to be quite a challenge, you know?" she said. "He has fire in his eyes."

"I've noticed that too," Zoey agreed, pursing her lips.

"And you really are a good, sweet girl. But what does your brother say about good girls?"

"They go to heaven. He's not the one that said that, Nana. He found it on the Internet."

"Whatever. It's true: bad girls go where they want."

She took her granddaughter's arm, hugged her tenderly and whispered, mischievously:

"Be a bad girl, sweetheart."

29
ENJOY

Matthew was nervously tapping on the dashboard when she joined him in the pickup that she'd used to drive to Nana's.

"Your grandmother is an exceptional person," he said as she slid in behind the wheel.

She gave Nana a last wave as her sparkling eyes followed from behind the window in her living room.

"Intrusive," she said, subconsciously realizing where she'd inherited this trait from.

She started the car and began driving out of town. When they reached the highway, they still hadn't said one word to each other.

"I think you took the wrong exit," Matthew said surprised.

"No, I don't think so."

She watched as his eyes follow the indications leading to a motel whose neon sign finally came into view.

"You want to take me to a motel?"

"That's correct."

The face he turned toward her was both shocked and horrified.

"You've given me no choice," she stated.

She slowed down as she approached the parking lot. The gray building in front of them gave her pause. She was, however, able to regain her composure and, determined, she parked as far from the entryway as she could.

"You could have waited till we got to your place," Matthew said.

"I don't recall you having been very patient in the past."

He smiled.

"I gave into the impulse of the moment. However, what you're doing here is premeditated."

"I admit it."

She removed her seat belt and bent toward him. His lips were deliciously warm. He tenderly took her in his arms. She pushed him away, hopped over the space separating them and over Matthew's legs, sliding in next to him. He smiled and began kissing her again, but without the passion of previous encounters. However, she recognized the ferocious glimmer in his eyes.

"I won't lose control this time," he said calmly.

Calm to all appearances, at least. She could feel his bulge against her thigh.

"Are you sure?" she breathed.

"Totally sure."

She pulled up his shirt and let her fingers explore his skin, dancing first along his neck and then over his chest. With a determined motion, she used one hand to undo the buttons of his jeans.

"Zoey, there are probably surveillance cameras," he groaned.

"No one will recognize us," she murmured.

"The name of your company is written on the side of the truck."

She sat up quickly.

It took some time to button his pants back up, cross the parking lot, and reserve a room under the bored eye of the hotel manager.

Zoey didn't even notice what the room looked like. As soon as the door was closed, Matthew was on her, not even trying to hide his impatience. She pushed him away again so that she could lead him to the bed. He fell on it without any resistance.

"Where were we?" she asked.

He didn't reply, watching her unbutton his pants again and slide them down his legs. She removed his shoes in the same fashion.

Balanced on his elbow, he took off his own shirt. Zoey was overtaken by a fever that she found difficult to contain. Panting, Matthew watched her use her tongue to lick his chest and then his belly.

All at once, he could no longer contain himself and pulled her to him, gripping her firmly under her arms. His mouth was on Zoey's and he was no longer holding back. With one hand, he began to undress her, breathing hard.

He bent down so that she could move under him, pulling on the buttons of her jeans, dropping them to her ankles.

Having arrived at her feet, he stopped for a moment. He seemed to be fighting something.

"Why do you wear these damn shoes?" he complained, frustrated with the laces.

"I hadn't planned on sleeping with you today."

She was happy to help him, undoing them herself, on tiptoe, then

238

removing her jeans and her panties. Once she was naked, lying on the bed cover, he looked at her for a moment.

"Me either," he replied somewhat contrarily, "but I didn't do a double knot for nothing."

He climbed back onto the bed and held her again, tenderly. She stayed like that for a moment, and then, with an exasperated sigh, escaped his grasp and stood over him. He raised his hand up to her and caressed her cheek.

"I need some time," he said.

She was not ready to wait. She leaned over him, brushing her lips over his warm skin, letting her nose take in his smell. Matthew arched his neck as she caressed it with her mouth.

"Is that enough?" she asked.

Without waiting for a reply, she went a bit lower and her tongue continued to explore every inch of his torso, from his hardened nipples to just below his stomach which was tightening abruptly. Matthew hands were in motion, to take his turn at touching her. She grabbed his wrists and held them firmly against the bed. He let out a stifled moan as she slid down till her knees reached the floor.

She lifted her head. He looked at her, his mouth open. Using her lips, she kissed his hard member. When she put her lips around it, she felt a shiver go through him and moan resonate throughout his chest. She paused, for the pleasure of seeing him move toward her again.

"Can you stop playing around?" he demanded in a hoarse voice.

"I'm not playing," Zoey replied. "I'm appreciating the power that I possess."

She flicked the tip of his manhood with her tongue. She was actually playing, and this game amused as much as it excited him.

"I really hate that you have the upper hand," he murmured.

"You're lying," she replied, without breaking his gaze.

"Definitely."

As she climbed back on top of him, he folded his hands behind his head, an elegant gesture of nonchalance that was so true to him, and he smiled.

30
FINISH

Fran ran the comb through her luxurious black hair one more time to tame an errant lock that only existed in her perfection-obsessed mind.

"Twenty-nine years of marriage! Do people have parties for that?" she griped in front of the entryway mirror.

Standing next to her, Zoey considered her own reflection without much hope. She had made an effort to put on makeup, but her hair was definitely out of control.

At the end of August, the weather had cooled and Fran gratefully accepted the shawl her husband placed over her shoulders. Joe briefly assessed his wife's annoyance level and did what he'd done for thirty years when she was like this: he took off.

"Stella has always been extremely competitive!" Fran continued. "And she totally ignores the rules. She must know that everyone can do the math! Adrian is over thirty!"

"There's no shame in bringing a baby into the world out of love," Zoey murmured.

"Because you think you weren't?" her mother said, looking at her, her face getting red. "Just because you weren't conceived in the back of a car doesn't mean you weren't conceived in love."

"Mom!"

"Don't be so uptight! Your grandmother says worse than that and you laugh. I'm your mother, not the mother superior in a convent. And the Peters, under their facade, are hippies."

Zoey laughed imagining Stella and Darryl Peters decked out in fringed jeans and flower shirts.

"Mom, how others live their lives is not always a direct affront to how

241

you live yours," she noted.

Fran stared at her, regal and intimidating.

"You have no idea of the wars that rampage through suburban life, my poor Zoey," she said quite seriously. "I have to use all the diplomatic skills at my disposal to maintain a certain balance within our circle of friends. Obviously, you don't care about these kinds of problems. You and your little gang are happy to throw yourselves on what you call couches and share some chips and beer. I am sure that Matthew feels out of place in all that."

In her mother's view of all that was masculine, Matthew was always uncomfortable, like Joe was always irritated or upset. Which neither of them ever were.

Zoey laughed to herself at the image of Matthew lying around with a bag of chips and some beer, especially since the last time she had seen him on her couch, he'd been totally naked, begging her to rock faster. Not really what Fran had in mind for the perfect son-in-law.

"I don't understand why you insist on acting like a teenager."

Their truce as a result of her mother's stroke had come to an end. Fran was once again her regal self and more dismissive than ever. But Zoey knew that her mother loved her and that was all that mattered. She was ready to accept this reprove with good grace when Matthew burst into the kitchen.

"Surely," she learned that from you, he said agreeably.

Fran smiled. She batted her eyes.

"I'm glad to see you agree with me."

Zoey rolled hers. Her mother could never admit that she'd lost a battle. And even less so a war.

Fran adjusted her collar by a millimeter and then indicated she was ready to leave.

"Zoey, if that pest Suzie Harting tries to minimize your new position, don't respond to her. I'll take care of it. I'm really sick of her talking about her idiotic daughter's fabulous wedding."

Her illness had changed her, actually. She was much funnier. She had Nana's sense of humor, in fact.

Like a general ready for battle, she walked gracefully to the driveway.

Matthew embraced Zoey affectionately.

"I want to thank you for putting up with my mother," she told him.

"I have been able to survive your entire family," he noted. "Does your Great Aunt Vicki ever stop talking?"

"No, she talks even more than you do."

By way of reply, Matthew buried his face in her hair.

"Would it be possible to be a little bit late?" he asked her, his hands already finding their way along her thighs.

Zoey awkwardly freed herself.

"My mother is waiting for us at the end of the driveway! If you think she's going to miss making her entrance on your arm..."

Matthew let out an annoyed whistle, but, a good sport, he quickly put on one of his most polite expressions.

He walked across the yard to the gate, where Fran was indeed waiting for them, adjusting her black silk shawl.

The Peters' yard was as full of guests, like the Westwood's had been two months before. Almost the same group of people were present. Zoey caught a glimpse of the large piano that had been moved to a platform, under a canvas tent. Adrian was sitting on the same stool that he'd had for twenty years, looking out vacantly, in despair. Apparently, his technique for finding his inner Zen wasn't really working this time and when he regained consciousness, he saw the dreadful situation with painful clarity. Marianita was next to him, going through sheet music, in a form-fitting, long white dress that sparkled in the candlelight.

Fran Westwood was going to hate that and make Dalton suffer terribly for it in the coming days. Zoey cackled.

She saw her mother move toward Stella, her most friendly expression plastered on her face, gushing about the decorations. A bit further away, Sally was talking to Darryl Peters. Seeing her with her parents' friends seemed strange, but not unpleasant. Sally's relationship with Adrian—which they refused to define—had made her more kind and indulgent.

In sum, a new Zoey. Not fundamentally different, just like Fran was not so different from what she had been before her stroke, but maybe less harsh and definitely less stressed.

She considered this summer's events her own personal "illness" that had forced her to address existential and emotional issues.

Matthew joined her once he was sure that Fran was well entrenched in her battle and no longer thinking about him. He was able to adapt with impressive skill.

"No one will notice if we aren't here," he whispered into her ear. "What's important is that they all saw us at the beginning of the party."

"You never give up," she replied, trying to ignore the look in his eye.

"Didn't you tell me there was a treehouse?"

She turned to scold him.

"I am no longer the Zoey who drank too much margarita who sneaks into the treehouse to make out with her boyfriend."

"That's too bad," Matthew murmured pulling her close. "That being said, last Monday, you did drink too much margarita in that restaurant and it seems to me that we..."

She put her hand over his mouth. Nearby, a couple, friends of her parents, glanced at them, amused.

Out of the corner of her eye, she saw Laurie and Spencer working their way through the crowd, holding hands. She stepped back and smiled at Matthew who, his eyes dark, kept his hands on her hips assertively, his right hand not leaving her side to shake Spencer's hand. She saw a different look come into his eye, much less welcoming than the one he reserved for her.

"Can I speak to you in private, Zoey?" Laurie asked, obviously very uncomfortable.

She was hopping from one foot to another, like a little girl who was embarrassed.

"We need drinks," Matthew said.

"Spencer, could you show me where the bar is?"

They left.

"Are the wedding preparations coming along?" Zoey asked as politely as she could.

"We still have time," Laurie replied, making a dismissive motion with her hand. "Actually, that's what I wanted to talk to you about—the wedding. We've never had the opportunity to put all of our cards on the table."

"I didn't know we were playing poker," Zoey rejoined.

Laurie blushed.

"You're not making it easy for me. I've always been a bit afraid to talk to you about it, you know."

"Because you seduced my fiancé? That's a good reason to avoid someone, isn't it?"

Laurie's grimace prompted Zoey to feel some pity but it was quickly swept away by the idea of how nice it would be to torture her like when they were kids.

"I didn't seduce Spencer," Laurie replied. "At least, I didn't do it on purpose. I fell in love and I was really upset with myself for it. You and I have never been friends and I couldn't talk to you. Now, you're with Matthew and it seems like you're happier. So, I thought we could bury the hatchet."

"I was never in a war with you, Laurie," Zoey emphasized, disingenuously. "I haven't lived here in a long time."

"You weren't particularly nice either."

"Should I have been?" Zoey snapped.

Laurie was getting on her nerves. She was certainly not going to apologize for having been upset that Spencer left her for her worst childhood enemy.

"At least somewhat," Laurie replied, standing up. "You could understand how we couldn't help ourselves. Spencer wasn't going to stay with you just because he met you first. You know exactly how he is. He's not good at expressing himself."

"I don't really feel like listening to you explain who Spencer is to me,"

Zoey replied. "I have been more than tolerant up till now."

"You, tolerant?"

The spontaneity of her statement was bothersome.

"Not really," she continued. "I spent my childhood and my adolescence putting up with your teasing—Adrian, Dalton and yours. You made me cry more than once. You were all so awful to me and you were so much better at everything than I was!"

"Excuse me?"

Zoey stared at her in sincere surprise.

"We were so much better at everything than you were?" she repeated.

"You were all much more relaxed, funnier, more talented. My mom constantly compared me to all of you."

This information brought on a wave of sympathy for Laurie, despite herself. She had also suffered from the terrible pressure of mothers worried about their children's success, especially as compared to others, within their little suburban bubble.

"Adrian and his piano, you and your cooking, Dalton and his law degree. And then me. Barely smart enough to be an acceptable housewife. My parents welcomed Spencer like he was the messiah, convinced he was going to make me a better person."

Zoey stopped herself from replying with the perfect comeback that this situation required and regretted that Adrian wasn't there to share this with her.

"It's very hard for me to tell you all this, you know, Laurie continued. I'd really like it if you would come to our wedding, with Matthew. It's important to me. It would mean that we'd really let bygones be bygones."

"Your mother would have a ball trying to interpret any expression that crossed my face."

Laurie let out a little laugh.

"Yours would criticize my dress and think the decorations were too gaudy."

"That's for sure. I'll come to the wedding. With or without Matthew."

"Thank you, Zoey," Laurie replied with a smile that lit up her pretty face. "I won't bother you anymore."

Zoey hesitated, and then, since she had decided that she was now a different Zoey and was feeling particularly confident, she held Laurie back.

"Laurie? Is Tina mad at me about Matthew ?"

"Not in the least," Laurie said kindly. "She was more interested in him for his professional connections than personally. Tina is not really looking for a serious relationship."

"What?" Zoey said, shocked.

"Really," Laurie laughed. "You should take the time to get to know her. She's fun and an excellent friend and not as conventional as you think. But, as part of a family, we always have to act the part. Except you, of course. You've always been free."

Zoey smiled. She didn't fit that image either.

"Not so much, actually," she murmured, remembering how she had been locked into the role of the impossible rebel and how she'd suffered from that.

Laurie moved away, in search of her fiancé. Dalton jumped into her spot. He was wearing one of the blue shirts that their mother continued to store in the closet of his room. He looked upset.

"Have you seen Marianita's dress?" was the first thing he said.

"Mom is going to kill you," Zoey announced, partly serious.

"She is going to kill me more than once if Marianita gives all Mom's old fogey friends erections."

"Dalton, I beg you, please spare me the details."

"The details may be pretty obvious, honey," he replied dryly.

"You are disgusting."

Her brother grinned slyly.

"I may be disgusting, but I'd like to point out that my room is located exactly between your room and the guest room where Mathew is sleeping. If you want me to forget about it, it's in your interest to side with me when Mom ambushes me to explain the difference between a dress and a stripper's outfit."

"You're exaggerating. She looks elegant and beautiful. If you prevent Matthew from joining me, you will get absolutely no help from me."

"Zoey, I really think that I became a lawyer so that I would have a chance at someday being a better negotiator than you. Now that I think about it, maybe I should have signed up with the mafia."

— "You still have a long way to go, son," she retorted, smiling.

She smiled again when Matthew joined her with a glass of champagne in each hand.

"No cocktail fountain this time," he said, handing her a glass. "They could really use one."

"Mom would never have let me cater this event—Stella either, actually."

"I just spent the most boring ten minutes of my life, he complained. That Spencer would put a team of Olympic sprinters to sleep."

He touched her waist. He had the sideways, dark look he'd had earlier with Spencer.

"I thought you weren't jealous," she said.

"I never said that. I said that I didn't like jealous women. Not that I wasn't."

"Oh, right. But, Spencer, seriously?"

"He has no personality whatsoever."

"That's almost insulting to me."

"It would have been if you had stayed with him."

He kissed her assertively, in front of everyone. Zoey had thought that he didn't like public displays of affection. Nearby, Dalton let out an exaggerated sound of disgust and moved away.

"Do you see any problem with me getting you out of here?" Matthew murmured.

"None at all," she replied, her breathing shallow.

They did stay at the party, however. Adrian played the pieces his mother required of him, and Marianita sang, which gave Dalton the opportunity to come up with arguments against his mother's future attack. Fran and Joe liked the music and it was obvious that Marianita was exceptionally talented.

The next morning, Zoey went to the kitchen, decked out in her teenage bathrobe, not wearing any makeup but with her hair in place for the most part. She found Fran busy preparing breakfast for everyone.

She was a little worried about what her mother was going to say. At the first streaks of dawn, Matthew had joined her, waking her up with kisses that were a bit too passionate for how (not) awake she was at the early time of day. However, it didn't take her much time to give up on sleeping in.

Fran stared at her for a moment, as if she were thinking about what she was going to say, eyebrow raised.

Zoey blushed. She was sure that they hadn't made any noise, even when he'd pushed her up against the wall in her room. She hadn't made a sound, since his hand had been over her mouth, gently, and having the opposite effect than what he'd intended—it made her even more aroused.

"If you could take care of the toast, honey, that would be helpful," her mother said in a friendly tone. "Make it just like your father likes. I've never understood how this toaster works. You are so much better than I am at that type of thing!"

Zoey refrained from pointing out that no talent was required to use a toaster and you just had to turn the dial to the desired temperature.

"Did you see that dress your brother's girlfriend was wearing?" Fran attacked while squeezing the oranges.

"I was focused on her gorgeous voice," Zoey replied, playing the game.

"Yes, of course. She sings very well. I hope she is able to make a living doing that. Dalton will never put up with a woman who doesn't have her own independence."

"He's very in love with her, Mom," Zoey pleaded.

"I was the one that raised him. He needs an independent woman who is at his level."

Zoey wanted to say that Marianita was likely going to inherit an empire that would make the house the Westwoods lived in look like a shack, by comparison.

She held her tongue. Her mother would feel threatened and she thought it best that Dalton take care of defending his girlfriend himself.

Fran gave her a cup of coffee. Zoey savored the calm in the kitchen for several minutes, as well as this improved version of her mother who was going to great lengths to prepare a proper breakfast, even though she had always hated that task. Her motive was most likely to impress Matthew. She had mentioned several times that he was an orphan and that he'd missed out on being part of a family. She was right about that, even though Zoey doubted that being served toast on dishware painted with purple pansies was the way to make up for it.

"You know, Zoey," Fran said out of the blue, "I hope that it didn't bother Matthew to have to sleep in the guest room. But, I think you understand that the rules are still the rules, right? I have no desire for you to parade other boyfriends here at your whim, if you are stupid enough to break up with this one."

Zoey opened her mouth to reply, but was able to refrain a second time. There was no point in explaining to Fran that she wasn't twenty years old anymore and that she would try her best to avoid breaking up with Matthew. She had even gotten used to the way he burst out laughing after making love.

"It's not really fair to your brother, obviously," Fran said, in thought. "I wasn't able to host Marianita, considering. I'm a little more leery with him, considering his past."

Fran never let go.

She placed the coffee cups on a tray, next to the pitcher of orange juice.

"His girlfriend seems particularly emotional, too. She's going to put him through the wringer. I'm sure she's moody. That's the worst. Living with someone like that is stressful. Believe me, I've been married to your father for thirty-five years!"

"Dad isn't moody."

Fran's lips thinned out.

"Zoey, you don't know what goes on under our roof. Just the other day, he disagreed with me about the garden. You should have heard the tone he used!"

Her nostrils flared with rage from the memory of it. Then, she put back on her smiling face and arranged the cups next to the linen napkins.

"You won't have to worry about that with Matthew. It seems like he appreciates you for who you are and respects your family, even though I know he went into your room this morning."

Zoey's eyes widened and she couldn't have been more embarrassed. Fran gave her a little smile.

"Well, he could have been a little more discrete. He woke up your father and me."

She wanted to disappear. She put her head in her hands, hiding behind her hair to mask her humiliation.

"Don't be so dramatic! I don't mind if he tells you good morning. I'm not as old as you think and I was once your age. It's just that, next time…"

Zoey lifted her head.

From the other side of the table, her mother looked at her, without any embarrassment, and added:

"…tell him to not laugh so loudly."

NANA'S LIME TART
by Zoey Westwood

One pie crust
Margarita mix (2 oz of tequila, 1 oz of Cointreau and the juice of two limes)
4 TBS of cornstarch
3/4 cup granulated sugar
zest of two lemons
3 egg yolk
4 TBS butter

Remove all ingredients from the refrigerator an hour before you begin.
When you are ready to start, put on Dalton's playlist (there's no Sinatra).
Bake the empty pie crust in a 400-degree oven for twenty minutes.
Mix the lime juice, tequila and Cointreau together to make a margarita. Taste it (margaritas are always too strong). Make another one. Make t wo more, while you're at it. Put one of them aside.
In a sauce pan, bring one of the margaritas to boil.
Beat the egg yolks and sugar until foamy. Gradually add the lime zest and cornstarch.
Thin the mixture with a bit of the warm margarita.
Pour back into the sauce pan and let thicken, stirring constantly over medium heat.
With your free hand, take your glass and sip the margarita you set aside.
Remove the sauce pan from the heat and carefully incorporate the butter.
Spread the cooled mixture on the pre-baked crust and bake for twenty minutes.
Let cool and refrigerate for at least three hours.
Serve to your guests. Avoid all closets.

ABOUT THE AUTHOR

Elie Grimes just has one recipe for a beautiful life: a big kitchen, slightly mad friends, a few spontaneous cocktails, good music and a steady supply of books. Inspiration that one day she decided to turn into stories... The rest of the time she lives between a Chinese supermarket and a Laundromat, only leaving her computer to keep up with the adventures of her two daughters and official self-made man.

ENJOYED THIS BOOK?

We recommend
I DON'T REALLY NEED YOU
by MARIE VAREILLE

The best-selling romance by France's answer to Sophie Kinsella finally available in English

More than 50,000 readers in France!
WINNER of the 2015 CONFIDENTIELLES ROMANTIC COMEDY prize

Chloe is the perfect Parisian: she's too skinny, smokes too much, and drinks too much. She also has the bad habit of getting into toxic relationships, particularly with her ex Guillaume who is engaged to another woman. Her friend Constance, however, is a hopeless romantic, spends all her money on Jane Austen memorabilia yet is unable to find her Mr. Darcy.

One day, the two friends make a bet: Chloe will spend one year in the countryside, far from men and temptations, to finally write the novel she has always dreamed of; Constance will let go of her foolish dreams of romance and start hooking up with perfect strangers.

From Paris to Bordeaux vineyards to London, this bet will have completely unintended consequences.

"The kind of chick-lit comedy we love: fresh, sparkly, romantic (...). A 100% feel good romance" – aufeminin.com
" THE romantic comedy to read this Summer" – SoBusyGirls.com

For fans of Sophie Kinsella, Marian Keyes, Helen Fielding and Emily Giffin

www.ingramcontent.com/pod-product-compliance
Lightning Source LLC
Chambersburg PA
CBHW021959170626
46808CB00001B/218